MW01193374

"[An] inventive collection. . . . ~~—~~
—*New York Times Book Review* (Editors' Choice)

"*20th Century Ghosts* is Hill's first collection of short stories
and displays consummate skill in a variety of genres. . . .
Amusing, moving, horrifying—*Ghosts* runs the full spec-
trum."   —*USA Today*

"Fully developed characters with complex emotional lives
enhance the fourteen stories in Joe Hill's extraordinary
collection, *20th Century Ghosts.* There's not a false note or
disappointing effort in this volume."
—*Publishers Weekly* (starred review)

"Melancholy and very fine . . . [*20th Century Ghosts*] should
establish its author as a major player in twenty-first-century
fantastic fiction. Hill's subject matter is steeped in the pop
culture and tabloid detritus of the last fifty years. . . . Hill's
best stories veer away from the well-trodden creep shows and
back alleys of genre writing into more dangerous territory:
suburban basements, ball fields, and schoolyards."
—*Washington Post*

"One of the best [horror] collections of the year. Hill is a
relative newcomer who consistently creates creepy, very
disturbing stories. His is the most important horror debut in
short fiction since Glen Hirshberg's *The Two Sams.*"
—*Locus*

"Pleasantly creepy. . . . Most of the stories display the un-
self-conscious dash that made Hill's novel an intelligent
pleasure. In addition to the touches of the supernatural,
some heavy, some light, the stories are largely united by
Hill's mastery of teenaged-male guilt and anxiety unrelieved
by garage-band success or ambition. . . . Not just for ghost
addicts."   —*Kirkus Reviews*

20TH CENTURY GHOSTS

20TH CENTURY GHOSTS

STORIES

20th Anniversary Edition

JOE HILL

Introduction by Christopher Golden

wm
WILLIAM MORROW
An Imprint of HarperCollins*Publishers*

These stories first appeared in the following publications:

"Best New Horror," *Postscripts*, issue 3, 2005; "20th Century Ghost," *The High Plains Literary Review*, vol. XVII, no. 1–3, 2002; "Pop Art," *With Signs and Wonders*, ed. Daniel Jaffe, Invisible Cities Press, 2001; "You Will Hear the Locust Sing," *The Third Alternative*, issue 37, 2004; "Abraham's Boys," *The Many Faces of Van Helsing*, ed. Jeanne Cavelos, Berkley, 2004; "Better Than Home," as a chapbook in the A. E. Coppard Long Fiction Prize series, published by the White Eagle Coffee Store Press, 1999; "The Black Phone," *The Third Alternative*, issue 39, 2004; "In the Rundown," *Crimewave*, issue 8, 2005; "Last Breath," *Subterranean Magazine*, issue 2, 2004; "Dead-Wood," Subterranean Press e-newsletter, February 2005; "The Widow's Breakfast," *The Clackamas Review*, vol. VI, 2002; "Bobby Conroy Comes Back from the Dead," *Postscripts*, issue 5, 2005; "Voluntary Committal," first published as a chapbook, Subterranean Press, 2005; "The Cape" and "My Father's Mask" are original to this collection.

First published in 2005 by PS Publishing Ltd, England.

A hardcover edition of this book was published in 2007 by HarperCollins Publishers.

A paperback edition of this book was published in 2021 by HarperCollins Publishers under the title *The Black Phone*.

HarperCollins books may be purchased for educational, business, or sales promotional use. For information please email the Special Markets Department at SPsales@harpercollins.com.

FIRST HARPER PAPERBACK PUBLISHED 2008.
FIRST WILLIAM MORROW PAPERBACK EDITION PUBLISHED 2021.
20TH ANNIVERSARY EDITION PUBLISHED 2025.

Designed by Renato Stanisic

Library of Congress Cataloging-in-Publication Data has been applied for.

ISBN 978-0-06-337493-5

25 26 27 28 29 RTLO 10 9 8 7 6 5 4 3 2 1

To Leanora and our kids:

ETHAN, AIDAN, AND RYAN

CONTENTS

INTRODUCTION

Modern horror is not often subtle. Most of those who practice the art of the unsettling far too often go for the jugular, forgetting that the best predators are stealthy. Nothing wrong with going for the jugular, of course, but writers of genuine skill and talent have more than one trick in their bags.

Not all of the stories in *20th Century Ghosts* are horror stories, by the by. Some are wistfully supernatural, some are darkly disturbing mainstream fiction, and one lacks any trace of nastiness and is actually quite sweet. But they are subtle, friends and neighbors. Joe Hill is one stealthy bastard. Even the one about the kid who turns into a giant bug is subtle, and, let's face it, how often can you say that?

I first encountered Joe Hill as a name on a list of contributors to an anthology called *The Many Faces of Van Helsing*, edited by Jeanne Cavelos. Though I also had a story in that volume, I confess that I had not read any of the others when the time came for a small group signing at Pandemonium, a specialty bookstore in Cambridge, Massachusetts. Joe Hill was there, along with Tom Monteleone, Jeanne, and me.

At that point I'd never read a word he'd written, but as the day went on, I found myself growing curious about Joe Hill. The most interesting thing, to me, that came out of our conversations was that while he had a love for horror stories, they were far from his only love. He had published mainstream stories in "literary" magazines (and, believe me, I use that word so loosely it might just fall off) and won awards for them. Yet he found himself coming home to horror and dark fantasy time and again.

Be glad of that. If you aren't now, you soon will be.

I would've gotten around to reading *The Many Faces of Van Helsing* eventually, but in large part due to meeting Joe I moved it to the top of the stack. His story therein, "Abraham's Boys," was a chilling, textured examination of children who have begun to realize—as all children do—that their father is imperfect. It reminded me in the very best ways of the deeply unsettling independent film *Frailty*. "Abraham's Boys" is an excellent story that falls about halfway through the book you're currently holding, and it was good enough that it made me want to seek out more work by Joe Hill. But he'd published only short stories, and most in places that I wasn't likely to run across casually. In the back of my head I made a note to watch for his name in the future.

When Peter Crowther asked me if I'd be willing to read *20th Century Ghosts* and write an introduction, I knew I shouldn't agree. I haven't time to do much of anything other than write and be with my family, but the truth is, I wanted to read this book. I wanted to satisfy my curiosity, to find out if Joe Hill was really as good as "Abraham's Boys" indicated he might be.

He wasn't.

He was oh-so-much better.

The title of this volume is appropriate in myriad ways. Many of the tales involve ghosts in one form or another, and others reflect the effects of the twentieth century's echoes. In "You Will Hear the Locust Sing," the author combines a fondness for and knowledge of the science fiction and monster films of the 1950s with the very same atomic fears that informed those films. The effect is both darkly humorous and heartfelt.

Yet perhaps the most significant way in which the title of this collection resonates is in the author himself. There is an elegance and tenderness to this work that is reminiscent of an earlier era, of Joan Aiken and Ambrose Bierce, of Beaumont and Matheson and Rod Serling.

At his best, Hill calls upon the reader to complete a scene, to provide the emotional response necessary for the story to truly be successful. And he elicits that response masterfully. These are collaborative stories that seem to exist only as the reader discovers them. They require your complicity to accomplish their ends. In the tale that leads off this volume, "Best New Horror," it is impossible not to recognize a certain familiarity and to realize where the tale is leading, but rather than a failing, this is its greatest achievement. Without the reader's feeling of almost jaded expectation, the story cannot succeed.

He draws you into the intimacy of "20th Century Ghost" and the desperation of "The Black Phone" so that you are a part of the tale, sharing the experience with the central characters.

Far too many writers seem to think there's no place in horror for genuine sentiment, substituting stock emotional response that has no more resonance than stage directions in a script. Not so in the work of Joe Hill. Oddly enough, one of the best examples of this is "Bobby Conroy Comes Back from the Dead," which is not a horror story at all, though it takes place on the set during the making of George Romero's classic film *Dawn of the Dead*.

I'd like to talk to you about every story in this book, but the danger of writing something that goes at the front of the book is in giving too much away. I can say that if it were possible to scour from my mind the memory of having read these stories, I would happily do so, just so that I could have the pleasure of reading them again for the first time.

"Better Than Home" and "Dead-Wood" are things of beauty. "The Widow's Breakfast" is a poignant snapshot of another era and of a man who has lost his way.

"20th Century Ghost" touches the nostalgic heart like many of my favorite episodes of *The Twilight Zone*. "You Will Hear the Locust Sing" is the love child of a ménage à trois with William Burroughs, Kafka, and the movie *Them!* "Last Breath" is flavored with a hint of Bradbury. All of these stories are wonderful, some of them startlingly good. "My Father's Mask" is so weird and upsetting that it made me giddy.

"Voluntary Committal," the piece that closes this collection, is among the best novellas I have ever read, and speaks to the maturity of Joe Hill as a storyteller. It happens so rarely for a writer to pop up fully formed like this. And when it does . . .

well, I confess I am the victim of inner turmoil as I struggle between elation and the urge to beat the crap out of him. "Voluntary Committal" is that good.

"Pop Art," though . . . "Pop Art" is transcendent. The single best short story I have read in years, it brings all of Joe Hill's abilities to bear in a few short pages—the weirdness, the tenderness, the complicity.

With the nascent efforts of a newly arrived author, fans and critics alike are wont to talk about their promise. Their potential.

The stories in *20th Century Ghosts* are promises fulfilled.

—*Christopher Golden*
Bradford, Massachusetts
January 15, 2005
Revised, March 21, 2007

BEST NEW HORROR

A month before his deadline, Eddie Carroll ripped open a manila envelope, and a magazine called *The True North Literary Review* slipped out into his hands. Carroll was used to getting magazines in the mail, although most of them had titles like *Cemetery Dance* and specialized in horror fiction. People sent him their books, too. Piles of them cluttered his Brookline townhouse, a heap on the couch in his office, a stack by the coffee maker. Books of horror stories, all of them.

No one had time to read them all, although once—when he was in his early thirties and just starting out as the editor of *America's Best New Horror*—he had made a conscientious effort to try. Carroll had guided sixteen volumes of *Best New Horror* to press, had been working on the series for over a third of his life now. It added up to thousands of hours of reading and proofing and letter-writing, thousands of hours he could never have back.

He had come to hate the magazines especially. So many of them used the cheapest ink, and he had learned to loathe the way it came off on his fingers, the harsh stink of it.

He didn't finish most of the stories he started anymore, couldn't bear to. He felt weak at the thought of reading another story about vampires having sex with other vampires. He tried to struggle through Lovecraft pastiches, but at the first painfully serious reference to the Elder Gods, he felt some important part of him going numb inside, the way a foot or a hand will go to sleep when the circulation is cut off. He feared the part of him being numbed was his soul.

At some point following his divorce, his duties as the editor of *Best New Horror* had become a tiresome and joyless chore. He thought sometimes, hopefully almost, of stepping down, but he never indulged the idea for long. It was twelve thousand dollars a year in the bank, the cornerstone of an income patched together from other anthologies, his speaking engagements and his classes. Without that twelve grand, his personal worst-case scenario would become inevitable: he would have to find an actual job.

The True North Literary Review was unfamiliar to him, a literary journal with a cover of rough-grained paper, an ink print on it of leaning pines. A stamp on the back reported that it was a publication of Katahdin University in upstate New York. When he flipped it open, two stapled pages fell out, a letter from the editor, an English professor named Harold Noonan.

The winter before, Noonan had been approached by a part-time man with the university grounds crew, a Peter Kilrue. He had heard that Noonan had been named the editor of *True North* and was taking open submissions, and asked him to look at a short story. Noonan promised he would, more to be polite than anything else. But when he finally read the manuscript, "Buttonboy: A Love Story," he was taken aback by both the supple force of its prose and the appalling nature of its subject matter. Noonan was new in the job, replacing the just-retired editor of twenty years, Frank McDane, and wanted to take the journal in a new direction, to publish fiction that would "rattle a few cages."

"In that I was perhaps too successful," Noonan wrote. Shortly after "Buttonboy" appeared in print, the head of the English department held a private meeting with Noonan to verbally assail him for using *True North* as a showcase for "juvenile literary practical jokes." Nearly fifty people cancelled their subscriptions—no laughing matter for a journal with a circulation of just a thousand copies—and the alumna who provided most of *True North*'s funding withdrew her financial support in outrage. Noonan himself was removed as editor, and Frank McDane agreed to oversee the magazine from retirement, in response to the popular outcry for his return.

Noonan's letter finished:

> *I remain of the opinion that (whatever its flaws),*
> *"Buttonboy" is a remarkable, if genuinely*
> *distressing, work of fiction, and I hope you'll give*
> *it your time. I admit I would find it personally*
> *vindicating if you decided to include it in your next*
> *anthology of the year's best horror fiction.*
>
> > *I would tell you to enjoy, but I'm not sure that's*
> *the word.*
>
> > > Best,
> > > Harold Noonan

Eddie Carroll had just come in from outside, and read Noonan's letter standing in the mudroom. He flipped to the beginning of the story. He stood reading for almost five minutes before noticing he was uncomfortably warm. He tossed his jacket at a hook and wandered into the kitchen.

He sat for a while on the stairs to the second floor, turning through the pages. Then he was stretched on the couch in his office, head on a pile of books, reading in a slant of late October light, with no memory of how he had got there.

He rushed through to the ending, then sat up, in the grip of a strange, bounding exuberance. He thought it was possibly the rudest, most awful thing he had ever read, and in his case that was saying something. He had waded through the rude and awful for most of his professional life, and in those flyblown and diseased literary swamps had discovered flowers of unspeakable beauty, of which he was sure this was one. It was cruel and perverse and he had to have it. He turned to the beginning and started reading again.

IT WAS ABOUT a girl named Cate—an introspective seventeen-year-old at the story's beginning—who one day is pulled into a car by a giant with jaundiced eyeballs and teeth in tin braces. He ties her hands behind her back and shoves her onto the backseat floor of his station wagon . . . where she discovers a boy about her age, whom she at first takes for dead and who has suffered an unspeakable disfiguration. His eyes are hidden behind a pair of round, yellow, smiley-face buttons. They've been pinned right through his eyelids—which have also been stitched shut with steel wire—and the eyeballs beneath.

As the car begins to move, though, so does the boy. He touches her hip and Cate bites back a startled scream. He moves his hand over her body, touching her face last. He whispers that his name is Jim, and that he's been traveling with the giant for a week, ever since the big man killed his parents.

"He made holes in my eyes and he said after he did it he saw my soul rush out. He said it made a sound like when you blow on an empty Coke bottle, real pretty. Then he put these over my eyes to keep my life trapped inside." As he speaks, Jim touches the smiley-face buttons. "He wants to see how long I can live without a soul inside me."

The giant drives them both to a desolate campground, in a nearby state park, where he forces Cate and Jim to fondle one another sexually. When he feels that Cate is failing to kiss Jim with convincing passion, he slashes her face, and removes her tongue. In the ensuing chaos—Jim shrieking in alarm, staggering about blindly, blood everywhere—Cate is able to escape into the trees. Three hours later she staggers out onto a highway, hysterical, drenched in blood.

Her kidnapper is never apprehended. He and Jim drive out of the national park and off the edge of the world. Investigators are unable to determine a single useful fact about the two. They don't know who Jim is or where he's from, and know even less about the giant.

Two weeks after her release from the hospital, a single clue turns up by U.S. mail. Cate receives an envelope containing a pair of smiley-face buttons—steel pins caked with dry blood—and a Polaroid of a bridge in Kentucky. The next morning a diver finds a boy there, on the river bottom, horribly decomposed, fish darting in and out of his empty eye sockets.

Cate, who was once attractive and well liked, finds herself the object of pity and horror among those who know her. She understands the way other people feel. The sight of her own face in the mirror repels her as well. She attends a special school for a time and learns sign language, but she doesn't stay long.

The other cripples—the deaf, the lame, the disfigured—disgust her with their neediness, their dependencies.

Cate tries, without much luck, to resume a normal life. She has no close friends, no employable skills, and is self-conscious about her looks, her inability to speak. In one particularly painful scene, Cate drinks her way into courage, and makes a pass at a man in a bar, only to be ridiculed by him and his friends.

Her sleep is troubled by regular nightmares, in which she relives unlikely and dreadful variations on her abduction. In some, Jim is not a fellow victim, but in on the kidnapping, and rapes her with vigor. The buttons stuck through his eyes are mirrored discs that show a distorted image of her own screaming face, which, with perfect dream logic, has already been hacked into a grotesque mask. Infrequently, these dreams leave her aroused. Her therapist says this is common. She fires the therapist when she discovers he's doodled a horrid caricature of her in his notebook.

Cate tries different things to help her sleep: gin, painkillers, heroin. She needs money for drugs and goes looking for it in her father's dresser. He catches her at it and chases her out. That night her mother calls to tell her Dad is in the hospital—he had a minor stroke—and please don't come to see him. Not long after, at a day care center for disabled children, where Cate is part-timing, one child pokes a pencil into another child's eye, blinding him. The incident clearly isn't Cate's fault, but in the aftermath, her assorted addictions become public knowledge. She loses her job and, even after kicking her habit, finds herself nearly unemployable.

Then, one cool fall day, she comes out of a local supermarket, and walks past a police car parked out back. The hood is up. A policeman in mirrored sunglasses is studying an overheated radiator. She happens to glance in the backseat—and there, with his hands cuffed behind his back, is her giant, ten years older and fifty pounds heavier.

The sight of him is nearly more of a shock than she can bear, splinters her usual reserve. She staggers toward the trooper working under the hood, crying out to him, the sort of bleating cries she was always making in the first days after her tongue was removed, and before she got used to not being able to talk. She hates these sounds, but for a few moments is helpless to quiet herself. She scrawls hurried, half-illegible notes, trying to explain who the giant is, what he did to her when she was seventeen. Her pen can't keep pace with her thoughts, and she knows that she isn't writing anything that really makes sense. The officer seems to get the gist almost immediately, however, hardly even seems to look at her scrambled, scribbled messages. He tells her it will be all right. He tells her not to be afraid.

The man in his backseat is under arrest for trying to shoplift duct tape and a hunting knife from a hardware store on Pleasant Street. This information sets Cate off on a trembling fit. She knows the hardware store in question. It's right around the corner from her apartment.

The policeman says that if he's done other things, things to her, then she needs to come with him to the precinct house. As he tells her this, he is guiding Cate to the passenger side door. The thought of getting in the same car with her abductor makes her light-headed with fear, but the police officer reminds her the giant is handcuffed in the back, and will not hurt her.

At last she settles into the passenger seat. At her feet is a winter jacket. The police officer says it's his coat, and she should put it on, it'll keep her warm, help with her shivering. She looks up at him, prepares to scratch out a thank you on her notepad—then goes still, finds herself unable to write. Something about the distorted reflection of her own face in the mirrored lenses of his sunglasses causes her to freeze up.

He closes the door and goes around to the front of the car to shut the hood. With numb fingers she reaches down to get his coat. Pinned to the front, one on each breast, are two smiley-face buttons. She knows who the police officer is, but the thought is too dizzying to accept and she tries to tell herself what she's thinking is crazy. Buttonboy was blind, and the policeman read her notes, and it isn't possible they can be the same person, there's no way, no chance. Except the policeman didn't read her notes. He never looked at a single one. She can see that now.

She reaches for the door, but it won't unlock. The window won't roll down. The hood slams. The man behind the sunglasses who is not a police officer is grinning a hideous grin. Buttonboy continues around the car, past the driver's side door, to let the giant out of the back. After all, a person needs eyes to drive.

In thick forest, it's easy for a person to get lost and walk around in circles, and for the first time, Cate can see this is what happened to her. She escaped Buttonboy and the giant by running into the woods, but she never made her way out—not really—has been stumbling around in the dark and the brush ever since, traveling in a great and pointless circle back to them. She's arrived where she was always headed, at last, and this thought, rather than terrifying her, is oddly soothing. It seems to her she belongs with them, and there is a kind of relief in that, in belonging somewhere. Cate relaxes into her seat, unconsciously pulling Buttonboy's coat around her against the cold.

IT DIDN'T SURPRISE Eddie Carroll to hear Noonan had been excoriated for publishing "Buttonboy." The story lingered on images of female degradation, and the heroine had been written as a somewhat willing accomplice to her own emotional, sexual, and spiritual mistreatment. This was bad . . . but Joyce Carol Oates wrote stories just like it for journals no different than *The True North Review*, and won awards for them. The really unforgivable literary sin was the shock ending.

Carroll had seen it coming—after reading almost ten thousand stories of horror and the supernatural, it was hard to sneak up on him—but he had enjoyed it nonetheless. Among the literary cognoscenti, though, a surprise ending (no matter how well executed) was the mark of childish, commercial fiction and bad TV. The readers of *The True North Review* were, he imagined, middle-aged academics, people who taught Grendel and Ezra Pound and who dreamed heartbreaking dreams about someday selling a poem to *The New Yorker*. For them, coming across a shock ending in a short story was akin to hearing a ballerina rip a noisy fart during a performance of *Swan Lake*—a faux pas so awful it bordered on the hilarious. Professor Harold Noonan either had not been rooming in the ivory tower for long or was subconsciously hoping someone would hand him his walking papers.

Although the ending was more John Carpenter than John Updike, Carroll hadn't come across anything like it in any of the horror magazines, either, not lately. It was, for twenty-five pages, the almost completely naturalistic story of a woman being destroyed a little at a time by the steady wear of survivor's guilt. It concerned itself with tortured family relationships, shitty jobs, the struggle for money. Carroll had forgotten what it was like to come across the bread of everyday life in a short story. Most horror fiction didn't bother with anything except rare bleeding meat.

He found himself pacing his office, too excited to settle, "Buttonboy" folded open in one hand. He caught a glimpse of his reflection in the window behind the couch and saw himself grinning in a way that was almost indecent, as if he had just heard a particularly good dirty joke.

Carroll was eleven years old when he saw *The Haunting* in The Oregon Theater. He had gone with his cousins, but when the lights went down, his companions were swallowed by the dark and Carroll found himself essentially alone, shut tight into his own suffocating cabinet of shadows. At times, it required all his will not to hide his eyes, yet his insides churned with a nervous-sick frisson of pleasure. When the lights finally came up, his nerve endings were ringing, as if he had for a moment grabbed a copper wire with live current in it. It was a sensation for which he had developed a compulsion.

Later, when he was a professional and it was his business, his feelings were more muted—not gone, but experienced distantly, more like the memory of an emotion than the thing itself. More recently, even the memory had fled, and in its place was a deadening amnesia, a numb disinterest when he looked at the piles of magazines on his coffee table. Or no—he was overcome with dread, but the wrong kind of dread.

This, though, here in his office, fresh from the depredations of "Buttonboy" . . . this was the authentic fix. It had clanged that inner bell and left him vibrating. He couldn't settle, wasn't used to exuberance. He tried to think when, if ever, he had last published a story he liked as much as "Buttonboy." He went to the shelf and pulled down the first volume of *Best New Horror* (still the best), curious to see what he had been excited about then. But looking for the table of contents, he flipped it open to the dedication, which was to his then-wife, Elizabeth. "Who helps me find my way in the dark," he had written, in a dizzy fit of affection. Looking at it now caused the skin on his arms to crawl.

Elizabeth had left him after he discovered she had been sleeping with their investment banker for over a year. She went to stay with her mother, and took Tracy with her.

"In a way I'm almost glad you caught us," she said, talking to him on the phone, a few weeks after her flight from his life. "To have it over with."

"The affair?" he asked, wondering if she was about to tell him she had broken it off.

"No," Lizzie said. "I mean all your horror shit, and all those people who are always coming to see you, the horror people. Sweaty little grubs who get hard over corpses. That's the best part of this. Thinking maybe now Tracy can have a normal childhood. Thinking I'm finally going to get to have a life with healthy, ordinary grown-ups."

It was bad enough she had fucked around like she had, but that she would throw Tracy in his face that way made him short of breath with hatred, even now. He flung the book back at the shelf and slouched away for the kitchen and lunch, his restless excitement extinguished at last. He had been looking to use up all that useless distracting energy. Good old Lizzie—still doing him favors, even from forty miles away and another man's bed.

THAT AFTERNOON HE e-mailed Harold Noonan, asking for Kilrue's contact information. Noonan got back to him less than an hour later, very much pleased to hear that Carroll wanted "Buttonboy" for *Best New Horror*. He didn't have an e-mail address for Peter Kilrue, but he did have an address of the more ordinary variety, and a phone number.

But the letter Carroll wrote came back to him, stamped RETURN TO SENDER, and when he rang the phone number, he got a recording: *This line has been disconnected*. Carroll called Harold Noonan at Katahdin University.

"I can't say I'm shocked," Noonan said, voice rapid and soft, hitching with shyness. "I got the impression he's something of a transient. I think he patches together part-time jobs to pay his bills. Probably the best thing would be to call Morton Boyd in the grounds department. I imagine they have a file on him."

"When's the last time you saw him?"

"I dropped in on him last March. I went by his apartment just after 'Buttonboy' was published, when the outrage was running at full boil. People saying his story was misogynistic hate speech, saying there should be a published apology and such nonsense. I wanted to let him know what was happening. I guess I was hoping he'd want to fire back in some way, write a defense of his story for the student paper or something . . . although he didn't. Said it would be weak. Actually, it was a strange kind of visit. He's a strange kind of guy. It isn't just his stories. It's him."

"What do you mean?"

Noonan laughed. "I'm not sure. What am I saying? You know how when you're running a fever, you'll look at something totally normal—like the lamp on your desk—and it'll seem somehow unnatural? Like it's melting or getting ready to waddle away? Encounters with Peter Kilrue can be kind of like that. I don't know why. Maybe because he's so intense about such troubling things."

Carroll hadn't even got in touch with him yet, and liked him already. "What things?"

"When I went to see him, his older brother answered the door. Half-dressed. I guess he was staying with him. And this guy was—I don't want to be insensitive—but I would say disturbingly fat. And tattooed. Disturbingly tattooed. On his stomach there was a windmill, with rotted corpses hanging from it. On his back, there was a fetus with—scribbled-over eyes. And a scalpel in one fist. And fangs."

Carroll laughed, but he wasn't sure it was funny.

Noonan went on, "But he was a good guy. Friendly as all get-out. Led me in, got me a can of soda, we all sat on the couch in front of the TV. And—this is very amusing—while we were talking, and I was catching them up on the outcry, the older brother sat on the floor, while Peter gave him a home-made piercing."

"He what?"

"Oh God, yes. Right in the middle of the conversation he forces a hot needle through the upper part of his brother's ear. Blood like you wouldn't believe. When the fat guy got up, it looked like he had been shot in the side of the head. His head is pouring blood. It's like the end of *Carrie*, like he just took a bath in it, and he asks if he can get me another Coke."

This time they laughed together, and after, for a moment, a friendly silence passed between them.

"Also they were watching about Jonestown," Noonan said suddenly—blurted it, really.

"Hm?"

"On the TV. With the sound off. While we talked and Peter stuck holes in his brother. In a way that was really the thing, the final weird touch that made it all seem so absolutely un- real. It was footage of the bodies in French Guyana. After they drank the Kool-Aid. Streets littered with corpses, and all the birds, you know . . . the birds picking at them." Noonan swal- lowed thickly. "I think it was a loop, because it seems like they watched the same footage more than once. They were watching like . . . like in a trance."

Another silence passed between them. On Noonan's part, it seemed to be an uncomfortable one. *Research*, Carroll thought—with a certain measure of approval.

"Didn't you think it was a remarkable piece of American fiction?" Noonan asked.

"I did. I do."

"I don't know how he'll feel about getting in your collection, but speaking for myself, I'm delighted. I hope I haven't creeped you out about him."

Carroll smiled. "I don't creep easy."

BOYD IN THE grounds department wasn't sure where he was either. "He told me he had a brother with public works in Poughkeepsie. Either Poughkeepsie or Newburgh. He wanted to get in on that. Those town jobs are good money, and the best thing is, once you're in, they can't fire you, it doesn't matter if you're a homicidal maniac."

Mention of Poughkeepsie stirred Carroll's interest. There was a small fantasy convention running there at the end of the month—Dark Wonder-con, or Dark Dreaming-con, or something. Dark Masturbati-con. He had been invited to attend, but had been ignoring their letters, didn't bother with the little cons anymore, and besides, the timing was all wrong, coming just before his deadline.

He went to the World Fantasy Awards every year, though, and Camp NeCon, and a few of the other more interesting get-togethers. The conventions were one part of the job he had not come entirely to loathe. His friends were there. And also, a part of him still liked *the stuff*, and the memories the stuff sometimes kicked loose.

Such as one time, when he had come across a bookseller offering a first edition of *I Love Galesburg in the Springtime*. He had not seen or thought of *Galesburg* in years, but as he stood turning through its browned and brittle pages, with their glorious smell of dust and attics, a whole vertiginous flood of memory poured over him. He had read it when he was thirteen, and it had held him rapt for two weeks. He had climbed out of his bedroom window onto the roof to read; it was the only place he could go to get away from the sounds of his parents fighting. He remembered the sandpaper texture of the roof shingles, the rubbery smell of them baking in the sun, the distant razz of a lawnmower, and most of all, his own blissful sense of wonder as he read about Jack Finney's impossible Woodrow Wilson dime.

Carroll rang public works in Poughkeepsie, was transferred to Personnel.

"Kilrue? Arnold Kilrue? He got the ax six months ago," said a man with a thin and wheezy voice. "You know how hard it is to get fired from a town job? First person I let go in years. Lied about his criminal record."

"No, not Arnold Kilrue. Peter. Arnold is maybe his brother. Was he overweight, lot of tattoos?"

"Not at all. Thin. Wiry. Only one hand. His left hand got ate up by a baler, said he."

"Oh," Carroll said, thinking this still somehow sounded like one of Peter Kilrue's relations. "What kind of trouble was he in?"

"Violatin' his restraining order."

"*Oh*," Carroll said. "Marital dispute?" He had sympathy for men who had suffered at the hands of their wives' lawyers.

"Hell no," Personnel replied. "Try his own mother. How the fuck do you like that?"

"Do you know if he's related to Peter Kilrue, and how to get in touch with him?"

"I ain't his personal secretary, buddy. Are we all through talking?"

They were all through.

HE TRIED INFORMATION, started calling people named Kilrue in the greater Poughkeepsie area, but no one he spoke to would admit to knowing a Peter, and finally he gave up. Carroll cleaned his office in a fury, jamming papers into the trash basket without looking at them, picking up stacks of books in one place and slamming them down in another, out of ideas and out of patience.

In the late afternoon, he flung himself on the couch to think, and fell into a furious doze. Even dreaming he was angry, chasing a little boy who had stolen his car keys through an empty movie theater. The boy was black and white and flickered like a ghost, or a character in an old movie, and was having himself a hell of a time, shaking the keys in the air and laughing hysterically. Carroll lurched awake, feeling a touch of feverish heat in his temples, thinking, *Poughkeepsie.*

Peter Kilrue lived somewhere in that part of New York, and on Saturday he would be at the Dark FutureCon in Poughkeepsie, would not be able to resist such an event. Someone there would know him. Someone would point him out. All Carroll needed was to be there, and they would find each other.

HE WASN'T GOING to stay overnight—it was a four-hour drive, he could go and come back late—and by six A.M. he was doing 80 in the left-hand lane on I-90. The sun rose behind him, filling his rearview mirror with blinding light. It felt good to squeeze the pedal to the floor, to feel the car rushing west, chasing the long thin line of its own shadow. Then he had the thought that his little girl belonged beside him, and his foot eased up on the pedal, his excitement for the road draining out of him.

Tracy loved the conventions, any kid would. They offered the spectacle of grown-ups making fools of themselves, dressed up as Pinhead or Elvira. And what child could resist the inevitable market, that great maze of tables and macabre exhibits to get lost in, a place where a kid could buy a rubber severed hand for a dollar. Tracy had once spent an hour playing pinball with Neil Gaiman at the World Fantasy Convention in Washington, D.C. They still wrote each other.

It was just noon when he found the Mid-Hudson Civic Center and made his way in. The marketplace was packed into a concert hall, and the floor was densely crowded, the concrete walls echoing with laughter and the steady hollow roar of overlapping conversations. He hadn't let anyone know he was coming, but it didn't matter, one of the organizers found him anyway, a chubby woman with frizzy red hair, in a pinstripe suit-jacket with tails.

"I had no idea—" she said, and, "We didn't hear from you!" and, "Can I get you a drink?"

Then there was a rum-and-Coke in one hand, and a little knot of the curious around him, chattering about movies and writers and *Best New Horror,* and he wondered why he had ever thought of not coming. Someone was missing for the 1:30 panel on the state of short horror fiction, and wouldn't that be perfect—? Wouldn't it, he said.

He was led to a conference room, rows of folding chairs, a long table at one end with a pitcher of ice water on it. He took a seat behind it, with the rest of the panel: a teacher who had written a book about Poe, the editor of an online horror magazine, a local writer of fantasy-themed children's books. The redhead introduced them to the two dozen people or so who filed in, and then everyone at the table had a chance to make some opening remarks. Carroll was the last to speak.

First he said that every fictional world was a work of fantasy, and whenever writers introduce a threat or a conflict into their story, they create the possibility of horror. He had been drawn to horror fiction, he said, because it took the most basic elements of literature and pushed them to their extremes. All fiction was make-believe, which made fantasy more valid (and honest) than realism.

He said that most horror and fantasy was worse than awful: exhausted, creatively bankrupt imitations of what was shit to begin with. He said sometimes he went for months without coming across a single fresh idea, a single memorable character, a single striking sentence.

Then he told them it had never been any different. It was probably true of any endeavor—artistic or otherwise—that it took a lot of people creating a lot of bad work to produce even a few successes. Everyone was welcome to struggle, get it wrong, learn from their mistakes, try again. And always there were rubies in the sand. He talked about Clive Barker and Kelly Link and Stephen Gallagher and Peter Kilrue, told them about "Buttonboy." He said for himself, anyway, nothing beat the high of discovering something thrilling and fresh, he would always love it, the happy horrible shock of it. As he spoke, he realized it was true. When he was done talking, a few in the back row began clapping, and the sound spread outward, a ripple in a pool, and as it moved across the room, people began to stand.

He was sweating as he came out from behind the table to shake a few hands, after the panel discussion was over. He took off his glasses to wipe his shirttail across his face, and before he had put them back on, he had taken the hand of someone else, a thin, diminutive figure. As he settled his glasses on his nose, he found he was shaking hands with someone he was not entirely pleased to recognize, a slender man with a mouthful of crooked, nicotine-stained teeth, and a mustache so small and tidy it looked penciled on.

His name was Matthew Graham and he edited an odious horror fanzine titled *Rancid Fantasies*. Carroll had heard that Graham had been arrested for sexually abusing his underage stepdaughter, although apparently the case had never gone to court. He tried not to hold that against the writers Graham published, but had still never found anything in *Rancid Fanta-*

sies even remotely worth reprinting in *Best New Horror*. Fiction about drug-addled morticians raping the corpses in their care, moronic hicks giving birth to shit-demons in outhouses located on ancient Indian burial grounds, work riddled with misspellings and grievous offenses to grammar.

"Isn't Peter Kilrue just something else?" Graham asked. "I published his first story. Didn't you read it? I sent you a copy, dear."

"Must've missed it," said Carroll. He had not bothered to look at *Rancid Fantasies* in over a year, although he had recently used an issue to line his catbox.

"You'd like him," Graham said, showing another flash of his few teeth. "He's one of us."

Carroll tried not to visibly shudder. "You've talked with him?"

"Talked with him? I had drinks with him over lunch. He was here this morning. You only just missed him." Graham opened his mouth in a broad grin. His breath stank. "If you want, I can tell you where he lives. He isn't far you know."

OVER A BRIEF late lunch, he read Peter Kilrue's first short story, in a copy of *Rancid Fantasies* that Matthew Graham was able to produce. It was titled "Piggies," and it was about an emotionally disturbed woman who gives birth to a litter of piglets. The pigs learn to talk, walk on their hind legs, and wear clothes, à la the swine in *Animal Farm*. At the end of the story, though, they revert to savagery, using their tusks to slash their mother to ribbons. As the story comes to a close, they are locked in mortal combat to see who will get to eat the tastiest pieces of her corpse.

It was a corrosive, angry piece, and while it was far and away the best thing *Rancid Fantasies* had ever published—written with care and psychological realism—Carroll didn't like it much. One passage, in which the piggies all fight to suckle at their mother's breasts, read like an unusually horrid and grotesque bit of pornography.

Matthew Graham had folded a blank piece of typing paper into the back of the magazine. On it he had drawn a crude map to Kilrue's house, twenty miles north of Poughkeepsie, in a little town called Piecliff. It was on Carroll's way home, up a scenic parkway, the Taconic, which would take him naturally back to I-90. There was no phone number. Graham had mentioned that Kilrue was having money troubles, and the phone company had shut him off.

By the time Carroll was on the Taconic, it was already getting dark, gloom gathering beneath the great oaks and tall firs that crowded the side of the road. He seemed to be the only person on the parkway, which wound higher and higher into hills and wood. Sometimes, in the headlights, he saw families of deer standing at the edge of the road, their eyes pink in the darkness, watching him pass with a mixture of fear and alien curiosity.

Piecliff wasn't much: a strip mall, a church, a graveyard, a Texaco, a single blinking yellow light. Then he was through it and following a narrow state highway through piney woods. By then it was full night and cold enough so he needed to switch on the heat. He turned off onto Tarheel Road, and his Civic labored through a series of switchbacks, up a hill so steep the engine whined with effort. He closed his eyes for a moment, and almost missed a hairpin turn, had to yank at the wheel to keep from crashing through brush and plunging down the side of the slope.

A half mile later the asphalt turned to gravel and he trolled through the dark, tires raising a luminescent cloud of chalky dust. His headlights rose over a fat man in a bright orange knit cap, shoving a hand into a mailbox. On the side of the mailbox, letters printed on reflective decals spelled **KIL U**. Carroll slowed.

The fat man held up a hand to shield his eyes, peering at Carroll's car. Then he grinned, tipped his head in the direction of the house, in a *follow-me* gesture, as if Carroll were an expected visitor. He started up the driveway, and Carroll rolled along behind him. Hemlocks leaned over the narrow dirt track. Branches swatted at the windshield, raked at the sides of his Civic.

At last the drive opened into a dusty dooryard before a great yellow farmhouse, with a turret and a sagging porch that wrapped around two sides. A plywood sheet had been nailed into a broken window. A toilet bowl lay in the weeds. At the sight of the place, Carroll felt the hairs stirring on his forearms. *Journeys end in lovers meeting*, he thought, and grinned at his own uneasy imagination. He parked next to an ancient tractor with wild stalks of Indian corn growing up through its open hood.

He shoved his car keys in his coat pocket and climbed out, started toward the porch, where the fat man waited. His walk took him past a brightly lit carriage house. The double doors were pulled shut, but from within he heard the shriek of a bandsaw. He glanced up at the house and saw a black, back-lit figure staring down at him from one of the second-floor windows.

Eddie Carroll said he was looking for Peter Kilrue. The fat man inclined his head toward the door, the same *follow-me* gesture he had used to invite Carroll up the driveway. Then he turned and let him in.

The front hall was dim, the walls lined with picture frames that hung askew. A narrow staircase climbed to the second floor. There was a smell in the air, a humid, oddly male scent . . . like sweat, but also like pancake batter. Carroll immediately identified it, and just as immediately decided to pretend he hadn't noticed anything.

"Bunch of shit in this hall," the fat man said. "Let me hang up your coat. Never be seen again." His voice was cheerful and piping. As Carroll handed him his coat, the fat man turned and hollered up the stairs, "*Pete! Someone here!*" The sudden shift from a conversational voice to a furious scream gave Carroll a bad jolt.

A floorboard creaked above them, and then a thin man, in a corduroy jacket and glasses with square, black plastic frames, appeared at the top of the steps.

"What can I do for you?" he asked.

"My name is Edward Carroll. I edit a series of books, *America's Best New Horror*?" He looked for some reaction on the thin man's face, but Kilrue remained impassive. "I read one of your stories, 'Buttonboy,' in *True North*, and I liked it quite a bit. I was hoping to use it in this year's collection." He paused, then added, "You haven't been so easy to get in touch with."

"Come up," Kilrue said, and stepped back from the top of the stairs.

Carroll started up the steps. Below, the fat brother began to wander down the hall, Carroll's coat in one hand, the Kilrue family mail in the other. Then, abruptly, the fat man stopped, looked up the stairwell, waggled a manila envelope.

"Hey, Pete! Mom's social security came!" His voice wavering with pleasure.

By the time Carroll reached the top of the staircase, Peter Kilrue was already walking down the hall, to an open door at the end. The corridor itself seemed crooked somehow. The floor felt tilted underfoot, so much so that once Carroll had to touch the wall to steady himself. Floorboards were missing. A chandelier hung with crystal pendants floated above the stairwell, furred with lint and cobwebs. In some distant, echoing room of Carroll's mind, a hunchback played the opening bars of *The Addams Family* on a glockenspiel.

Kilrue had a small bedroom located under the pitch of the roof. A card table with a chipped wooden surface stood against one wall, with a humming Selectric typewriter set upon it, a sheet of paper rolled into the platen.

"Were you working?" Carroll asked.

"I can't stop," Kilrue said.

"Good."

Kilrue sat on the cot. Carroll came a step inside the door, couldn't go any further without ducking his head. Peter Kilrue had oddly colorless eyes, the lids red-rimmed as if irritated, and he regarded Carroll without blinking.

Carroll told him about the collection. He said he could pay two hundred dollars, plus a percentage of shared royalties. Kilrue nodded, seemed neither surprised nor curious about the details. His voice was breathy and girlish. He said thank you.

"What did you think of my ending?" Kilrue asked, without forewarning.

"Of 'Buttonboy'? I liked it. If I didn't, I wouldn't want to reprint it."

"They hated it down at Katahdin University. All those co-eds with their pleated skirts and rich daddies. They hated a lot of stuff about the story, but especially my ending."

Carroll nodded. "Because they didn't see it coming. It probably gave a few of them a nasty jolt. The shock ending is out of fashion in mainstream literature."

Kilrue said, "The way I wrote it at first, the giant is strangling her, and just as she's passing out, she can feel the other one using buttons to pin her twat shut. But I lost my nerve and cut it out. Didn't think Noonan would publish it that way."

"In horror, it's often what you leave out that gives a story its power," Carroll said, but it was just something to say. He felt a cool tingle of sweat on his forehead. "I'll go get a permissions form from my car." He wasn't sure why he said that either. He didn't have a permissions form in the car, just felt a sudden intense desire to catch a breath of cold fresh air.

He ducked back through the door into the hall. He found it took an effort to keep from breaking into a trot.

At the bottom of the staircase, Carroll hesitated in the hall, wondering where Kilrue's obese older brother had gone with his jacket. He started down the corridor. The way grew darker the further he went.

There was a small door beneath the stairs, but when he tugged on the brass handle it wouldn't open. He proceeded down the hall, looking for a closet. From somewhere nearby he heard grease sizzling, smelled onions, and heard the whack of a knife. He pushed open a door to his right and looked into a formal dining room, the heads of animals mounted on the walls. An oblong shaft of wan light fell across the table. The tablecloth was red and had a swastika in the center.

Carroll eased the door shut. Another door, just down the hall and to the left, was open, and offered a view of the kitchen. The fat man stood behind a counter, bare-chested and tattooed, chopping what looked like liver with a meat cleaver. He had iron rings through his nipples. Carroll was about to call to him, when the fat Kilrue boy came around the counter and walked to the gas range, to stir what was in the pan. He wore only a jock strap now, and his surprisingly scrawny, pale buttocks trembled with each step. Carroll shifted further back into the darkness of the hall, and after a moment continued on, treading silently.

The corridor was even more crooked than the one upstairs, visibly knocked out of true, as if the house had been jarred by some seismic event, and the front end no longer lined up with the back. He didn't know why he didn't turn back; it made no sense just wandering deeper and deeper into a strange house. Still his feet carried him on.

Carroll opened a door to the left, close to the end of the hall. He flinched from the stink and the furious humming of flies. An unpleasant human warmth spilled out and over him. It was the darkest room yet, a spare bedroom, and he was about to close the door when he heard something shifting under the sheets of the bed. He covered his mouth and nose with one hand and willed himself to take a step forward, and to wait for his eyes to adjust to the light.

A frail old woman was in the bed, the sheet tangled at her waist. She was naked, and he seemed to have caught her in the act of stretching, her skeletal arms raised over her head.

"Sorry," Carroll muttered, looking away. "So sorry."

Once more he began to push the door shut, then stopped, looked back into the room. The old woman stirred again beneath the sheets. Her arms were still stretched over her head. It was the smell, the human reek of her, that made him hold up, staring at her.

As his eyes adjusted to the gloom, he saw the wire around her wrists, holding her arms to the headboard. Her eyes were slitted and her breath rattled. Beneath the wrinkled, small sacks of her breasts, he could see her ribs. The flies whirred. Her tongue popped out of her mouth and moved across her dry lips, but she didn't speak.

Then he was moving down the hall, going at a fast walk on stiff legs. As he passed the kitchen, he thought the fat brother looked up and saw him, but Carroll didn't slow down. At the edge of his vision he saw Peter Kilrue standing at the top of the stairs, looking down at him, head cocked at a questioning angle.

"Be right back with that thing," Carroll called up to him, without missing a step. His voice was surprisingly casual.

He hit the front door, banged through it. He didn't leap the stairs, but took them one at a time. When you were running from someone, you never jumped the stairs; that was how you twisted an ankle. He had seen it happen in a hundred horror movies. The air was so frosty it burned his lungs.

One of the carriage house doors was open now. He had a look into it on his way past. He saw a smooth dirt floor, rusted chains and hooks dangling from the beams, a chain saw hanging from the wall. Behind a table saw stood a tall, angular man with one hand. The other was a stump, the tormented skin shiny with scar tissue. He regarded Carroll without speaking, his colorless eyes judging and unfriendly. Carroll smiled and nodded.

He opened the door of his Civic and heaved himself in behind the wheel . . . and in the next moment felt a spoke of panic pierce him through the chest. His keys were in his coat. His coat was inside. He almost cried out at the awful shock of it, but when he opened his mouth what came out was a frightened sob of laughter instead. He had seen this in a hundred horror movies too, had read this moment in three hundred stories. They never had the keys, or the car wouldn't start, or—

The brother with one hand appeared at the door of the carriage house, and stared across the drive at him. Carroll waved. His other hand was disconnecting his cell phone from the charger. He glanced at it. There was no reception up here. Somehow he wasn't surprised. He laughed again, a choked, nerve-jangling sound.

When he looked up, the front door of the house was open, and two figures stood in it, staring down at him. All the brothers were staring at him now. He climbed out of the car and started walking swiftly down the driveway. He didn't start to run until he heard one of them shout.

At the bottom of the driveway, he did not turn to follow the road, but went straight across it and crashed through the brush, into the trees. Whip-thin branches lashed at his face. He tripped and tore the knee of his pants, got up, kept going.

The night was clear and cloudless, the sky filled to its limitless depth with stars. He paused, on the side of a steep slope, crouching among rocks, to catch his breath, a stitch in one side. He heard voices up the hill from him, branches breaking. He heard someone pull the ripcord on a small engine, once, twice, then the noisy unmuffled scream-and-roar of a chain saw coming to life.

He got up and ran on, pitching himself down the hill, flying through the branches of the firs, leaping roots and rocks without seeing them. As he went, the hill got steeper and steeper, until it was really like falling. He was going too fast and he knew when he came to a stop, it would involve crashing into something, and shattering pain.

Only as he went on, picking up speed all the time, until with each leap he seemed to sail through yards of darkness, he felt a giddy surge of emotion, a sensation that might have been panic but felt strangely like exhilaration. He felt as if at any moment his feet might leave the ground and never come back down. He knew this forest, this darkness, this night. He knew his chances: not good. He knew what was after him. It had been after him all his life. He knew where he was—in a story about to unfold an ending. He knew better than anyone how these stories went, and if anyone could find their way out of these woods, it was him.

20TH CENTURY GHOST

The best time *to see her is when the place is almost full.*

There is the well-known story of the man who wanders in for a late show and finds the vast six-hundred-seat theater almost deserted. Halfway through the movie, he glances around and discovers her sitting next to him, in a chair that only moments before had been empty. Her witness stares at her. She turns her head and stares back. She has a nosebleed. Her eyes are wide, stricken. My head hurts, *she whispers.* I have to step out for a moment. Will you tell me what I miss? *It is in this instant that the person looking at her realizes she is as insubstantial as the shifting blue ray of light cast by the projector. It is possible to see the next seat over through her body. As she rises from her chair, she fades away.*

Then there is the story about the group of friends who go into the Rosebud together on a Thursday night. One of the bunch sits down next to a woman by herself, a woman in blue. When the movie doesn't start right away, the person who sat down beside her decides to make conversation. What's playing tomorrow? *he asks her.* The theater is dark tomorrow, *she whispers.* This is the last show. *Shortly after the movie begins she vanishes. On the drive home, the man who spoke to her is killed in a car accident.*

These, and many of the other best-known legends of the Rosebud, are false . . . the ghost stories of people who have seen too many horror movies and who think they know exactly how a ghost story should be.

Alec Sheldon, who was one of the first to see Imogene Gilchrist, owns the Rosebud, and at seventy-three still operates the projector most nights. He can always tell, after talking to someone for just a few moments, whether or not they really saw her, but what he knows he keeps to himself, and he never publicly discredits anyone's story . . . that would be bad for business.

He knows, though, that anyone who says they could see right through her didn't see her at all. Some of the put-on artists talk about blood pouring from her nose, her ears, her eyes; they say she gave them a pleading look, and asked for them to find somebody, to bring help. But she doesn't bleed that way, and when she wants to talk, it isn't to tell someone to bring a doctor. A lot of the pretenders begin their stories by saying, You'll never believe what I just saw. *They're right.* He won't, although he will listen to all that they have to say, with a patient, even encouraging, smile.

The ones who have seen her don't come looking for Alec to tell him about it. More often than not he finds them, comes across them wandering the lobby on unsteady legs; they've had a bad shock, they don't feel well. They need to sit down a while. They don't ever say, You won't believe what I just saw. The experience is still too immediate. The idea that they might not be believed doesn't occur to them until later. Often they are in a state that might be described as subdued, even submissive. When he thinks about the effect she has on those who encounter her, he thinks of Steven Greenberg coming out of The Birds one cool Sunday afternoon in 1963. Steven was just twelve then, and it would be another twelve years before he went and got so famous; he was at that time not a golden boy, but just a boy.

Alec was in the alley behind the Rosebud, having a smoke, when he heard the fire door into the theater clang open behind him. He turned to see a lanky kid leaning in the doorway—just leaning there, not going in or out. The boy squinted into the harsh white sunshine, with the confused, wondering look of a small child who has just been shaken out of a deep sleep.

Alec could see past him into a darkness filled with the shrill sounds of thousands of squeaking sparrows. Beneath that, he could hear a few in the audience stirring restlessly, beginning to complain.

Hey, kid, in or out? *Alec said.* You're lettin' the light in.

The kid—Alec didn't know his name then—turned his head and stared back into the theater for a long, searching moment. Then he stepped out and the door settled shut behind him, closing gently on its pneumatic hinge. And still he didn't go anywhere, didn't say anything. The Rosebud had been showing The Birds *for two weeks, and although Alec had seen others walk out before it was over, none of the early exits had been twelve-year-old boys. It was the sort of film most boys of that age waited all year to see, but who knew? Maybe the kid had a weak stomach.*

I left my Coke in the theater, *the kid said, his voice distant, almost toneless.* I still had a lot of it left.

You want to go back in and look for it?

And the kid lifted his eyes and gave Alec a bright look of alarm, and then Alec knew. No.

Alec finished his cigarette, pitched it.

I sat with the dead lady, *the kid blurted.*

Alec nodded.

She talked to me.

What did she say?

He looked at the kid again, and found him staring back with eyes that were now wide and round with disbelief.

I need someone to talk to, she said. When I get excited about a movie I need to talk.

Alec knows when she talks to someone she always wants to talk about the movies. She usually addresses herself to men, although sometimes she will sit and talk with a woman—Lois Weisel most notably. Alec has been working on a theory of what it is that causes her to show herself. He has been keeping notes in a yellow legal pad. He has a list of who she appeared to and in what movie and when (Leland King, Harold and Maude, *'72; Joel Harlowe,* Eraserhead, *'77; Hal Lash,* Blood Simple, *'85; and all the others). He has, over the years, developed clear ideas about what conditions are most likely to produce her, although the specifics of his theory are constantly being revised.*

As a young man, thoughts of her were always on his mind, or simmering just beneath the surface; she was his first and most strongly felt obsession. Then for a while he was better—when the theater was a success, and he was an important business-man in the community, chamber of commerce, town planning board. In those days he could go weeks without thinking about her; and then someone would see her, or pretend to have seen her, and stir the whole thing up again.

But following his divorce—she kept the house, he moved into the one-bedroom under the theater—and not long after the 8-screen cineplex opened just outside of town, he began to obsess again, less about her than about the theater itself (is there any difference, though? Not really, he supposes, thoughts of one always circling around to thoughts of the other). He never imag-ined he would be so old and owe so much money. He has a hard time sleeping, his head is so full of ideas—wild, desperate ideas—about how to keep the theater from failing. He keeps himself awake thinking about income, staff, salable assets. And when he can't think about money anymore, he tries to picture where he will go if the theater closes. He envisions an old folks' home, mattresses that reek of Ben-Gay, hunched geezers with their den-tures out, sitting in a musty common room watching daytime sitcoms; he sees a place where he will passively fade away, like wallpaper that gets too much sunlight and slowly loses its color.

This is bad. What is more terrible is when he tries to imag-ine what will happen to her if the Rosebud closes. He sees the theater stripped of its seats, an echoing empty space, drifts of dust in the corners, petrified wads of gum stuck fast to the ce-ment. Local teens have broken in to drink and screw; he sees scattered liquor bottles, ignorant graffiti on the walls, a single, grotesque, used condom on the floor in front of the stage. He sees the lonely and violated place where she will fade away.

Or won't fade . . . the worst thought of all.

Alec saw her—spoke to her—for the first time when he was fifteen, six days after he learned his older brother had been killed in the South Pacific. President Truman had sent a letter expressing his condolences. It was a form letter, but the signature on the bottom—that was really his. Alec hadn't cried yet. He knew, years later, that he spent that week in a state of shock, that he had lost the person he loved most in the world and it had badly traumatized him. But in 1945 no one used the word "trauma" to talk about emotions, and the only kind of shock anyone discussed was "shell—."

He told his mother he was going to school in the mornings. He wasn't going to school. He was shuffling around downtown looking for trouble. He shoplifted candy-bars from the American Luncheonette and ate them out at the empty shoe factory—the place closed down, all the men off in France, or the Pacific. With sugar zipping in his blood, he launched rocks through the windows, trying out his fastball.

He wandered through the alley behind the Rosebud and looked at the door into the theater and saw that it wasn't firmly shut. The side facing the alley was a smooth metal surface, no door handle, but he was able to pry it open with his fingernails. He came in on the 3:30 P.M. show, the place crowded, mostly kids under the age of ten and their mothers. The fire door was halfway up the theater, recessed into the wall, set in shadow. No one saw him come in. He slouched up the aisle and found a seat in the back.

"I heard Jimmy Stewart went to the Pacific," his brother had told him while he was home on leave, before he shipped out. They were throwing the ball around out back. "Mr. Smith is probably carpet-bombing the red fuck out of Tokyo right this instant. How's that for a crazy thought?" Alec's brother, Ray, was a self-described film freak. He and Alec went to every single movie that opened during his monthlong leave: *Bataan*, *The Fighting Seabees*, *Going My Way*.

Alec waited through an episode of a serial concerning the latest adventures of a singing cowboy with long eyelashes and a mouth so dark his lips were black. It failed to interest him. He picked his nose and wondered how to get a Coke with no money. The feature started.

At first Alec couldn't figure out what the hell kind of movie it was, although right off he had the sinking feeling it was going to be a musical. First the members of an orchestra filed onto a stage against a bland blue backdrop. Then a starched shirt came out and started telling the audience all about the brand-new kind of entertainment they were about to see. When he started blithering about Walt Disney and his artists, Alec began to slide downwards in his seat, his head sinking between his shoulders. The orchestra surged into big dramatic blasts of strings and horns. In another moment his worst fears were realized. It wasn't just a musical; it was also a *cartoon*. Of course it was a cartoon, he should have known—the place crammed with little kids and their mothers—a 3:30 show in the middle of the week that led off with an episode of The Lipstick Kid, singing sissy of the high plains.

After a while he lifted his head and peeked at the screen through his fingers, watched some abstract animation: silver raindrops falling against a background of roiling smoke, rays of molten light shimmering across an ashen sky. Eventually he straightened up to watch in a more comfortable position. He was not quite sure what he was feeling. He was bored, but interested too, almost a little mesmerized. It would have been hard not to watch. The visuals came at him in a steady hypnotic assault: ribs of red light, whirling stars, kingdoms of cloud glowing in the crimson light of a setting sun.

The little kids were shifting around in their seats. He heard a little girl whisper loudly, "Mom, when is there going to be *Mickey*?" For the kids it was like being in school. But by the time the movie hit the next segment, the orchestra shifting from Bach to Tchaikovsky, he was sitting all the way up, even leaning forward slightly, his forearms resting on his knees. He watched fairies flitting through a dark forest, touching flowers and spiderwebs with enchanted wands and spreading sheets of glittering, incandescent dew. He felt a kind of baffled wonder watching them fly around, a curious feeling of yearning. He had the sudden idea he could sit there and watch forever.

"I could sit in this theater forever," whispered someone beside him. It was a girl's voice. "Just sit here and watch and never leave."

He didn't know there was someone sitting beside him and jumped to hear a voice so close. He thought—no, he knew—

that when he sat down, the seats on either side of him were empty. He turned his head.

She was only a few years older than him, couldn't have been more than twenty, and his first thought was that she was very close to being a fox; his heart beat a little faster to have such a girl speaking to him. He was already thinking, *Don't blow it.* She wasn't looking at him. She was staring up at the movie, and smiling in a way that seemed to express both admiration and a child's dazed wonder. He wanted desperately to say something smooth, but his voice was trapped in his throat.

She leaned towards him without glancing away from the screen, her left hand just touching the side of his arm on the armrest.

"I'm sorry to bother you," she whispered. "When I get excited about a movie I want to talk. I can't help it."

In the next moment he became aware of two things, more or less simultaneously. The first was that her hand against his arm was cold. He could feel the deadly chill of it through his sweater, a cold so palpable it startled him a little. The second thing he noticed was a single teardrop of blood on her upper lip, under her left nostril.

"You have a nosebleed," he said, in a voice that was too loud. He immediately wished he hadn't said it. You only had one opportunity to impress a fox like this. He should have found something for her to wipe her nose with, and handed it to her, murmured something real Sinatra: *You're bleeding, here.* He pushed his hands into his pockets, feeling for something she could wipe her nose with. He didn't have anything.

But she didn't seem to have heard him, didn't seem the slightest bit aware he had spoken. She absent-mindedly brushed the back of one hand under her nose, and left a dark smear of blood over her upper lip . . . and Alec froze with his hands in his pockets, staring at her. It was the first he knew there was something wrong about the girl sitting next to him, something slightly *off* about the scene playing out between them. He instinctively drew himself up and slightly away from her without even knowing he was doing it.

She laughed at something in the movie, her voice soft, breathless. Then she leaned towards him and whispered,

"This is all wrong for kids. Harry Parcells loves this theater, but he plays all the wrong movies—Harry Parcells who runs the place?"

There was a fresh runner of blood leaking from her left nostril and blood on her lips, but by then Alec's attention had turned to something else. They were sitting directly under the projector beam, and there were moths and other insects whirring through the blue column of light above. A white moth had landed on her face. It was crawling up her cheek. She didn't notice, and Alec didn't mention it to her. There wasn't enough air in his chest to speak.

She whispered, "He thinks just because it's a cartoon they'll like it. It's funny he could be so crazy for movies and know so little about them. He won't run the place much longer."

She glanced at him and smiled. She had blood staining her teeth. Alec couldn't get up. A second moth, ivory white, landed just inside the delicate cup of her ear.

"Your brother Ray would have loved this," she said.

"Get away," Alec whispered hoarsely.

"You belong here, Alec," she said. "You belong here with me."

He moved at last, shoved himself up out of his seat. The first moth was crawling into her hair. He thought he heard himself moan, just faintly. He started to move away from her. She was staring at him. He backed a few feet down the aisle and bumped into some kid's legs, and the kid yelped. He glanced away from her for an instant, down at a fattish boy in a striped T-shirt who was glaring back at him: *Watch where you're going, meathead.*

Alec looked at her again and now she was slumped very low in her seat. Her head rested on her left shoulder. Her legs hung lewdly open. There were thick strings of blood, dried and crusted, running from her nostrils, bracketing her thin-lipped mouth. Her eyes were rolled back in her head. In her lap was an overturned carton of popcorn.

Alec thought he was going to scream. He didn't scream. She was perfectly motionless. He looked from her to the kid he had almost tripped over. The fat kid glanced casually in the direction of the dead girl, showed no reaction. He turned his gaze back to Alec, his eyes questioning, one corner of his mouth turned up in a derisive sneer.

"Sir," said a woman, the fat kid's mother. "Can you move, *please?* We're trying to watch the movie."

Alec threw another look towards the dead girl, only now the chair where she had been was empty, the seat folded up. He started to retreat, bumping into knees, almost falling over once, grabbing someone for support. Then suddenly the room erupted into cheers, applause. His heart throbbed. He cried out, looked wildly around. It was Mickey, up there on the screen in droopy red robes—Mickey had arrived at last.

He backed up the aisle, swatted through the padded leather doors into the lobby. He flinched at the late-afternoon brightness, narrowed his eyes to squints. He felt dangerously sick. Then someone was holding his shoulder, turning him, walking him across the room, over to the staircase up to balcony-level. Alec sat down on the bottom step, sat down hard.

"Take a minute," someone said. "Don't get up. Catch your breath. Do you think you're going to throw up?"

Alec shook his head.

"Because if you think you're going to throw up, hold on till I can get you a bag. It isn't so easy to get stains out of this carpet. Also when people smell vomit they don't want popcorn."

Whoever it was lingered beside him for another moment, then without a word turned and shuffled away. He returned maybe a minute later.

"Here. On the house. Drink it slow. The fizz will help with your stomach."

Alec took a wax cup sweating beads of cold water, found the straw with his mouth, sipped icy cola bubbly with carbonation. He looked up. The man standing over him was tall and slope-shouldered, with a sagging roll around the middle. His hair was cropped to a dark bristle and his eyes, behind his absurdly thick glasses, were small and pale and uneasy.

Alec said, "There's a dead girl in there." He didn't recognize his own voice.

The color drained out of the big man's face and he cast an unhappy glance back at the doors into the theater. "She's never been in a matinee before. I thought only night shows, I thought—for God's sake, it's a kid's movie. What's she trying to do to me?"

Alec opened his mouth, didn't even know what he was going to say, something about the dead girl, but what came out instead was: "It's not really a kid's film."

The big man shot him a look of mild annoyance. "Sure it is. It's Walt Disney."

Alec stared at him for a long moment, then said, "You must be Harry Parcells."

"Yeah. How'd you know?"

"Lucky guesser," Alec said. "Thanks for the Coke."

ALEC FOLLOWED HARRY Parcells behind the concessions counter, through a door and out onto a landing at the bottom of some stairs. Harry opened a door to the right and let them into a small, cluttered office. The floor was crowded with steel film cans. Fading film posters covered the walls, overlapping in places: *Boys Town, David Copperfield, Gone With the Wind.*

"Sorry she scared you," Harry said, collapsing into the office chair behind his desk. "You sure you're all right? You look kind of peaked."

"Who is she?"

"Something blew out in her brain," he said, and pointed a finger at his left temple, as if pretending to hold a gun to his head. "Six years ago. During *The Wizard of Oz*. The very first show. It was the most terrible thing. She used to come in all the time. She was my steadiest customer. We used to talk, kid around with each other—" His voice wandered off, confused and distraught. He squeezed his plump hands together on the desktop in front of him, said finally, "Now she's trying to bankrupt me."

"You've seen her." It wasn't a question.

Harry nodded. "A few months after she passed away. She told me I don't belong here. I don't know why she wants to scare me off when we used to get along so great. Did she tell you to go away?"

"Why is she here?" Alec said. His voice was still hoarse, and it was a strange kind of question to ask. For a while, Harry just peered at him through his thick glasses with what seemed to be total incomprehension.

Then he shook his head and said, "She's unhappy. She died before the end of *The Wizard* and she's still miserable about it. I understand. That was a good movie. I'd feel robbed too."

"Hello?" someone shouted from the lobby. "Anyone there?"

"Just a minute," Harry called out. He gave Alec a pained look. "My concession-stand girl told me she was quitting yesterday. No notice or anything."

"Was it the ghost?"

"Heck no. One of her paste-on nails fell into someone's food so I told her not to wear them anymore. No one wants to get a fingernail in a mouthful of popcorn. She told me a lot of boys she knows come in here and if she can't wear her nails she wasn't going to work for me no more so now I got to do everything myself." He said this as he was coming around the desk. He had something in one hand, a newspaper clipping. "This will tell you about her." And then he gave Alec a look—it wasn't a glare exactly, but there was at least a measure of dull warning in it—and he added: "Don't run off on me. We still have to talk."

He went out, Alec staring after him, wondering what that last funny look was about. He glanced down at the clipping. It was an obituary—her obituary. The paper was creased, the edges worn, the ink faded; it looked as if it had been handled often. Her name was Imogene Gilchrist, she had died at nineteen, she worked at Water Street Stationery. She was survived by her parents, Colm and Mary. Friends and family spoke of her pretty laugh, her infectious sense of humor. They talked about how she loved the movies. She saw all the movies, saw them on opening day, first show. She could recite the entire cast from almost any picture you cared to name, it was like a party trick—she even knew the names of actors who had had just one line. She was president of the drama club in high school, acted in all the plays, built sets, arranged lighting. "I always thought she'd be a movie star," said her drama professor. "She had those looks and that laugh. All she needed was someone to point a camera at her and she would have been famous."

When Alec finished reading he looked around. The office was still empty. He looked back down at the obituary, rubbing the corner of the clipping between thumb and forefinger. He felt sick at the unfairness of it, and for a moment there was a pressure at the back of his eyeballs, a tingling, and he had the ridiculous idea he might start crying. He felt ill to live in a world where a nineteen-year-old girl full of laughter and life could be struck down like that, for no reason. The intensity of what he was feeling didn't really make sense, considering he had never known her when she was alive; didn't make sense until he thought about Ray, thought about Harry Truman's letter to his mom, the words *died with bravery, defending freedom, America is proud of him*. He thought about how Ray had taken him to *The Fighting Seabees*, right here in this theater, and they sat together with their feet up on the seats in front of them, their shoulders touching. "Look at John Wayne," Ray said. "They oughta have one bomber to carry him, and another one to carry his balls." The stinging in his eyes was so intense he couldn't stand it, and it hurt to breathe. He rubbed at his wet nose, and focused intently on crying as soundlessly as possible.

He wiped his face with the tail of his shirt, put the obituary on Harry Parcells' desk, looked around. He glanced at the posters, and the stacks of steel cans. There was a curl of film in the corner of the room, just eight or so frames—he wondered where it had come from—and he picked it up for a closer look. He saw a girl closing her eyes and lifting her face, in a series of little increments, to kiss the man holding her in a tight embrace; giving herself to him. Alec wanted to be kissed that way sometime. It gave him a curious thrill to be holding an actual piece of a movie. On impulse he stuck it into his pocket.

He wandered out of the office and back onto the landing at the bottom of the stairwell. He peered into the lobby. He expected to see Harry behind the concession stand, serving a customer, but there was no one there. Alec hesitated, wondering where he might have gone. While he was thinking it over, he became aware of a gentle whirring sound coming from the top of the stairs. He looked up them, and it clicked—the projector. Harry was changing reels.

Alec climbed the steps and entered the projection room, a dark compartment with a low ceiling. A pair of square windows looked into the theater below. The projector itself was pointed through one of them, a big machine made of brushed stainless steel, with the word VITAPHONE stamped on the case. Harry stood on the far side of it, leaning forward, peering out the same window through which the projector was casting its beam. He heard Alec at the door, shot him a brief look. Alec expected to be ordered away, but Harry said nothing, only nodded and returned to his silent watch over the theater.

Alec made his way to the VITAPHONE, picking a path carefully through the dark. There was a window to the left of the projector that looked down into the theater. Alec stared at it for a long moment, not sure if he dared, and then put his face close to the glass and peered into the darkened room beneath.

The theater was lit a deep midnight blue by the image on the screen: the conductor again, the orchestra in silhouette. The announcer was introducing the next piece. Alec lowered his gaze and scanned the rows of seats. It wasn't much trouble to find where he had been sitting, an empty cluster of seats close to the back, on the right. He half-expected to see her there, slid down in her chair, face tilted up towards the ceiling and blood all down it—her eyes turned perhaps to stare up at *him*. The thought of seeing her filled him with both dread and a strange nervous exhilaration, and when he realized she wasn't there, he was a little surprised by his own disappointment.

Music began: at first the wavering skirl of violins, rising and falling in swoops, and then a series of menacing bursts from the brass section, sounds of an almost military nature. Alec's gaze rose once more to the screen—rose and held there. He felt a chill race through him. His forearms prickled with gooseflesh. On the screen the dead were rising from their graves, an army of white and watery specters pouring out of the ground and into the night above. A square-shouldered demon, squatting on a mountain-top, beckoned them. They came to him, their ripped white shrouds fluttering around their gaunt bodies, their faces anguished, sorrowing. Alec caught his breath and held it, watched with a feeling rising in him of mingled shock and wonder.

The demon split a crack in the mountain, opened Hell. Fires leaped, the Damned jumped and danced, and Alec knew what he was seeing was about the war. It was about his brother dead for no reason in the South Pacific, *America is proud of him*, it was about bodies damaged beyond repair, bodies sloshing this way and that while they rolled in the surf at the edge of a beach somewhere in the Far East, getting soggy, bloating. It was about Imogene Gilchrist, who loved the movies and died with her legs spread open and her brain swelled full of blood and she was nineteen, her parents were Colm and Mary. It was about young people, young healthy bodies, punched full of holes and the life pouring out in arterial gouts, not a single dream realized, not a single ambition achieved. It was about young people who loved and were loved in return, going away, and not coming back, and the pathetic little remembrances that marked their departure, *my prayers are with you today, Harry Truman,* and *I always thought she'd be a movie star.*

A church bell rang somewhere, a long way off. Alec looked up. It was part of the film. The dead were fading away. The churlish and square-shouldered demon covered himself with his vast black wings, hiding his face from the coming of dawn. A line of robed men moved across the land below, carrying softly glowing torches. The music moved in gentle pulses. The sky was a cold, shimmering blue, light rising in it, the glow of sunrise spreading through the branches of birch trees and northern pine. Alec watched with a feeling in him like religious awe until was over.

"I liked *Dumbo* better," Harry said.

He flipped a switch on the wall, and a bare lightbulb came on, filling the projection room with harsh white light. The last of the film squiggled through the VITAPHONE and came out at the other end, where it was being collected on one of the reels. The trailing end whirled around and around and went *slap, slap, slap.* Harry turned the projector off, looked at Alec over the top of the machine.

"You look better. You got your color back."

"What did you want to talk about?" Alec remembered the

vague look of warning Harry gave him when he told him not to go anywhere, and the thought occurred to him now that maybe Harry knew he had slipped in without buying a ticket, that maybe they were about to have a problem.

But Harry said, "I'm prepared to offer you a refund or two free passes to the show of your choice. Best I can do."

Alec stared. It was a long time before he could reply.

"For what?"

"For what? To shut up about it. You know what it would do to this place if it got out about her? I got reasons to think people don't want to pay money to sit in the dark with a chatty dead girl."

Alec shook his head. It surprised him that Harry thought it would keep people away if it got out that the Rosebud was haunted. Alec had an idea it would have the opposite effect. People were happy to pay for the opportunity to experience a little terror in the dark—if they weren't, there wouldn't be any business in horror pictures. And then he remembered what Imogene Gilchrist had said to him about Harry Parcells: *He won't run the place much longer.*

"So what do you want?" Harry asked. "You want passes?"

Alec shook his head.

"Refund then."

"No."

Harry froze with his hand on his wallet, flashed Alec a surprised, hostile look. "What do you want then?"

"How about a job? You need someone to sell popcorn. I promise not to wear my paste-on nails to work."

Harry stared at him for a long moment without any reply, then slowly removed his hand from his back pocket.

"Can you work weekends?" he asked.

IN OCTOBER, ALEC *hears that Steven Greenberg is back in New Hampshire, shooting exteriors for his new movie on the grounds of Phillips Exeter Academy—something with Tom Hanks and Haley Joel Osment, a misunderstood teacher inspiring troubled kid-geniuses. Alec doesn't need to know any more than that to know it smells like Steven might be on his way* to *winning another Oscar. Alec, though, preferred the earlier work, Steven's fantasies and suspense thrillers.*

He considers driving down to have a look, wonders if he could talk his way onto the set—Oh yes, I knew Steven when he was a boy—*wonders if he might even be allowed to speak with Steven himself. But he soon dismisses the idea. There must be hundreds of people in this part of New England who could claim to have known Steven back in the day, and it isn't as if they were ever close. They only really had that one conversation, the day Steven saw her. Nothing before; nothing much after.*

So it is a surprise when one Friday afternoon close to the end of the month Alec takes a call from Steven's personal assistant, a cheerful, efficient-sounding woman named Marcia. She wants Alec to know that Steven was hoping to see him, and if he can drop in—is Sunday morning all right?—there will be a set pass waiting for him at Main Building, on the grounds of the Academy. They'll expect to see him around 10:00 A.M., she says in her bright chirp of a voice, before ringing off. It is not until well after the conversation has ended that Alec realizes he has received not an invitation, but a summons.

A goateed P.A. meets Alec at Main and walks him out to where they're filming. Alec stands with thirty or so others, and watches from a distance, while Hanks and Osment stroll together across a green quad littered with fallen leaves, Hanks nodding pensively while Osment talks and gestures. In front of them is a dolly, with two men and their camera equipment sitting on it, and two men pulling it. Steven and a small group of others stand off to the side, Steven observing the shot on a video monitor. Alec has never been on a movie set before, and he watches the work of professional make-believe with great pleasure.

After he has what he wants, and has talked with Hanks for a few minutes about the shot, Steven starts over towards the crowd where Alec is standing. There is a shy, searching look on his face. Then he sees Alec and opens his mouth in a gap-toothed grin, lifts one hand in a wave, looks for a moment very much the lanky boy again. He asks Alec if he wants to walk to craft services with him, for a chili dog and a soda.

On the walk Steven seems anxious, jingling the change in his pockets and shooting sideways looks at Alec. Alec knows he wants to talk about Imogene, but can't figure how to broach the subject. When at last he begins to talk, it's about his memories of the Rosebud. He talks about how he loved the place, talks about all the great pictures he saw for the first time there. Alec smiles and nods, but is secretly a little astounded at the depths of Steven's self-deception. Steven never went back after The Birds. *He didn't see any of the movies he says he saw there.*

At last, Steven stammers, What's going to happen to the place after you retire? Not that you should retire! I just mean—do you think you'll run the place much longer?

Not much longer, *Alec replies—it's the truth—but says no more. He is concerned not to degrade himself asking for a handout—although the thought is in him that this is in fact why he came. That ever since receiving Steven's invitation to visit the set he had been fantasizing that they would talk about the Rosebud, and that Steven, who is so wealthy, and who loves movies so much, might be persuaded to throw Alec a life preserver.*

The old movie houses are national treasures, *Steven says.* I own a couple, believe it or not. I run them as revival joints. I'd love to do something like that with the Rosebud someday. That's a dream of mine, you know.

Here is his chance, the opportunity Alec was not willing to admit he was hoping for. But instead of telling him that the Rosebud is in desperate straits, sure to close, Alec changes the subject . . . ultimately lacks the stomach to do what must be done.

What's your next project? *Alec asks.*

After this? I was considering a remake, *Steven says, and gives him another of those shifty sideways looks from the corners of his eyes.* You'd never guess what. *Then, suddenly, he reaches out, touches Alec's arm.* Being back in New Hampshire has really stirred some things up for me. I had a dream about our old friend, would you believe it?

Our old—*Alec starts, then realizes who he means.*

I had a dream the place was closed. There was a chain on

the front doors, and boards in the windows. I dreamed I heard a girl crying inside, *Steven says, and grins nervously. Isn't that the funniest thing?*

Alec drives home with a cool sweat on his face, ill at ease. He doesn't know why he didn't say anything, why he couldn't *say anything; Greenberg was practically begging to give him some money. Alec thinks bitterly that he has become a very foolish and useless old man.*

At the theater there are nine messages on Alec's machine. The first is from Lois Weisel, whom Alec has not heard from in years. Her voice is brittle. She says, Hi, Alec, Lois Weisel at B.U. *As if he could have forgotten her. Lois saw Imogene in* Midnight Cowboy. *Now she teaches documentary filmmaking to graduate students. Alec knows these two things are not unconnected, just as it is no accident Steven Greenberg became what he became.* Will you give me a call? I wanted to talk to you about—I just—will you call me? *Then she laughs, a strange, frightened kind of laugh, and says,* This is crazy. *She exhales heavily.* I just wanted to find out if something was happening to the Rosebud. Something bad. So—call me.

The next message is from Dana Llewellyn, who saw her in The Wild Bunch. *The message after that is from Shane Leonard, who saw Imogene in* American Graffiti. *Darren Campbell, who saw her in* Reservoir Dogs. *Some of them talk about the dream, a dream identical to the one Steven Greenberg described, boarded-over windows, chain on the doors, girl crying. Some only say they want to talk. By the time the answering machine tape has played its way to the end, Alec is sitting on the floor of his office, his hands balled into fists—an old man weeping helplessly.*

Perhaps twenty people have seen Imogene in the last twenty-five years, and nearly half of them have left messages for Alec to call. The other half will get in touch with him over the next few days, to ask about the Rosebud, to talk about their dream. Alec will speak with almost everyone living who has ever seen her, all of those Imogene felt compelled to speak to: a drama professor, the manager of a video rental store, a retired financier who in his youth wrote angry, comical film reviews for The Lansdowne Record, *and others. A whole congregation of people who flocked to the Rosebud instead of church on Sundays, those whose prayers were written by Paddy Chayefsky and whose hymnals were composed by John Williams and whose intensity of faith is a call Imogene is helpless to resist. Alec himself.*

AFTER THE SALE, *the Rosebud is closed for two months to refurbish. New seats, state-of-the-art sound. A dozen artisans put up scaffolding and work with little paintbrushes to restore the crumbling plaster molding on the ceiling. Steven adds personnel to run the day-to-day operations. Although it's his place now, Alec has agreed to stay on to manage things for a little while.*

Lois Weisel drives up three times a week to film a documentary about the renovation, using her grad students in various capacities, as electricians, sound people, grunts. Steven wants a gala reopening to celebrate the Rosebud 's past. When Alec hears what he wants to show first—a double feature of The Wizard of Oz *and* The Birds—*his forearms prickle with gooseflesh; but he makes no argument.*

On reopening night, the place is crowded like it hasn't been since Titanic. *The local news is there to film people walking inside in their best suits. Of course, Steven is there, which is why all the excitement . . . although Alec thinks he would have a sell-out even without Steven, that people would have come just to see the results of the renovation. Alec and Steven pose for photographs, the two of them standing under the marquee in their tuxedoes, shaking hands. Steven's tuxedo is Armani, bought for the occasion. Alec got married in his.*

Steven leans into him, pressing a shoulder against his chest. What are you going to do with yourself?

Before Steven's money, Alec would have sat behind the counter handing out tickets, and then gone up himself to start the projector. But Steven hired someone to sell tickets and run the projector. Alec says, Guess I'm going to sit and watch the movie.

Save me a seat, *Steven says.* I might not get in until *The Birds,* though. I have some more press to do out here.

Lois Weisel has a camera set up at the front of the theater, turned to point at the audience, and loaded with high-speed film for shooting in the dark. She films the crowd at different times, recording their reactions to The Wizard of Oz. This was to be the conclusion of her documentary—a packed house enjoying a twentieth-century classic in this lovingly restored old movie palace—but her movie wasn't going to end like she thought it would.

In the first shots on Lois's reel it is possible to see Alec sitting in the back left of the theater, his face turned up towards the screen, his glasses flashing blue in the darkness. The seat to the left of him, on the aisle, is empty, the only empty seat in the house. Sometimes he can be seen eating popcorn. Other times he is just sitting there watching, his mouth open slightly, an almost worshipful look on his face.

Then in one shot he has turned sideways to face the seat to his left. He has been joined by a woman in blue. He is leaning over her. They are unmistakably kissing. No one around them pays them any mind. The Wizard of Oz is ending. We know this because we can hear Judy Garland, reciting the same five words over and over in a soft, yearning voice, saying—well, you know what she is saying. They are only the loveliest five words ever said in all of film.

In the shot immediately following this one, the house lights are up, and there is a crowd of people gathered around Alec's body, slumped heavily in his seat. Steven Greenberg is in the aisle, yelping hysterically for someone to bring a doctor. A child is crying. The rest of the crowd generates a low rustling buzz of excited conversation. But never mind this shot. The footage that came just before it is much more interesting.

It is only a few seconds long, this shot of Alec and his unidentified companion—a few hundred frames of film—but it is the shot that will make Lois Weisel's reputation, not to mention a large sum of money. It will appear on television shows about unexplained phenomena, it will be watched and rewatched at gatherings of those fascinated with the supernatural. It will be studied, written about, debunked, confirmed, and celebrated. Let's see it again.

He leans over her. She turns her face up to his, and closes her eyes and she is very young and she is giving herself to him com-

pletely. Alec has removed his glasses. He is touching her lightly at the waist. This is the way people dream of being kissed, a movie star kiss. Watching them, one almost wishes the moment would never end. And over all this, Dorothy's small, brave voice fills the darkened theater. She is saying something about home. She is saying something everyone knows.

POP ART

My best friend when I was twelve was inflatable. His name was Arthur Roth, which also made him an inflatable Hebrew, although in our now-and-then talks about the afterlife, I don't remember that he took an especially Jewish perspective. Talk was mostly what we did—in his condition rough-house was out of the question—and the subject of death, and what might follow it, came up more than once. I think Arthur knew he would be lucky to survive high school. When I met him, he had already almost been killed a dozen times, once for every year he had been alive. The afterlife was always on his mind; also the possible lack of one.

When I tell you we talked, I mean only to say we communicated, argued, put each other down, built each other up. To stick to facts, *I* talked—Art couldn't. He didn't have a mouth. When he had something to say, he wrote it down. He wore a pad around his neck on a loop of twine, and carried crayons in his pocket. He turned in school papers in crayon, took tests in crayon. You can imagine the dangers a sharpened pencil would present to a four-ounce boy made of plastic and filled with air.

I think one of the reasons we were best friends was because he was such a great listener. I needed someone to listen. My mother was gone and my father I couldn't talk to. My mother ran away when I was three, sent my dad a rambling and confused letter from Florida, about sunspots and gamma rays and the radiation that emanates from power lines, about how the birthmark on the back of her left hand had moved up her arm and onto her shoulder. After that, a couple postcards, then nothing.

As for my father, he suffered from migraines. In the afternoons, he sat in front of soaps in the darkened living room, wet-eyed and miserable. He hated to be bothered. You couldn't tell him anything. It was a mistake even to try.

"Blah blah," he would say, cutting me off in mid-sentence. "My head is splitting. You're killing me here with blah blah this, blah blah that."

But Art liked to listen, and in trade, I offered him protection. Kids were scared of me. I had a bad reputation. I owned a switchblade, and sometimes I brought it to school and let other kids see; it kept them in fear. The only thing I ever stuck it into, though, was the wall of my bedroom. I'd lie on my bed and flip it at the corkboard wall, so that it hit, blade-first, *thunk!*

One day when Art was visiting he saw the pockmarks in my wall. I explained, one thing led to another, and before I knew it he was begging to have a throw.

"What's wrong with you?" I asked him. "Is your head completely empty? Forget it. No way."

Out came a Crayola, burnt-sienna. He wrote:

So at least let me look.

I popped it open for him. He stared at it wide-eyed. Actually, he stared at everything wide-eyed. His eyes were made of glassy plastic, stuck to the surface of his face. He couldn't blink or anything. But this was different than his usual bug-eyed stare. I could see he was really fixated.

He wrote:

I'll be careful I totally promise please!

I handed it to him. He pushed the point of the blade into the floor so it snicked into the handle. Then he hit the button and it snicked back out. He shuddered, stared at it in his hand. Then, without giving any warning, he chucked it at the wall. Of course it didn't hit tip-first; that takes practice, which he hadn't had, and coordination, which, speaking honestly, he wasn't ever going to have. It bounced, came flying back at him. He sprang into the air so quickly it was like I was watching his ghost jump out of his body. The knife landed where he had been and clattered away under my bed.

I yanked Art down off the ceiling. He wrote:

You were right, that was dumb. I'm a loser—a jerk.

"No question," I said.

But he wasn't a loser or a jerk. My dad is a loser. The kids at school were jerks. Art was different. He was all heart. He just wanted to be liked by someone.

Also, I can say truthfully, he was the most completely harmless person I've ever known. Not only would he not hurt a fly, he *couldn't* hurt a fly. If he slapped one, and lifted his hand, it would buzz off undisturbed. He was like a holy person in a Bible story, someone who can heal the ripped and infected parts of you with a laying-on of hands. You know how Bible stories go. That kind of person, they're never around long. Losers and jerks put nails in them and watch the air run out.

THERE WAS SOMETHING special about Art, an invisible special something that just made other kids naturally want to kick his ass. He was new at our school. His parents had just moved to town. They were normal, filled with blood not air. The condition Art suffered from is one of these genetic things that plays hopscotch with the generations, like Tay-Sachs (Art told me once that he had had a grand-uncle, also inflatable, who flopped one day into a pile of leaves and burst on the tine of a buried rake). On the first day of classes, Mrs. Gannon made Art stand at the front of the room, and told everyone all about him, while he hung his head out of shyness.

He was white. Not Caucasian, *white*, like a marshmallow, or Casper. A seam ran around his head and down his sides. There was a plastic nipple under one arm, where he could be pumped with air.

Mrs. Gannon told us we had to be extra careful not to run with scissors or pens. A puncture would probably kill him. He couldn't talk; everyone had to try and be sensitive about that. His interests were astronauts, photography, and the novels of Bernard Malamud.

Before she nudged him towards his seat, she gave his shoulder an encouraging little squeeze and as she pressed her fingers into him, he whistled gently. That was the only way he ever made sound. By flexing his body he could emit little squeaks and whines. When other people squeezed him, he made a soft, musical hoot.

He bobbed down the room and took an empty seat beside me. Billy Spears, who sat directly behind him, bounced thumbtacks off his head all morning long. The first couple times Art pretended not to notice. Then, when Mrs. Gannon wasn't looking, he wrote Billy a note. It said:

Please stop! I don't want to say anything to Mrs. Gannon but it isn't safe to throw thumbtacks at me. I'm not kidding.

Billy wrote back:

You make trouble, and there won't be enough of you left to patch a tire. Think about it.

It didn't get any easier for Art from there. In biology lab, Art was paired with Cassius Delamitri, who was in sixth grade for the second time. Cassius was a fat kid, with a pudgy, sulky face, and a disagreeable film of black hair above his unhappy pucker of a mouth.

The project was to distill wood, which involved the use of a gas flame—Cassius did the work, while Art watched and wrote notes of encouragement:

I can't believe you got a D- on this experiment when you did it last year—you totally know how to do this stuff!!

and

my parents bought me a lab kit for my birthday. You could come over and we could play mad scientist sometime—want to?

After three or four notes like that, Cassius had read enough, got it in his head Art was some kind of homosexual . . . especially with Art's talk about having him over to play doctor or whatever. When the teacher was distracted helping some other kids, Cassius shoved Art under the table and tied him around one of the table legs, in a squeaky granny knot, head, arms, body, and all. When Mr. Milton asked where Art had gone, Cassius said he thought he had run to the bathroom.

"Did he?" Mr. Milton asked. "What a relief. I didn't even know if that kid *could* go to the bathroom."

Another time, John Erikson held Art down during recess and wrote KOLLOSTIMY BAG on his stomach with indelible marker. It was spring before it faded away.

The worst thing was my mom saw. Bad enough she has to know I get beat up on a daily basis. But she was really upset it was spelled wrong.

He added:

I don't know what she expects—this is 6th grade. Doesn't she remember 6th grade? I'm sorry, but realistically, what are the odds you're going to get beat up by the grand champion of the spelling bee?

"The way your year is going," I said, "I figure them odds might be pretty good."

HERE IS HOW Art and I wound up friends:

During recess periods, I always hung out at the top of the monkey bars by myself, reading sports magazines. I was cultivating my reputation as a delinquent and possible drug pusher. To help my image along, I wore a black denim jacket and didn't talk to people or make friends.

At the top of the monkey bars—a dome-shaped construction at one edge of the asphalt lot behind the school—I was a good nine feet off the ground, and had a view of the whole yard. One day I watched Billy Spears horsing around with Cassius Delamitri and John Erikson. Billy had a wiffle ball and a bat, and the three of them were trying to bat the ball in through an open second-floor window. After fifteen minutes of not even coming close, John Erikson got lucky, swatted it in.

Cassius said, "Shit—there goes the ball. We need something else to bat around."

"Hey," Billy shouted. "Look! There's Art!"

They caught up to Art, who was trying to keep away, and Billy started tossing him in the air and hitting him with the bat to see how far he could knock him. Every time he struck Art with the bat it made a hollow, springy *whap!* Art popped into the air, then floated along a little ways, sinking gently back to the ground. As soon as his heels touched earth he started to run, but swiftness of foot wasn't one of Art's qualities. John and Cassius got into the fun by grabbing Art and drop-kicking him, to see who could punt him highest.

The three of them gradually pummeled Art down to my end of the lot. He struggled free long enough to run in under the monkey bars. Billy caught up, struck him a whap across the ass with the bat, and shot him high into the air.

Art floated to the top of the dome. When his body touched the steel bars, he stuck, face-up—static electricity.

"Hey," Billy hollered. "Chuck him down here!"

I had, up until that moment, never been face-to-face with Art. Although we shared classes, and even sat side-by-side in Mrs. Gannon's homeroom, we had not had a single exchange. He looked at me with his enormous plastic eyes and sad blank face, and I looked right back. He found the pad around his neck, scribbled a note in spring green, ripped it off and held it up at me.

I don't care what they do, but could you go away? I hate to get the crap knocked out of me in front of spectators.

"What's he writin'?" Billy shouted.

I looked from the note, past Art, and down at the gathering of boys below. I was struck by the sudden realization that I could *smell* them, all three of them, a damp, *human* smell, a sweaty-sour reek. It turned my stomach.

"Why are you bothering him?" I asked.

Billy said, "Just screwin' with him."

"We're trying to see how high we can make him go," Cassius said. "You ought to come down here. You ought to give it a try. We're going to kick him onto the roof of the friggin' school!"

"I got an even funner idea," I said, *funner* being an excellent word to use if you want to impress on some other kids that you might be a mentally retarded psychopath. "How about we see if I can kick your lardy ass up on the roof of the school?"

"What's your problem?" Billy asked. "You on the rag?"

I grabbed Art and jumped down. Cassius blanched. John Erikson tottered back. I held Art under one arm, feet sticking towards them, head pointed away.

"You guys are dicks," I said—some moments just aren't right for a funny line.

And I turned away from them. The back of my neck crawled at the thought of Billy's wiffle ball bat clubbing me one across the skull, but he didn't do a thing, let me walk.

We went out on the baseball field, sat on the pitcher's mound. Art wrote me a note that said thanks, and another that said I didn't have to do what I had done but that he was glad I had done it, and another that said he owed me one. I shoved each note into my pocket after reading it, didn't think why. That night, alone in my bedroom, I dug a wad of crushed notepaper out of my pocket, a lump the size of a lemon, peeled each note free and pressed it flat on my bed, read them all over again. There was no good reason not to throw them away, but I didn't, started a collection instead. It was like some part of me knew, even then, I might want to have something to remember Art by after he was gone. I saved hundreds of his notes over the next year, some as short as a couple words, a few six-page-long manifestos. I have most of them still, from the first note he handed me, the one that begins, *I don't care what they do,* to the last, the one that ends:

I want to see if it's true. If the sky opens up at the top.

*　　*　　*

AT FIRST MY father didn't like Art, but after he got to know him better he really hated him.

"How come he's always mincing around?" my father asked. "Is he a fairy or something?"

"No, Dad. He's inflatable."

"Well, he acts like a fairy," he said. "You better not be queering around with him up in your room."

Art tried to be liked—he tried to build a relationship with my father. But the things he did were misinterpreted; the statements he made were misunderstood. My dad said something once about a movie he liked. Art wrote him a message about how the book was even better.

"He thinks I'm an illiterate," my dad said, as soon as Art was gone.

Another time, Art noticed the pile of worn tires heaped up behind our garage, and mentioned to my dad about a recycling program at Sears, bring in your rotten old ones, get twenty percent off on brand-new Goodyears.

"He thinks we're trailer trash," my dad complained, before Art was hardly out of earshot. "Little snotnose."

One day Art and I got home from school, and found my father in front of the TV, with a pit bull at his feet. The bull erupted off the floor, yapping hysterically, and jumped up on Art. His paws made a slippery zipping sound sliding over Art's plastic chest. Art grabbed one of my shoulders and vaulted into the air. He could really jump when he had to. He grabbed the ceiling fan—turned off—and held on to one of the blades while the pit bull barked and hopped beneath.

"What the hell is that?" I asked.

"Family dog," my father said. "Just like you always wanted."

"Not one that wants to eat my friends."

"Get off the fan, Artie. That isn't built for you to hang off it."

"This isn't a dog," I said. "It's a blender with fur."

"Listen, do you want to name it, or should I?" Dad asked.

Art and I hid in my bedroom and talked names.

"Snowflake," I said. "Sugarpie. Sunshine."

How about Happy? That has a ring to it, doesn't it?

We were kidding, but Happy was no joke. In just a week, Art had at least three life-threatening encounters with my father's ugly dog.

If he gets his teeth in me, I'm done for. He'll punch me full of holes.

But Happy couldn't be housebroken, left turds scattered around the living room, hard to see in the moss brown rug. My dad squelched through some fresh leavings once, in bare feet, and it sent him a little out of his head. He chased Happy all through the downstairs with a croquet mallet, smashed a hole in the wall, crushed some plates on the kitchen counter with a wild backswing.

The very next day he built a chain-link pen in the sideyard. Happy went in, and that was where he stayed.

By then, though, Art was nervous to come over, and preferred to meet at his house. I didn't see the sense. It was a long walk to get to his place after school, and my house was right there, just around the corner.

"What are you worried about?" I asked him. "He's in a pen. It's not like Happy is going to figure out how to open the door to his pen, you know."

Art knew . . . but he still didn't like to come over, and when he did, he usually had a couple patches for bicycle tires on him, to guard against dark happenstance.

ONCE WE STARTED going to Art's every day, once it came to be a habit, I wondered why I had ever wanted us to go to my house instead. I got used to the walk—I walked the walk so many times I stopped noticing that it was long bordering on never-ending. I even looked forward to it, my afternoon stroll through coiled suburban streets, past houses done in Disney pastels: lemon, seashell, tangerine. As I crossed the distance between my house and Art's house, it seemed to me that I was moving through zones of ever-deepening stillness and order, and at the walnut heart of all this peace was Art's.

Art couldn't run, talk, or approach anything with a sharp edge on it, but at his house we managed to keep ourselves entertained. We watched TV. I wasn't like other kids, and didn't know anything about television. My father, I mentioned already, suffered from terrible migraines. He was home on disability, lived in the family room, and hogged our TV all day long, kept track of five different soaps. I tried not to bother him, and rarely sat down to watch with him—I sensed my presence was a distraction to him at a time when he wanted to concentrate.

Art would have watched whatever I wanted to watch, but I didn't know what to do with a remote control. I couldn't make a choice, didn't know how. Had lost the habit. Art was a NASA buff, and we watched anything to do with space, never missed a space shuttle launch. He wrote:

> I want to be an astronaut. I'd adapt really well to being weightless. I'm <u>already</u> mostly weightless.

This was when they were putting up the International Space Station. They talked about how hard it was on people to spend too long in outer space. Your muscles atrophy. Your heart shrinks three sizes.

> The advantages of sending me into space keep piling up. I don't have any muscles to atrophy. I don't have any heart to shrink. I'm telling you. I'm the ideal spaceman. I <u>belong</u> in orbit.

"I know a guy who can help you get there. Let me give Billy Spears a call. He's got a rocket he wants to stick up your ass. I heard him talking about it."

Art gave me a dour look, and a scribbled two-word response.

Lying around Art's house in front of the tube wasn't always an option, though. His father was a piano instructor, tutored small children on the baby grand, which was in the living room along with their television. If he had a lesson, we had to find something else to do. We'd go into Art's room to play with his computer, but after twenty minutes of *row-row-row-your-boat* coming through the wall—a shrill, out-of-time plinking—we'd shoot each other sudden wild looks, and leave by way of the window, no need to talk it over.

Both Art's parents were musical, his mother a cellist. They had wanted music for Art, but it had been let-down and disappointment from the start.

I can't even kazoo

Art wrote me once. The piano was out. Art didn't have any fingers, just a thumb, and a puffy pad where his fingers belonged. Hands like that, it had been years of work with a tutor just to learn to write legibly with a crayon. For obvious reasons, wind instruments were also out of the question; Art didn't have lungs, and didn't breathe. He tried to learn the drums, but couldn't strike hard enough to be any good at it.

His mother bought him a digital camera. "Make music with color," she said. "Make melodies out of light."

Mrs. Roth was always hitting you with lines like that. She talked about oneness, about the natural decency of trees, and she said not enough people were thankful for the smell of cut grass. Art told me when I wasn't around, she asked questions about me. She was worried I didn't have a healthy outlet for my creative self. She said I needed something to feed the inner me. She bought me a book about origami and it wasn't even my birthday.

"I didn't know the inner me was hungry," I said to Art.

That's because it already starved to death

Art wrote.

She was alarmed to learn that I didn't have any sort of religion. My father didn't take me to church or send me to Sunday school. He said religion was a scam. Mrs. Roth was too polite to say anything to me about my father, but she said things about him to Art, and Art passed her comments on. She told Art that if my father neglected the care of my body like he neglected the care of my spirit, he'd be in jail, and I'd be in a foster home. She also told Art that if I was put in foster care, she'd adopt me, and I could stay in the guest room. I loved her, felt my heart surge whenever she asked me if I wanted a glass of lemonade. I would have done anything she asked.

"Your mom's an idiot," I said to Art. "A total moron. I hope you know that. There isn't any oneness. It's every man for himself. Anyone who thinks we're all brothers in the spirit winds up sitting under Cassius Delamitri's fat ass during recess, smelling his jock."

Mrs. Roth wanted to take me to the synagogue—not to convert me, just as an educational experience, exposure to other cultures and all that—but Art's father shot her down, said not a chance, not our business, and what are you crazy? She had a bumper sticker on her car that showed the Star of David and the word PRIDE with a jumping exclamation point next to it.

"So, Art," I said another time. "I got a Jewish question I want to ask you. Now you and your family, you're a bunch of hardcore Jews, right?"

I don't know that I'd describe us as <u>hardcore</u> exactly. We're actually pretty lax. But we go to synagogue, observe the holidays—things like that.

"I thought Jews had to get their joints snipped," I said, and grabbed my crotch. "For the faith. Tell me—"
But Art was already writing.

No not me. I got off. My parents were friends with a progressive Rabbi. They talked to him about it first thing after I was born. Just to find out what the official position was.

"What'd he say?"

He said it was the official position to make an exception for anyone who would actually explode during the circumcision. They thought he was joking, but later on my mom did some research on it. Based on what she found out, it looks like I'm

in the clear—Talmudically speaking. Mom says the foreskin
has to be <u>skin</u>. If it isn't, it doesn't need to be cut.

"That's funny," I said. "I always thought your mom didn't
know dick. Now it turns out your mom *does* know dick. She's
an expert even. Shows what I know. Hey, if she ever wants to do
more research, I have an unusual specimen for her to examine."

And Art wrote how she would need to bring a microscope,
and I said how she would need to stand back a few yards when
I unzipped my pants, and back and forth, you don't need me
to tell you, you can imagine the rest of the conversation for
yourself. I rode Art about his mother every chance I could get,
couldn't help myself. Started in on her the moment she left the
room, whispering about how for an old broad she still had an
okay can, and what would Art think if his father died and I
married her. Art, on the other hand, never once made a punch
line out of my dad. If Art ever wanted to give me a hard time,
he'd make fun of how I licked my fingers after I ate, or how I
didn't always wear matching socks. It isn't hard to understand
why Art never stuck it to me about my father, like I stuck it to
him about his mother. When your best friend is ugly—I mean
bad ugly, *deformed*—you don't kid them about shattering mirrors. In a friendship, especially in a friendship between two
young boys, you are allowed to inflict a certain amount of pain.
This is even expected. But you must cause no serious injury;
you must never, under any circumstances, leave wounds that
will result in permanent scars.

ARTHUR'S HOUSE WAS also where we usually settled to do
our homework. In the early evening, we went into his room to
study. His father was done with lessons by then, so there wasn't
any plink-plink from the next room to distract us. I enjoyed
studying in Art's room, responded well to the quiet, and liked
working in a place where I was surrounded by books; Art had
shelves and shelves of books. I liked our study time together,
but mistrusted it as well. It was during our study sessions—surrounded by all that easy stillness—that Art was most likely to
say something about dying.

When we talked, I always tried to control the conversation, but Art was slippery, could work death into anything.

"Some Arab *invented* the idea of the number zero," I said. "Isn't that weird? Someone had to think zero up."

Because it isn't obvious—that nothing can be something. That something which can't be measured or seen could still exist and have meaning. Same with the soul, when you think about it.

"True or false," I said another time, when we were studying for a science quiz. "Energy is never destroyed, it can only be changed from one form into another."

I hope it's true—it would be a good argument that you continue to exist after you die, even if you're transformed into something completely different than what you had been.

He said a lot to me about death and what might follow it, but the thing I remember best was what he had to say about Mars. We were doing a presentation together, and Art had picked Mars as our subject, especially whether or not men would ever go there and try to colonize it. Art was all for colonizing Mars, cities under plastic tents, mining water from the icy poles. Art wanted to go himself.

"It's fun to imagine, maybe, fun to think about it," I said. "But the actual thing would be bullshit. Dust. Freezing cold. Everything red. You'd go blind looking at so much red. You wouldn't really want to do it—leave this world and never come back."

Art stared at me for a long moment, then bowed his head, and wrote a brief note in robin's egg blue.

But I'm going to have to do that anyway. Everyone has to do that.

Then he wrote:

POP ART

You get an astronaut's life whether you want it or not.
Leave it all behind for a world you know nothing about.
That's just the deal.

In the Spring, Art invented a game called Spy Satellite. There was a place downtown, the Party Station, where you could buy a bushel of helium-filled balloons for a quarter. I'd get a bunch, meet Art somewhere with them. He'd have his digital camera.

Soon as I handed him the balloons, he detached from the earth and lifted into the air. As he rose, the wind pushed him out and away. When he was satisfied he was high enough, he'd let go a couple balloons, level off, and start snapping pictures. When he was ready to come down, he'd just let go a few more. I'd meet him where he landed and we'd go over to his house to look at the pictures on his laptop. Photos of people swimming in their pools, men shingling their roofs; photos of me standing in empty streets, my upturned face a miniature brown blob, my features too distant to make out; photos that always had Art's sneakers dangling into the frame at the bottom edge.

Some of his best pictures were low-altitude affairs, things he snapped when he was only a few yards off the ground. Once he took three balloons and swam into the air over Happy's chain-link enclosure, off at the side of our house. Happy spent all day in his fenced-off pen, barking frantically at women going by with strollers, the jingle of the ice cream truck, squirrels. Happy had trampled all the space in his penned-in plot of earth down to mud. Scattered about him were dozens of dried piles of dog crap. In the middle of this awful brown turdscape was Happy himself, and in every photo Art snapped of him, he was leaping up on his back legs, mouth open to show the pink cavity within, eyes fixed on Art's dangling sneakers.

I feel bad. What a horrible place to live.

"Get your head out of your ass," I said. "If creatures like Happy were allowed to run wild, they'd make the whole world look that way. He doesn't want to live somewhere else. Turds and mud—that's Happy's idea of a total garden spot."

I STRONGLY disagree

Arthur wrote me, but time has not softened my opinions on this matter. It is my belief that, as a rule, creatures of Happy's ilk—I am thinking here of canines and men both—more often run free than live caged, and it is in fact a world of mud and feces they desire, a world with no Art in it, or anyone like him, a place where there is no talk of books or God or the worlds beyond this world, a place where the only communication is the hysterical barking of starving and hate-filled dogs.

ONE SATURDAY MORNING, mid-April, my dad pushed the bedroom door open, and woke me up by throwing my sneakers on my bed. "You have to be at the dentist's in half an hour. Put your rear in gear."

I walked—it was only a few blocks—and I had been sitting in the waiting room for twenty minutes, dazed with boredom, when I remembered I had told Art that I'd be coming by his house as soon as I got up. The receptionist let me use the phone to call him.

His mom answered. "He just left to see if he could find you at your house," she told me.

I called my dad.

"He hasn't been by," he said. "I haven't seen him."

"Keep an eye out."

"Yeah, well. I've got a headache. Art knows how to use the doorbell."

I sat in the dentist's chair, my mouth stretched open and tasting of blood and mint, and struggled with unease and an impatience to be going. Did not perhaps trust my father to be decent to Art without myself present. The dentist's assistant kept touching my shoulder and telling me to relax.

When I was all through and got outside, the deep and vivid blueness of the sky was a little disorientating. The sunshine was headache-bright, bothered my eyes. I had been up for two hours, still felt cotton-headed and dull-edged, not all the way awake. I jogged.

The first thing I saw as I approached my house was Happy, free from his pen. He didn't so much as bark at me. He was on his belly in the grass, head between his paws. He lifted sleepy eyelids to watch me approach, then let them sag shut again. His pen door stood open in the side yard.

I was looking to see if he was lying on a heap of tattered plastic when I heard the first feeble tapping sound. I turned my head and saw Art in the back of my father's station wagon, smacking his hands on the window. I walked over and opened the door. At that instant, Happy exploded from the grass with a peal of mindless barking. I grabbed Art in both arms, spun and fled. Happy's teeth closed on a piece of my flapping pant leg. I heard a tacky ripping sound, stumbled, kept going.

I ran until there was a stitch in my side and no dog in sight—six blocks, at least. Toppled over in someone's yard. My pant leg was sliced open from the back of my knee to the ankle. I took my first good look at Art. It was a jarring sight. I was so out of breath, I could only produce a thin, dismayed little squeak—the sort of sound Art was always making.

His body had lost its marshmallow whiteness. It had a gold-brown duskiness to it now, so it resembled a marshmallow lightly toasted. He seemed to have deflated to about half his usual size. His chin sagged into his body. He couldn't hold his head up.

Art had been crossing our front lawn when Happy burst from his hiding place under one of the hedges. In that first crucial moment, Art saw he would never be able to outrun our family dog on foot. All such an effort would get him would be an ass full of fatal puncture wounds. So instead, he jumped into the station wagon, and slammed the door.

The windows were automatic—there was no way to roll them down. Any door he opened, Happy tried to jam his snout in at him. It was seventy degrees outside the car, over a hundred inside. Art watched in dismay as Happy flopped in the grass beside the wagon to wait.

Art sat. Happy didn't move. Lawn mowers droned in the distance. The morning passed. In time Art began to wilt in the heat. He became ill and groggy. His plastic skin started sticking to the seats.

Then you showed up. Just in time. You saved my life.

But my eyes blurred and tears dripped off my face onto his note. I hadn't come just in time—not at all.

Art was never the same. His skin stayed a filmy yellow, and he developed a deflation problem. His parents would pump him up, and for a while he'd be all right, his body swollen with oxygen, but eventually he'd go saggy and limp again. His doctor took one look and told his parents not to put off the trip to Disney World another year.

I wasn't the same either. I was miserable—couldn't eat, suffered unexpected stomachaches, brooded and sulked.

"Wipe that look off your face," my father said one night at dinner. "Life goes on. Deal with it."

I was dealing, all right. I knew the door to Happy's pen didn't open itself. I punched holes in the tires of the station wagon, then left my switchblade sticking out of one of them, so my father would know for sure who had done it. He had police officers come over and pretend to arrest me. They drove me around in the squad car and talked tough at me for a while, then said they'd bring me home if I'd "get with the program." The next day I locked Happy in the wagon and he took a shit on the driver's seat. My father collected all the books Art had got me to read, the Bernard Malamud, the Ray Bradbury, the Isaac Bashevis Singer. He burned them on the barbecue grill.

"How do you feel about that, smart guy?" he asked me, while he squirted lighter fluid on them.

"Okay with me," I said. "They were on your library card."

That summer, I spent a lot of time sleeping over at Art's.

Don't be angry. No one is to blame.

Art wrote me.

"Get your head out of your ass," I said, but then I couldn't say anything else because it made me cry just to look at him.

*   *   *

LATE AUGUST, ART left a note for me, stuck in the mailbox among the bills. It was a hilly four miles to Scarswell Cove, where he wanted us to meet, but by then months of hoofing it to Art's after school had hardened me to long walks. I had plenty of balloons with me, just like he asked.

Scarswell Cove is a sheltered, pebbly beach on the sea, where people go to stand in the tide and fish in waders. There was no one there except a couple old fishermen and Art, sitting on the slope of the beach. His body looked soft and saggy, and his head lolled forward, bobbled weakly on his nonexistent neck. I sat down beside him. Half a mile out, the dark blue waves were churning up icy combers.

"What's going on?" I asked.

Art thought a bit. Then he began to write.

He wrote:

Do you know people have made it into outer space without rockets? Chuck Yeager flew a high-performance jet so high it started to tumble—it tumbled <u>upwards</u>, not downwards. He ran so high, gravity lost hold of him. His jet was tumbling up out of the stratosphere. All the color melted out of the sky. It was like the blue sky was paper, and a hole was burning out the middle of it, and behind it, everything was black. Everything was full of stars. Imagine falling <u>UP</u>.

I looked at his note, then back to his face. He was writing again. His second message was simpler.

I've had it. Seriously—I'm all done. I deflate 15–16 times a day. I need someone to pump me up practically every hour. I feel sick all the time and I hate it. This is no kind of life.

"Oh no," I said. My vision blurred. Tears welled up and spilled over my eyes. "Things will get better."

No. I don't think so. It isn't about whether I die. It's about figuring out where. And I've decided.

I'm going to see how high I can go. I want to see if it's true. If the sky opens up at the top.

I don't know what else I said to him. A lot of things, I guess. I asked him not to do it, not to leave me. I said that it wasn't fair. I said that I didn't have any other friends. I said that I had always been lonely. I talked until it was all blubber and strangled, helpless sobs, and he reached his crinkly plastic arms around me and held me while I hid my face in his chest.

He took the balloons from me, got them looped around one wrist. I held his other hand and we walked to the edge of the water. The surf splashed in and filled my sneakers. The sea was so cold it made the bones in my feet throb. I lifted him and held him in both arms, and squeezed until he made a mournful squeak. We hugged for a long time. Then I opened my arms. I let him go. I hope if there is another world, we will not be judged too harshly for the things we did wrong here—that we will at least be forgiven for the mistakes we made out of love. I have no doubt it was a sin of some kind, to let such a one go.

He rose away and the airstream turned him around so he was looking back at me as he bobbed out over the water, his left arm pulled high over his head, the balloons attached to his wrist. His head was tipped at a thoughtful angle, so he seemed to be studying me.

I sat on the beach and watched him go. I watched until I could no longer distinguish him from the gulls that were wheeling and diving over the water, a few miles away. He was just one more dirty speck wandering the sky. I didn't move. I wasn't sure I could get up. In time, the horizon turned a dusky rose and the blue sky above deepened to black. I stretched out on the beach, and watched the stars spill through the darkness overhead. I watched until a dizziness overcame me, and I could imagine spilling off the ground, and falling up into the night.

I DEVELOPED EMOTIONAL problems. When school started again, I would cry at the sight of an empty desk. I couldn't answer questions or do homework. I flunked out and had to go through seventh grade again.

Worse, no one believed I was dangerous anymore. It was impossible to be scared of me after you had seen me sobbing my guts out a few times. I didn't have the switchblade anymore; my father had confiscated it.

Billy Spears beat me up one day, after school—mashed my lips, loosened a tooth. John Erikson held me down, wrote COLLISTAMY BAG on my forehead in Magic Marker. Still trying to get it right. Cassius Delamitri ambushed me, shoved me down and jumped on top of me, crushing me under his weight, driving all the air out of my lungs. A defeat by way of deflation; Art would have understood perfectly.

I avoided the Roths'. I wanted more than anything to see Art's mother, but stayed away. I was afraid if I talked to her, it would come pouring out of me, that I had been there at the end, that I stood in the surf and let Art go. I was afraid of what I might see in her eyes; of her hurt and anger.

Less than six months after Art's deflated body was found slopping in the surf along North Scarswell beach, there was a For Sale sign out in front of the Roths' ranch. I never saw either of his parents again. Mrs. Roth sometimes wrote me letters, asking how I was and what I was doing, but I never replied. She signed her letters *love*.

I went out for track in high school, and did well at pole vault. My track coach said the law of gravity didn't apply to me. My track coach didn't know fuck all about gravity. No matter how high I went for a moment, I always came down in the end, same as anyone else.

Pole vault got me a state college scholarship. I kept to myself. No one at college knew me, and I was at last able to rebuild my long-lost image as a sociopath. I didn't go to parties. I didn't date. I didn't want to get to know anybody.

I was crossing the campus one morning, and I saw coming towards me a young girl, with black hair so dark it had the cold blue sheen of rich oil. She wore a bulky sweater and a librarian's ankle-length skirt; a very asexual outfit, but all the same you could see she had a stunning figure, slim hips, high ripe breasts. Her eyes were of staring blue glass, her skin as white as Art's. It was the first time I had seen an inflatable person since Art drifted away on his balloons. A kid walking behind me wolf-whistled at her. I stepped aside, and when he went past, I tripped him up and watched his books fly everywhere.

"Are you some kind of psycho?" he screeched.

"Yes," I said. "Exactly."

Her name was Ruth Goldman. She had a round rubber patch on the heel of one foot where she had stepped on a shard of broken glass as a little girl, and a larger square patch on her left shoulder where a sharp branch had poked her once on a windy day. Home schooling and obsessively protective parents had saved her from further damage. We were both English majors. Her favorite writer was Kafka—because he understood the absurd. My favorite writer was Malamud—because he understood loneliness.

We married the same year I graduated. Although I remain doubtful about the life eternal, I converted without any prodding from her, gave in at last to a longing to have some talk of the spirit in my life. Can you really call it a conversion? In truth, I had no beliefs to convert from. Whatever the case, ours was a Jewish wedding, glass under white cloth, crunched beneath the boot heel.

One afternoon I told her about Art.

That's so sad. I'm so sorry.

she wrote to me in wax pencil. She put her hand over mine.

What happened? Did he run out of air?

"Ran out of sky," I said.

YOU WILL HEAR THE LOCUST SING

1.

Francis Kay woke from dreams that were not uneasy, but exultant, and found himself an insect. He was not surprised, had thought this might happen. Or not thought: hoped, fantasized, and if not for this precise thing, then something like it. He had believed for a while he would learn to control cockroaches by telepathy, that he would master a glistening brown-backed horde of them, and send them clattering to battle for him. Or like in that movie with Vincent Price, he would only be partly transformed, his head become the head of a fly, sprouting obscene black hairs, his bulging, faceted eyes reflecting a thousand screaming faces.

He still wore his former skin like a coat, the skin of who he had been when he was human. Four of his six legs poked through rents in the damp, beige, pimpled, mole-studded, tragic, reeking cape of flesh. At the sight of his ruined, castaway skin he felt a little thrill of ecstasy and thought good riddance to it. He was on his back, and his legs—segmented, and jointed so they bent backwards—wavered helplessly above his body. His legs were armored in curved plates of brilliant metallic green, as shiny as polished chrome, and in the sun that slanted through his bedroom windows, splashes of unwholesome iridescence raced across their surfaces. His appendages ended in curved hooks of hardened black enamel, filigreed with a thousand blade-like hairs.

Francis wasn't all the way awake yet. He feared the moment

when his head would clear and it would all be over, his coat of skin buttoned back up, the insect shape gone, nothing more than a particularly intense dream that had persisted for a few minutes after waking. He thought if it turned out he was only imagining it, the disappointment would crack him open, would be too awful to bear. At the very least he would have to skip school.

Then he remembered he had been planning to skip school anyway. Huey Chester had thought Francis was giving him faggot looks in the locker room after gym, when they were both getting undressed. Huey scooped a turd out of the toilet with a lacrosse stick and flung it at Francis to teach him something about staring at other guys, and it was so funny he said it ought to be a new sport. Huey and the other kids argued over what to call it. Dodge-a-shit was one favorite. Long-Range Shit Launching was another. Francis had decided right then and there to stay clear of Huey Chester and gym—of the whole school—for a day or two.

Huey had liked Francis once; or not liked him exactly, but enjoyed showing him off to others. He liked Francis to eat bugs for his friends. This was in fourth grade. The summer before, Francis had lived with his grand-aunt Reagan, in her trailer over in Tuba City. Reagan smothered crickets in molasses and served them in the afternoon with tea. It was really something, watching them cook. Francis would lean over the gently bubbling pot of molasses with its tarry, awful-sweet reek, and go into a happy kind of trance, watching the slow-motion struggles of the crickets as they drowned. He liked candied crickets, the sweet crunch of them, the oily-grassy taste at the center, and he liked Reagan, and wished he could stay with her forever, but his father came and got him anyway, of course.

So one day at school Francis told Huey about eating crickets, and Huey wanted to see, only they didn't have either molasses or crickets, so Francis caught a cockroach and ate it while it was alive. It was salty and bitter, with a harsh, metallic aftertaste, terrible really. But Huey laughed, and Francis experienced a swell of pride so intense, he couldn't breathe for an instant; like a cricket drowning in molasses, he felt suffocated by sweetness.

After that, Huey gathered his friends for afternoon horror shows in the playground. Francis ate cockroaches they brought him. He crushed a moth with splendid pale green wings into his mouth and munched it slowly; the children quizzed him as to what he was feeling, how it tasted. "Hungry," he told them in answer to the first question. "Like someone's lawn," he said in answer to the second. He poured honey to attract ants and inhaled them out of the gleaming lump of amber with a straw. The ants went *phut-phut-phut* on their way up through the plastic tube. Groans rose from his audience, and he beamed, intoxicated by his newfound celebrity.

Only he had never been famous before, and he misjudged what his fans would tolerate and what they wouldn't. On a different afternoon, he captured flies swarming around a calcified pile of dogshit, inhaling them by the handful. Again he was delighted by the moans of those who gathered to watch. But flies off dogshit were somehow different than honey-coated ants. The latter was comically gruesome. The former was pathologically disturbing. After that they started calling him the shiteater and the dung beetle. One day someone planted a dead rat in his lunchbox. In biology, Huey and his friends pelted him with half-dissected salamanders, while Mr. Krause was out of the room.

Francis let his gaze drift across his ceiling. Strips of flypaper, curling in the heat, drifted about in the breeze made by the humming, elderly fan in the corner. He lived alone with his father, and his father's girlfriend, in the rooms behind the filling station. His windows looked down through sage and brush, into a culvert mounded with garbage, the back end of the town dump. On the other side of the culvert was a low rise, and beyond that, the painted red flats, where on some nights they still lit The Bomb. He had seen it once—The Bomb. It was when he was eight. He came awake to the wind rushing against the back of the gas station, tumbleweeds flying through the air. He stood on his bed, to peer through one of the windows high in the wall, saw the sun rising in the west at two in the morning, a gassy ball of blood-colored neon light, boiling up into the sky on a slender column of smoke. He watched until he felt a transcendent pain flaring at the back of his eyeballs.

He wondered if it was late. He didn't have a clock, didn't worry about being places on time anymore. His teachers rarely noticed if he was in classes, or when he entered the room. He listened for some sound of the world beyond his room, and heard the television, which meant Ella was awake. Ella was his father's mountainous girlfriend, a woman with fat legs and varicose veins, who spent the entire day on the couch.

He was hungry; he would have to get up soon. It came to him then that he was still an insect, a realization that surprised and galvanized him. His old skin had slid down off his arms and hung in a rubbery mass from his—what were they, shoulders?—anyway, lay beneath him like a wrinkled sheet of some stretchy synthetic material. He wanted to flip over, get down on the floor, and have a look at the old skin. He wondered if he could find his face somewhere in all that, a shriveled mask with holes where his eyes had been.

He tried to reach for the wall, meaning to use it to turn himself. But his movements were uncoordinated, and his legs jerked and twitched in every direction except the one he wanted. As he struggled with his limbs, he felt a gaseous pressure building in his lower abdomen. He tried to sit up, and at that instant, the pressure blew out his rear end, with a hard hissing sound, like all the air going out of a tire at once: *paffff*. He felt an unnatural warmth around his back legs, and glanced down in time to see a rippling distortion pass through the air, like heat rising off a distant, sun-struck road.

This was funny. A monster insect fart; or maybe a monster insect bowel movement. He wasn't sure, but he thought he felt wetness down there. He shivered with laughter, and for the first time became aware of some impossibly thin, impossibly hard plates, trapped between the curve of his back and the bunched-up lumps of his former flesh. He considered what they might be. They were a part of him, and it felt as if he might be able to move them about like his arms, only they weren't arms.

He wondered if anyone would check on him, imagined Ella rapping on the door, then sticking her head in . . . and how she would scream, mouth falling open so wide it would make four double chins, her piggy close-set eyes shiny with terror. But no; Ella wouldn't check. It was too much trouble for her to get off the couch. For a while he daydreamed about marching out of his room on all six legs, walking straight past her, and how she would shriek and cringe. Was it possible she might die of a heart attack? He imagined her cries becoming choked, the skin under her pancake make-up turning an unpleasant cast of gray, her eyelids fluttering and the eyes themselves rolling back to show the glistening whites.

He found he could hump his way along by heaving his whole body up and to the side, moving in little increments towards the edge of the cot. As he twitched closer to the edge, he tried to imagine what he would do *after* giving Ella the heart attack. He envisioned letting himself out into the hot glare of the Arizona morning, scrabbling right down the middle of the highway. He could see it already: cars swerving to avoid hitting him, horns blaring, the shrill whine of tires, people driving their pickups into telephone poles, hillbillies screaming, *What the fuck is that thing*, then grabbing for their shotguns on the rifle rack . . . on second thought, maybe it would be better to stay off the highway.

He wanted to make his way over to Eric Hickman's house, scuttle into the basement and wait for him there. Eric was a scrawny seventeen-year-old with a skin disorder that had caused dozens of moles to erupt on his face, most of them sprouting bunches of wiry pubic hair; he also had a filmy black mustache, growing thick at the corners of his mouth, like the whiskers of a catfish. He was for this reason known around school as the cuntfish. Eric and Francis met for movies sometimes. They had seen the Vincent Price picture *The Fly* together; also *Them!* twice. Eric loved *Them!* He was going to wet himself when he saw what had happened. Eric was smart—he had read everything Mickey Spillane had ever written—and they could make plans about what to do next. Also maybe Eric would get him something to eat. Francis wanted something sweet. Ding-Dongs. Twinkies. His stomach rumbled dangerously.

In the next moment, Francis heard—no, *sensed*—his father entering the living room. Each step Buddy Kay took set off a subtle vibration Francis could feel in the iron frame of his cot, and humming in the dry hot air around his head. The stucco walls of the filling station were relatively thick, and absorbed sounds well. He had never before been able to clearly hear a conversation going on in the next room. Now, though, he *felt*, rather than heard, what Ella was saying and how his father answered her; felt their voices as a series of low reverberations, which stirred the exquisitely sensitive antennae at the top of his head. Their voices were distorted, and deeper than normal—as if their conversation were taking place underwater—but perfectly understandable.

She said, "You know he never went to school."

"What are you talking about?" Buddy asked.

"He never went to school is what. He's been in there all mornin'."

"Is he awake?"

"I don't know."

"Din't you look?"

"You know I don't like to put no weight on my laig."

"You fuckin' lazy cow," his father said, and began to stride towards Francis's door. Each step sent another shivering jolt of pleasure and alarm through Francis's antennae.

By then, Francis had reached the edge of the bed. The skin of his old body, however, hadn't come along with him, and lay in a knotted mess in the center of the mattress, a boneless canoe filled with blood. Francis balanced on the iron rail that ran along the outside of his cot. He tried to shuffle another inch or two closer to the side, not sure yet how to get down, and turned over. His old skin yanked at his limbs, the weight of it pulling him back. He heard his father's boot heels ringing on the other side of the door, and he heaved himself forward, alarmed at the thought of being found helpless on his back. His father might not recognize him and go for the gun—which was on the wall in the living room, only a few steps away—and blow open his segmented belly in a whitish-green gush of bug innards.

When Francis threw himself at the edge of the bed, the rags of his old flesh came apart, with a ripping sound like someone tearing a bedsheet; he fell; flipped at the same time; and landed with a springy lightness on all six feet, with a grace he had never known in his days as a human.

His back was to the bedroom door. He didn't have time to think, and for that reason, perhaps, his legs did just what they were supposed to. He spun around, his rear legs running to the right while his front legs scrabbled to the left, turning the low, narrow five-foot length of him. He felt the microthin plates or shields on his back flutter strangely, and had just an instant to wonder again what they were. Then his father was braying at the door.

"What the fuck you doin' in there, you asshole? Get the fuck to school—"

The door banged open. Francis reared back, lifting his front two legs off the floor. His mandibles made a rapid clattering sound, like a fast typist giving a manual typewriter a workout. Buddy hung in the open door, one hand still gripping the doorknob. His gaze fell upon the crouched figure of his transformed son. The color drained from his starved, whiskery face, until he looked like a waxwork of himself.

Then he shrieked, a shrill piercing sound that sent a white electric throb of pure stimulation shooting down Francis's antennae. Francis shrieked himself, although what came out in no way resembled a human cry. It was the sound instead of someone shaking a thin sheet of aluminum, an undulating, inhuman warble.

He looked for a way out. There were windows high in the wall above his bed, but they weren't big enough, just a series of wide slots barely a foot tall. His glance fell upon his bed and held there for a startled instant. He had thrown his sheets off in the night, kicking them to the far end of the mattress. Now they were lathered in some kind of white spittle, and they were *dissolving* in it . . . had liquefied and blackened at the same time, becoming a mass of fizzing organic sludge.

The bed sagged deeply in the center. The castoff raiment of his flesh was there, a one-piece boy costume that had been ripped apart up the middle. He didn't get a look at his face, but he did see one hand, a crinkly flesh-colored glove with nothing in it, fingers curling inwards. The foam that had melted the sheets was trickling down towards his former skin, and where it touched it, the tissue blistered and smoked. Francis remembered farting, and the feeling of liquid trickling between his hind legs. *He* had done this somehow.

The air shuddered with a sudden heavy crash. He looked back and saw his father on the floor, his toes pointing outwards. Stared past him into the living room, where Ella was struggling to sit up from the couch. Instead of turning gray and grabbing her chest, she stiffened at the sight of him, her expression going fixed and blank. She had a bottle of Coke in one hand—it wasn't yet ten in the morning—and she sat frozen with it raised halfway to her lips.

"Oh God," she said, in a dazed, but relatively normal tone of voice. "Just look at you."

Coke began to spill out of the bottle, drizzling down her breasts. She didn't notice.

He would have to go, and there was only one way out. He jogged forward, erratically at first—he zagged a little too hard to the right on his way through the doorway and clouted his side, although he barely felt it—and climbed over the body of his unconscious father. He continued on, squeezing between the couch and the coffee table, aiming himself at the screen door. Ella daintily lifted her feet onto the couch to let him pass. She was whispering to herself now, so softly a person sitting right next to her might not have been aware she was doing it. Francis, however, didn't miss a word, his antennae trembling at every syllable.

"Then from the smoke came locusts on the earth, and they were given power like the power of scorpions of the earth, and they were told not to harm the grass of the earth or any green growth or any tree—" He was at the door now; he paused, listening. "—but only those of mankind who have not the seal of God upon their foreheads; they were allowed to torture them for five months, but not to kill them, and their torture was like the torture of a scorpion, when it stings a man. And in those days men will seek death and will not find it; they will long to die, and death flies from them."

He shivered, although he could not have said why; her words stirred and thrilled him. He lifted his front legs to the door and shoved it open, and clambered out into the blinding white heat of the day.

2.

The culvert was filled with garbage for half a mile, the combined trash of five towns. Garbage collection was Calliphora's main industry. Two of every five grown men in town had a job in trash; one out of five was in the army's radiological division and stationed at Camp Calliphora, a mile to the north; the other two stayed home to watch television, scratch lottery tickets, and eat the frozen dinners they bought with their food stamps. Francis's father was the rare exception, someone who owned his own business. Buddy called himself an entrepreneur. He had had an idea which he thought might revolutionize the filling station business. It was called self-serve. It meant you let the customer fill his own Goddamn tank, and you charged them just the same as they did at the full-service place.

Down in the culvert, it was difficult to see anything of Calliphora on the shelf of rock above. When Francis peered up the steep incline, he could make out just a single identifiable landmark, the top of the great flagpole in front of his father's gas station. The flag itself was reckoned to be the biggest in the state. It was easily large enough to drape over the cab of an eighteen-wheeler, and too heavy to move even in very strong winds. Francis had seen it rippling only once—in the gales that boomed across Calliphora after they dropped The Bomb.

His father got a lot of army business. Whenever he had to come out of his office for some reason, say, to look at someone's overheated Jeep, he usually threw the top half of his fatigues on over his T-shirt. Medals bounced and flashed on the left breast. None of them were his—he had bought them one afternoon at the pawn—but the uniform he had at least come by honestly, in World War II. His father had liked the war.

"There isn't any pussy like what you get in a country you just shelled into the dirt," he said one night, lifting a can of Buckhorn as if in a toast, his rheumy eyes glistening with fond memories.

Francis hid in the garbage, squeezing himself into a soft depression between bulging plastic bags, and waited fearfully for police cruisers, listening for the dreadful, thunderous beat of helicopters, his antennae twitching and erect. But there were no cruisers, and there were no helicopters. Once or twice a pickup came rattling down the dirt road winding between the trash heaps, and he'd squirm desperately backwards, burrowing so far into the garbage that only his antennae stuck out. But that was all. There was little traffic at this end of the dump, which was almost half a mile from the processing center where the real work was done.

Later, he scuttled up onto one of the great mounds of garbage, to make sure he wasn't quietly being encircled. He wasn't, and he didn't remain in the open for long. He didn't like the direct glare of the sun. After only a moment in it, he felt a numbing lassitude creeping over him, as if he had been pumped full of novocaine. In the very back of the dump, though, where the culvert narrowed, he spied a trailer on cement blocks. He climbed down and waddled over to it. He had thought it looked abandoned and it was. The space beneath it was filled with deliciously cool shadows. Climbing under the trailer was as refreshing as a dip into a lake.

He rested. It was Eric Hickman who woke him; not that Francis had been asleep in the literal sense. He had settled instead into a state of intensely felt stillness, in which he knew nothing and yet was completely alert. He heard the scrape and drag of Eric's feet from forty feet away, and lifted his head. Eric was squinting through his glasses in the afternoon sunlight. He was always squinting—to read things, or just when he was thinking hard—a habit which never failed to put a kind of simian grimace on his face. It was such an unpleasant expression, it just naturally made other people want to give him something to grimace about.

"Francis," Eric whispered loudly. He carried a grease-spattered brown paper bag that might've contained his lunch, and at the sight Francis felt a sharp twinge of hunger, but he didn't come out.

"Francis, are you down here somewhere?" Eric whisper-shouted one more time before he tracked on out of sight.

Francis had wanted to show himself, but couldn't. What had stopped him was the idea that Eric was only there to lure him out in the open. Francis imagined a team of snipers crouched on the hills of garbage, watching the road through their rifle sights for some sign of the giant killer cricket. He held his ground, crouched and tense, monitoring the mounds of trash for movement. He held his breath. A can fell clanking. It was only a crow.

Eventually, he had to admit he had let anxiety get the better of him. Eric had come alone. This was followed a moment later by the understanding that no one was looking for him, because no one would believe his father when Buddy said what he had seen. If he tried to tell them he had discovered a giant insect in his son's bedroom, crouched beside the eviscerated body of his boy, he'd be lucky not to wind up in the back of a police car, on his way to the psychiatric ward in Tucson. They would not even believe him when he said his son was dead. After all, there was no body, and no discarded skin either. The milky excretion that had bubbled out of Francis's rear would've melted it away.

Only last Halloween, his father had sweated out the DTs in the county jail, and could hardly be considered a credible witness. Ella might back up his story, but her word was worth no more than his, and possibly less. She called the offices of the *Calliphora Happenings*, sometimes as often as once a month, to report seeing clouds that looked like Jesus. She had a whole photo album of clouds she said bore the face of Her Savior. Francis had flipped through it, but was unable to recognize any religious notables, although he was willing to admit there was one cloud that might've been a fat man in a fez.

The local police would be on the lookout for Francis himself, of course, but he wasn't sure how hard they'd actively search. He was eighteen—free to do as he chose—and often missed school without explanation. There were just four law enforcement officers in Calliphora: Sheriff George Walker, and three part-timers. That allowed for only a very limited search party, and besides, there were other things to do on a pretty, windless day like this one: hassle wetbacks for example, or sit in the speed-trap and wait for teenagers to burn by on their way to Phoenix.

It was getting hard, anyway, to worry much about whether anyone was looking for him. He was daydreaming about Little Debbie snacks again. He could not remember the last time he had been so hungry.

Although the sky was bright and hard, a blue enameled surface, afternoon shadows had eased out across the culvert, as the sun slipped behind the shelf of red rock to the west. He scuttled out from under the trailer, and picked through the litter, stopping at a bag that had split open and spilled its contents. He prodded the leavings with his antennae. Amidst the crushed papers, exploded Styrofoam cups, and balled-up diapers, he discovered a dirt-speckled red lollipop. He leaned forward and clumsily took the whole thing into his mouth, bent cardboard stick and all, grasping at it with his mandibles, drool spattering into the dust.

For an instant, the inside of his mouth was filled with an overpowering burst of sugary sweetness, and he felt blood rush to his heart. But an instant later he became conscious of an awful tickling in the thorax, and his throat seemed to close. His stomach lurched. He spat the lollipop out in disgust. It was no better with the half-eaten chicken wings he discovered. The few scraps of meat and fat on the bones tasted rancid and he gagged reflexively.

Bluebottle flies buzzed greedily around the pile of waste. He glared at them resentfully, considered snapping them up. Some bugs ate other bugs—but he didn't know how to catch them with no hands (although he sensed he was quick enough), and he could hardly ease his suffering with a half dozen bluebottles. Headachy and edgy with hunger, he thought of the candied crickets and all the other bugs he had eaten. It was because of them this had happened to him, he supposed, and his mind leaped to the sun rising at two A.M., and the way the wind came at the filling station in superheated blasts, slamming into the building so hard, dust trickled from the ceiling.

Huey Chester's father, Vern, had hit a rabbit in his driveway once, got out and discovered a thing with unnatural pink eyes—four of them. He brought it into town to show it off, but then a biologist, accompanied by a corporal and two privates with machine guns, turned up to claim it, and they paid Vern five hundred dollars to sign a statement agreeing he wouldn't talk about it. Then once, just a week after one of the tests in the desert, a dense, moist fog that smelled horribly of bacon had billowed over the entire town. It was so thick they cancelled school, and closed the supermarket and the post office. Owls flew in the daytime, and low booms and rumbles of thunder sounded at all hours, out in the roiling wet murk. The scientists in the desert were tearing holes through the sky and the earth out there, and maybe the tissue of the universe itself. They set fire to the clouds. For the first time Francis understood clearly that he was a contaminated thing, an aberration to be squashed and covered up, by a corporal with a government checkbook and a briefcase of binding legal documents. It had been hard for him to recognize this at first, perhaps because Francis had *always* felt contaminated, a thing others wanted not to see.

In frustration he shoved himself away from the split bag of garbage, moving without thought. His spring-loaded back legs launched him into the air, and the hardened petals on his back whipped furiously about him. His stomach plunged. The hard-baked, litter-strewn ground bobbed recklessly below him. He waited to fall, but didn't, found himself veering through the air, landing a moment later on one of the massive hills of trash, settling in a spot still in the sunlight. His breath exploded from his body; he didn't even know he had been holding it.

For a moment he balanced there, overcome by a sensation of shock that he felt a pins-and-needles prickling at the tips of his antennae. He had climbed, scrambled, swam—no, by Jesus, he had flown!—through thirty feet of Arizona air. He didn't consider what had happened for long, was afraid to think it over too closely. He fired himself into the air again. His wings made a buzzing sound that was almost mechanical, and he found himself swooping drunkenly through the sky, over the sea of decomposing disposable goods below. He forgot for a moment that he needed to eat. He forgot that only a few seconds before, he had felt close to hopelessness. He clutched his legs to his armored sides, and with the air rushing in his face, he stared down at the wasteland a hundred feet below, held entranced by the sight of his unlikely shadow skipping across it.

3.

After the sun went down, but while a little light remained in the sky, Francis returned home. He had nowhere else to go and he was so hungry. There was Eric's, of course, but to get to his house he would have to cross several streets, and his wings wouldn't carry him high enough not to be seen.

He crouched for a long time in the brush at the back edge

of the lot around the filling station. The pumps were switched off, the lights above them turned out, the blinds down across the windows of the front office. His father had never closed the place so early. It was utterly still at this end of Estrella Avenue, and except for the occasional passing truck, there was no sign of life or movement anywhere. He wondered if his father was home, but could not imagine any other possibility. Buddy Kay had nowhere else to go.

Francis staggered, light-headed, across the gravel to the screen door. He lifted himself on his back legs, and peeked into the living room. What he saw there was so unlike anything he had ever seen before, it disorientated him, and he swayed as a sudden weak spell passed over him.

His father was sprawled on the couch, turned on his side, his face crushed into Ella's bosom. They seemed to be asleep. Ella clasped Buddy about the shoulders, her plump, ring-covered fingers folded across his back. He was barely on the couch— there wasn't room for him—and it looked as if he might suffocate with his face squashed against her tits like that. Francis could not remember the last time he had seen Buddy and Ella embracing one another, and he had forgotten how small his father seemed in comparison to Ella's bulk. With his face buried in her chest, he resembled a child who has cried himself to sleep against his mother's bosom. They were so old and friendless, so defeated looking even in sleep, and the sight of them that way—two figures huddled together against a shearing wind—gave him a wrenching sensation of regret. His next thought was that his life with them was over. If they woke and saw him, it would be shrieking and fainting again, it would be guns and police.

He despaired, was about to back away from the door and return to the dump, when he saw the bowl on the table, to the right of the door. Ella had made a taco salad. He couldn't see into the bowl, but knew what it was by the smell, he was smelling everything now, the rusty tang of the screen door, the mildew in the shag carpeting, and he could smell salty corn chips, hamburger that had simmered in taco sauce, the peppery zing of salsa. He imagined big flaps of lettuce, soggy with taco juices, and his mouth filled with saliva.

Francis leaned forward, craning his neck for some kind of look into the bowl. The serrated hooks at the front of his forelegs were already pressed to the screen door, and before he realized what he was doing, the weight of his body had pushed it halfway open. He eased himself inside, casting a furtive glance at his father and Ella. Neither moved.

The spring on the inside of the door was old, and pulled out of shape. When he had slipped through it, the door did not smash shut behind him, but closed with a dry whine, thudding gently against the frame. That soft thud was loud enough to make Francis's heart rear up against the inside of his chest. But his father only seemed to squirm deeper into the wrinkled cleft between Ella's breasts. Francis crept to the side of the table, and bent over the bowl. There was almost nothing left, except for a greasy soup of taco sauces, and a few soggy pieces of romaine sticking to the inside of the dish. He tried to fish one out, but his hands weren't hands anymore. The trowel-like blade at the end of his foreleg rapped against the inside of the bowl, turning it onto its side. He tried to catch it as it went over the edge of the table, but it only deflected off the hook-shaped paw, and fell to the floor with a brittle crack.

Francis dropped low, stiffening. Ella made a muzzy, confused, waking sound behind him. It was followed by a steely snap. He looked back. His father was on his feet, not a yard away. He had been awake even before the bowl fell—Francis saw this immediately—had perhaps been feigning sleep from the beginning. Buddy held the shotgun in one hand, broke open to be loaded, the butt clenched in his armpit. In the other hand was a box of shells. He had been holding the gun all along, had been laying there with it hidden between his body and Ella's.

Buddy's upper lip curled back in a look of wondering disgust. He was missing some teeth, and the ones that were left were blackened and rotting out of his head.

"You fuckin' nasty thing," he said. He thumbed open the box of shells. "I guess they're gonna believe me now."

Ella shifted her weight, pushed herself up to look over the back of the couch, and let out a strangled cry. "Oh my God. Oh my Jesus."

Francis tried to speak. He tried to say no, not to hurt him, that he wouldn't hurt them. But what came out was that sound, like someone furiously shaking a flexible piece of metal.

"Why is it makin' that noise?" Ella cried. She was trying to get to her feet, but was sunk too deeply into the couch, couldn't pry herself out. "Get away from it, Buddy!"

Buddy glanced back at her. "What do you mean, get away? I'm gonna fuckin' blast the thing. I'll show that shithead George Walker . . . stan' there, laughin' at me." His father laughed himself, but his hands were shaking, and shells fell in a clattering shower to the floor. "They're gonna put my picture on the front page of the paper tomorrow mornin'."

His fingers found a shell at last, and he poked it into the shotgun. Francis gave up trying to talk and held his forelegs up in front of him, serrated hooks raised, in a gesture of surrender.

"It's doin' somethin'!" Ella screamed.

"Will you shut the fuck up, you noisy bitch?" Buddy said. "It's just a bug, I don't care how big it is. It doesn't have the faintest fuckin' idea what I'm doin'." He snapped his wrist, and the barrel locked into place.

Francis lunged, meant to shove Buddy back, burst for the door. His right foreleg fell, and the emerald scimitar at the end of it drew a red slash across the length of Buddy's face. The gash started at his right temple, skipped over his eye socket, dashed across the bridge of his nose, jumped the other eye socket, and then ran four inches across his left cheek. Buddy's mouth fell open, so he appeared to be gaping in surprise, a man accused of a shocking thing and at a loss for words. The gun discharged with a stunning boom that sent a white throb of pain down the sensitive wands of Francis's antennae. Some of the spray caught his shoulder in a stinging burst; most of the rest of the shot thumped into the plaster wall behind him. Francis shrieked in terror and pain: another of those distorted, singing-sheet-metal sounds, only urgent and shrill this time. His other hooked leg fell, a hatchet swung with all his weight straight down. It slammed into his father's chest. He felt the impact shiver all the way up into the first joint in his arm.

Francis tried to take it back, to yank his arm out of his father's torso. Instead he pulled him off the floor and into the air. Ella was screaming, clawing at her face with both hands. He swung his arm up and down, trying to shake his father off the scythe at the end of it. Buddy was suddenly boneless, arms and legs flopping uselessly about. The sound of Ella's shrieking was so painful, Francis thought he might pass out from it. He slammed his father against the wall. The filling station shook. This time when he pulled his arm away, Buddy came unpinned. He slid down the wall, hands folded over the puncture wound in his chest. He left a dark smear on the plaster behind him. Francis didn't know what had happened to the gun. Ella knelt on the couch, rocking back and forth, screeching and scratching at her face unconsciously. Francis fell upon her, chopping at her with his bladed hands. It sounded like a team of men driving shovels into wet mud. For several minutes the room was noisy with the sound of furious digging.

4.

For a long time after, Francis hid under the table and waited for someone to come and end it. His shoulder throbbed. His pulse was a hard rapid ticking in the throat. No one came.

Later, he scuttled out and squatted over his father. Buddy had slid all the way down the wall so only his head rested against it, his body sprawled across the floor. His father had always been a scrawny, half-starved man, but sitting like he was, with his chin resting against his chest, he suddenly seemed fat and unlike himself, with two chins and loose hanging jowls. Francis found he could cup his head in the curved, edged scoops that served as his hands now—the murder weapons. He couldn't bear to look at what he had done to Ella.

His stomach was upset. The sharp, gassy pressure of the early morning had returned. He wanted to tell someone he was sorry, it was awful, he wished he could take it back, but there was no one to tell, and no one could have understood his new grasshopper voice even if there was. He wanted to sob. He farted instead, and his rear end gushed the foaming white carbolic in a few spasmodic bursts. It spattered against his father's torso, soaking his T-shirt, eating through it with a sputtering hiss. Francis turned Buddy's face this way and that, hoping he would look more like himself from a different angle, but no matter which way Francis turned him, he was always unfamiliar, a stranger.

A smell, like burnt bacon fat, caught Francis's attention, and when he glanced down he saw his father's stomach had caved in and become a bowl overbrimming with watery pink chowder; the red bones of his ribs glistened, stringy knots of half-dissolved tissue clinging to them. Francis felt his stomach constrict in painful, desperate hunger. He bent closer to investigate the mess with his antennae; but he couldn't wait any longer, couldn't hold himself back. He swallowed his father's puddled innards in great gulping mouthfuls, his mandibles clicking wetly. Ate him from the outside in, then staggered away, half-drunk, his ears buzzing, his belly aching from fullness. He waddled under the table and rested.

Through the screen door he could see a piece of the highway. In an overstuffed daze, he watched the occasional truck shush past, racing into the desert, headlights skimming along the blacktop, over a small rise, then racing all heedless out of view. The sight of those headlights gliding effortlessly through the dark brought to mind what it had felt like to soar, climbing into the sky in a great leaping rush.

The thought of whistling through the warm fresh air made him want to breathe some. He swatted through the screen door. He was too full to fly. His belly still hurt. He walked to the middle of the gravel parking lot, tipped his head back, and regarded the night. The Milky Way was a frothing river of brilliance. He could hear very clearly the crickets in the weeds, the weird theremin music they made, a plaintive humming that rose and fell, rose and fell. They had always been calling to him, he supposed now.

He walked unafraid up the middle of the highway, waiting for a truck to come, for its headlights to pour over him . . . waited for the shriek of brakes, and the hoarsened, frightened shout. But no traffic passed along the road. He was very full and he went slowly. He wasn't worried about what would happen to him next. He didn't know where he was headed, and didn't care. His shoulder ached just slightly. The shotgun pellets hadn't punctured his armor—of course they couldn't—and had only lightly bruised the flesh beneath.

Once, he and his father had gone to the dump together, with the shotgun, and took turns with it, picking off cans, rats, seagulls. "Imagine the fuckin' krauts are coming," his father said. Francis didn't know what German soldiers looked like, so he pretended he was shooting the kids at school instead. The memory of that day in the dump made him a little sentimental for his father—they had had some good times together, and Buddy had made a decent meal in the end. Really, what else could you ask from a parent?

He found himself behind the school when the first flush of rose was bleeding into the east. He had come there without meaning to, brought perhaps by his memory of the afternoon he went shooting with his father. He studied the long brick edifice, with its rows of small windows, thought what an ugly little hive. Even wasps had it better, built their homes in the high branches of trees, where in the spring they would be hidden in sweet-smelling masses of blossoms, nothing to disturb them except the cool trickle of the breeze.

A car turned into the parking lot, and Francis scuttled to the side of the building, then edged around the corner to stay out of sight. He heard a car door slam. He continued to crawl backwards, then happened to glance down and to the side, and saw the line of windows looking into the basement. The first one he pushed his head against swung in on its forty-year-old hinges, and in a moment he fell through it.

Francis waited in perfect stillness in one corner of the cellar, behind some pipes beaded with icy water, while sunshine rose against the row of windows high up in the wall. First the light was weak and gray, then a delicate shade of lemon, and it lit slowly the basement world around him, revealing a lawn mower, rows of folding metal chairs, stacked cans of paint. For a long time he rested without sleeping, thoughtless but alert, as he had the day before when he took refuge beneath the old trailer in the dump. The sun was shining silver against the eastern-facing windows when he heard the first lockers slamming above him, feet tramping across the floors overhead, loud, exuberant voices.

He crossed to the stairs, and clambered up them. As he moved towards the sounds, though, they paradoxically fell away from him, as if he was rising into an envelope of silence. He thought of The Bomb, the red sun boiling off the desert floor at two in the morning, the wind hammering the filling station; then from the smoke came locusts on the earth. As he climbed, he felt a building exuberance of his own, a sudden, intense, thrilling sense of purpose. The door at the top was shut and he didn't know how to open it. He banged one of his hooks against it. The door shook thunderously in its frame. He waited.

At last the door opened. On the other side stood Eric Hickman. Behind him, the hall was thronged with kids, putting things away in their lockers, holding shouted conversations with one another, but it was like watching a movie without sound. A few kids glanced his way, saw him, and went rigid, fixing themselves into frozen, unnatural poses next to their lockers. A sandy-haired girl opened her mouth to scream; she was holding an armful of books, and one by one they slid out of her grasp and crashed noiselessly to the floor.

Eric peered at him through the grease-spotted lenses of his ridiculously thick glasses. He twitched in shock, and lurched back a step, but then his mouth opened in a disbelieving grin.

"Awesome," Eric said. Francis heard him distinctly.

Francis lunged, and snapped through Eric's neck with his mandibles, using them like an oversized pair of hedge-clippers. He killed him first—because he loved him. Eric fell with his legs kicking in a brainless dying jig, and his blood sprayed across the sandy-haired girl, who did not move but only stood there screaming. And all the sounds rushed in at once, in a roar of banging lockers, running feet, and cries to God. Francis scrambled forward, propelling himself with the great springs of his back legs, effortlessly knocking people aside, or driving them face-first to the floor. He caught Huey Chester at the end of the hall, trying to run for an exit, and pounded one shovel-blade claw through the small of his back and out the other side, thrust him into the air. Huey slid down along Francis's green-armored arm, making choking sounds. His feet went on pedaling comically through the air, as if he were still trying to run.

Francis went back the way he had come, slashing and snapping, although he left the sandy-haired girl, who had dropped to her knees and was praying over her folded hands. He killed four in the hall before he went upstairs. He found six more huddled under the tables in one of the biology labs, and killed them too. Then he thought he would kill the sandy-haired girl after all, but when he went back downstairs she had left.

Francis was tearing pieces off of Huey Chester and eating them when he heard the distorted echo of a bullhorn outside. He leaped onto the wall, and climbed upside down across the ceiling, scrambling to a dusty window. There were army trucks parked on the far side of the street, and soldiers throwing down sandbags. He heard a loud, steely clanking, and the sputter-and-rumble of a massive engine, and glanced up Estrella Avenue. They had a tank too. Well, he thought. They were going to need it.

Francis drove one spear-tipped claw through the window before him, and blades of glass whirled through the air. In the bright, dust-blowing day outside, men began to shout. The tank ground to a stop, and the turret began to turn. Someone was yelling orders through a megaphone. Soldiers were hitting the deck. Francis pitched himself out and up into the sky, his wings whirring with the mechanical sound of wood being fed to a buzzsaw. As he rose above the school, he began to sing.

ABRAHAM'S BOYS

Maximilian searched for them in the carriage house and the cattle shed, even had a look in the springhouse, although he knew almost at first glance he wouldn't find them there. Rudy wouldn't hide in a place like that, dank and chill, no windows and so no light, a place that smelled of bats. It was too much like a basement. Rudy never went in their basement back home if he could help it, was afraid the door would shut behind him, and he'd find himself trapped in the suffocating dark.

Max checked the barn last, but they weren't hiding there either, and when he came into the dooryard, he saw with a shock that dusk had come. He had never imagined it could be so late.

"No more this game," he shouted. "Rudolf! We have to go." Only when he said *have* it came out *hoff*, a noise like a horse sneezing. He hated the sound of his own voice, envied his younger brother's confident American pronunciations. Rudolf had been born here, had never seen Amsterdam. Max had lived the first five years of his life there, in a dimly lit apartment that smelled of mildewed velvet curtains and the latrine stink of the canal below.

Max hollered until his throat was raw, but in the end, all his shouting brought only Mrs. Kutchner, who shuffled slowly across the porch, hugging herself for warmth, although it was not cold. When she reached the railing she took it in both hands and sagged forward, using it to hold herself up.

This time last fall, Mrs. Kutchner had been agreeably plump, dimples in her fleshy cheeks, her face always flushed from the heat of the kitchen. Now her face was starved, the skin pulled tight across the skull beneath, her eyes feverish and bird-bright in their bony hollows. Her daughter, Arlene—who at this very moment was hiding with Rudy somewhere—had whispered that her mother kept a tin bucket next to the bed, and when her father carried it to the outhouse in the morning to empty it, it sloshed with a quarter inch of bad-smelling blood.

"You'n go on if you want, dear," she said. "I'll tell your brother to run on home when he crawls out from whatever hole he's in."

"Did I wake you, Mrs. Kutchner?" he asked. She shook her head, but his guilt was not eased. "I'm sorry to get you out of bed. My loud mouth." Then, his tone uncertain: "Do you think you should be up?"

"Are you doctorin me, Max Van Helsing? You don't think I get enough of that from your daddy?" she asked, one corner of her mouth rising in a weak smile.

"No, ma'am. I mean, yes, ma'am."

Rudy would've said something clever to make her whoop with laughter and clap her hands. Rudy belonged on the radio, a child star on someone's variety program. Max never knew what to say, and anyway, wasn't suited to comedy. It wasn't just his accent, although that was a source of constant discomfort for him, one more reason to speak as little as possible. But it was also a matter of temperament; he often found himself unable to fight his way through his own smothering reserve.

"He's pretty strict about havin you two boys in before dark, isn't he?"

"Yes, ma'am," he said.

"There's plenty like him," she said. "They brung the old country over with them. Although I would have thought a doctor wouldn't be so superstitious. Educated and all."

Max suppressed a shudder of revulsion. Saying that his father was superstitious was an understatement of grotesquely funny proportions.

"You wouldn't think he'd worry so much about one like

you," she went on. "I can't imagine you've ever been any trouble in your life."

"Thank you, ma'am," said Max, when what he really wanted to say was he wished more than anything she'd go back inside, lie down and rest. Sometimes it seemed to him he was allergic to expressing himself. Often, when he desperately wanted to say a thing, he could actually feel his windpipe closing up on him, cutting off his air. He wanted to offer to help her in, imagined taking her elbow, leaning close enough to smell her hair. He wanted to tell her he prayed for her at night, not that his prayers could be assumed to have value; Max had prayed for his own mother, too, but it hadn't made any difference. He said none of these things. *Thank you, ma'am* was the most he could manage.

"You go on," she said. "Tell your father I asked Rudy to stay behind, help me clean up a mess in the kitchen. I'll send him along."

"Yes, ma'am. Thank you, ma'am. Tell him hurry, please."

When he was in the road he looked back. Mrs. Kutchner clutched a handkerchief to her lips, but she immediately removed it, and flapped it in a gay little wave, a gesture so endearing it made Max sick to his bones. He raised his own hand to her and then turned away. The sound of her harsh, barking coughs followed him up the road for a while—an angry dog, slipped free of its tether and chasing him away.

When he came into the yard, the sky was the shade of blue closest to black, except for a faint bonfire glow in the west where the sun had just disappeared, and his father was sitting on the porch waiting with the quirt. Max paused at the bottom of the steps, looking up at him. His father's eyes were hooded, impossible to see beneath the bushy steel-wool tangles of his eyebrows.

Max waited for him to say something. He didn't. Finally, Max gave up and spoke himself. "It's still light."

"The sun is down."

"We are just at Arlene's. It isn't even ten minutes away."

"Yes, Mrs. Kutchner's is very safe. A veritable fortress. Protected by a doddering farmer who can barely bend over, his rheumatism pains him so, and an illiterate peasant whose bowels are being eaten by cancer."

"She is not illiterate," Max said. He heard how defensive he sounded, and when he spoke again, it was in a tone of carefully modulated reason. "They can't bear the light. You say so yourself. If it isn't dark there is nothing to fear. Look how bright the sky."

His father nodded, allowing the point, then said, "And where is Rudolf?"

"He is right behind me."

The old man craned his head on his neck, making an exaggerated show of searching the empty road behind Max.

"I mean, he is coming," Max said. "He stops to help clean something for Mrs. Kutchner."

"Clean what?"

"A bag of flour, I think. It breaks open, scatters on everything. She's going to clean herself, but Rudy say no, he wants to do it. I tell them I will run ahead so you will not wonder where we are. He'll be here any minute."

His father sat perfectly still, his back rigid, his face immobile. Then, just when Max thought the conversation was over, he said, very slowly, "And so you left him?"

Max instantly saw, with a sinking feeling of despair, the corner he had painted himself into, but it was too late now, no talking his way back out of it. "Yes, sir."

"To walk home alone? In the dark?"

"Yes, sir."

"I see. Go in. To your studies."

Max made his way up the steps, towards the front door, which was partly open. He felt himself clenching up as he went past the rocking chair, expecting the quirt. Instead, when his father lunged, it was to clamp his hand on Max's wrist, squeezing so hard Max grimaced, felt the bones separating in the joint.

His father sucked at the air, a hissing indraw of breath, a sound Max had learned was often prelude to a right cross. "You know our enemies? And still you dally with your friends until the night come?"

Max tried to answer, but couldn't, felt his windpipe closing, felt himself choking again on the things he wanted, but didn't have the nerve, to say.

"Rudolf I expect not to learn. He is American. Here they believe the child should teach the parent. I see how he look at me when I talk. How he try not to laugh. This is bad. But you. At least when Rudolf disobey, it is deliberate, I feel him *engaging* me. You disobey in a stupor, without considering, and then you wonder why sometime I can hardly stand to look at you. Mr. Barnum has a horse that can add small numbers. It is considered one of the great amazements of his circus. If you were once to show the slightest comprehension of what things I tell you, it would be wonder on the same order." He let go of Max's wrist, and Max took a drunken step backwards, his arm throbbing. "Go inside and out of my sight. You will want to rest. That uncomfortable buzzing in your head is the hum of thought. I know the sensation must be quite unfamiliar." Tapping his own temple to show where the thoughts were.

"Yes, sir," Max said, in a tone—he had to admit—which sounded stupid and churlish. Why did his father's accent sound cultured and worldly, while the same accent made himself sound like a dull-witted Dutch farmhand, someone good at milking the cows maybe, but who would goggle in fear and confusion at an open book? Max turned into the house, without looking where he was going, and batted his head against the bulbs of garlic hanging from the top of the door frame. His father snorted at him.

Max sat in the kitchen, a lamp burning at the far end of the table, not enough to dispel the darkness gathering in the room. He waited, listening, his head cocked so he could see through the window and into the yard. He had his English Grammar open in front of him, but he didn't look at it, couldn't find the will to do anything but sit and watch for Rudy. In a while it was too dark to see the road, though, or anyone coming along it. The tops of the pines were black cutouts etched across a sky that was a color like the last faint glow of dying coals. Soon even that was gone, and into the darkness was cast a handful of stars, a scatter of bright flecks. Max heard his father in the rocker, the soft whine-and-thump of the curved wooden runners going back and forth over the boards of the porch. Max shoved his hands through his hair, pulling at it, chanting to himself, *Rudy, come on*, wanting more than anything for the waiting to be over. It might've been an hour. It might've been fifteen minutes.

Then he heard him, the soft chuff of his brother's feet in the chalky dirt at the side of the road; he slowed as he came into the yard, but Max suspected he had just been running, a hypothesis that was confirmed as soon as Rudy spoke. Although he tried for his usual tone of good humor, he was winded, could only speak in bursts.

"Sorry, sorry. Mrs. Kutchner. An accident. Asked me to help. I know. Late."

The rocker stopped moving. The boards creaked, as their father came to his feet.

"So Max said. And did you get the mess clean up?"

"Yuh. Uh-huh. Arlene and I. Arlene ran through the kitchen. Wasn't looking. Mrs. Kutchner—Mrs. Kutchner dropped a stack of plates—"

Max shut his eyes, bent his head forward, yanking at the roots of his hair in anguish.

"Mrs. Kutchner shouldn't tire herself. She's unwell. Indeed, I think she can hardly rise from bed."

"That's what—that's what I thought. Too." Rudy's voice at the bottom of the porch. He was beginning to recover his air. "It's not really all the way dark yet."

"It isn't? Ah. When one get to my age, the vision fail some, and dusk is often mistake for night. Here I was thinking sunset has come and gone twenty minutes ago. What time—?" Max heard the steely snap of his father opening his pocket watch. He sighed. "But it's too dark for me to read the hands. Well. Your concern for Mrs. Kutchner, I admire."

"Oh it—it was nothing—" Rudy said, putting his foot on the first step of the porch.

"But really, you should worry more about your own well-being, Rudolf," said their father, his voice calm, benevolent, speaking in the tone Max often imagined him employing when addressing patients he knew were in the final stages of a fatal illness. It was after dark and the doctor was in.

Rudy said, "I'm sorry, I'm—"

"You're sorry now. But your regret will be more palpable momentarily."

The quirt came down with a meaty smack, and Rudy, who would be ten in two weeks, screamed. Max ground his teeth, his hands still digging in his hair; pressed his wrists against his ears, trying vainly to block out the sounds of shrieking, and of the quirt striking at flesh, fat and bone.

With his ears covered he didn't hear their father come in. He looked up when a shadow fell across him. Abraham stood in the doorway to the hall, hair disheveled, collar askew, the quirt pointed at the floor. Max waited to be hit with it, but no blow came.

"Help your brother in."

Max rose unsteadily to his feet. He couldn't hold the old man's gaze so he lowered his eyes, found himself staring at the quirt instead. The back of his father's hand was freckled with blood. Max drew a thin, dismayed breath.

"You see what you make me do."

Max didn't reply. Maybe no answer was necessary or expected.

His father stood there for a moment longer, then turned, and strode away into the back of the house, towards the private study he always kept locked, a room in which they were forbidden to enter without his permission. Many nights he nodded off there, and could be heard shouting in his sleep, cursing in Dutch.

"Stop running," Max shouted. "I catch you eventually."

Rudolf capered across the corral, grabbed the rail and heaved himself over it, sprinted for the side of the house, his laughter trailing behind him.

"Give it back," Max said, and he leaped the rail without slowing down, hit the ground without losing a step. He was angry, really angry, and in his fury possessed an unlikely grace; unlikely because he was built along the same lines as his father, with the rough dimensions of a water buffalo taught to walk on its back legs.

Rudy, by contrast, had their mother's delicate build, to go with her porcelain complexion. He was quick, but Max was closing in anyway. Rudy was looking back over his shoulder too much, not concentrating on where he was going. He was almost to the side of the house. When he got there, Max would have him trapped against the wall, could easily cut off any attempt to break left or right.

But Rudy didn't break to the left or right. The window to their father's study was pushed open about a foot, revealing a cool library darkness. Rudy grabbed the windowsill over his head—he still held Max's letter in one hand—and with a giddy glance back, heaved himself into the shadows.

However their father felt about them arriving home after dark, it was nothing compared to how he would feel to discover that either one of them had gained entry to his most private sanctum. But their father was gone, had taken the Ford somewhere, and Max didn't slow down to think what would happen if he suddenly returned. He jumped and grabbed his brother's ankle, thinking he would drag the little worm back out into the light, but Rudy screamed, twisted his foot out of Max's grasp. He fell into darkness, crashed to the floorboards with an echoing thud that caused glass to rattle softly against glass somewhere in the office. Then Max had the windowsill and he yanked himself into the air—

"Go slow, Max, it's a . . ." his brother cried.

—and he thrust himself through the window.

"Big drop," Rudy finished.

Max had been in his father's study before, of course (sometimes Abraham invited them in for "a talk," by which he meant he would talk and they would listen), but he had never entered the room by way of the window. He spilled forward, had a startling glance of the floor almost three feet below him, and realized he was about to dive into it face-first. At the edge of his vision he saw a round end table, next to one of his father's armchairs, and he reached for it to stop his fall. His momentum continued to carry him forward, and he crashed to the floor. At the last moment, he turned his face aside and most of his weight came down on his right shoulder. The furniture leaped. The end table turned over, dumping everything on it. Max heard a bang, and a glassy crack that was more painful to him than the soreness he felt in either head or shoulder.

Rudy sprawled a yard away from him, sitting on the floor, still grinning a little foolishly. He held the letter half-crumpled in one hand, forgotten.

The end table was on its side, fortunately not broken. But an empty inkpot had smashed, lay in gleaming chunks close to Max's knee. A stack of books had been flung across the Persian carpet. A few papers swirled overhead, drifting slowly to the floor with a swish and a scrape.

"You see what you make me do," Max said, gesturing at the inkpot. Then he flinched, realizing that this was exactly what his father had said to him a few nights before; he didn't like the old man peeping out from inside him, talking through him like a puppet, a hollowed-out, empty-headed boy of wood.

"We'll just throw it away," Rudy said.

"He knows where everything in his office is. He will notice it missing."

"My balls. He comes in here to drink brandy, fart in his couch and fall asleep. I've been in here lots of times. I took his lighter for smokes last month and he still hasn't noticed."

"You what?" Max asked, staring at his younger brother in genuine surprise, and not without a certain envy. It was the older brother's place to take foolish risks and be casually detached about it later.

"Who's this letter to, that you had to go and hide somewhere to write it? I was watching you work on it over your shoulder. 'I still remember how I held your hand in mine.' " Rudy's voice swooping and fluttering in mock-romantic passion.

Max lunged at his brother, but was too slow, Rudy had flipped the letter over and was reading the beginning. The smile began to fade, thought lines wrinkling the pale expanse of his forehead; then Max had ripped the sheet of paper away.

"Mother?" Rudy asked, thoroughly nonplussed.

"It was assignment for school. We were ask if you wrote a letter to anyone, who would it be? Mrs. Louden tell us it could be someone imaginary or—or historic figure. Someone dead."

"You'd turn that in? And let Mrs. Louden read it?"

"I don't know. I am not finish yet." But as Max spoke, he was already beginning to realize he had made a mistake, allowed himself to get carried away by the fascinating possibilities of the assignment, the irresistible *what if* of it, and had written things too personal for him to show anyone. He had written *you were the only one I knew how to talk to* and *I am sometimes so lonely.* He had really been imagining her reading it, somehow, somewhere—perhaps as he wrote it, some astral form of her staring over his shoulder, smiling sentimentally as his pen scratched across the page. It was a mawkish, absurd fantasy and he felt a withering embarrassment to think he had given in to it so completely.

His mother had already been weak and ill when the scandal drove their family from Amsterdam. They lived for a while in England, but word of the terrible thing their father had done (whatever it was—Max doubted he would ever know) followed them. On they had gone to America. His father believed he had acquired a position as a lecturer at Vassar College, was so sure of this he had ladled much of his savings into the purchase of a handsome nearby farm. But in New York City they were met by the dean, who told Abraham Van Helsing that he could not, in good conscience, allow the doctor to work unsupervised with young ladies who were not yet at the age of consent. Max knew now his father had killed his mother as surely as if he had held a pillow over her face in her sickbed. It wasn't the travel that had done her in, although that was bad enough, too much for a woman who was both pregnant and weak with a chronic infection of the blood which caused her to bruise at the slightest touch. It was humiliation. Mina had not been able to survive the shame of what he had done, what they were all forced to run from.

"Come on," Max said. "Let's clean up and get out of here."

He righted the table and began gathering the books, but turned his head when Rudy said, "Do you believe in vampires, Max?"

Rudy was on his knees in front of an ottoman across the room. He had hunched over to collect a few papers which had settled there, then stayed to look at the battered doctor's bag tucked underneath it. Rudy tugged at the rosary knotted around the handles.

"Leave that alone," Max said. "We need to clean, not make bigger mess."

"Do you?"

Max was briefly silent. "Mother was attacked. Her blood was never the same after. Her illness."

"Did *she* ever say she was attacked, or did he?"

"She died when I was six. She would not confide in a child about such a thing."

"But . . . do you think we're in danger?" Rudy had the bag open now. He reached in to remove a bundle, carefully wrapped in royal purple fabric. Wood clicked against wood inside the velvet. "That vampires are out there, waiting for a chance at us. For our guard to drop?"

"I would not discount possibility. However unlikely."

"However unlikely," his brother said, laughing softly. He opened the velvet wrap and looked in at the nine-inch stakes, skewers of blazing white wood, handles wrapped in oiled leather. "Well, I think it's all bullshit. *Bullll*-shit." Singing a little.

The course of the discussion unnerved Max. He felt, for an instant, light-headed with vertigo, as if he suddenly found himself peering over a steep drop. And perhaps that wasn't too far off. He had always known the two of them would have this conversation someday and he feared where it might take them. Rudy was never happier than when he was making an argument, but he didn't follow his doubts to their logical conclusion. He could say it was all bullshit, but didn't pause to consider what that meant about their father, a man who feared the night as a person who can't swim fears the ocean. Max almost *needed* it to be true, for vampires to be real, because the other possibility—that their father was, and always had been, in the grip of a psychotic fantasy—was too awful, too overwhelming.

He was still considering how to reply when his attention was caught by a picture frame, slid halfway in under his father's armchair. It was facedown, but he knew what he'd see when he turned it over. It was a sepia-toned calotype print of his mother, posed in the library of their townhouse in Amsterdam. She wore a white straw hat, her ebon hair fluffed in airy curls beneath it. One gloved hand was raised in an enigmatic gesture, so that she almost appeared to be waving an invisible cigarette in the air. Her lips were parted. She was saying something, Max often wondered what. He for some reason imagined himself to be standing just out of the frame, a child of four, staring solemnly up at her. He felt that she was raising her hand to wave him back, keep him from wandering into the shot. If this was so, it seemed reasonable to believe she had been caught forever in the act of saying his name.

He heard a scrape and tinkle of falling glass as he picked the picture frame up and turned it over. The plate of glass had shattered in the exact center. He began wiggling small gleaming fangs of glass out of the frame and setting them aside, concerned that none should scratch the glossy calotype beneath. He pulled a large wedge of glass out of the upper corner of the frame, and the corner of the print came loose with it. He reached up to poke the print back into place . . . and then hesitated, frowning, feeling for a moment that his eyes had crossed and he was seeing double. There appeared to be a second print behind the first. He tugged the photograph of his mother out of the frame, then stared without understanding at the picture that had been secreted behind it. An icy numbness spread through his chest, crawling into his throat. He glanced around and was relieved to see Rudy still kneeling at the ottoman, humming to himself, rolling the stakes back up into their shroud of velvet.

He looked back at the secret photograph. The woman in it was dead. She was also naked from the waist up, her gown torn open and yanked to the curve of her waist. She was sprawled in a four-poster bed—pinned there by ropes wound around her throat, and pulling her arms over her head. She was young and maybe had been beautiful, it was hard to tell; one eye was shut, the other open in a slit that showed the unnatural glaze on the eyeball beneath. Her mouth was forced open, stuffed with an obscene misshapen white ball. She was actually biting down on it, her upper lip drawn back to show the small, even row of her upper teeth. The side of her face was discolored with bruises. Between the milky, heavy curves of her breasts was a spoke of white wood. Her left rib cage was painted with blood.

Even when he heard the car in the drive, he couldn't move, couldn't pry his gaze from the photograph. Then Rudy was up, pulling at Max's shoulder, telling him they had to go. Max clapped the photo to his chest to keep his brother from seeing. He said go, I'll be right behind you, and Rudy took his hand off his arm and went on.

Max fumbled with the picture frame, struggling to fit the calotype of the murdered woman back into place . . . then saw something else, went still again. He had not until this instant taken note of the figure to the far left in the photograph, a man on the near side of the bed. His back was to the photographer, and he was so close in the foreground that his shape was a blurred, vaguely rabbinical figure, in a flat-brimmed black hat and black overcoat. There was no way to be sure who this man was, but Max *was* sure, knew him from the way he held his head, the careful, almost stiff way it was balanced on the thick barrel of his neck. In one hand he held a hatchet. In the other a doctor's bag.

The car died with an emphysemic wheeze and tinny clatter. He squeezed the photograph of the dead woman into the frame, slid the portrait of Mina back on top of it. He set the picture, with no glass in it, on the end table, stared at it for a beat, then saw with horror that he had stuck Mina in upside down. He started to reach for it.

"*Come on!*" Rudy cried. "*Please, Max.*" He was outside, standing on his tiptoes to look back into the study.

Max kicked the broken glass under the armchair, stepped to the window, and screamed. Or tried to—he didn't have the air in his lungs, couldn't force it up his throat.

Their father stood behind Rudy, staring in at Max over Rudy's head. Rudy didn't see, didn't know he was there, until their father put his hands on his shoulders. Rudolf had no trouble screaming at all, and leaped as if he meant to jump back into the study.

The old man regarded his eldest son in silence. Max stared back, head half out the window, hands on the sill.

"If you like," his father said, "I could open the door and you could effect your exit by the hallway. What it lacks in drama, it makes up in convenience."

"No," Max said. "No thank you. Thank you. I'm—we're—this is—mistake. I'm sorry."

"Mistake is not knowing capital of Portugal on a geography test. This is something else." He paused, lowering his head, his face stony. Then he released Rudy, and turned away, opening a hand and pointing it at the yard in a gesture that seemed to mean, *step this way*. "We will discuss what at later date. Now if it is no trouble, I will ask you to leave my office."

Max stared. His father had never before delayed punishment—breaking and entering his study at the least deserved a vigorous lashing—and he tried to think why he would now. His father waited. Max climbed out, dropped into the flower bed. Rudy looked at him, eyes helpless, pleading, asking him what they ought to do. Max tipped his head towards the stables—their own private study—and started walking slowly and deliberately away. His little brother fell into step beside him, trembling continuously.

Before they could get away, though, his father's hand fell on Max's shoulder.

"My rules are to protect you always, Maximilian," he said. "Maybe you are tell me now you don't want to be protect any longer? When you were little I cover your eyes at the theater, when come the murderers to slaughter Clarence in *Richard*. But then, later, when we went to *Macbeth*, you shove my hand away, you *want* to see. Now I feel history repeats, nuh?"

Max didn't reply. At last his father released him.

They had not gone ten paces when he spoke again. "Oh I almost forget. I did not tell you where or why I was gone and I have piece of news I know will make sad the both of you. Mr. Kutchner run up the road while you were in school, shouting doctor, doctor, come quick, my wife. As soon as I see her, burning with fever, I know she must travel to Dr. Rosen's infirmary in town, but alas, the farmer come for me too late. Walking her to my car, her intestines fall out of her with a *slop*." He made a soft clucking sound with his tongue, as of disapproval. "I will have our suits cleaned. The funeral is on Friday."

ARLENE KUTCHNER WASN'T in school the next day. They walked past her house on the way home, but the black shutters were across the windows, and the place had a too-silent, abandoned feel to it. The funeral would be in town the next morning, and perhaps Arlene and her father had already gone there to wait. They had family in the village. When the two boys tramped into their own yard, the Ford was parked alongside the house, and the slanted double doors to the basement were open.

Rudy pointed himself towards the barn—they owned a single horse, a used-up nag named Rice, and it was Rudy's day to muck out her stable—and Max went into the house alone. He was at the kitchen table when he heard the doors to the cellar crash shut outside. Shortly afterwards his father climbed the stairs, appeared in the basement doorway.

"Are you work on something down there?" Max asked.

His father's gaze swept across him, but his eyes were deliberately blank.

"Later I shall unfold to you," he said, and Max watched him while he removed a silver key from the pocket of his waistcoat and turned it in the lock to the basement door. It had never been used before, and until that moment, Max had not even known a key existed.

Max was on edge the rest of the afternoon, kept looking at the basement door, unsettled by his father's promise: *Later I shall unfold to you*. There was of course no opportunity to talk to Rudy about it over dinner, to speculate on just *what* might be unfolded, but they were also unable to talk afterwards, when they remained at the kitchen table with their schoolbooks. Usually, their father retired early to his study to be alone, and they wouldn't see him again until morning. But tonight he seemed restless, always coming in and out of the room, to wash a glass, to find his reading spectacles, and finally, to light a lantern. He adjusted the wick, so a low red flame wavered at the bottom of the glass chimney, and then set it on the table before Max.

"Boys," he said, turning to the basement, unlocking the bolt. "Go downstairs. Wait for me. Touch nothing."

Rudy threw a horrified, whey-faced look at Max. Rudy couldn't bear the basement, its low ceiling and its smell, the lacy veils of cobwebs in the corners. If Rudy was ever given a chore there, he always begged Max to go with him. Max opened his mouth to question their father, but he was already slipping away, out of the room, disappearing down the hall to his study.

Max looked at Rudy. Rudy was shaking his head in wordless denial.

"It will be all right," Max promised. "I will take care of you."

Rudy carried the lantern, and let Max go ahead of him down the stairs. The reddish-bronze light of the lamp threw shadows that leaned and jumped, a surging darkness that lapped at the walls of the stairwell. Max descended to the basement floor and took a slow, uncertain look around. To the left of the stairs was a worktable. On top of it was a pile of something, covered in a piece of grimy white tarp—stacks of bricks maybe, or heaps of folded laundry, it was hard to tell in the gloom without going closer. Max crept in slow, shuffling steps until he had crossed most of the way to the table, and then he stopped, suddenly knowing what the sheet covered.

"We need to go, Max," Rudy peeped, right behind him. Max hadn't known he was there, had thought he was still standing on the steps. "We need to go right now." And Max knew he didn't mean just get out of the basement, but get out of the house, run from the place where they had lived ten years and not come back.

But it was too late to pretend they were Huck and Jim and light out for the territories. Their father's feet fell heavily on the dusty wood planks behind them. Max glanced up the stairs at him. He was carrying his doctor's bag.

"I can only deduce," their father began, "from your ransack of my private study, you have finally develop interest in the secret work to which I sacrifice so much. I have in my time kill six of the Undead by my own hand, the last the diseased bitch in the picture I keep hid in my office—I believe you have both see it." Rudy cast a panicked look at Max, who only shook his head, *Be silent.* Their father went on: "I have train others in the art of destroying the vampire, including your mother's unfortunate first husband, Jonathan Harker, Gott bless him, and so I can be held indirectly responsible for the slaughter of perhaps fifty of their filthy, infected kind. And it is now, I see, time my own boys learn how it is done. How to be sure. So you may know how to strike at those who would strike at you."

"I don't want to know," Rudy said.

"He didn't see picture," Max said at the same time.

Their father appeared not to hear either of them. He moved past them to the worktable, and the canvas-covered shape upon it. He lifted one corner of the tarp and looked beneath it, made a humming sound of approval, and pulled the covering away.

Mrs. Kutchner was naked, and hideously withered, her cheeks sunken, her mouth gaping open. Her stomach was caved impossibly in beneath her ribs, as if everything in it had been sucked out by the pressure of a vacuum. Her back was bruised a deep bluish violet by the blood that had settled there. Rudy moaned and hid his face against Max's side.

Their father set his doctor's bag beside her body, and opened it.

"She isn't, of course, Undead. Merely dead. True vampires are uncommon, and it would not be practicable, or advisable, for me to find one for you to rehearse on. But she will suit for purposes of demonstration." From within his bag he removed the bundle of stakes wrapped in velvet.

"What is she doing here?" Max asked. "They bury her tomorrow."

"But today I am to make autopsy, for purposes of my private research. Mr. Kutchner understand, is happy to cooperate, if it mean one day no other woman die in such a way." He had a stake in one hand, a mallet in the other.

Rudy began to cry.

Max felt he was coming unmoored from himself. His body stepped forward, without him in it; another part of him remained beside Rudy, an arm around his brother's heaving shoulders. Rudy was saying, *Please I want to go upstairs.* Max watched himself walk, flat-footed, to his father, who was staring at him with an expression that mingled curiosity with a certain quiet appreciation.

He handed Max the mallet, and that brought him back. He was in his own body again, conscious of the weight of the hammer, tugging his wrist downwards. His father gripped Max's other hand and lifted it, drawing it towards Mrs. Kutchner's meager breasts. He pressed Max's fingertips to a spot between two ribs, and Max looked into the dead woman's face. Her mouth open as to speak. *Are you doctorin' me, Max Van Helsing?*

"Here," his father said, folding one of the stakes into his hand. "You drive it in here. To the hilt. In an actual case, the first blow will be follow by wailing, profanity, a frantic struggle to escape. The accursed never go easily. Bear down. Do not desist from your work until you have impale her and she has give up her struggle against you. It will be over soon enough."

Max raised the mallet. He stared into her face and wished he could say he was sorry, that he didn't want to do it. When he slammed the mallet down, with an echoing bang, he heard a high, piercing scream and almost screamed himself, believing for an instant it was her, still somehow alive; then realized it was Rudy. Max was powerfully built, with his deep water-buffalo chest and Dutch farmer's shoulders. With the first blow he had driven the stake over two-thirds of the way in. He only needed to bring the mallet down once more. The blood that squelched up around the wood was cold and had a sticky, viscous consistency.

Max swayed, his head light. His father took his arm.

"*Goot,*" Abraham whispered into his ear, his arms around him, squeezing him so tightly his ribs creaked. Max felt a little thrill of pleasure—an automatic reaction to the intense, unmistakable affection of his father's embrace—and was sickened by it. "To do offense to the house of the human spirit, even after its tenant depart, is no easy thing, I know."

His father went on holding him. Max stared at Mrs. Kutchner's gaping mouth, the delicate row of her upper teeth, and found himself remembering the girl in the calotype print, the ball of garlic jammed in her mouth.

"Where were her fangs?" Max said.

"*Hm?* Whose? What?" his father said.

"In the photograph of the one you kill," Max said, turning his head and looking into his father's face. "She didn't have fangs."

His father stared at him, his eyes blank, uncomprehending. Then he said, "They disappear after the vampire die. *Poof.*"

He released him, and Max could breathe normally again. Their father straightened.

"Now, there remain one thing," he said. "The head must be remove, and the mouth stuff with garlic. Rudolf!"

Max turned his head slowly. His father had moved back a step. In one hand he held a hatchet, Max didn't know where it had come from. Rudy was on the stairs, three steps from the bottom. He stood pressed against the wall, his left wrist shoved in his mouth to quell his screaming. He shook his head, back and forth, frantically.

Max reached for the hatchet, grabbed it by the handle. "I do it." He would too, was confident of himself. He saw now he had always had it in him: his father's brusque willingness to puncture flesh and toil in blood. He saw it clear, and with a kind of dismay.

"No," his father said, wrenching the hatchet away, pushing Max back. Max bumped the worktable, and a few stakes rolled off, clattering to the dust. "Pick those up."

Rudy bolted, but slipped on the steps, falling to all fours and banging his knees. Their father grabbed him by the hair and hauled him backwards, throwing him to the floor. Rudy thudded into the dirt, sprawling on his belly. He rolled over. When he spoke, his voice was unrecognizable.

"*Please!*" he screamed. "*Please don't! I'm scared. Please, Father, don't make me.*"

The mallet in one hand, half a dozen stakes in the other, Max stepped forward, thought he would intervene, but his father swiveled, caught his elbow, shoved him at the stairs.

"Up. Now." Giving him another push as he spoke.

Max fell on the stairs, barking one of his own shins.

Their father bent to grab Rudy by the arm, but he squirmed away, crabwalking over the dirt for a far corner of the room.

"Come. I help you," their father said. "Her neck is brittle. It won't take long."

Rudy shook his head, backed further into the corner by the coal bin.

His father flung the axe in the dirt. "Then you will remain here until you are in a more complaisant state of mind."

He turned, took Max's arm and thrust him towards the top of the steps.

"*No!*" Rudy screamed, getting up, lunging for the stairs.

The handle of the hatchet got caught between his feet, though, and he tripped on it, crashed to his knees. He got back up, but by then their father was pushing Max through the door at the top of the staircase, following him through. He slammed it behind them. Rudy hit the other side a moment later, as their father was turning that silver key in the lock.

"Please!" Rudy cried. "I'm scared! I'm scared! I want to come out!"

Max stood in the kitchen. His ears were ringing. He wanted to say stop it, open the door, but couldn't get the words out, felt his throat closing. His arms hung at his sides, his hands heavy, as if cast from lead. No—not lead. They were heavy from the things in them. The mallet. The stakes.

His father panted for breath, his broad forehead resting against the shut door. When he finally stepped back, his hair was scrambled, and his collar had popped loose.

"You see what he make me do?" he said. "Your mother was also so, just as unbending and hysterical, just as in need of firm instruction. I tried, I—"

The old man turned to look at him, and in the instant before Max hit him with the mallet, his father had time to register shock, even wonder. Max caught him across the jaw, a blow that connected with a bony clunk, and enough force to drive a shivering feeling of impact up into his elbow. His father sagged to one knee, but Max had to hit him again to sprawl him on his back.

Abraham's eyelids sank as he began to slide into unconsciousness, but they came up again when Max sat down on top of him. His father opened his mouth to say something, but Max had heard enough, was through talking, had never been much when it came to talk anyway. What mattered now was the work of his hands; work he had a natural instinct for, had maybe been born to.

He put the tip of the stake where his father had showed him and struck the hilt with the mallet. It turned out it was all true, what the old man had told him in the basement. There was wailing and profanity and a frantic struggle to get away, but it was over soon enough.

BETTER THAN HOME

My father is on the television about to be thrown out of a game again. I can tell. Some of the fans watching at Tiger Stadium know too and they're making rude, happy noises about it. They want him to be thrown out. They're looking forward to it.

I know he's going to be thrown out because the home plate umpire is trying to walk away from him but my father is following him everywhere he goes. My father has all the fingers of his right hand stuck down the front of his pants, while the left gestures angrily in the air. The announcers are chattering happily away to tell everyone watching at home about what my father is trying to tell the umpire that the umpire is working so hard not to hear.

"You just had an idea from the way things were going that emotions were sure to boil over sooner rather than later," says one of the announcers.

My aunt Mandy laughs nervously. "Jessica, you might want to see this. Ernie is getting himself all worked up."

My mother steps into the kitchen doorway and sees what is happening on the television and leans against the doorframe with her arms crossed.

"I can't watch," Mandy says. "This is *so* upsetting."

Aunt Mandy is at one end of the couch. I'm at the other, with my feet under me and my heels pressed into my buttocks.

I'm rocking back and forth. I can't stay still. Something in me just needs to rock. My mouth is open and doing the thing it does when I'm nervous. I don't even know I'm doing it until I feel the warm dribbling wetness at the corner of my mouth. When I'm tense, and my mouth is stretched open like that, water runs out at the corner and eventually leaks down my chin. When I'm wired up tight with nerves like I am now, I spend a lot of time making these little sucking sounds, sucking the spit back into my head.

The third-base umpire, Comins, inserts himself between my father and Welkie, the home-plate umpire, allowing Welkie the chance to slip off. My father could just step around Comins, but he does not. This is an unexpected positive development, a sign the worst may yet be averted. His mouth is opening and closing, the left hand waving, and Comins is listening and smiling and shaking his head in a way that is good-natured and understanding yet firm. My father is unhappy. Our Team is losing four to one. Detroit has a rookie throwing the ball, a man who has never won a major league game in his life, a man who has in fact lost all five of his starts so far, but in spite of his well-established mediocrity he now has eight strike-outs in only five innings. My father is unhappy about the last strike-out, which came on a checked swing. He's unhappy because Welkie called it a strike without looking at the third-base umpire to see if the batter checked his swing or not. That's what he's supposed to do, but he didn't do it.

But Welkie didn't need to check with Comins down at third base. It was obvious the batter, Ramon Diego, let the head of the bat fly out over the plate, and then tried to snap it back with a flick of his wrists, to fool the umpire into thinking he didn't swing, but he did swing, everyone saw him swing, everyone knows he was fooled on a sinker that almost skipped off the dirt in front of home plate, everyone except for my father, that is.

At last my father says a few final words to Comins, turns, and starts back to the dugout. He's halfway there, almost free and clear, when he pivots and hollers a fare-thee-well to home-plate umpire Welkie. Welkie has his back to him. Welkie is bent over to brush the plate off with his little sweeper, his broad asscheeks spread apart, his not inconsiderable rear pointed my father's way.

Whatever it is my father shouts, Welkie wheels around and goes up on one foot in a jiggling fat man's hop and punches his finger into the air. My father whips his cap into the dirt and comes back to home plate in a loping run.

When it happens the first thing that goes insane is my father's hair. It has spent six innings trapped in his hat. When it springs out it is lathered in sweat. The gusting wind in Detroit catches it and messes it all around. One side is flattened and the other side is sticking up as if he slept on it wet. Hair is pasted damp against the sunburned and sweaty back of his neck. Hair blowing around as he screams.

Mandy says, "Oh my God. Look at him."

"Yes. I see," says my mother. "Another shining moment for the Ernie Feltz highlight reel."

Welkie crosses his arms over his chest. He has no more to say and regards my father with hooded eyes. My father kicks loose dirt over his shoes. Again Comins tries to get in between them, but my father kicks loose dirt at him. My father rips off his jacket and hurls it on the field. Then he kicks that. He kicks it up the third-base line. Then he picks it up and tries to throw it in the outfield, though it only goes a few feet. Some Tigers have collected out on the pitcher's mound. Their second baseman quickly puts his glove over his mouth so my father will not see him laughing. He turns his face into the loose group of men, his shoulders trembling.

My father leaps into the dugout. Stacked on the wall of the dugout are three towers of waxed Gatorade cups. He hits them with both hands and they explode across the grass. He does not touch the Gatorade coolers themselves, which some of the guys will be wanting to drink from, but he does take a batting helmet by the bill and he flips it out over the grass where it bounces, and rolls to the third-base bag. My insane father screams something more to Welkie and Comins and then crosses the dugout and goes down some steps and is gone. Except he isn't gone, he is suddenly once more at the top of the steps like the thing in the hockey mask in all those movies, the wretched creature you keep thinking has been destroyed and put out of the picture and his misery, but who always lurches back into things anyway to kill and kill again, and he pulls an armful of bats out of one of the deep cubbyholes for bats and throws the whole crashing heap of wood onto the grass. Then he stands there screaming and shouting with spit flying and eyes watering. The bat boy has by this time retrieved my father's jacket and brought it to the dugout steps, but is afraid to come any closer, so my father has to climb up to him and yank it from his hands. He shouts a last round of endearments and puts his jacket on inside out with the tag waving at the back of his neck and disappears now once and for all. I let out an unsteady breath that I didn't know I was holding.

"That was quite the episode," says my aunt.

"Time for that bath, kid," says my mother, coming up behind me and pushing her fingers through my hair. "Best part of the game is over."

In the bedroom I strip to my underwear. I start down the hall for the bathroom but when the phone rings I veer into my parents' bedroom and throw myself belly first on the bed and scoop the phone off the end table.

"Feltz residence."

"Hey, Homer," my father says. "I had a free minute. I thought I'd give a call and say good night. You watching the game?"

"Uh-huh," I say, and suck a little drool.

It's not the kind of thing I want him to hear but he hears me anyway. "Are you okay?"

"It's my mouth. It's just doing it. I can't help it."

"Are you getting yourself all tied in knots?"

"No."

"Who are you talking to, honey?" my mother calls out.

"Dad!"

"Did you think he broke his swing?" my father asks, shooting it to me point-blank.

"I wasn't sure he went around at first, but then I watched it on the replay and you can tell he went."

"Oh, shit," my father says, and then my mother picks up the extension in the kitchen and joins us on the line.

"Hey," she says. "It's a call from the Good Sport."

"How's it going?" my father says. "I had a free second, I thought I'd call up and say good night to the kid."

"From where I'm sitting it looks like you ought to have the rest of the evening free."

"I'm not going to tell you I think I was appropriate."

"Inappropriate, maybe," she says. "But inspiring, absolutely One of those special baseball moments that make the human spirit sing. Like seeing someone jack a big home-run, or hearing the third strike smack into the catcher's glove. There's just something a little magical about watching Ernie Feltz calling the umpire a butt-sucking rat-bastard and getting dragged off the field in a straitjacket by the men in white coats."

"Okay," is what he says. "I know. It looked really bad."

"It's something to work on."

"Well, goddamn it. I'm sorry. I mean that. No kidding—I am sorry," he says. "Hey, but will you tell me something?"

"What?"

"Did you see the replay? Did it look like he went around to you?"

THE LEAK I get at the corner of my mouth when I'm feeling tense, that isn't the only thing I'm struggling with, just one of the more obvious things, which is why I go see Dr. Faber twice a month. Dr. Faber and me get together to talk about strategies for coping with the things that stress me. There are lots of things that stress me; for example, I can't even look at tin foil without going weak and sick, and the sound of someone crunching tin foil brings on an ill ache that goes all through my teeth and up into my eardrums. Also I can't stand it when the VCR rewinds. I have to leave the room because of the way the machine sounds when the tape is whining backwards through the spools. And the smell of fresh paint or uncapped Magic Markers—let's not even talk about it.

Also nobody likes that I take apart my food to inspect the components. I mostly do this with hamburgers. I was deeply affected by a special I saw on television once about what can happen if you get a bad hamburger. They had E.Coli on; they had mad cow; they even showed a mad cow, wrenching its head to one side and staggering around a pen bawling. When we get hamburgers from Wendy's, I have my dad unwrap it from the foil for me, and then I lay all the parts out and discard any vegetables that look suspect, and give the patty a good long sniff to make sure it isn't spoiled. Not once but twice I've actually discovered a spoiled one and refused to eat. On both occasions my refusal precipitated a royal screaming match between my mother and me over whether it was really spoiled or not, and of course such meetings of the minds inevitably can end in only one way, with me doing the kicking thing I sometimes do, where I lay on the floor and scream and kick at anyone who tries to touch me, which is one of what Dr. Faber calls my hysterical compulsions. Mostly what I do now is get rid of the hamburger in the trash without discussing it and just eat the roll. It isn't any pleasure, I can tell you, to have my dietary problems. I hate the taste of fish. I won't eat pork because pork has little white worms in it that boil out of the raw meat when you pour alcohol on it. What I really like is breakfast cereal. I'd have Kix three times a day if it was up to me. Cans of fruit salad also go over well with me. When I'm at the park I enjoy a bag of peanuts, although I wouldn't eat a hot dog for all the tea in China (which I wouldn't want anyway since for me caffeine triggers shrill, hyper behavior and impromptu nosebleeds).

Dr. Faber's a good guy. We sit on the floor of his office and play Candy Land and hash it out.

"I've heard crazy before, but that's just nuts," my psychiatrist says. "You think McDonald's would serve spoiled hamburger? They'd lose their shirts! You'd sue their ass!" He pauses to move a piece, then looks up, and says, "You and me, we got to start talking about these miserable feelings that come over you whenever you stick lunch in your mouth. I think you're blowing things out of proportion. Letting your imagination freak you out. I'll tell you something else. Let's say you did get some goofy food, which I claim is very unlikely, because the McDonald's chain has a vested interest in not getting their asses sued, *even if*—people do manage to eat some pretty foul stuff without, you know, *death*."

"Todd Dickey, who plays third base for us? He ate a squirrel once," I say. "For a thousand dollars. It was back when he was in the minors. The team bus crunched it backing up and he ate it. He says people where he's from just eat them."

Dr. Faber stares at me dumbly, his round, pleasant face struck blank with disgust. "Where's he from?"

"Minnesota. Pretty much everyone there lives on squirrel. That's what Todd says. That way they have more money for the important things at the supermarket—like beer and lottery tickets."

"He ate it—raw?"

"Oh no. He fried it. With canned chili. He said it was the easiest money he ever made. The thousand dollars. That's a lot of money in the minors. Ten different guys had to pony up a hundred dollars apiece. He said it was like getting paid a grand to eat a Whopper."

"Right," he says. "That brings us back to the McDonald's issue. If Todd Dickey can eat a squirrel he scraped up out of the parking lot—a menu I can't, as your doctor, recommend—and suffer no ill effects, then you can handle a Big Mac."

"Uh-huh."

And I see his point. I really do. He's saying Todd Dickey is a strapping young professional athlete, and here he eats all this awful stuff like squirrel chili and Big Macs that squirt grease when you bite into them and *he* doesn't die of mad cow disease. I'm just not going to argue after a certain point. But I know Todd Dickey, and that's not a guy who is all right. Deep down something's wrong with him.

When Todd gets into a game and he's out on third he does this thing where he's always pressing his mouth into his glove and it seems like he's whispering into the palm of it. Ramon Diego, our shortstop and one of my best friends, says that he *is* whispering. He's looking at the batter coming to the plate and he's whispering:

"Beat 'em or burn 'em. They go up pretty quick. Beat 'em or burn 'em. Or *fuck* 'em. Either way. Either way beat 'em burn 'em or fuck 'em, fuck 'em, fuck this guy fucking *fuck* this guy!" Ramon says Todd gets spit all over his glove.

Also when the guys get talking about all the ball-club groupies they've made (I'm not supposed to hear this kind of talk but just try being around professional athletes and not catching some of it), Todd, who is one of these big ballplayers for Holy Everlasting Jesus!, listens with a face that seems swollen, and a weird intense look in his eyes, and sometimes without warning the muscles in the left side of his face all at once will start jumping and rippling unnaturally, and *he doesn't even know his face is doing what it's doing when it's doing it.*

Ramon Diego thinks he's weird and so do I. No parking-lot squirrel for me. There's a difference between being a stone-cold Colt .45–drinking hayseed redneck and being some kind of whispering psycho killer with a degenerative nerve condition in your face.

MY DAD DEALS really well with all my issues, like the time he took me road-tripping with him and we stayed at the Four Seasons in Chicago for a three-spot with the White Sox.

We settle into a suite with a big living room, and at one end is a door into his bedroom, and at the other is a door into mine. We stay up until midnight watching a movie on hotel cable. For dinner we order Froot Loops from room service (his idea—I didn't even ask). He sits slumped low in his chair, naked except for his jockey shorts, and the fingers of his right hand stuck in under the elastic waistband as they always are except in my mother's presence, watching the television in a drowsy, absent-minded sort of way. I don't remember falling asleep with the movie on. What I remember is that I wake up when he lifts me out of the cool leather couch to haul me into my bedroom, and my face is turned into his chest, and I'm breathing in the good smell of him. I can't tell you what that smell is, except that it has grass and clean earth in it, and sweat and locker rooms, and also the inherent sweetness of aged, lived-in skin. I bet farmers smell good just the same way.

After he's gone I'm laying alone in the dark, as comfortable as can be in my icy nestle of sheets, when for the first time I notice a thin, shrill whine, bad like when someone is rewinding a tape in the VCR. Almost the instant I'm aware of it I receive the first sick pulse in my back teeth. I'm not sleepy anymore—being carried has jostled me partly awake, and the cold sheets have shocked me the rest of the way—so I sit up and listen to the light-starved world around me. The traffic in the street whooshes along and horns bleat from a long distance off. I hold the clock-radio to my ear, but that isn't what's doing it. I hoist myself out of bed. On with the light. It has to be the air conditioner. In most hotels the air conditioner is usually a steel cabinet against the wall beneath the window, but not the Four Seasons, which is too good for that. The only air conditioning component I can track down is a slotted gray vent in the ceiling, and standing beneath it I can hear that this is the culprit. The whine is more than I can stand. My eardrums hurt. I snatch a hardcover I've been reading out of my tote and stand beneath the vent throwing the book up at it.

"Be quiet! Shut up! Stop it! *No more!*" I hit the vent a couple good shots with the book, too—clang! whang! A screw pops out of one corner and the whole vent falls loose at one side, but no luck—not only does it still whine but now it is also sometimes producing a delicate buzz, as if a piece of metal somewhere inside has been knocked loose and is shuddering a little. A cool wetness trickles at the edge of my mouth. I suck spit and give one last helpless look at the busted vent, and then I go into the living room with my fingers jamming my ears to get away from it, but the whine is whining even worse in there. There is no place to go and the fingers in my ears are no help.

The sound drives me into my father's bedroom.

"Dad," I say and wipe my chin on my shoulder—my jaw is slathered in spit—and go on, "Dad, can I sleep with you?"

"Huh? Okay. I got the farts, though. Watch out."

I scramble into his bed and pull the sheets over me. In his room too there is of course the thin piercing whine.

"Are you all right?" he asks.

"The air conditioner. The air conditioner has a noise. It's hurting my teeth. I couldn't find how to turn it off."

"Switch is in the living room. Right by the front door."

"I'll go get it," I say and I skitter to the edge of the bed.

"Hey," he says and clasps my upper arm. "You better not. This is Chicago in June. It was a hundred and three today. It'll get too stuffy. I mean it, we'll die in here."

"But I can't listen to it. Do you hear it? Do you hear the way it's making that noise? It hurts my teeth. It's as bad as when people crunch tinfoil, Dad, it's as bad as that."

"Yeah," he replies. He falls quiet and for a long moment seems to be listening to it himself. Then he says, "You're right. The air conditioner in this place sucks. It's a necessary evil, though. We'll suffocate in here like bugs screwed into a jar if we don't have air conditioning."

It has a steadying effect on me, the sound of his talk. Also, although when I climbed into the bed, the sheets had that crisp hotel room cold to them, by now I have warmed back up, and I'm not shivering so badly anymore. I feel better, although there are still the steady shoots of pain going through my jaw and up into my eardrums and then into my head. He has the farts, too, just as he warned me, but somehow even the reeky yellow smell of them, even that seems vaguely reassuring.

"All right," he decides. "Here's what we'll do. Come on."

He slips out of bed. I follow him through the dark to the bathroom. He clicks on the light. The bathroom is a vast expanse of beige-colored marble, and the sink has golden faucets, and in the corner is a shower with a door of rippled glass. It is pretty much the hotel bathroom of your dreams. By the sink is a collection of little bottles of shampoo and conditioner and skin lotion and boxes of soaps, a plastic jar of Q-tips, another of cotton balls. My father pops open the jar of cotton balls and crams one into each ear. I giggle at the sight of him—the sight of him standing there with a loose fluff of cotton hanging out of his big sunburned ears.

"Here," he said. "Put some of this in."

I force a few cotton balls deep into my ears. With the cotton in place, the world fills with a deep, hollow rushing roar. *My* roar, a steady flow of my own personal sound, a sound I find exceedingly pleasant.

I look at my father. He says, "Homkhmy chmn yhmu sthmll hhmhrmr thrm hrrr chmndhuthmmnhar?"

"What?" I yell happily.

He nods and makes an O with his thumb and index finger and we both go back to bed, which is what I mean about how my father deals really well with my issues. We both have a great night of sleep and the next morning my dad makes room service bring us cans of fruit salad and a can opener for breakfast.

NOT EVERYONE OUT there deals so well with my problems, case in point my aunt Mandy.

Aunt Mandy has tried her hand at a lot of things, but none of it has gone anywhere. Mom and Dad helped to pay for her to go to art school because she thought she was going to be a photographer for a while. After she gave that up, they also helped her start an art gallery in Cape Cod, but like Aunt Mandy says, it never *gelled*, it didn't come together, the click never clicked. She went to film school in L.A., and had a cup of coffee as a screenwriter—no dice. She married a man she thought was going to be a novelist, but he turned out to just be an English teacher, and furthermore not a very happy one, and Aunt Mandy had to pay *him* alimony for a little while, so even being a married person didn't come together so well.

What Aunt Mandy would say about it is that she's still trying to figure out what it is she's supposed to be. What my father would say is Mandy is wrong if she thinks the question hasn't been answered yet—she already is the person she was always sure to become. It's like Brad McGuane, who was the right-fielder when my father took over managing the Team, who is a lifetime .292 batter but who only hits about .200 with men in scoring position and has never had a postseason hit, in spite of about twenty-five at-bats the last time he got to the playoffs. He's a meltdown case—that's what my father calls him. McGuane has drifted from team to team to team and people keep hiring him because of his good numbers in general and because they think someone with such a good bat is bound to *develop*, but what they don't see is that he *did* develop, and this is what he developed into. His click already clicked and it sure seems that there are not many fresh clicks out there for those sweet young men who find themselves in the game of baseball, or for middle-aged women either who marry the wrong people and who are never happy doing what they're doing but can only think of what else the world has to offer that might be better, or for any of us really, which I suppose is what I'm afraid of in my own case, since I think it's pretty clear despite what Dr. Faber says about it that I'm not really a lot better but actually about the same as I've ever been which we all can safely say is not the ideal.

Needless to say, as you would guess based on their differences of philosophy and world view, et al., Aunt Mandy and my father don't really like each other, although they pretend otherwise for my mother's sake.

Mandy and I went up to North Altamont just the two of us on a Sunday, because Mom thought I had spent too much of the summer at the park. What really bothered her was that The Team had been pounded five straight and Mom was worried I was getting all wound up about it. She was right as far as that goes. The losing streak was really getting to me. The leak had never leaked so much as during the last homestand.

I don't know why North Altamont. When Aunt Mandy talks about it, she always talks about going up to "*do* Lincoln Street," as if Lincoln Street in North Altamont is one of those famous places everyone knows about and always means to *do*, the way when people are passing through Florida they *do* Walt Disney World, or when they're in New York City they *do* a Broadway show. Lincoln Street is pretty, though, in a quiet little New England township kind of way. It's on a steep hill, and the road is made of brick, and no cars are allowed, although people walk horses right up the middle, and there are occasional dry, green horse-turd pies scattered over the road. I mean—*scenic.*

We visit a series of poorly lit patchouli-smelling shops. We go into one store where they're hawking bulky sweaters made out of Vermont-bred llama wool, and there's this music playing down low, some kind of music that incorporates flutes, blurred harpsichord sounds, and the shrill whistles of birds. In another store we peruse the work of local artisans—glistening ceramic cows, their pink ceramic udders waving beneath them as they leap over ceramic moons—while from the store's sound-system comes the reedy choogling of the Grateful Dead.

After a dozen stores I'm bored of it. I have been sleeping badly all week—nightmares, plus the shivers, and so on—and all the walking around has made me tired and grouchy. It doesn't help my mood that the last place we go into, an antique shop in a renovated carriage house, has on neither New Age music or hippie music, but more awful sounds yet—the Sunday game. Here is no store-wide sound-system, only a little table-top stereo on the front desk. The proprietor, an old man in bib overalls, listens to the game with his thumb stuck in his mouth. In his eyes is a stunned, hopeless daze.

I hang around by the desk to listen in and find out what all the misery is about. We're at the plate. Our first guy pops out to left, and our second guy pops out to right. Hap Diehl comes up planning to swing and racks up a couple strikes in practically no time.

"Hap Diehl has been just *atrocious* with the lumber lately," says the announcer. "He's hitting an *excruciating* .160 over the last eight days, and when do you have to start questioning Ernie's decision to leave him in there day after day, when he's just getting *killed* at the plate. Partridge sets now and delivers and—oh, Hap Diehl *swung* at a *bad one*, I mean *bad*, a fastball that was a *mile* over his head—wait, he fell over, I actually think he's *hurt*—"

Aunt Mandy says we'll walk down to Wheelhouse Park and have a picnic. I'm used to city parks, open grassy areas with asphalt paths and Rollerblading girls in spandex. Wheelhouse Park is *dimmer* somehow than a city park, crowded with great old New England firs. The paths are of Rollerblade-unfriendly blue gravel. No playground. No tennis courts. *No* ballpark. Only the mysterious pine-sweet gloom—in under the over-spreading branches of the Christmas trees there is no real direct sunshine—and the sometimes gentle swoosh of wind. We pass no one.

"There's a good place to sit up ahead," my aunt says. "Just over this cute little covered bridge."

We approach a clearing, although even here the light is somehow obscured and dimmish. The path wanders unevenly to a covered bridge suspended only a yard above a wide, slow-moving river. On the other side of the bridge is a grassy sward with some benches in it.

One look and I am not a fan of this covered bridge, which sags obviously in the middle. Once a long time ago the bridge was a firetruck red, but rot and rain have stripped most of the paint away and there has been no effort to touch up, and the wood revealed is dried-out, splintery, and untrustworthy in character. Inside the tunnel is a scatter of garbage bags, ruptured and spilling litter. I hesitate an instant and in that time Aunt Mandy plunges on ahead. I straggle along behind with such a lack of enthusiasm that she is soon across, and I have not even gone in.

At the entrance I pause once more. Sickly sweet smells: the smell of rot and fungus. A narrow track passes between the heaps of garbage bags. I am disconcerted by the smell and the sewer gloom, but Aunt Mandy is on the other side, indeed, already gone on out of my direct view, and it makes me nervous to think of being left behind. I hurry on.

What happens next, though, is I get only a few yards, and then take a deep breath and what I smell makes me stop walking all at once and stick in place, unable to go on. What I have noticed is a rodent smell, a heated dandruffy rodent smell, mixed with a whiff of ammonia, a smell like I have smelled before in attics and basements, a rank *bat stink*. Suddenly I'm imagining a ceiling covered with bats. I imagine tipping my head back and seeing a colony of thousands of bats covering the roof in a squirming surface of brown-furred bodies, torsos wrapped in membrane-thin wings. I imagine the faint bat squeaks so like the sub-audible squeak of bad air conditioners and VCRs on rewind. I imagine bats, but cannot make myself glance up to look for them. The fright would kill me if I saw one. I take a few tense mincing steps forward and put my foot down on some ancient newspaper. There is an unfortunate crunch. I jump back, the sound giving my heart a stiff wrench in my chest.

My foot comes down on something, a log maybe, that rolls beneath my heel. I totter backwards, wheeling my arms about to catch my balance, and at last manage to steady myself without falling over. I twist around to look at whatever it is I just stepped on.

It is not a log at all but a man's leg. A man lays on his side in a drift of leaves. He wears a filthy baseball cap—Our Team's cap, once dark blue, but now faded almost white around the rim where it is blotched by dried salts left by old sweats—and denim jeans, and a lumberjack's plaid shirt. His beard has leaves in it. I stare down at him, the first thrill of panic shooting through me. I just stepped on him—and he *didn't wake up.*

I stare at his face and like in the comic books I am tingling with horror. A little flicker of movement catches my eye. I see a fly crawling on his upper lip. The fly's body gleams like an ingot of greased metal. It hesitates at the corner of his mouth, then climbs in and disappears and *he does not wake up.*

I shriek; no other word for it. I turn and run back to my side of the bridge where I shriek myself hoarse for Mandy.

"Aunt Mandy, come back! Come back *right now!*"

In a moment, she appears at the far end of the bridge.

"What are you screaming your head off for?"

"Aunt Mandy, come back, come back, *please!*" I suck at some drool. For the first time I am aware of drool all down my chin.

She starts across the bridge, coming at me with her head lowered as if she were walking into a bitter wind. "You can stop that screaming right now. Just stop! What are you yelling about?"

I point. "Him! *Him!*"

She stops a quarter of the way across and looks at the stiff old goner lying there in the garbage. She stares at him for a few seconds, and then says, "Oh. Him. Well, come on. He'll be all right, Homer. You let him mind his business and we'll mind ours."

"No, Aunt Mandy, we have to go! Please come back, please!"

"I'm not going to listen to a second more foolishness. Come over here."

"No!" I scream. "No, I *won't!*"

I pivot and run, the panic swelling through me, sick to my stomach, sick of the garbage smell and the bats and the dead man and the terrible crunch of old newspaper, the stink of bat piss, the way Hap Diehl was swinging at shit and Our Team was going into the toilet just like last year, and I run gushing tears, and wiping miserably at the spit on my face, and finding that no matter how hard I sobbed I could hardly get any air into my lungs.

"Stop it!" Mandy hollers when she catches up to me. She throws our bagged lunch aside to have both hands free. "You stop it! Jesus—*shut up!*"

She captures me around the waist. I flail about, shrieking, not wanting to be lifted, not wanting to be handled. I snap back an elbow that cracks sharply against a bony eye socket. She cries out and we both go staggering to the ground, Mandy on top of me. Her chin clouts the top of my skull. I scream at the sharp little flash of pain. Her teeth clack together and she gasps, and her grip goes loose. I leap and almost get free but she grabs me with both hands by the elastic band of my shorts.

"Goddamn it, you stop!"

My face glows with an infernal heat. "No! No I won't go back I won't go back let me go!"

I surge forward again, coming off the ground like a runner jumping from the blocks and suddenly, in an instant, I am out from under her and tramping full-speed up the path, listening to her squall behind me.

"Homer!" she squalls. "Homer, come back here *right now!*"

I have gone almost all the way back to Lincoln Street when I feel a gush of cool air between my legs and look down and observe for the first time how it is that I have escaped. She had been holding me by the shorts, and I have come right out of them—shorts, Mark McGwire Underoos, and all. I look down at my male equipment, pink and smooth and small, jouncing from thigh to thigh as I run. The sight of all this bareness below gives me an unexpected rush of exhilaration.

She catches me again halfway to the car on Lincoln Street. A crowd watches while she yanks me off my feet by my hair and we wrestle together on the ground.

"Sit down, you weird shit!" she shouts. "You crazy little asshole!"

"Fat bitch whore!" I yell. "Parasitic capitalist!"

Well, no. But along those lines.

*   *   *

I DON'T KNOW but it might be that what happened up at Wheel-house Park was the last straw, because two weeks later, when The Team is taking an off-day, the folks and me are driving to Vermont to tour a boarding school called Biden Academy that my mom wants us to look at. She tells me it's a prep school, but I've seen the brochure, which is full of code words—special needs, stable environment, social normalization—so I know what kind of school we're really going to look at.

A young man in a worn blue shirt, jeans, and hiking boots meets us on the steps in front of Main Building. He introduces himself as Archer Grace. He's with admissions. He's going to show us around. Biden Academy is in the White Mountains. The breeze swishing in the pines has a brisk chill to it, so that although it is August, the afternoon has the exciting, chilly feel of World Series time. Mr. Grace takes us on a stroll around the campus. We look at a couple of brick buildings smothered in fresh green ivy. We look inside at empty classrooms. We walk through an auditorium with dark wood paneling and a bunch of heavy crimson curtains hanging around. At one side of the room is a bust of Benjamin Franklin chiseled in milky blond marble. At the other, a bust of Martin Luther King in dark on-yxlike stone. Ben is scowling across the room at the reverend, who looks as if he has just woken up and is still puffy with sleep.

"Is it just me or is it really stuffy in here?" my father asks. "Like, short on oxygen?"

"It gets a good airing out before the fall semester begins," replies Mr. Grace. "There isn't anyone here hardly except for a few of the summer-program kids."

We perambulate together outside and into a grove of enor-mous trees with slippery-looking gray bark. At one end of the grove is a half-shell amphitheater and terraced seats, where they have graduations and occasionally hold productions or shows for the kids.

"What's that smell?" my father asks. "Does this place smell funny?"

What is interesting is that my mother and Mr. Grace are pretending not to hear him. My mother has lots of questions for Mr. Grace about the school productions. It's like my father isn't there.

"What are these beautiful trees?" my mother asks, as we're on our way out of the grove.

"Gingko," Mr. Grace replies. "Do you know there are no trees in the world like the Gingko? They're sole survivors of an ancient prehistoric tree family that has been wiped completely off the earth."

My father stops by the trunk of one of them. He scratches a thumb along the bark. Then he gives his thumb a sniff. He makes a disgusted face.

"So *that's* what stinks," he says. "You know, extinction is not always a bad thing."

We look at a swimming pool. Mr. Grace talks about physical therapy. He shows us a running track. He talks about the junior Special Olympics. He shows us the ballpark.

"So you get a team together," my father says. "And you play some games. Is that right?"

"Yes. A team, a few games. But this is more than just play, what we're doing out here," Mr. Grace says. "At Biden we challenge children to squeeze learning out of everything they do. Even their games. This is a classroom too. We see this as a place to develop in the children some of the most crucial life skills, like negotiating conflict, and building interpersonal relationships, and releasing stress through physical activity. It's like, you know that old cliché—it's not whether you win or lose, it's what you take away from the game, how much you learn about yourself, about emotional growth."

Mr. Grace turns and starts away.

"What did he just tell me?" my father says. "That was like in a different language."

My mother starts to walk away too.

"I didn't get him," my father says. "But I think he just told me they have one of these pity-party teams where no one ever strikes out."

Mr. Grace takes us last to the library and it's here that we meet one of the summer-session kids. We enter a large circular room, with rosewood bookcases wrapped around the walls. A distant computer clickety-clicks. A boy about my age is lying on the floor. A woman in a plaid dress has him by the right arm. I think she's trying to get him on his feet, but all she's managing to do is drag him around in circles.

"Jeremy?" she says. "If you won't get up, then we can't go play with the computer. Do you hear me?"

Jeremy doesn't respond and she just keeps dragging him around and around. Once when she has him turned around to face us, he looks at me briefly with vacant eyes. He has the leak too—drool all over his chin.

"*Wanna,*" he drones in a long, stupid voice. "*Wannaaa.*"

"The library just installed four new computers," says Mr. Grace. "Internet-ready."

"Look at this marble," my mother says.

My father puts his hand on my shoulder and squeezes me gently.

THE FIRST SUNDAY in September I go to the park with my father, and of course it is early when we get there, so early that no one is there, only a couple of rookie call-ups who have been in since the dawn to impress my father. My father is sitting in the stands behind the screen overlooking home plate and talking with Shaughnessy for the sports pages, and at the same time the two of us are playing a game, it's called the secret things game, where he makes out a list of things for me to look for, each item worth a different number of points, and I have to run around the park and try and hunt them down (no digging through the trash which he should know I would not do anyway): a ballpoint pen, a quarter, a lady's glove, et cetera. No easy task after the crews have been out cleaning.

As I find things on the list I run them back to him, ballpoint pen, string of black licorice, steel button. Then one time when I return, Shaughnessy has gone off and my father is just sitting there with his hands laced behind his head and an open plastic bag of peanuts in his lap and his feet up on the seat in front of him and he says, "Why don't you set awhile?"

"Look: I found a matchbook. Forty points," I say, and I plop into the seat beside him.

"Get a load of this," my father says. "Look how nice it is when no one is here. When you get the place quiet. You know what I like best about it? The way it is right now?"

"What do you like best about it?"

"You can get some thinking done, and eat peanuts at the same time," he tells me and cracks a peanut open.

It is cool out, the sky a whitish-blue arctic color. A seagull floats above the outfield, wings spread, not seeming to move. The rookies are stretching in the outfield and chatting. One of them laughs, strong, young, healthy laughter.

"Where do you think better?" I ask. "Here or home?"

"This is better than home," he says. "Better for eating peanuts too, because you can't just throw the shells on the floor at home." He throws a few shells on the floor. "Not unless you want Mom to hand you an ass-kicking."

We were quiet. A steady cool stream of air was blowing in from the outfield and into our faces. No one was going to hit any home runs today—not with that steady wind blowing in against us.

"Well," I say, popping up. "Forty points. Here's my matchbook. I better get back to it. I've almost found everything I'm looking for."

"Lucky you," he tells me.

"This is a good game," I say. "I bet we could play at home. You could send me out to look for things and I could hunt around and find them. How come we never do that? How come we never play the game where we look for secret things at home?"

"Because it's just better here," he says.

At that point I run off to look for what's left on the list—a shoelace, a lucky rabbit's foot key chain—and leave my father behind, but the conversation came back to me later on and is kind of stuck in my head so that I think about it all the time and sometimes I wonder if that was one of those moments you aren't supposed to forget when you think your father is saying one thing, but actually he's saying another, when there's meaning buried in some comments that seemed really ordinary. I like to think that. It's a nice memory of my father sitting with his hands cupped behind his head and the wintry blue sky over the both of us. It's a nice memory with that old seagull floating over the outfield and not going anywhere, just hanging in place with its wings spread, never traveling any closer to wherever it was heading. It's a nice memory to have in your head. Everyone should have a memory just like it.

THE BLACK PHONE

1.

The fat man on the other side of the road was about to drop his groceries. He had a paper bag in each arm, and was struggling to jam a key into the back door of his van. Finney sat on the front steps of Poole's Hardware, a bottle of grape soda in one hand, watching it all. The fat man was going to lose his groceries the moment he got the door open. The one in his left arm was already sliding free.

He wasn't any kind of fat, but grotesquely fat. His head had been shaved to a glossy polish, and there were two plump folds of skin where his neck met the base of his skull. He wore a loud Hawaiian shirt—toucans nestled among hanging creepers—although it was too cool for short sleeves. The wind had a brisk edge, so that Finney was always hunching and turning his face away from it. He wasn't dressed for the weather either. It would've made more sense for him to wait for his father inside, only John Finney didn't like the way old Tremont Poole was always eyeballing him, half-glaring, as if he expected him to break or shoplift something. Finney only went in for grape soda, which he had to have, it was an addiction.

The lock popped and the rear door of the van sprang open. What happened next was such a perfect bit of slapstick it might have been practiced—and only later did it occur to Finney that probably it had been. The back of the van contained a gathering of balloons, and the moment the door was open, they shoved their way out in a jostling mass . . . thrusting themselves at the fat man, who reacted as if he had no idea they would be there. He leaped back. The bag under his left arm fell, hit the ground, split open. Oranges rolled crazily this way and that. The fat man wobbled and his sunglasses slipped off his face. He recovered and hopped on his toes, snatching at the balloons, but it was already too late, they were sailing away, out of reach.

The fat man cursed and waved a hand at them in a gesture of angry dismissal. He turned away, squinted at the ground and then sank to his knees. He set his other bag in the back of the van and began to explore the pavement with his hands, feeling for his glasses. He put a hand down on an egg, which splintered beneath his palm. He grimaced, shook his hand in the air. Shiny strings of egg white spattered off it.

By then, Finney was already trotting across the road, left his soda behind on the stoop. "Help, mister?"

The fat man peered blearily up at him without seeming to see him. "Did you observe that bullshit?"

Finney glanced down the road. The balloons were thirty feet off the ground by now, following the double line along the middle of the road. They were black . . . all of them, as black as sealskin.

"Yeah. Yeah, I—" he said, and then his voice trailed off and he frowned, watching the balloons bobbing into the low overcast of the sky. The sight of them disturbed him in some way. No one wanted black balloons; what were they good for, anyway? Festive funerals? He stared, briefly transfixed, thinking of poisoned grapes. He moved his tongue around in his mouth, and noticed for the first time that his beloved grape soda left a disagreeable metallic aftertaste, a taste like he had been chewing an exposed copper wire.

The fat man brought him out of it. "See my glasses?"

Finney lowered himself to one knee, leaned forward to look beneath the van. The fat man's glasses were under the bumper.

"Got 'em," he said, stretching an arm past the fat man's leg to pick them up. "What were the balloons for?"

"I'm a part-time clown," said the fat man. He was reaching into the van, getting something out of the paper bag he had set down there. "Call me Al. Hey, you want to see something funny?"

Finney glanced up, had time to see Al holding a steel can, yellow and black, with pictures of wasps on it. He was shaking it furiously. Finney began to smile, had the wild idea that Al was about to spray him with silly string.

The part-time clown hit him in the face with a blast of white foam. Finney started to turn his head away, but was too slow to avoid getting it in his eyes. He screamed and took some in the mouth, tasted something harsh and chemical. His eyes were coals, cooking in their sockets. His throat burned; in his entire life he had never felt any pain like it, a searing icy-heat. His stomach heaved and the grape soda came back up in a hot, sweet rush.

Al had him by the back of the neck and was pulling him forward, into the van. Finney's eyes were open but all he could see were pulsations of orange and oily brown that flared, dripped, ran into one another and faded. The fat man had a fistful of his hair and another hand between his legs, scooping him up by the crotch. The inside of Al's arm brushed his cheek. Finney turned his head and bit down on a mouthful of wobbling fat, squeezed until he tasted blood.

The fat man wailed and let go and for a moment Finney had his feet on the ground again. He stepped back and put his heel on an orange. His ankle folded. He tottered, almost fell and then the fat man had him by the neck again. He shoved him forward. Finney hit one of the van's rear doors, head-first, with a low bonging sound, and all the strength went out of his legs.

Al had an arm under his chest, and he tipped him forward, into the back of the van. Only it wasn't the back of a van. It was a coal chute, and Finney dropped, with a horrifying velocity, into darkness.

2.

A door banged open. His feet and knees were sliding across linoleum. He couldn't see much, was pulled through darkness toward a faint fluttering moth of gray light that was always dancing away from him. Another door went crash and he was dragged down a flight of stairs. His knees clubbed each step on the way down.

Al said, "Fucking arm. I ought to snap your neck right now, what you did to my arm."

Finney thought of resisting. They were distant, abstract thoughts. He heard a bolt turn, and he was pulled through a last door, across cement, and finally to a mattress. Al flipped him onto it. The world did a slow, nauseating roll. Finney sprawled on his back and waited for the feeling of motion sickness to pass.

Al sat down beside him, panting for breath.

"Jesus, I'm covered in blood. Like I killed someone. Look at this arm," he said. Then he laughed, husky, disbelieving laughter. "Not that you can see anything."

Neither of them spoke, and an awful silence settled upon the room. Finney shook continuously, had been shivering steadily, more or less since regaining consciousness.

At last Al spoke. "I know you're scared of me, but I won't hurt you anymore. What I said about I ought to snap your neck, I was just angry. You did a number on my arm, but I won't hold it against you. I guess it makes us even. You don't need to be scared because nothing bad is going to happen to you here. You got my word, Johnny."

At the mention of his name, Finney went perfectly still, abruptly stopped trembling. It wasn't just that the fat man knew his name. It was the way he said it . . . his breath a little trill of excitement. *Johnny.* Finney felt a ticklish sensation crawling across his scalp, and realized Al was playing with his hair.

"You want a soda? Tell you what, I'll bring you a soda and then—wait! Did you hear the phone?" Al's voice suddenly wavered a little. "Did you hear a phone ringing somewhere?"

From an unguessable distance, Finney heard the soft burr of a telephone.

"Oh, shit," Al said. He exhaled unsteadily. "That's just the phone in the kitchen. Of course it's just the phone in—okay. I'll go see who it is and get you that soda and come right back and then I'll explain everything."

Finney heard him come up off the mattress with a labored sigh, followed the scuffle of his boots as he moved away. A door thumped shut. A bolt slammed. If the phone upstairs rang again, Finney didn't hear it.

3.

He didn't know what Al was going to say when he came back, but he didn't need to explain anything. Finney already knew all about it.

The first child to disappear had been taken two years ago, just after the last of the winter's snow melted. The hill behind St. Luke's was a lumpy slope of greasy mud, so slippery that kids were going down it on sleds, cracking each other up when they crashed at the bottom. A nine-year-old named Loren ran into the brush on the far side of Mission Road to take a whiz, and never came back. Another boy went missing two months later, on the first of June. The papers named the kidnapper The Galesburg Grabber, a name Finney felt lacked something on Jack the Ripper. He took a third boy on the first of October, when the air was aromatic with the smell of dead leaves crunching underfoot.

That night John and his older sister Susannah sat at the top of the stairs and listened to their parents arguing in the kitchen. Their mother wanted to sell the house, move away, and their father said he hated when she got hysterical. Something fell over or was thrown. Their mother said she couldn't stand him anymore, was going crazy living with him. Their father said so don't and turned on the TV.

Eight weeks later, at the very end of November, the Galesburg Grabber took Bruce Yamada.

Finney wasn't friends with Bruce Yamada, had never even had a conversation with him—but he had known him. They had pitched against each other, the summer before Bruce disappeared. Bruce Yamada was maybe the best pitcher the Galesburg Cardinals had ever faced; certainly the hardest thrower. The ball sounded different when he threw it in the catcher's glove, not like it sounded when other kids threw. When Bruce Yamada threw, it was like the sound of someone opening champagne.

Finney pitched well himself, giving up just a pair of runs, and those only because Jay McGinty dropped a big lazy fly to left that anyone else would've caught. After the game—Galesburg lost five to one—the teams formed into two lines and started to march past each other, slapping gloves. It was when Bruce and Finney met each other to touch gloves that they spoke to each other for the one and only time in Bruce's life.

"You were dirty," Bruce said.

Finney was flustered with happy surprise, opened his mouth to reply—but all that came out was, "good game," same as he said to everyone. It was a thoughtless, automatic line, repeated twenty straight times, and it was said before he could help himself. Later, though, he wished he had come up with something as cool as *You were dirty*, something that really smoked.

He didn't run into Bruce again the rest of the summer, and when he did finally happen to see him—coming out of the movies that fall—they didn't speak, just nodded to each other. A few weeks later, Bruce strolled out of the Space Port arcade, told his friends he was walking home, and never got there. The dragnet turned up one of his sneakers in the gutter on Circus Street. It stunned Finney to think a boy he knew had been stolen away, yanked right out of his shoes, and was never coming back. Was already dead somewhere, with dirt in his face and bugs in his hair and his eyes open and staring at exactly nothing.

But then a year passed, and more, and no other kids disappeared, and Finney turned thirteen, a safe age—the person snatching children had never bothered with anyone older than twelve. People thought the Galesburg Grabber had moved away, or been arrested for some other crime, or died. Maybe Bruce Yamada killed him, Finney thought once, after hearing two adults wonder aloud whatever happened to the Grabber. Maybe Bruce Yamada picked up a rock as he was being kidnapped, and later saw a chance to show the Galesburg Grabber his fastball. There was a hell of an idea.

Only Bruce didn't kill the Grabber, the Grabber had killed him, like he had killed three others, and like he was going to kill Finney. Finney was one of the black balloons now. There was no one to pull him back, no way to turn himself around. He was sailing away from everything he knew, into a future that stretched open before him, as vast and alien as the winter sky.

4.

He risked opening his eyes. The air stung his eyeballs, and it was like looking through a Coke bottle, everything distorted and tinted an unlikely shade of green, although that was an improvement on not being able to see at all. He was on a mattress at one end of a room with white plaster walls. The walls seemed to bend in at the top and bottom, enclosing the world between like a pair of white parentheses. He assumed—hoped—this was only an illusion created by his poisoned eyes.

Finney couldn't see to the far end of the room, couldn't see the door he had been brought in through. He might have been underwater, peering into silty jade depths, a diver in the cabin room of a sunken cruise liner. To his left was a toilet with no seat. To his right, midway down the room, was a black box or cabinet bolted to the wall. At first he couldn't recognize it for what it was, not because of his unclear vision, but because it was so out of place, a thing that didn't belong in a prison cell.

A phone. A large, old-fashioned, black phone, the receiver hanging from a silver cradle on the side.

Al wouldn't have left him in a room with a working phone. If it worked, one of the other boys would've used it. Finney knew that, but he felt a thrill of hope anyway, so intense it almost brought tears to his eyes. Maybe he had recovered faster than the other boys. Maybe the others were still blind from the wasp poison when Al killed them, never even knew about the phone. He grimaced, appalled by the force of his own longing. But then he started crawling toward it, plunged off the edge of the mattress and fell to the floor, three stories below. His chin hit the cement. A black flashbulb blinked in the front of his brain, just behind his eyes.

He pushed himself up on all fours, shaking his head slowly from side to side, insensible for a moment, then recovering himself. He started to crawl. He crossed a great deal of floor without seeming to get any closer to the phone. It was as if he were on a conveyer belt, bearing him steadily back, even as he plodded forward on hands and knees. Sometimes when he squinted at the phone, it seemed to be breathing, the sides swelling and then bending inward. Once, Finney had to stop to rest his hot forehead against the icy concrete. It was the only way to make the room stop moving.

When he next looked up, he found the phone directly above him. He pulled himself to his feet, grabbing the phone as soon as it was in reach and using it to hoist himself up. It was not quite an antique, but certainly old, with a pair of round silver bells on top and a clapper between them, a dial instead of buttons. Finney found the receiver and held it to his ear, listened for a dial tone. Nothing. He pushed the silver cradle down, let it spring back up. The black phone remained silent. He dialed for the operator. The receiver went click-click-click in his ear, but there was no ring on the other end, no connection.

"It doesn't work," Al said. "It hasn't worked since I was a kid."

Finney swayed on his heels, then steadied himself. He for some reason didn't want to turn his head and make eye contact with his captor, and he allowed himself only a sideways glance at him. The door was close enough to see now, and Al stood in it.

"Hang up," he said, but Finney stood as he was, the receiver in one hand. After a moment, Al went on. "I know you're scared and you want to go home. I'm going to take you home soon. I just—everything's all fucked up and I have to be upstairs for a while. Something's come up."

"What?"

"Never mind what."

Another helpless, awful surge of hope. Poole maybe—old Mr. Poole had seen Al shoving him into the van and called the police. "Did someone see something? Are the police coming? If you let me go, I won't tell, I won't—"

"No," the fat man said, and laughed, harshly and unhappily. "Not the police."

"Someone, though? Someone's coming?"

The kidnapper stiffened, and the close-set eyes in his wide, homely face were stricken and wondering. He didn't reply, but he didn't need to. The answer Finney wanted was there in his look, his body language. Either someone was on the way—or already there, upstairs somewhere.

"I'll scream," Finney said. "If there's someone upstairs, they'll hear me."

"No he won't. Not with the door shut."

"He?"

Al's face darkened, the blood rushing to his cheeks. Finney watched his hands squeeze into fists, then open slowly again.

"When the door's shut you can't hear anything down here," Al went on in a tone of forced calm. "I soundproofed it myself. So shout if you want, you won't bother anyone."

"You're the one who killed those other kids."

"No. Not me. That was someone else. I'm not going to make you do anything you won't like."

Something about the construction of this phrase—*I'm not going to make you do anything you won't like*—brought a fever heat to Finney's face and left his body cold, roughened with gooseflesh.

"If you try to touch me, I'll scratch your face, and whoever is coming to see you will ask why."

Al gazed at him blankly for a moment, absorbing this, then said, "You can hang up the phone now."

Finney set the receiver back in the cradle.

"I was in here and it rang once," Al said. "Creepiest thing. I think static electricity does it. It went off once when I was standing right beside it, and I picked it up, without thinking, you know, to see if anyone was there."

Finney didn't want to make conversation with someone who meant to kill him at the first convenient opportunity, and was taken by surprise when he opened his mouth and heard himself asking a question. "Was there?"

"No. Didn't I say it doesn't work?"

The door opened and shut. In the instant it was ajar, the great, ungainly fat man slipped himself out, bouncing on his toes—a hippo performing ballet—and was gone before Finney could open his mouth to yell.

5.

He screamed anyway. Screamed and threw himself at the door, crashing his whole body against it, not imagining it could be knocked open, but thinking if there was someone upstairs they might hear it banging in the frame. He didn't shout until his throat was raw, though; a few times was enough to satisfy him that no one was going to hear.

Finney quit hollering to peer around his underwater compartment, trying to figure where the light was coming from. There were two little windows—long glass slots—set high in the wall, well out of easy reach, emitting some faint, weed-green light. Rusty grilles had been bolted across them.

Finney studied one of the windows for a long time, then ran at the wall, didn't give himself time to think how drained and sick he was, planted a foot against the plaster and leaped. For one moment he grabbed the grille, but the steel links were too close together to squeeze a finger in, and he dropped back to his heels, then fell on his rear, shivering violently. Still. He had been up there long enough to get a glimpse through the filth-obscured glass. It was a double window, ground-level, almost completely hidden behind strangling brush. If he could break it, someone might hear him shouting.

They all thought of that, he thought. *And you see how far it got them.*

He went around the room again, and found himself standing before the phone once more. Studying it. His gaze tracked a slender black wire, stapled to the plaster above it. It climbed the wall for about a foot, then ended in a spray of frayed copper filaments. Finney discovered he was holding the receiver again, had picked it up without knowing he was doing it, was even holding it to his ear . . . an unconscious act of such hopeless, awful want, it made him shrink into himself a little. Why would anyone put a phone in their basement? But then there was the toilet, too. Maybe, probably—awful thought—someone had once lived in this room.

Then he was on the mattress, staring through the jade murk at the ceiling. He noted, for the first time, that he hadn't cried, and didn't feel like he was going to. He was very intentionally resting, building up his energy for the next round of exploration and thought. Would be circling the room, looking for an advantage, something he could use, until Al came back. Finney could hurt him if he had anything, anything at all, to use as a weapon. A piece of broken glass, a rusted spring. Were there springs in the mattress? When he had the energy to move again he'd try to figure out.

By now his parents had to know something had happened to him. They had to be frantic. But when he tried to picture the search, he didn't visualize his weeping mother answering a detective's questions in her kitchen, and he didn't see his father, out in front of Poole's Hardware, turning away from the sight of a policeman carrying an empty bottle of grape soda in an evidence bag.

Instead he imagined Susannah, standing on the pedals of her ten-speed and gliding down the center of one wide residential avenue after another, the collar of her denim jacket turned up, grimacing into the icy sheer of the wind. Susannah was three years older than Finney, but they had both been born on the same day, June 21, a fact she held to be of mystical importance. Susannah had a lot of occultish ideas, owned a deck of Tarot cards, read books about the connection between Stonehenge and aliens. When they were younger, Susannah had a toy stethoscope, which she would press to his head, in an attempt to listen in on his thoughts. He had once drawn five cards out of a deck at random and she had guessed all of them, one after another, holding the end of the stethoscope to the center of his forehead—five of spades, six of clubs, ten and jack of diamonds, ace of hearts—but she had never been able to repeat the trick.

Finney saw his older sister searching for him down streets that were, in his imagination, free of pedestrians or traffic. The wind was in the trees, flinging the bare branches back and forth so they appeared to rake futilely at the low sky. Sometimes Susannah half-closed her eyes, as if to better concentrate on some distant sound calling to her. She was listening for him, for his unspoken cry, hoping to be guided to him by some trick of telepathy.

She made a left, then a right, moving automatically, and discovered a street she had never seen before, a dead end road. On either side of it were disused-looking ranches with unraked front lawns, children's toys left out in driveways. At the sight of this street, her blood quickened. She felt strongly that Finney's kidnapper lived somewhere on this road. She biked more slowly, turning her head from side to side, making an uneasy inspection of each house as she went by. The whole road seemed set in a state of improbable silence, as if every person on it had been evacuated weeks ago, taking their pets with them, locking all the doors, turning out all the lights. *Not this one*, she thought. *Not that one*. And on and on, to the dead end of the street, and the last of the houses.

She put a foot down, stood in place with her bike under her. She hadn't felt hopeless yet, but standing there, chewing her lip and looking around, the thought began to form that she wasn't going to find her brother, that no one was going to find him. It was an awful street, and the wind was cold. She imagined she could feel that cold inside her, a ticklish chill behind the breastbone.

In the next moment she heard a sound, a tinny twanging, which echoed strangely. She glanced around, trying to place it, lifted her gaze to the last telephone pole on the street. A mass of black balloons were caught there, snarled in the lines. The wind was wrestling to wrench them free, and they bobbled and weaved, pulling hard to escape. The wires held the balloons implacably where they were. She recoiled at the sight of them. They were dreadful—somehow they were dreadful—a dead spot in the sky. The wind plucked at the wires and made them ring.

When the phone rang Finney opened his eyes. The vivid little story he had been telling himself about Susannah fleeted away. Only a story, not a vision; a ghost story, and he was the ghost, or would be soon. He lifted his head from the mattress, startled to find it almost dark . . . and his gaze fell upon the black phone. It seemed to him that the air was still faintly vibrating, from the brash firehouse clang of the steel clapper on the rusty bells.

He pushed himself up. He knew the phone couldn't really ring—that hearing it had just been a trick of his sleeping mind—yet he half-expected it to ring again. It had been stupid to lie there, dreaming the daylight away. He needed an advantage, a bent nail, a stone to throw. In a short time it would be dark, and he couldn't search the room if he couldn't see. He stood.

He felt spacey, empty-headed and cold; it was cold in the basement. He walked to the phone, put the receiver to his ear.

"Hello?" he asked.

He heard the wind sing, outside the windows. He listened to the dead line. As he was about to hang up, he thought he heard a click on the other end.

"Hello?" he asked.

6.

When the darkness gathered itself up and fell upon him, he curled himself on the mattress, with his knees close to his chest. He didn't sleep. He hardly blinked. He waited for the door to open and the fat man to come in and shut it behind him, for the two of them to be alone in the dark together, but Al didn't come. Finney was empty of thought, all his concentration bent to the dry rap of his pulse and the distant rush of the wind beyond the high windows. He was not afraid. What he felt was something larger than fear, a narcotic terror that numbed him completely, made it impossible to imagine moving.

He did not sleep, he was not awake. Minutes did not pass, collecting into hours. There was no point in thinking about time in the old way. There was only one moment and then another moment, in a string of moments that went on in a quiet, deadly procession. He was roused from his dreamless paralysis only when one of the windows began to show, a rectangle of watery gray floating high in the darkness. He knew, without knowing at first how he could know, that he wasn't meant to live to see the window painted with dawn. The thought didn't inspire hope exactly, but it did inspire movement, and with great effort he sat up.

His eyes were better. When he stared at the glowing window, he saw twinkling, prismatic lights at the edge of his vision . . . but he was seeing the window clearly, nonetheless. His stomach cramped from emptiness.

Finney forced himself to stand and he began to patrol the room again, looking for his advantage. In a back corner of the room, he found a place where a patch of cement floor had crumbled into granular, popcorn-size chunks, with a layer of

sandy earth beneath. He was putting a handful of carefully se-
lected nuggets into his pocket when he heard the thump of the
bolt turning.

The fat man stood in the doorway. They regarded each other
across a distance of five yards. Al wore striped boxers and a
white undershirt, stained down the front with old sweat. His
fat legs were shocking in their paleness.

"I want breakfast," Finney said. "I'm hungry."

"How's your eyes?"

Finney didn't reply.

"What are you doing over there?"

Finney squatted in the corner, glaring.

Al said, "I can't bring you anything to eat. You'll have to
wait."

"Why? Is there someone upstairs who would see you taking
me food?"

Again, Al's face darkened, his hands squeezed into fists.
When he replied, however, his tone was not angry, but glum
and defeated. "Never mind." Finney took that to mean *yes.*

"If you aren't going to feed me why did you even come down
here?" Finney asked him.

Al shook his head, staring at Finney with a kind of morose
resentment, as if this was another unfair question he couldn't
possibly be expected to answer. But then he shrugged and said,
"Just to look at you. I just wanted to look at you." Finney's upper lip drew back from his teeth in an unreasoned expression of
disgust, and Al visibly wilted. "I'll go."

When he opened the door, Finney sprang to his feet and began to scream *help.* Al stumbled over the doorjamb in his haste
to back out and almost fell, then slammed the door.

Finney stood in the center of the room, sides heaving for
breath. He had never really imagined he could get past Al and
out the door—it was too far away—had only wanted to test
his reaction time. Fatty was even slower than he thought. He
was slow, and there was someone else in the house, someone
upstairs. Almost against his will, Finney felt a building sense of
charge, a nervous excitement that was almost like hope.

For the rest of the day, and all that night, Finney was alone.

7.

When the cramps came again, late on his third day in the basement, he had to sit down on the striped mattress to wait for them to pass. It was like someone had thrust a spit through his side and was turning it slowly. He ground his back teeth until he tasted blood.

Later, Finney drank out of the tank on the back of the toilet, and then stayed there, on his knees, to investigate the bolts and the pipes. He didn't know why he hadn't thought of the toilet before. He worked until his hands were raw and abraded, trying to unscrew a thick iron nut, three inches in diameter, but it was caked with rust, and he couldn't budge it.

He lurched awake, the light coming through the window on the west side of the room, falling in a beam of bright yellow sunshine filled with scintillating mica-flecks of dust. It alarmed him that he couldn't remember lying down on the mattress to nap. It was hard to piece thoughts together, to reason things through. Even after he had been awake for ten minutes, he felt as if he had only just come awake, empty-headed and disorientated.

For a long time he was unable to rise, and sat with his arms wound around his chest, while the last of the light fled, and the shadows rose around him. Sometimes a fit of shivering would come over him, so fierce his teeth chattered. As cold as it was, it would be worse after dark. He didn't think he could wait out another night as cold as the last one. That was Al's plan maybe. To starve and freeze the fight out of him. Or maybe there was no plan, maybe the fat man had keeled over of a heart attack, and this was just how Finney was going to die, one cold minute at a time. The phone was breathing again. Finney stared at it, watching as the sides inflated, withdrew, and inflated again.

"Stop that," he said to it.

It stopped.

He walked. He had to, to stay warm. The moon rose, and for a while it lit the black phone like a bone-colored spotlight. Finney's face burned and his breath smoked, as if he were more demon than boy.

He couldn't feel his feet. They were too cold. He stomped

around, trying to bring the life back into them. He flexed his hands. His fingers were cold too, stiff and painful to move. He heard off-key singing and realized it was him. Time and thought were coming in leaps and pulses. He fell over something on the floor, then went back, feeling around with both hands, trying to figure out what had tripped him up, if it was something he could use as a weapon. He couldn't find anything and finally had to admit to himself he had tripped over his own feet. He put his head on the cement and shut his eyes.

He woke to the sound of the phone ringing again. He sat up and looked across the room at it. The eastern-facing window was a pale, silvery shade of blue. He was trying to decide if it had really rung, or if he had only dreamed it ringing, when it rang once more, a loud, metallic clashing.

Finney rose, then waited for the floor to stop heaving underfoot; it was like standing on a waterbed. The phone rang a third time, the clapper clashing at the bells. The abrasive reality of the sound had the effect of sweeping his head clear, returning him to himself.

He picked up the receiver and put his ear to it.

"Hello?" he asked.

He heard the snowy hiss of static.

"John," said the boy on the other end. The connection was so poor, the call might have been coming from the other side of the world. "Listen, John. It's going to be today."

"Who is this?"

"I don't remember my name," the boy said. "It's the first thing you lose."

"First thing you lose when?"

"You know when."

But Finney thought he recognized the voice, even though they had only spoken to each other that one time.

"Bruce? Bruce Yamada?"

"Who knows?" the boy said. "Tell me if it matters."

Finney lifted his eyes to the black wire traveling up the wall, stared at the spot where it ended in a spray of copper needles. He decided it didn't matter.

"What's going to be today?" Finney asked.

"I was calling to say he left you a way to fight him."

"What way?"

"You're holding it."

Finney turned his head, looked at the receiver in his hand. From the earpiece, which was no longer against his ear, he heard the faraway hiss of static and the tinny sound of the dead boy saying something else.

"What?" Finney asked, putting the receiver to his ear once more.

"Sand," Bruce Yamada told him. "Make it heavier. It isn't heavy enough. Do you understand?"

"Did the phone ring for any of the other kids?"

"Ask not for whom the phone rings," Bruce said, and there came soft, childish laughter. Then he said, "None of us heard it. It rang, but none of us heard. Just you. A person has to stay here a while, before you learn how to hear it. You're the only one to last this long. He killed the other children before they recovered, but he can't kill you, can't even come downstairs. His brother sits up all night in the living room making phone calls. His brother is a coke-head who never sleeps. Albert hates it, but he can't make him leave."

"Bruce? Are you really there or am I losing my mind?"

"Albert hears the phone too," Bruce replied, continuing as if Finney had said nothing. "Sometimes when he's down in the basement we prank-call him."

"I feel weak all the time and I don't know if I can fight him the way I feel."

"You will. You'll be dirty. I'm glad it's you. You know, she really found the balloons, John. Susannah did."

"She did?"

"Ask her when you get home."

There was a click. Finney waited for a dial tone, but there was none.

8.

A wheat-colored light had begun to puddle into the room when Finney heard the familiar slam of the bolt. His back was to the door, he was kneeling in the corner of the room, at the place where the cement had been shattered to show the sandy earth beneath. Finney still had the bitter taste of old copper in his mouth, a flavor like the bad aftertaste of grape soda. He turned his head but didn't rise, shielding what was in his hands with his body.

He was so startled to see someone besides Albert, he cried out, sprang unsteadily to his feet. The man in the doorway was small, and although his face was round and plump, the rest of his body was too tiny for his clothes: a rumpled army jacket, a loose cable-knit sweater. His unkempt hair was retreating from the egg-shaped curve of his forehead. One corner of his mouth turned up in a wry, disbelieving smile.

"Holy shit," said Albert's brother. "I knew he had something he didn't want me to see in the basement but I mean holy shit."

Finney staggered toward him, and words came spilling out in an incoherent, desperate jumble, like people who have been stuck for a night in an elevator, finally set free. "Please—my mom—help—call help—call my sister—"

"Don't worry. He's gone. He had to run into work," said the brother. "I'm Frank. Hey, calm down. Now I know why he was freaking out about getting called in. He was worried I'd find you while he's out."

Albert stepped into the light behind Frank with a hatchet, and lifted it up, cocked it like a baseball bat over one shoulder. Albert's brother went on, "Hey, do you want to know the story how I found you?"

"No," Finney said. "No, no, no."

Frank made a face. "Sure. Whatever. I'll tell you some other time. Everything's okay now."

Albert brought the hatchet down into the back of his younger brother's skull with a hard, wet clunk. The force of the impact threw blood into Al's face. Frank toppled forward. The ax stayed in his head, and Albert's hands stayed on the handle. As Frank fell, he pulled Al over with him.

Albert hit the basement floor on his knees, drew a sharp breath through clenched teeth. The ax-handle slipped out of his hands and his brother fell onto his face with a heavy boneless thump. Albert grimaced, then let out a strangled cry, staring at his brother with the ax in him.

Finney stood a yard away, breathing shallowly, holding the receiver to his chest in one hand. In the other hand was a coil of black wire, the wire that had connected the receiver to the black phone. It had been necessary to chew through it to pull it off. The wire itself was straight, not curly, like on a modern phone. He had the line wrapped three times around his right hand.

"You see this," Albert said, his voice choked, uneven. He looked up. "You see what you made me do?" Then he saw what Finney was holding, and his brow knotted with confusion. "What the fuck you do to the phone?"

Finney stepped toward him and snapped the receiver into his face, across Al's nose. He had unscrewed the mouthpiece and filled the mostly hollow receiver with sand, and screwed the mouthpiece back in to hold it all in place. It hit Albert's nose with a brittle snap like plastic breaking, only it wasn't plastic breaking. The fat man made a sound, a choked cry, and blood blurted from his nostrils. He lifted a hand. Finney smashed the receiver down and crushed his fingers.

Albert dropped his shattered hand and looked up, an animal sound rising in his throat. Finney hit him again to shut him up, clubbed the receiver against the bare curve of his skull. It hit with a satisfying knocking sound, and a spray of glittering sand leaped into the sunlight. Screaming, the fat man propelled himself off the floor, staggering forward, but Finney skipped back—so much faster than Albert—striking him across the mouth, hard enough to turn his head halfway around, then in the knee to drop him, to make him stop.

Al fell, throwing his arms out, caught Finney at the waist and slammed him to the floor. He came down on top of Finney's legs. Finney struggled to pull himself out from under. The fat man lifted his head, blood drizzling from his mouth, a furious moan rising from somewhere deep in his chest. Finney still held the receiver in one hand, and three loops of black wire in the other. He sat up, meant to club Albert with the receiver again, but then his hands did something else instead. He put the wire around the fat man's throat and pulled tight, crossing his wrists behind Al's neck. Albert got a hand on his face and scratched him, flaying Finney's right cheek. Finney pulled the wire a notch tighter and Al's tongue popped out of his mouth.

Across the room, the black phone rang. The fat man choked. He stopped scratching at Finney's face and set his fingers under the wire around his throat. He could only use his left hand, because the fingers of his right were shattered, bent in unlikely directions. The phone rang again. The fat man's gaze flicked toward it, then back to Finney's face. Albert's pupils were very wide, so wide the golden ring of his irises had shrunk to almost nothing. His pupils were a pair of black balloons, obscuring twin suns. The phone rang and rang. Finney pulled at the wire. On Albert's dark, bruise-colored face was a horrified question.

"It's for you," Finney told him.

IN THE RUNDOWN

Kensington came to work Thursday afternoon with a piercing. Wyatt noticed because she kept lowering her head and pressing a wadded-up Kleenex to her open mouth. In a short time, the little knot of tissue paper was stained a bright red. He positioned himself at the computer terminal to her left, and watched her from the corners of his eyes, while he busied himself with a stack of returned videos, bleeping them back into the inventory with the scanner. The next time she lifted the Kleenex to her mouth, he caught a direct glimpse of the stainless steel pin stuck through her blood-stained tongue. It was an interesting development in the Sarah Kensington story.

She was going punk, a little at a time. When he first started working at Best Video, she was chunky and plain, with short-cropped brown hair, and small, close-set eyes; she went around with the brusque, standoffish attitude of a person who is used to not being liked. Wyatt had a streak of that himself, and had imagined they might get along, but it was nothing doing. She never looked at him if she could help it, and often pretended not to hear him when he spoke to her. In time he came to feel that getting to know her was too much effort. It was easier to loathe and shun her.

One day, an old guy had come into the store, a forty-year-old carnival freak with a shaved head and a dog collar cinched around his neck, a leash dangling from it. He wanted a copy of

Sid & Nancy. He asked Kensington to help him find it and they chatted a while. Kensington laughed at everything he said, and when it was her turn to speak, the words came falling out of her mouth in a noisy, excited rush. It was a hell of a thing, watching her turn herself inside out like that over someone. Then when Wyatt showed up at work the next afternoon, the two of them were around the side of the store that couldn't be seen from the street. The circus gimp had her flattened against the wall. They were holding hands, their fingers entwined together, while she poked her tongue desperately into cue-ball's mouth. Now, a few months later, Kensington's hair was an alien shade of bright copper, and she wore biker boots and haunted-house eye shadow. The stud in her tongue, though, that was all-new.

"Why's it bleeding?" he asked her.

"Because I just got it," she said, without looking up. She said it bitchy too. Love had not made her warm and expressive; she still sulked and glared when Wyatt spoke to her, avoiding him as if the air around him was poisonous, abhorring him as she always had, for reasons that had not and never would be defined.

"I figured maybe you got it stuck in a zipper or something," he said. Then he added, "I guess that's one way to keep him interested in you. He isn't going to hang around for your good looks."

Kensington was a pretty hard case and her reaction caught him off guard. She glanced up at him, with startled, miserable eyes, her chin quivering. In a voice he hardly recognized, she said, "Leave me alone."

Wyatt didn't like suddenly feeling bad for her. He wished he hadn't said anything at all, and never mind that he had been provoked. She turned away from him, and he started to reach out, thought he would snag her sleeve, keep her there until he could figure out some way to apologize, without actually saying he was sorry. But then she spun back and glared at him through her watery eyes. She muttered something, he only caught part of it—she said *retard*, and then something about knowing how to read—but what he heard was more than enough. He felt a sudden, almost painful coldness spreading across his chest.

"Open your mouth one more time and I'll yank that pin right out of your tongue, you little bitch."

Kensington's eyes dulled with fury. *There* was the Kensington he was used to. Then she was moving, her short thick legs carrying her around the counter, and along the far wall towards the back of the store. A sour-sick feeling came over him, mingled with a sudden irritability. She was headed for the office, and Mrs. Badia; running to tell on him.

He decided he was going on break, grabbed his army jacket and shoved through the Plexiglas doors. He lit an American Spirit, and stood against the stucco wall outside, shoulders hunched. He smoked and shivered, glaring across the street in the direction of Miller's Hardware.

Wyatt watched Mrs. Prezar swing her station wagon into Miller's parking lot, her two boys in the car with her. Mrs. Prezar lived at the end of his street in a house the color of a strawberry milk shake. He had mowed her lawn—not anytime recently, but a few years ago, back when he mowed people's lawns.

Mrs. Prezar got out and moved briskly towards the doors of the Hardware. She left the car running. Her face was thick and heavily made up, but not bad-looking. There was something about her mouth—she had a plump, sexy underlip—that Wyatt had always liked. Her expression, as she went inside, was a robotic blank.

She left a boy in the front seat and another in back, strapped into a baby seat. The boy in front—his name was Baxter, Wyatt didn't know why he remembered that—was skinny and long, had a delicate build that must've come to him by way of his father. From where Wyatt was standing, he couldn't see much of the one in the baby seat, just a thatch of dark hair and a pair of chubby waving hands.

As soon as Mrs. Prezar slipped into the store, the older boy, Baxter, screwed himself around to look into the back. He had a Twizzler in one hand and he held it out for his baby brother. When his brother reached for it, though, Baxter jerked it out of reach. Then he held it out again. When his brother refused to be goaded into making a second grab, Baxter swatted him with it. The game continued along these lines for a while, until Baxter stopped to unwrap the Twizzler and pop one end into his mouth for a lazy taste. He had on a Twin City Pizza cap—Wyatt's old team. Wyatt tried to figure if Baxter could be old enough to play in Little League. It didn't seem it, but maybe they let them in younger now.

Wyatt had good memories of Little League. In Wyatt's last year with Twin City, he almost set a league record for stolen bases. It was one of the few moments in his life when he had known for sure that he was better at something than anyone else his age. By the end of the season he had nine steals total, and had only been caught once. A doughy-faced left-handed pitcher got him leading off first, before Wyatt had a chance to get his feet under him, and all at once he was racing back and forth in the middle of a rundown, while the first baseman and second baseman closed in from either side, softly lobbing the ball back and forth between them. Wyatt had tried, at the end, to burst for second, hoping to drop and slide in under the tag . . . but almost as soon as he made his decision he knew it was the wrong one, and a feeling of hopelessness, of racing towards the inescapable, had come over him. The second baseman—a kid Wyatt knew, Treat Rendell, the star of the other team—was planted right in the way, waiting for him with his feet spread apart, and for the first time Wyatt could ever remember, it seemed that no matter how fast he ran he was getting no closer to where he was headed. He didn't actually remember being called out, only running, and the way Treat Rendell had been there in his path, waiting with his eyes narrowed to slits.

That was almost the end of the season, and Wyatt was hitless his last two games, missed the record by two stolen bases. He never got a chance to find out what he could do in high school. He didn't play in a single game, was always on academic or disciplinary probation. Midway through his junior year he was diagnosed with a reading disability—Wyatt had trouble connecting things all together when a sentence got more than four or five words long, had for years found it a struggle to interpret anything longer than a movie title—and was dropped into a remedial program with a bunch of mental deficients. The program was called Super-Tools, but was known around school by a variety of other monikers: Stupid-Drools, Super-Fools. Wyatt had come across some graffiti in the men's room once that read *I em in Sooper Tules & I em reel prowd.*

He spent his senior year on the fringe, didn't look at people when he walked by them in the hall, didn't try out for base-ball. Treat Rendell, on the other hand, made varsity as a sopho-more, hit everything in sight, and led the team to two regional championships. Now he was a state trooper, drove a souped-up Crown Victoria, and was married to Ellen Martin, an ice-white blonde, and undoubtedly the best looking of all the cheerlead-ers Treat was rumored to have banged.

Mrs. Prezar came out. She had only been inside a minute and hadn't bought anything. She was holding her jacket tightly shut with one hand, perhaps against the gusting wind. Her eyes passed right over him a second time, no sign she recognized him or even noticed he was there. She dropped into the front seat, and banged the door shut, backed out so fast she squealed the tires a little.

She hadn't ever looked at him much when he mowed her lawn, either. He remembered one time, after he finished in her yard, he had let himself into the house, through a slid-ing glass door into the living room. He had been cutting her lawn all morning—she was rich, her husband was an execu-tive with a company that sold broadband capacity, she had the most yard on the street—and Wyatt was sunburned and itchy, grass stuck to his face and arms. She was on the phone. Wyatt stood just inside the door, waiting for her to acknowl-edge him.

She took her time. She was sitting at a small desk, twirl-ing a coil of yellow hair with one finger, rocking back in her chair, laughing now and then. She had credit cards spread out in front of her and was absentmindedly moving them around with her pinkie. Even when he cleared his throat to get her at-tention, she didn't so much as glance at him. He waited a full ten minutes, and then she hung up and swiveled to face him, instantly all business. She told him she had been watching him while he worked, and she wasn't paying him to talk to everyone who went by on the sidewalk. Also she had heard him go over a rock, and if the lawn mower blade was chipped, she'd make sure he paid for a new one. The job was twenty-eight dollars.

She gave him thirty and said he was lucky to get any tip at all. When he went out she was laughing on the phone again, moving the credit cards around, pushing them into a pattern, the letter P.

There wasn't much left of Wyatt's cigarette, but he was figuring one more and then he'd go in, when the door opened behind him. Mrs. Badia stepped out, dressed only in her black sweater and the white vest with the name tag pinned to it, *Pat Badia, Manager.* She grimaced at the cold and hugged herself.

"Sarah told me what you said," Mrs. Badia began.

Wyatt nodded, waited. He liked Mrs. Badia okay. He could kid her sometimes.

"Why don't you go home, Wyatt," she said.

He flipped his butt onto the blacktop. "Okay. I'll come back in and make up my hours tomorrow. She isn't working then." Gesturing towards the store with his head.

"No," Mrs. Badia said. "Don't come back tomorrow. Come back next Tuesday to pick up your last check."

It took him a moment to figure that out, for some reason. Then he got it, and felt an unwholesome heat rising to his face.

Mrs. Badia was talking again. She said, "You can't threaten the people you work with, Wyatt. I'm sick to death of hearing people complain about you. I'm tired of one incident after another." She made a face and glanced back at the store. "She's going through a hard time right now, and you're in there telling her you're going to rip her tongue out."

"I *didn't* say—it was the pin in her—do you want to know what she said to me?"

"Not particularly. What?"

But Wyatt didn't reply. He couldn't tell her what Kensington had said, because he didn't know, hadn't caught all of it . . . and he might not have told Mrs. Badia even if he did know. Whatever she had said, it was something about how he couldn't read. Wyatt always tried to avoid talking about the trouble he had with grammar and spelling and all the rest; it was a subject that inevitably brought more embarrassment than he could stand.

Mrs. Badia stared at him, waiting for him to speak. When

he didn't, she said, "I gave you as many chances as I thought I could. But at a certain point, it isn't fair to the people you work with, to ask them to put up with it." She stared a while longer, sucking thoughtfully on her lower lip. Then she cast a careless glance at his feet, and as she turned away, she said, "Tie your shoes, Wyatt."

She went back in and he stood there, flexing his hands in the frigid air. He walked slowly along the front of the video store, around the corner, to the side of the store that couldn't be seen from the street. He bent and spat. He tilted another cigarette out of the pack, lit it and inhaled, waited for his legs to stop shaking.

He had thought Mrs. Badia liked him. He had stayed behind late sometimes to help her close up—something he didn't have to do—just because she was easy to talk to. They talked about movies, or about weird customers, and she listened to his stories and opinions as if she were really interested. It had been an unusual experience for him, to get along with an employer. But now here it turned out to be the same old crap in the end. Someone had a personal grievance against him, an axe to grind, and there was no due process, no effort to hear everyone out and get all the information. She said, *I'm sick to death of hearing people complain,* but not which people or what complaints. She said, *I'm tired of one incident after another,* but didn't you have to judge this incident on its own merits, and all the other so-called incidents on theirs?

He flicked his cigarette away—it hit the asphalt and red sparks jumped—turned and started moving. He came around the corner at a fast walk. The windows had a lot of movie posters taped in them. Kensington was staring out at the parking lot through a gap between posters for *Pitch Black* and *The Others.* Her eyes were bloodshot, a little unfocused. He could tell from the moony expression on her face that she believed he was long gone, and before he could stop himself he lunged at the glass and banged his middle finger against it, right up against her face. She jerked back, mouth opening in a shocked O.

He spun away and lurched across the parking lot. A car swung in suddenly from the road, and the driver had to slam on the brakes to keep from hitting him. The driver gave his horn an angry poke. Wyatt lifted his upper lip in a sneer, flipped him off too. Then he was on the other side of the parking lot and plunging into the scrubby, littered woods.

He made his way along a narrow path; it was the way he always went home when he didn't have a ride. Among the trees were rotting, water-logged mattresses, filled-to-bursting bags of trash and rust-streaked kitchen appliances. There was a little freshet which had its headwaters at the Queen Bee Car Wash. He couldn't see it, but he could hear it trickling through the undergrowth, and the smell of cheap car wax and cherry-scented carpet-shampoo was occasionally very strong. He was moving more slowly now, head hunched between his shoulders. In the gathering dimness of early evening, it was hard to see the most slender branches that stuck into the path, and he didn't want to walk into one.

The trail came out at the dead-end of a dirt lane which curled along one side of a shallow, famously polluted pond. The lane would take him out to 17K, and a short distance along that was the road into Ronald Reagan Park, where Wyatt lived alone in a one-story no-basement ranch with his mother, his father having run for the hills years before and good riddance. The lane was weedy and disused. People parked there sometimes, though, for the reasons people usually drove to such spots, and as Wyatt rustled through the last of the undergrowth, up towards the road, he saw there was a car there now.

By then the shadows beneath the trees had massed together into a darkness only a few degrees from full night—although when he looked straight up he could still see some color in the sky, a pale violet shading into an apricot yellow. The car was on a slight rise and he didn't recognize it until he was close. It was Mrs. Prezar's station wagon. The driver's side door was cocked open.

Wyatt hesitated a few paces away from it, the wind catching strangely in his lungs, he didn't know why. At first, he thought the car was empty. No sound came from it, except for some soft ticking noises beneath the hood, as the engine cooled. Then he saw the black-haired four-year-old in the back, still strapped into the baby seat. The boy's chin rested on his chest and his eyes were shut. He looked asleep.

Wyatt glanced around for Mrs. Prezar, for Baxter, scanned

the trees, the edge of the pond. He couldn't imagine why anyone would leave the boy asleep there like that. But then, when he glanced back at the car, he saw Mrs. Prezar. She was in the driver's seat, but hunched over, so that from where he stood, only the crown of her shiny blonde head was visible above the steering wheel.

It was a moment before he could move. He found it hard to start forward again, was badly unsettled, for no reason he could pinpoint, by the scene before him. The little boy asleep in the backseat frightened him. In the twilight, the kid's face was fat and tinged faintly blue.

He stepped carefully around to the side of the car and stopped again. What he saw drove the air out of him. Mrs. Prezar was rocking back and forth just slightly. Baxter was faceup in her lap. His eyes were open and staring. He had lost his Twin City Pizza cap somewhere. His head was shaved to a fine, colorless bristle. His lips were so bright red, he might have been wearing lipstick. Baxter's head was tipped back so he appeared to be staring at Wyatt. Wyatt saw the slash in his throat first, a glistening black line in the approximate shape of a fishhook. There was another wound in his cheek. It almost looked like a long black slug resting on his very white face.

Mrs. Prezar's eyes were open wide, too, and they were red and raw with tears, and yet she made no sound as she wept. There were four long smears of blood on the side of her face, marks left by a child's fingers. She took one long, shuddering breath after another.

"Oh God." She was whispering on each exhalation. "Oh Baxter. Oh God."

Wyatt took a step back, unconsciously recoiling, and put his foot down on the plastic lid of a discarded soda cup, heard it splinter under his heel. Her shoulders jumped in a reflexive shrug and she cast a wild look up at him.

"Mrs. Prezar," he said, in a voice he hardly recognized, hushed and gravelly.

He expected wailing and cries, but when she spoke it was in a benumbed whisper. "Please help us." For the first time he noticed her purse was on the ground, by the car door, some of the contents spilled out into the mud.

"I'll go get someone," he said, and he was already twisting at the waist, preparing to turn, to fly up the lane. He could be at 17K in a minute, could flag down a passing car.

"No," she said in a tone of sudden, frightened urgency. "Don't go. I'm scared. I don't know where he went. He could still be somewhere nearby. He might of just gone to wash himself off." Throwing a panicked look at the pond.

"Who?" Wyatt asked, glancing over at the pond himself—the steep embankment, the close stands of ratty little trees—with a withering feeling of alarm.

She didn't answer him, said, "I've got a cell phone. I don't know where it is. He took it, but I think he dropped it on the ground next to the car. Oh God oh God. Will you look for it? Oh God please don't let him come back."

Wyatt was dry-mouthed and his insides felt sick, but he moved forward automatically, gaze sweeping the area around the dropped purse. He crouched, in part so he could see the ground better, and in part so he would be invisible to anyone approaching the car from the other side, the side facing the pond. Some papers and a tangle of scarf had fallen out of her bag. One end of the scarf—silk, shimmers of yellow and red—was floating on a puddle.

"In your purse?" he asked, pulling it open.

"Maybe. I don't know."

He dug through it, found more papers, a lipstick, a compact, little brushes for her face, no cell phone. He dropped the purse and stared intently along the length of the station wagon, but it was difficult to make out much of anything in the early evening shadows.

"He walked towards the water?" Wyatt asked, his pulse banging steadily in his throat.

"I don't know. He got in at the stoplight. When I was waiting for it to turn green at the corner of Union. He said he wouldn't hurt us if I did what he said. Oh God, Baxter. I'm sorry. I'm so sorry he hurt you. I'm so sorry he made you cry."

At the mention of Baxter's name, Wyatt glanced up, was helpless not to, could not hear the boy mentioned without feeling a dreadful compulsion to look at him again. He was surprised at how close Baxter's face was to his own. The boy's head was hanging over his mother's thigh, less than a yard away from him. Wyatt was seeing Baxter's face upside down, the dark stab wound in his cheek, the clown-red lips—red from the Twizzler, not the blood, Wyatt realized, in a sudden flash of remembering—the wide, stricken eyes. Baxter was gazing blankly past Wyatt's shoulder with glazed eyes; then those eyes twitched slightly and fixed on him.

Wyatt screamed. He lurched to his feet.

"He's not—" Wyatt said, gasping, his lungs sucking at the air. It was hard to get enough oxygen to speak. He swallowed, tried again, "He's not—" and he looked at Mrs. Prezar and stopped once more.

He had not, until now, been at an angle to see her right hand. It rested on Baxter's leg. It was closed around the handle of a knife.

He thought he recognized it. They had a couple clear plastic cases of them in Miller's Hardware, on a counter to the left of the door, just past the racks of camouflage jackets. Wyatt remembered one in particular, with a ten-inch blade, one edge serrated, the steel polished to a mirror-brightness. Wyatt had been in there looking once, he had noticed it. He might even have asked to see it. It was the first one anyone would notice. And he remembered the way she had come out of Miller's, how she held one arm clutched stiffly across her overcoat, how she came out without a bag.

She saw him looking at it. She glanced away from him, and stared down at it herself for a moment, looking at it with an expression of bewilderment, as if she had no idea how such a thing had come into her possession. As if, perhaps, she had no idea what such an instrument might even be for. Then she looked back.

"He dropped it," she said, staring at Wyatt with a look that was almost pleading. "His hands were bloody and he got it stuck in Baxter. When he tried to pull it out, it slipped out of his hands. It fell on the floor and I picked it up. That's why he didn't kill me. Because I had the knife. That's when he ran away."

The hand closed around the Teflon grip of the knife was stained deeply with blood; blood darkened every groove across her knuckles, the cuticle around her thumbnail. Drops of blood were still falling off the waterproof sleeve of her jacket, dripping onto the leather seat.

"I'll run and get help," he said, but he wasn't sure she heard him. He spoke so softly he could hardly hear himself. He was holding his hands up in front of him, the palms turned outward, in a defensive gesture. He didn't know how long he had been holding them that way.

She put one foot out on the ground, started to rise. The sudden movement alarmed him and he staggered back. And then there was something wrong with his right foot, he was trying to take a step back, but it was pinned to the ground somehow, wouldn't move. He glanced down in time to see he was standing on an untied shoelace, and then he was tottering off balance, pitching backwards.

The impact was hard enough to drive the breath out of him. He sprawled on his back across a moist carpet of fallen leaves. He stared up at the sky, which was now a deep violet hue, and scattered here and there with the first and brightest of the early evening stars. His eyes watered. He blinked and sat up.

She was out of the car, a yard away from him. She held his sneaker in one hand, the knife in the other. He had come right out of his shoe. His right foot was clad now only in a gray athletic sock, and was cold in the frozen damp.

"He dropped it," she said. "The man who attacked us. I wouldn't. My babies. I wouldn't hurt them. I just picked it up."

He scrambled up off the ground and hopped a step away from her, putting very little weight on the right foot, to keep it from sinking into the cold mush of the leaves. He wanted the shoe back before he ran. He looked at the sneaker—she was holding it outstretched towards him—and then at the knife. Her right hand, with the knife in it, hung limply at her side.

Once again she followed his gaze, looked down at the knife, looked back. She shook her head slowly from side to side in some kind of mute denial.

"I wouldn't," she said, and dropped the knife. She leaned towards him, holding out the shoe. "Here."

He edged a step closer to her, and took the shoe and tugged on it, only she wouldn't let go of it at first, and then she did, but only to grab his arm. Her fingernails sank into the soft underside of his wrist, digging painfully into the skin. It frightened him, how suddenly she grabbed him, how tightly she had hold of him.

"I didn't," she said. He tried to wrench his arm free. Her other hand was grabbing at the front of his open jacket, at his sweater, smearing blood on him. She said, "What are you going to say to people?"

In his panic, he wasn't sure he had heard her right and didn't care. He wanted her to let go. Her fingernails were biting painfully into his flesh, but worse than that, she was getting blood on him, all over his hand, his wrist, his sweater. It was sticky and unpleasantly warm and more than anything he didn't want her streaking it on his bare skin. He grabbed her left hand at the wrist, and tried to make her let him go, squeezed until he could feel the bones in her wrist separating from their joints. She was blubbering, crowding him. Her right hand closed on his shoulder, fingers boring into the socket, and he struck her arm aside, and shoved her, not hard, just to drive her back. Her eyes flew open and she made a horrid, choked little cry. Her right hand flew up and suddenly she was scratching his face, he felt her fingernails laying him open, felt the hot sting of blood in fresh cuts.

He grabbed the hand raking at his cheek, and bent her fingers straight back until they were almost touching the back of her hand. Then he punched her in the breastbone and heard the air gush out of her, and as she bent forward he hit her in the face, a driving downward blow that split his knuckles. She staggered drunkenly forward and grabbed his sweater and when she went down she pulled him down with her. She still had him by the wrist, her fingernails tearing at him. More than ever he needed to make her let go. He grabbed some of her hair and yanked her head straight backwards, twisted it back until she was baring her neck to him, until her head couldn't be forced any further back. She gasped and let go of his wrist and tried to slap at his face and he punched her in the throat.

She choked. He let go of her hair and her head fell forward. She held her neck in both hands and sat there on her knees, her shoulders hunched, and her hair hiding her face, breathing raggedly. Then her head swiveled. She looked at the knife on the ground behind her. She let go of her neck with her right hand and started to reach for it, but she was slow, and he shoved himself past her and snatched it off the ground. He turned and hacked it in the air to warn her away.

He stood a few feet off from her, his own breathing labored, watching her. She stared back at him. Her hair was in her face, but she looked at him through the frazzled, blood-knotted coils of it. All he could see were the whites of her eyes. She was breathing more slowly now. They regarded each other in this way for perhaps five seconds.

"Help," she said, in a hoarsened voice. "Help."

He stared at her.

She rose unsteadily to her feet.

"Help," she called out for the third time.

The left side of his face stung where she had scratched him. The stinging was especially bad at the corner of his eye.

"I'll tell people what you did," he said.

She stared at him a moment longer and then turned and started to run.

"Help me," she shouted. "Somebody help me." He thought he might run after her and make her stop it, only he didn't know how he would make her stop it if he caught up to her, so he let her go.

He took a few steps towards the car, and put one arm on the open door, resting his weight against it. He felt light-headed. She was already a long ways down the lane, a dark figure against the paler darkness of the woods.

For a short time Wyatt stood there, panting. Then his gaze happened to fall, and he saw Baxter staring up at him, his eyes large and round in his slender, fine-boned face. Wyatt saw, with a fresh wave of shock, the boy's tongue moving around in his open red mouth, as if perhaps he had some intention of speaking.

Wyatt's stomach plunged. He felt weak through the legs, looking at the boy again, at the slash across his neck, that almost fishhook shape that started behind the right ear and curved down to just below his Adam's apple. Looking straight down at him, Wyatt could see blood yet surging from this wound in thick, slow pulses. The seat under Baxter's head was puddled with it.

He stepped around the open door and stood over Baxter. He looked to see if the car keys were still in the ignition slot, thought maybe he could just drive the car up to 17K and then—but they weren't and who knew where they were. The bleeding—the important thing to do in a situation like this was stop the bleeding. He had seen about it on F. R. You found a towel and balled it up, pressed it into the wound and applied pressure until help arrived. He didn't have a towel, but there was the scarf, on the ground beside the car. He dropped to his knees by the open door and the overturned purse, and grabbed the scarf. One end was soaked and dripping mud. He hesitated for a single squeamish-sick instant, then wadded it up and pressed it against the slash across the boy's neck. He could feel the blood pumping against it.

The scarf was a thin, almost transparent piece of silk, already wet from the puddle it had been half-lying in, and in a moment it was saturated, and blood was leaking down his hands, the insides of his arms. He let go, let the scrap of silk fall away, wiped his hands compulsively against his shirt front. Baxter was watching him with stunned, fascinated eyes. Blue like his mother's.

Wyatt began to cry. He had not known he was going to do it until he was doing it. He could not remember the last time he had wept openly. He grabbed some of the papers that had spilled out of Mrs. Prezar's purse, and tried squeezing these into the wound, but they were even more useless than the scarf. They were shiny white papers, not at all absorbent, several pages stapled together; in the twilight Wyatt saw he was holding a credit card statement. Stamped across the top of the first page were the words PAYMENT OVERDUE in red ink.

He thought of dumping out what was left in her purse, looking for something else to use as a compress, then shucked off his jacket, pulled off the white vest that he wore to work, balled the vest up and pressed that into the wound. He held both hands over it and pushed down with the greater portion of his weight. The vest was an almost luminescent white in the gloom; but then, as he pressed down on it, he saw a dark stain spreading upwards through it, soaking into the fabric. He tried to think what to do now, but nothing would come. He flashed to a memory of Kensington, dabbing at her tongue with Kleenex, the way each ball of tissue paper was soon soaked red. He had a thought, strange for him, a thought that connected Kensington and the silver pin in her tongue and the slash across Baxter's throat; he thought how the young are pierced by love, innocent bodies torn and ruined for no reason, save that it suited someone who held them dear.

Baxter's left hand floated up from his side. Wyatt almost cried out when he saw it at the edge of his vision, a ghastly white shape gliding through the darkness. Baxter's fingers wavered in the general direction of his throat. Wyatt had an idea. He took Baxter's left hand and pressed it down to the compress. He reached into the car, found Baxter's other hand, placed it on top of the first. When he let go, the hands remained on top of the blood-soaked vest. They held it only loosely—but it stayed in place.

"I'll just go for a minute," Wyatt said. He was shivering violently. "I'll just run and bring someone back. I'll get to the road and I'll bring someone back and we'll take you to the hospital. You'll be okay. Just hold that against your neck. You'll be okay, I promise."

Baxter stared blankly up at him. His eyes had a dull, glazed look that Wyatt didn't like. He got to his feet and started to run. He went a few yards and then kicked off the one sneaker he still had on and started again.

He ran at a full, long-legged sprint, gasping in the wet cold air. The only sound was the heavy thud of his feet on the hard earth. It seemed to him, though, that he used to be faster than he was, that when he was younger, running was less of an effort. He had not gone far before he felt the sharp bite of a cramp in one side. Although he took great sucking breaths, he could not seem to bring enough air down into his lungs. It was the cigarettes maybe. He lowered his head and ran on, biting his lip, trying not to think about how much faster he might have been if only his side didn't hurt. Wyatt looked back, and saw he had only traveled a hundred yards or so, the car still in sight. He was crying again. As he ran he said a prayer. Words came out in whispered bursts, each time he exhaled.

"Please, God," he whispered into the February darkness. He ran and ran but didn't feel that he was getting any closer to the highway. It was like being in the rundown again, same feeling of hopelessness, of rushing towards the inescapable. He said, "Please make me fast. Make me fast again. Make me fast like I was."

At the next bend in the road, 17K came into sight, less than a quarter of a mile off. There was a streetlamp at the end of the lane, and a car idling underneath it. It was a tan Crown Victoria with police lights on top, switched off—a state trooper's car, Wyatt thought with relief. It was funny that he should just be thinking about the rundown again; maybe it would turn out to be Treat Rendell. A man—just a black silhouette at this distance—got out and stood by the front end. Wyatt began shouting, and waving his arms for help.

THE CAPE

We were little.

I was the Red Bolt and I went up the dead elm in the corner of our yard to get away from my brother, who wasn't anyone, just himself. He had friends coming over and he wanted me not to exist, but I couldn't help it: I existed.

I had his mask and I said when his friends got there I was going to reveal his secret identity. He said I was lunch meat, and stood below, chucking stones at me, but he threw like a girl, and I quickly climbed out of range.

He was too old to play superheroes. It had happened all of a sudden, with no warning. He had spent whole days leading up to Halloween dressed as The Streak, who was so fast the ground melted under his feet as he ran. Then Halloween was over and he didn't want to be a hero anymore. More than that, he wanted everyone to forget he had ever been one, wanted to forget himself, only I wouldn't let him, because I was up in a tree with his mask, and his friends were coming over.

The elm had been dead for years. Whenever it was windy, the gusts sheared off branches and flung them across the lawn. The scaly bark splintered and snapped away under the toes of my sneakers. My brother wasn't inclined to follow—beneath his dignity—and it was intoxicating to escape from him.

At first I climbed without thought, scrambling higher than I ever had before. I went into a kind of tree-climbing trance, getting off on altitude and my own seven-year-old agility. Then I heard my brother shout up that he was ignoring me (sure proof that he wasn't) and I remembered what had sent me up the elm in the first place. I set my eye on a long, horizontal branch, a place where I could sit, dangle my feet, and taunt my brother into a frenzy without fear of repercussions. I swept the cape back over my shoulders and climbed on, with a purpose.

The cape had started life as my lucky blue blanket and had kept me company since I was two. Over the years, the color had faded from a deep, lustrous blue to a tired pigeon gray. My mother had cut it down to cape size and stitched a red felt lightning bolt in the center of it. Also sewn to it was a Marine's patch, one of my father's. It showed the number 9, speared through by a lightning bolt. It had come home from Vietnam in his foot locker. He hadn't come with it. My mother flew the black P.O.W. flag from the front porch, but even then I knew no one was holding my father prisoner.

I put the cape on as soon as I came home from school, sucked on the sateen hem while I watched TV, wiped my mouth with it at the dinner table, and most nights, fell asleep wrapped in it. It pained me to take it off. I felt undressed and vulnerable without it. It was just long enough to make trouble underfoot if I was incautious.

I reached the high branch, threw a leg over and straddled it. If my brother wasn't there to witness what happened next, I wouldn't have believed it myself. Later, I would've told myself it was a panicked fantasy, a delusion that gripped me in a moment of terror and shock.

Nicky was sixteen feet below, glaring up at me and talking about what he was going to do to me when I came down. I held up his mask, a black Lone Ranger thing with holes for the eyes, and waggled it.

"Come and get me, Streak," I said.

"You better be planning to live up there."

"I found streaks in my underwear that smell better than you."

"Okay. Now you're fucking dead," he said. My brother hurled comebacks like he hurled rocks: badly.

"Streak, Streak, Streak," I said, because the name was taunt enough.

I was crawling out along the branch as I chanted. I put my right hand down on the cape, which had slid off my shoulder. The next time I tried to move forward, the cape pulled taut and unbalanced me. I heard cloth tear. I toppled hard against the branch, scraping my chin, throwing my arms around it. The branch sank beneath me, sprang up, sank again . . . and I heard a crack, a brittle snap that carried sharply in the crisp November air. My brother blanched.

"Eric," he shouted. "Hold on, Eric!"

Why did he tell me to hold on? The branch was breaking—I needed to get off it. Was he too shocked to know that, or did some unconscious part of him want to see me fall? I froze, struggling mentally to unscramble what to do, and in the moment I hesitated, the branch gave way.

My brother leaped back. The broken limb, all five feet of it, hit the ground at his feet and shattered, bark and twigs flying. The sky wheeled above me. My stomach did a nauseating somersault.

It took an instant to register that I wasn't falling. That I was staring out over the yard as if still seated on a high tree branch.

I shot a nervous look at Nicky. He stared back—gaping up at me.

My knees were hitched to my chest. My arms were spread out to either side, as for balance. I floated in the air, nothing holding me up. I wobbled to the right. I rolled to the left. I was an egg that wouldn't quite fall over.

"Eric?" my brother said, his voice weak.

"Nicky?" I said, my voice the same. A breeze wafted through the elm's bare branches, so they clicked and clattered against one another. The cape stirred at my shoulders.

"Come down, Eric," my brother said. "Come down."

I gathered my nerve and forced myself to glance over my knees at the ground directly below. My brother stood holding his arms outstretched to the sky, as if to grab my ankles and pull me down, although he was too far below me and standing too far back from the tree for any hope of that.

Something glittered at the edge of my vision and I lifted my gaze. The cape had been held around my neck by a golden safety pin, hooked through two opposing corners of the blanket. But the pin had ripped right through one of the corners, and hung uselessly from the other. I remembered, then, the tearing sound I had heard as I collapsed on the branch. Nothing was holding the cape on me.

The wind gusted again. The elm groaned. The breeze raced through my hair and snatched the cape off my back. I saw it dance away, as if being jerked along by invisible wires. My support danced away with it. In the next instant, I rolled forward, and the ground came at me in a hideous rush, so quickly there was no time even to scream.

I hit the hard earth, landing atop the shattered branch. One long skewer of wood punctured my chest, just beneath the collarbone. When it healed, it left a shiny scar in the shape of a crescent moon, my most interesting feature. I broke my fibula, pulverized my left kneecap and fractured my skull in two places. I bled from my nose, my mouth, my eyes.

I don't remember the ambulance, although I have heard I never truly lost consciousness. I do remember my brother's white and frightened face bending over mine, while we were still in the yard. My cape was balled up in his fists. He was twisting it, unconsciously, into knots.

If I had any doubts about whether it really happened, they were removed two days later. I was still in the hospital, when my brother tied the cape around his neck and leaped from the top of the front stairs, at home. He fell the whole way, eighteen steps in all, hit the last riser on his face. The hospital was able to place him in the same room with me, but we didn't talk. He spent most of the day with his back turned to me, staring at the wall. I don't know why he wouldn't look at me—maybe he was angry because the cape hadn't worked for him, or angry with himself for thinking it would, or just sick at the thought of how the other kids were going to make fun of him, when they learned he had smashed his face trying to be Superman—but at least I could understand why we didn't talk. His jaw was wired shut. It took six pins and two corrective surgeries to rebuild his face into something like its former appearance.

The cape was gone by the time we both got out of the hospital. My mother told us in the car. She had packed it into the trash and sent it to the dump to be incinerated. There would be no more flying in the Shooter household.

I was a different kid after my accident. My knee throbbed when I did too much walking, when it rained, when it was cold. Bright lights gave me explosive migraines. I had trouble concentrating for long stretches of time, found it difficult to follow a lecture from start to finish, sometimes drifted off into daydreams in the middle of tests. I couldn't run, so I was lousy at sports. I couldn't think, so I was worse at schoolwork.

It was misery to try and keep up with other kids, so I stayed inside after school and read comic books. I couldn't tell you who my favorite hero was. I don't remember any of my favorite stories. I read comics compulsively, without any particular pleasure, or any particular thought, read them only because when I saw one I couldn't not read it. I was in thrall to cheap newsprint, lurid colors, and secret identities. The comics had a druglike hold over me, with their images of men shooting through the sky, shredding the clouds as they passed through them. Reading them felt like life. Everything else was a little out of focus, the volume turned too low, the colors not quite bright enough.

I didn't fly again for over ten years.

I WASN'T A collector, and if not for my brother I would've just left my comics in piles. But Nick read them as compulsively as I did, was as much under their spell. For years, he kept them in slippery plastic bags, arranged alphabetically in long white boxes.

Then, one day, when I was fifteen, and Nick was beginning as a senior at Passos High, he came home with a girl, an unheard-of event. He left her in the living room with me, said he wanted to drop his backpack upstairs, and then ran up to our room and threw our comics away, all of them, his and mine, almost eight hundred issues. Dumped them in two big Glad bags and snuck them out back.

I understand why he did it. Dating was hard for Nick. He was insecure about his rebuilt face, which didn't look so bad really. His jaw and chin were maybe a bit too square, the skin stretched too tightly over them, so at times he resembled a caricature of some brooding comic book hero. He was hardly The Elephant Man, although there was something terrible about his pinched attempts to smile, the way it seemed to pain him to move his lips and show his white, strong, Clark Kent–straight false teeth. He was always looking at himself in the mirror, searching for some sign of disfigurement, for the flaw that made others avoid his company. He wasn't easy at being around girls. I had been in more relationships, and was three years younger. With all that against him, he couldn't afford to be uncool too. Our comics had to go.

Her name was Angie. She was my age, a transfer student, too new at school to know that my brother was a dud. She smelled of patchouli and wore a hand-knit cap in the red-gold-and-green of the Jamaican flag. We had an English class together and she recognized me. There was a test on *Lord of the Flies* the next day. I asked what she thought of the book, and she said she hadn't finished it yet, and I said I'd help her study if she wanted.

By the time Nick got back from disposing of our comic collection, we were lying on our stomachs, side by side in front of MTV's *Spring Break*. I had the novel out and was going through some passages I had highlighted . . . something I usually never did. As I said, I was a poor, unmotivated student, but *Lord of the Flies* had excited me, distracted my imagination for a week or so, made me want to live barefoot and naked on an island, with my own tribe of boys to dominate and lead in savage rituals. I read and reread the parts about Jack painting his face, smitten with a desire to smear colored muds on my own face, to be primitive and unknowable and free.

Nick sat on the other side of her, sulking because he didn't want to share her with me. Nick couldn't talk about the book with us—he had never read it. Nick had always been in Advanced English courses, where the assigned reading was Milton and Chaucer. Whereas I was pulling Cs in Adventures in English!, a course for the world's future janitors and air conditioner repairmen. We were the dumb kids, going nowhere, and for our stupidity, we were rewarded with all the really fun books.

Now and then Angie would stop and check out what was on TV and ask a provocative question: *Do you guys think that girl is totally hot? Would it be embarrassing to be beaten by a female mud wrestler, or is that the whole point?* It was never clear who she was talking to, and usually I answered first, just to fill the silences. Nick acted like his jaw was wired shut again, and smiled his angry pinched smile when my answers made her laugh. Once, when she was laughing especially hard, she put a hand on my arm. He sulked about that too.

ANGIE AND I were friends for two years, before the first time we kissed, in a closet, both of us drunk at a party, with others laughing and shouting our names through the door. We made love for the first time three months later, in my room, with the windows open and a cool breeze that smelled sweetly of pines blowing in on us. After that first time, she asked what I wanted to do with myself when I grew up. I said I wanted to learn how to hang-glide. I was eighteen, she was eighteen. This was an answer that satisfied us both.

Later, not long after she finished nursing school, and we settled into an apartment together downtown, she asked me again what I wanted to do. I had spent the summer working as a house painter, but that was over. I hadn't found another job to replace it yet, and Angie said I ought to take the time to think about the long term.

She wanted me to get back into college. I told her I'd think about it, and while I was thinking, I missed the enrollment period for the next semester. She said why not learn to be an EMT, and spent several days collecting paperwork for me to fill out, so I could get in the program: applications, questionnaires, financial aid forms. The pile of them sat by the fridge, collecting coffee stains, until one of us threw them out. It wasn't laziness that held me back. I just couldn't bring myself to do it. My brother was studying to be a doctor in Boston. He'd think I was, in some needy way, trying to be like him, an idea that gave me shivers of loathing.

Angie said there had to be something I wanted to do with myself. I told her I wanted to live in Barrow, Alaska, at the edge of the arctic circle, with her, and raise children, and malamutes, and have a garden in a greenhouse: tomatoes, string beans, a plot of mellow weed. We'd earn our living taking tourists dog sledding. We would shun the world of supermarkets, broadband Internet, and indoor plumbing. We would leave the TV behind. In the winter, the northern lights would paint the sky above us all day long. In the summers, our children would live half-wild, skiing unnamed backcountry hills, feeding playful seals by hand from the dock behind our house.

We had only just set out on the work of being adults, and were in the first stages of making a life with one another. In those days, when I talked about our children feeding seals, Angie would look at me in a way that made me feel both faintly weak and intensely hopeful . . . hopeful about myself and who I might turn out to be. Angie had the too-large eyes of a seal herself, brown, with a ring of brilliant gold around her pupil. She'd stare at me without blinking, listening to me tell it, lips parted, as attentive as a child hearing her favorite bedtime story.

But after my D.U.I., any mention of Alaska would cause her to make faces. Getting arrested cost me my job, too—no great loss, I admit, since I was temping as a pizza delivery man at the time—and Angie was desperate trying to keep up with the bills. She worried, and she did her worrying alone, avoiding me as much as possible, no easy task, considering we shared a three-room apartment.

I brought up Alaska now and then, anyway, trying to draw her back to me, but it only gave her a place to concentrate her anger. She said if I couldn't keep the apartment clean, at home alone all day, what was our lodge going to be like? She saw our children playing amid piles of dogshit, the front porch caving in, rusting snowmobiles and deranged half-breed dogs scattered about the yard. She said hearing me talk about it made her want to scream, it was so pathetic, so disconnected from our lives. She said she was scared I had a problem, alcoholism maybe, or clinical depression. She wanted me to see someone, not that we had the money for that.

None of this explains why she walked out—fled without warning. It wasn't the court case, or my drinking, or my lack of direction. The real reason we split was more terrible than that, so terrible we could never talk about it. If she had brought it up, I would've ridiculed her. And I couldn't bring it up, because it was my policy to pretend it hadn't happened.

I was cooking breakfast for supper one night, bacon and eggs, when Angie arrived home from work. I always liked to have supper ready for her when she got back, part of my plan to show her I was down but not out. I said something about how we were going to have our own pigs up in the Yukon, smoke our own bacon, kill a shoat for Christmas dinner. She said I wasn't funny anymore. It was her tone more than what she said. I sang the song from *Lord of the Flies*—*kill the pig, drain her blood*—trying to squeeze a laugh out of what hadn't been funny in the first place, and she said *Stop it*, very shrill, *just stop it*. At this particular moment I happened to have a knife in my hand, what I had used to cut open the pack of bacon, and she was leaning with her rump resting against the kitchen counter a few feet away. I had a sudden, vivid picture in my head, imagined turning and slashing the knife across her throat. In my mind I saw her hand fly to her neck, her baby seal eyes springing open in astonishment, saw blood the bright red of cranberry juice gushing down her V-neck sweater.

As this thought occurred to me, I happened to glance at her throat—then at her eyes. And she was staring back at me and she was afraid. She set her glass of orange juice down, very gently, in the sink, and said she wasn't hungry and maybe she needed to lie down. Four days later I went around the corner for bread and milk and she was gone when I got back. She called from her parents to say we needed some time.

It was just a thought. Who doesn't have a thought like that now and then?

WHEN I WAS two months behind on the rent and my landlord was saying he could get an order to have me thrown out, I moved home myself. My mother was remodeling and I said I wanted to help. I did want to help. I was desperate for something to do. I hadn't worked in four months and had a court date in December.

My mother had knocked down the walls in my old bedroom, pulled out the windows. The holes in the wall were covered with plastic sheeting, and the floor was littered in chunks of plaster. I made a nest for myself in the basement, on a cot across from the washer and dryer. I put my TV on a milk crate at the foot of the bed. I couldn't leave it behind in the apartment, needed it for company.

My mother was no company. The first day I was home, she only spoke to me to tell me I couldn't use her car. If I wanted to get drunk and crash a set of wheels, I could buy my own. Most of her communication was nonverbal. She'd let me know it was time to wake up by stomping around over my head, feet booming through the basement ceiling. She told me I disgusted her by glaring at me over her crowbar, as she pulled boards out of my bedroom floor, yanking them up in a silent fury, as if she wanted to tear away all the evidence of my childhood in her home.

The cellar was unfinished, with a pitted cement floor and a maze of low pipes hanging from the ceiling. At least it had its own bathroom, an incongruously tidy room with a flower-pattern linoleum floor and a bowl of woodland-scented pot-pourri resting on the tank of the toilet. When I was in there taking a leak, I could shut my eyes and inhale that scent and imagine the wind stirring in the tops of the great pines of northern Alaska.

I woke one night, in my basement cell, to a bitter cold, my breath steaming silver and blue in the light from the TV, which I had left on. I had finished off a couple beers before bed and now I needed to urinate so badly it hurt.

Normally, I slept beneath a large quilt, hand-stitched by my grandmother, but I had spilled Chinese on it and tossed it in the wash, then never got around to drying it. To replace it, I had raided the linen closet, just before bed, gathering up a stack of old comforters from my childhood: a puffy blue bedspread decorated with characters from *The Empire Strikes Back*, a red blanket with fleets of Fokker triplanes soaring across it. None of them, singly, was large enough to cover me, but I had spread the different blankets over my body in overlapping patterns, one for my feet, another for my legs and crotch, a third for my chest.

They had kept me cozy enough to fall asleep, but now were in disarray, and I was huddled for warmth, my knees pulled almost to my chest, my arms wrapped around them, my bare feet sticking into the cold. I couldn't feel my toes, as if they had already been amputated for frostbite.

My head was muddy. I was only half-awake. I needed to pee. I had to get warm. I rose and floated to the bathroom through the dark, the smallest blanket thrown over my shoulders to keep the cold off. I had the sleep-addled idea that I was still balled up to stay warm, with my knees close to my chest, although I was nevertheless moving forward. It was only when I was over the toilet, fumbling with the fly of my boxers, that I happened to look down and saw my knees *were* hitched up, and that my feet weren't touching the floor. They dangled a full foot over the toilet seat.

The room swam around me and I felt momentarily light-headed, not with shock so much as a kind of dreaming wonder. Shock didn't figure into it. I suppose some part of me had been waiting, all that time, to fly again, had almost been expecting it.

Not that what I was doing could really be described as fly-ing. It was more like controlled floating. I was an egg again, tippy and awkward. My arms waved anxiously at my sides. The fingertips of one hand brushed the wall and steadied me a little.

I felt fabric shift across my shoulders and carefully dropped my gaze, as if even a sudden movement of the eyes could send me sprawling to the ground. At the edge of my vision I saw the blue sateen hem of a blanket, and part of a patch, red and yel-low. Another wave of dizziness rolled over me and I wobbled in the air. The blanket slipped, just as it had done that day almost fourteen years before, and slid off my shoulders. I dropped in the same instant, clubbed a knee against the side of the toilet, shoved a hand into the bowl, plunging it deep into freezing water.

*   *   *

I SAT WITH the cape spread across my knees, studying it as the first silvery flush of dawn lit the windows high along the basement walls.

The cape was even smaller than I remembered, about the length of a large pillowcase. The red felt lightning bolt was still sewn to the back, although a couple of stitches had popped free, and one corner of the bolt was sticking up. My father's Marine patch was still sewn on as well, was what I had seen from the corner of my eye: a slash of lightning across a background like fire.

Of course my mother hadn't sent it to the dump to be incinerated. She never got rid of anything, on the theory she might find a use for it later. Hoarding what she had was a mania, not spending money an obsession. She didn't know anything about home renovation, but it never would've crossed her mind to pay anyone to do the work for her. My bedroom would be torn open to the elements and I would be sleeping in the basement until she was in diapers and I was in charge of changing them. What she thought of as self-reliance was really a kind of white-trash mulishness, and I had not been home long before it got under my skin and I had quit helping her out.

The sateen edge of the cape was just long enough for me to tie it around my neck.

I sat on the edge of my cot for a long time, perched with my feet up, like a pigeon on a ledge, and the blanket trailing to the small of my back. The floor was half a foot below, but I stared over the side as if looking at a forty-foot drop. At last, I pushed off.

And hung. Bobbled unsteadily, frontward and backways, but did not fall. My breath got caught behind my diaphragm and it was several moments before I could force myself to exhale, in a great equine snort.

I ignored my mother's wooden-heeled shoes banging overhead at nine in the morning. She tried again at ten, this time opening the door to shout down, *Are you ever getting up?* I yelled back that I *was* up. It was true: I was two feet off the ground.

By then I had been flying for hours . . . but again, describing it as flight probably brings to mind the wrong sort of image. You see Superman. Imagine, instead, a man sitting on a magic carpet, with his knees pulled to his chest. Now take away the magic carpet and you'll be close.

I had one speed, which I would call stately. I moved like a float in a parade. All I had to do to glide forward was look forward, and I was going, as if driven by a stream of powerful but invisible gas, the flatulence of the Gods.

For a while, I had trouble turning, but eventually, I learned to change direction in the same way one steers a canoe. As I moved across the room, I'd throw an arm in the air and pull the other in. And effortlessly, I'd veer to the right or left, depending on which metaphorical oar I stuck in the water. Once I got the hang of it, the act of turning became exhilarating, the way I seemed to accelerate into the curves, in a sudden rush that produced a ticklish feeling in the pit of my stomach.

I could rise by leaning back, as if into a recliner. The first time I tried it, I swooped upward so quickly, I bashed a head against a brass pipe, hard enough to make constellations of black dots wheel in front of my eyes. But I only laughed and rubbed at the stinging lump in the center of my forehead.

When I finally quit, at almost noon, I was exhausted, and I lay in bed, my stomach muscles twitching helplessly from the effort it had required to keep my knees hitched up all that time. I had forgotten to eat, and I felt light-headed from low blood sugar. And still, even lying down, under my sheets, in the slowly warming basement, I felt as if I were soaring. I shut my eyes and sailed away into the limitless reaches of sleep.

IN THE LATE afternoon, I took the cape off and went upstairs to make bacon sandwiches. The phone rang and I answered automatically. It was my brother.

"Mom tells me you aren't helping upstairs," he said.

"Hi. I'm good. How are you?"

"She also said you sit in the basement all day watching TV."

"That's not all I do," I said. I sounded more defensive than I liked. "If you're so worried about her, why don't you come home and play handyman one of these weekends?"

"When you're third-year premed, you can't just take off whenever you feel like it. I have to schedule my BMs in advance. One day last week I was in the ER for ten hours. I should've left, but this old woman came in with heavy vaginal bleeding—" At this, I giggled, a reaction that was met with a long moment of disapproving silence. Then Nick went on, "I stayed at work another hour to make sure she was okay. That's what I want for you. Get you doing something that will lift you up above your own little world."

"I've got things I'm doing."

"What things? For example, what have you done with yourself today?"

"Today—today isn't a normal day. I didn't sleep all night. I've just been—sort of—floating from here to there." I couldn't help it; I giggled again.

He was silent for a while. Then he said, "If you were in total freefall, Eric, do you think you'd even know it?"

I SLIPPED OFF the edge of the roof like a swimmer sliding from the edge of the pool into the water. My insides churned and my scalp prickled, icy-hot, my whole body clenching up, waiting for freefall. This is how it ends, I thought, and it crossed my mind that the entire morning, all that flying around the basement, had been a delusion, a schizophrenic fantasy, and now I would drop and shatter, gravity asserting its reality. Instead I dipped, then rose. My child's cape fluttered at my shoulders.

While waiting for my mother to go to bed, I had painted my face. I had retreated into the basement bathroom, and used one of her lipsticks to draw an oily red mask, a pair of linked loops, around my eyes. I did not want to be spotted while I was out flying, and if I was, I thought the red circles would distract any potential witnesses from my other features. Besides, it felt good to paint my face, was oddly arousing, the sensation of the lipstick rolling hard and smooth across my skin. When I was done, I stood admiring myself in front of the bathroom mirror for a while. I liked my red mask. It was a simple thing, but made my features strange and unfamiliar. I was curious about this new person staring back at me out of the mirror glass. About what he wanted. About what he could do.

After my mother closed herself in her bedroom for the night, I had crept upstairs, out the hole in my bedroom wall where the dormer window had been, and onto the roof. A few of the black tar shingles were missing, and others were loose, hanging askew. Something else my mother could try and fix herself in the interest of saving a few nickels. She would be lucky not to slide off the roof and snap her neck. Anything could happen out there where the world touches the sky. No one knew that better than me.

The cold stung my face, numbed my hands. I had sat flexing my fingers for a long time, building up the nerve to overcome a hundred thousand years of evolution, screaming at me that I would die if I went over the edge. Then I was over the edge, and suspended in the clear, frozen air, thirty feet above the lawn.

You want to hear now that I felt a rush of excitement, whooped at the thrill of flight. I didn't. What I felt was something much more subtle. My pulse quickened. I caught my breath for a moment. Then I felt a stillness settling into me, like the stillness of the air. I was drawn completely into myself, concentrating on staying balanced atop the invisible bubble beneath me (which perhaps gives the impression that I could feel something beneath me, some unseen cushion of support; I could not, which was why I was constantly squirming around for balance). Out of instinct, as much as habit, I held my knees up to my chest, and kept my arms out to the side.

The moon was only a little bigger than a quarter full, but bright enough to etch intensely dark, sharp-edged shadows on the ground, and to make the frosty yards below shine as if the grass were blades of chrome.

I glided forward. I did some loops around the leafless crown of a red maple. The dead elm was long gone, had split in two in a windstorm almost eight years before. The top half had come down against the house, a long branch shattering one of my bedroom windows, as if reaching in for me, still trying to kill me.

It was cold, and the chill intensified as I climbed. I didn't care. I wanted to get above everything.

The town was built on the slopes of a valley, a crude black bowl, a-glitter with lights. I heard a mournful honking in my left ear, and my heart gave a lunge. I looked through the inky dark and saw a mallard, with a liquid black head and a throat of startling emerald, beating its wings and staring curiously back at me. He did not remain by my side for long, but dove, swooped to the south, and was gone.

For a while I didn't know where I was going. I had a nervous moment, when I wasn't sure how I'd get back down without falling eight hundred feet. But when I couldn't bend my fingers anymore, or feel any sensation in my face, I tilted forward slightly and began to sink back to earth, gently descending, in the way I had practiced hour on hour in the basement.

By the time I leveled off over Powell Avenue, I knew where I was headed. I floated three blocks, rising once to clear the wire suspending a stoplight, then hung a left and soared on, dream-like, to Angie's house. She would just be getting off her shift at the hospital.

Only she was almost an hour late. I was sitting on the roof of the garage when she turned into the driveway in the old bronze Civic we had shared, bumper missing and hood battered from where I had crashed it into a Dumpster, at the end of my low-speed attempt to evade the police.

Angie was made up and dressed in her lime-colored skirt with tropical flowers printed on it, the one she only wore to staff meetings at the end of the month. It wasn't the end of the month. I sat on the tin roof of the garage and watched her totter to the front door in her heels and let herself in.

Usually she showered when she got home. I didn't have anything else to do.

I slid off the peak of the garage roof, bobbled and rose like a black balloon toward the third floor of her parents' tall, narrow Victorian. Her bedroom was dark. I leaned toward the glass, peering in, looking toward her door and waiting for it to open. But she was already there, and in the next moment she snapped on a lamp, just to the left of the window, on a low dresser. She stared out the window at me and I stared right back, didn't move—couldn't move, was too shocked to make a sound. She regarded me wearily, without interest or surprise. She didn't see me. She couldn't make me out past her own reflection. I wondered if she had ever been able to see me.

I floated outside the window while she stripped her skirt off over her head and wiggled out of plain girdle underwear. A bathroom adjoined her bedroom, and she considerately left the door open between the two. I watched her shower through the clear glass of the shower cabinet. She showered a long time, lifting her arms to throw her honey-colored hair back, hot water pelting her breasts. I had watched her shower before, but it hadn't been this interesting in a long time. I wished she'd masturbate with the flexible showerhead, something she said she had done as a teenager, but she didn't.

In a while the window steamed over and I couldn't see as clearly. I watched her pink pale form move here and there. Then I heard her voice. She was on the phone. She asked someone why they were studying on a Saturday night. She said she was bored, she wanted to play a game. She pleaded in tones of erotic petulance.

A circle of clear glass appeared in the center of the window and began to expand as the condensation in her room evaporated, giving me a slow reveal. She was in a clinging white halter and a pair of black cotton panties, sitting at a small desk, hair wrapped in a towel. She had hung up the phone, but was playing cribbage on her computer, typing occasionally to send an instant message. She had a glass of white wine. I watched her drink it. In movies, voyeurs watch models prance about in French lingerie, but the banal is kinky enough, lips on a wineglass, the band of simple panties against a white buttock.

When she got off-line she seemed happy with herself but restless. She got into bed, switched on her little TV and flipped through the channels. She stopped on the Think! channel to watch seals fucking. One climbed on the back of the other and began humping away, blubber shaking furiously. She looked longingly at the computer.

"Angie," I said.

It seemed to take her a moment to register she had heard anything. Then she sat up and leaned forward, listening to the house. I said her name again. Her eyelashes fluttered nervously. She turned her head to the window almost reluctantly, but again, didn't see me past her reflection . . . until I tapped on the glass.

Her shoulders jumped in a nervous reflex. Her mouth opened in a cry, but she didn't make a sound. After a moment, she came off the bed and approached the window on stiff legs. She stared out. I waved hello. She looked beneath me for the ladder, then lifted her gaze back to my face. She swayed, put her hands on her dresser to steady herself.

"Unlock it," I said.

Her fingers struggled with the locks for a long time. She pulled the window up.

"Oh my God," she said. "Oh my God. Oh my God. How are you doing that?"

"I don't know. Can I come in?"

I eased myself up onto the windowsill, turning and shifting, so one arm was in her room, but my legs hung out.

"No," she said. "I don't believe it."

"Yes. Real."

"How?"

"I don't know. Honest." I picked at the edge of the cape. "But I did it once before. A long time back. You know my knee and the scar on my chest? I told you I did all that falling out of a tree, you remember?"

A look of surprise, mingled with sudden understanding, spread across her face. "The branch broke and fell. But you didn't. Not at first. You stayed in the air. You were in your cape and it was like magic and you didn't fall."

She already knew. She already knew and I didn't know how, because I had never told her. I could fly; she was psychic.

"Nicky told me," she said, seeing my confusion. "He said when the tree branch fell, he thought he saw you fly. He said he was so sure he tried to fly himself and that's what happened to his face. We were talking and he was trying to explain how he wound up with false teeth. He said he was crazy back then. He said you both were."

"When did he tell you about his teeth?" I asked. My brother never got over being insecure about his face, his mouth especially, and he didn't like people to know about the teeth.

She shook her head. "I don't remember."

I turned on the windowsill and put my feet up on her dresser. "Do you want to see what it's like to fly?"

Her eyes were glassy with disbelief. Her mouth was open in a blank, dazed smile. Then she tilted her head to one side and narrowed her eyes.

"How are you doing it?" she asked. "Really."

"It's something about the cape. I don't know what. Magic, I guess. When I put it on, I can fly. That's all."

She touched the corner of one of my eyes, and I remembered the mask I had drawn with lipstick. "What about this stuff on your face? What's that do?"

"Makes me feel sexy."

"Holy shit, you're weird. And I lived with you for two years." She was laughing, though.

"Do you want to fly?"

I slid the rest of the way into the room, toward her, and hung my legs over the side of the dresser.

"Sit in my lap. I'll ride you around the room."

She looked from my lap to my face, her smile sly and distrustful now. A breeze trickled in through the window behind me, stirring the cape. She hugged herself and shivered, then glanced down at herself and noticed she was in her underwear. She shook her head, twisted the towel off her still-damp hair.

"Hold on a minute," she said.

She went to her closet and folded back the door and dug in a cubby for sweats. While she was looking, there came a pitiful shriek from the television, and my gaze shifted toward the screen. One seal was biting the neck of another, furiously, while his victim wailed. A narrator said dominant males would use all the natural weapons at their disposal to drive off any rival that might challenge them for access to the females of the herd. The blood looked like a splash of cranberry juice on the ice.

Angie had to clear her throat to get my attention again, and when I glanced at her, her mouth was, for a moment, thin and pinched, the corners crimped downward in a look of irritation. It only took a moment sometimes for me to drift away from myself and into some television program, even something I had no interest in at all. I couldn't help myself. It's like I'm a negative, and the TV is a positive. Together we make a circuit, and nothing outside the circuit matters. It was the same way when I read comics. It's a weakness, I admit, but it darkened my mood to catch her there, judging me.

She tucked a strand of wet hair behind one ear and showed me a quick, elfin grin, tried to pretend she hadn't just been giving me The Look. I leaned back, and she pulled herself up, awkwardly, onto my thighs.

"Why do I think this is some perverted prank to get me in your lap?" she asked. I leaned forward, made ready to push off. She said, "We're going to fall on our a—"

I slipped off the side of the dresser and into the air. I wobbled forward and back and forward again, and she wrapped her arms around my neck and cried out, a happy, laughing, frightened sort of cry.

I'm not particularly strong, but it wasn't like picking her up . . . it was really as if she were sitting on my lap and we were together in an invisible rocking chair. All that had changed was my center of gravity, and now I felt tippy, a canoe with too many people in it.

I floated her around her bed, then up and over it. She screamed-laughed-screamed again.

"This is the craziest—" she said. "Oh my God no one will believe it," she said. "Do you know you're going to be the most famous person in human history?" Then she just stared into my face, her wide eyes shining, the way they used to when I talked about Alaska.

I made as if to fly back to my perch on the dresser, but when I got to it, I just kept going, ducked my head and carried us right out the open window.

"No! What are you doing? Holy Jesus it's cold!" She was squeezing me so tightly around the neck it was hard to breathe.

I rose toward the slash of silver moon.

"Be cold," I said. "Just for a minute. Isn't it worth it—for this? To fly like this? Like you do in dreams?"

"Yes," she said. "Isn't this the most incredible thing?"

"Yes."

She shivered furiously, which set off an interesting vibration in her breasts, under the thin shirt. I kept climbing, toward a flotilla of clouds, edged in mercury. I liked the way she clung to me, and I liked the way it felt when she trembled.

"I want to go back," she said.

"Not yet."

My shirt was open a little, and she snuggled into it, her icy nose touching my flesh.

"I've wanted to talk to you," she said. "I wanted to call you tonight. I was thinking about you."

"Who did you call instead?"

"Nobody," she said, and then realized I had been outside the window listening. "Hannah. You know. From work."

"Is she studying for something? I heard you ask why she was studying on a Saturday."

"Let's go back."

"Sure."

She buried her face against my chest again. Her nose grazed my scar, a silver slash like the silver slash of the moon. I was still climbing toward the moon. It didn't seem so far away. She fingered the old scar.

"It's unbelievable," she whispered. "Think how lucky you were. A few inches lower and that branch might've gone right through your heart."

"Who said it didn't?" I said, and leaned forward and let her go.

She held onto my neck, kicking, and I had to peel her fingers off, one at a time, before she fell.

WHENEVER MY BROTHER and I played superheroes, he always made me be the bad guy.

Someone has to be.

MY BROTHER HAS been telling me I ought to fly down to Boston one of these nights, so we can do some drinking together. I think he wants to share some big-brother advice, tell me I have to pick myself up, have to move on. Maybe he also wants to share some grief. I'm sure he's in grief too.

One of these nights, I think I will . . . fly on down to see him.

Show him the cape. See if he'll try it on. See if he wants to take a leap out his fifth-floor window.

He might not want to. Not after what happened last time. He might need some encouragement; a little nudge from little brother.

And who knows? Maybe if he goes out the window in my cape, he will rise instead of fall, float away into the cool, still embrace of the sky.

But I don't think so. It didn't work for him when we were children. Why would it now? Why would it ever?

It's my cape.

LAST BREATH

A family walked in for a look around, a little before noon, a man, a woman, and their son. They were the first visitors of the day—for all Alinger knew they would be the only visitors of the day, the museum was never busy—and he was free to give them the tour.

He met them in the coatroom. The woman still stood with one foot out on the front steps, hesitant to come in any further. She was staring over her son's head at her husband, giving him a doubting, uneasy look. The husband frowned back at her. His hands were on the lapels of his shearling overcoat, but he seemed undecided whether to take it off or not. Alinger had seen it a hundred times before. Once people were inside and had looked beyond the foyer into the funeral home gloom of the parlor, they had second thoughts, wondered if they had come to the right place, began to entertain ideas of backing out. Only the little boy seemed at ease, was already stripping off his jacket and hanging it over one of the child-level hooks on the wall.

Before they could get away from him, Alinger cleared his throat to draw their attention. No one ever left once they had been spotted; in the battle between anxiety and social custom, social custom almost always won. He folded his hands together and smiled at them, in a way he hoped was reassuring, grandfatherly. The effect, though, was rather the opposite. Alinger was cadaverous, ten inches over six feet, his temples sunk into shadowed hollows. His teeth (at eighty, still his own) were small and gray and gave the unpleasant impression of having been filed. The father shrank away a little. The woman unconsciously reached for her son's hand.

"Good morning. I'm Dr. Alinger. Please come in."

"Oh—hello," said the father. "Sorry to bother."

"No bother. We're open."

"You are. Good!" he said, with a not quite convincing enthusiasm. "So what do we—" And his voice trailed off and he fell quiet, either had forgotten what he was going to say, or wasn't sure how to put it, or lacked the nerve.

His wife took over. "We were told you have an exhibition here? That this is some kind of scientific museum?"

Alinger showed them the smile again, and the father's right eyelid began to twitch helplessly.

"Ah. You misheard," Alinger said. "You were expecting a museum of science. This is the museum of *silence*."

"Hmm?" the father said.

The mother frowned. "I think I'm still mishearing."

"Come on, Mom," said the boy, pulling his hand free from her grip. "Come on, Dad. I want to look around. I want to see."

"Please," Alinger said, stepping back from the coatroom, gesturing with one gaunt, long-fingered hand into the parlor. "I would be glad to offer you the guided tour."

THE SHADES WERE drawn, so the room, with its mahogany paneling, was as dim as a theater in the moment before the curtain is pulled back on the show. The display stands, though, were lit from above by tightly focused spotlights, recessed in the ceiling. On tables and pedestals stood what appeared to be empty glass beakers, polished to a high shine, bulbs glowing so brilliantly they made the darkness around them that much darker.

Each beaker had what appeared to be a stethoscope attached to it, the diaphragm stuck right to the glass, sealed there with a clear adhesive. The earpieces waited for someone to pick them up and listen. The boy led the way, followed by his parents, and then Alinger. They stopped before the first display, a jar on a marble pedestal, located just beyond the parlor entrance, set right in their path.

"There's nothing in it," the boy said. He peered all around, surveying the entire room, the other sealed beakers. "There's nothing in any of them. They're just empty like "

"Ha," said the father, humorlessly.

"Not quite empty," Alinger said. "Each jar is airtight, hermetically sealed. Each one contains someone's dying breath. I have the largest collection of last breaths in the world, over a hundred. Some of these bottles contain the final exhalations of some very famous people."

Now the woman began to laugh; real laughter, not laughter for show. She clapped a hand over her mouth and shivered, but couldn't manage to completely stifle herself. Alinger smiled. He had been showing his collection for years. He was used to every kind of reaction.

The boy, however, had turned back to the beaker directly before him, his eyes rapt. He picked up the earpieces of the device that looked like but was not a stethoscope.

"What's this?" he asked.

"The deathoscope," Alinger said. "Very sensitive. Put it on if you like, and you can hear the last breath of William R. Sied."

"Is he someone famous?" the boy said.

Alinger nodded. "For a while he was a celebrity . . . in the way criminals sometimes become celebrities. A source of public outrage and fascination. Forty-two years ago he took a seat in the electric chair. I issued his death certificate myself. He has a place of honor in my museum. His was the first last breath I ever captured."

By now the woman had recovered herself, although she held a wadded-up handkerchief to her lips and looked as if she were only containing a fresh outburst of mirth with great effort.

"What did he do?" the boy asked.

"Strangled children," Alinger said. "He preserved them in a freezer, and took them out now and then to look at them. People will collect anything, I always say." He crouched to the boy's level, and looked into the jar with him. "Go ahead and listen if you want."

The boy lifted the earpieces and put them on, his gaze fixed and unblinking on the vessel brimming with light. He listened intently for a while, and then his brow knotted and he frowned.

"I can't hear anything." He started to reach up to remove the earpieces.

Alinger stopped his hand. "Wait. There are all different kinds of silence. The silence in a seashell. The silence after a gunshot. His last breath is still in there. Your ears need time to acclimate. In a while you'll be able to make it out. His own particular final silence."

The boy bent his head and shut his eyes. The adults watched him together.

Then his eyes sprang open and he looked up, his plump face shining a little with eagerness.

"Did you hear?" Alinger asked him.

The boy pulled off the earphones. "Like a hiccup, only inside-out! You know? Like—" He stopped and sucked in a short, soundless little gasp.

Alinger tousled his hair and stood.

The mother dabbed at her eyes with her kerchief. "And you're a doctor?"

"Retired."

"Don't you think this is a little unscientific? Even if you really did manage to capture the last tiny bit of carbon monoxide someone exhaled—"

"Dioxide," he said.

"It wouldn't make a sound. You can't bottle the sound of someone's last breath."

"No," he agreed. "But it isn't a sound being bottled. Only a certain silence. We all have our different silences. Does your husband have one silence when he's happy and another when he's angry with you, missus? Your ears can discern even between specific kinds of nothing."

She didn't like being called *missus*, narrowed her eyes at him, and opened her mouth to say something disagreeable, but her husband spoke first, giving Alinger a reason to turn away from her. Her husband had drifted to a jar on a table against the wall, next to a dark, padded loveseat.

"How do you collect these breaths?"

"With an aspirator. A small pump that draws a person's exhalations into a vacuum container. I keep it in my doctor's bag at all times, just in case. It's a device of my own design, although similar equipment has been around since the beginning of the nineteenth century."

"This says Poe," the father said, fingering an ivory card set on the table before the jar.

"Yes," Alinger said. He coughed shyly. "People have been collecting last breaths for as long as the machinery has existed to make my hobby possible. I admit I paid twelve-thousand dollars for that. It was offered to me by the great-grandson of the doctor who watched him die."

The woman began to laugh again.

Alinger continued patiently, "That may sound like a lot of money, but believe me, it was a bargain. Scrimm, in Paris, recently paid three times that for the last breath of Enrico Caruso."

The father fingered the deathoscope attached to the jar marked for Poe.

"Some silences seem to resonate with feeling," Alinger said. "You can almost sense them trying to articulate an idea. Many who listen to Poe's last breath begin in a while to sense a single word not being said, the expression of a very specific want. Listen and see if you sense it too."

The father hunched and put on the earpieces.

"This is ridiculous," the woman said.

The father listened intently. His son crowded him, squeezing himself tight to his leg.

"Can I listen, Dad?" the boy said. "Can I have a turn?"

"Sh," his father said.

They were all silent, except for the woman, who was whispering to herself in a tone of agitated bemusement.

"Whiskey," the father mouthed, just moving his lips.

"Turn over the card with his name on it," said Alinger.

The father turned over the ivory card that said POE on one side. On the other side, it read "WHISKEY."

He removed the earpieces, his face solemn, eyes lowered respectfully to the jar.

"Of course. The alcoholism. Poor man. You know—I memorized 'The Raven,' when I was in sixth grade," the father said. "And recited it before my entire class without a mistake."

"Oh, come on," said the woman. "It's a trick. There's probably a speaker hidden under the jar, and when you listen you can hear a recording, someone whispering *whiskey*."

"I didn't hear a whisper," the father said. "I just had a thought—like someone's voice in my head—such disappointment—"

"The volume turned low," she said. "So it's all subliminal. Like what they do to you at drive-in movies."

The boy put on the earpieces to not-hear the same thing his father had not-heard.

"Are they *all* famous people?" the father asked. His features were pale, although there were little spots of red high on his cheeks, as if he had a fever.

"Not at all," Alinger said. "I've bottled the dying sighs of graduate students, bureaucrats, literary critics—any number of assorted nobodies. One of the most exquisite silences in my collection is the last breath of a janitor."

"Carrie Mayfield," said the woman, reading from a card in front of a tall, dusty jar. "Is that one of your nobodies? I'm guessing housewife."

"No," Alinger said. "No housewives in my collection yet. Carrie Mayfield was a young Miss Florida, beautiful in the extreme, on her way to New York City with her parents and fiancé, to pose for the cover of a woman's magazine. Her big break. Only her jet crashed in the Everglades. Lots of people died, it was a famous air disaster. Carrie, though, survived. For a time. She splashed through burning jet fuel while escaping the wreck, and over eighty percent of her body was burned. She lost her voice screaming for help. She lasted, in intensive care, just over a week. I was teaching then, and brought my medical students in to see her. As a curiosity. At the time, it was rare to view someone, still alive, who had been burned that way. So comprehensively. Parts of her body fused to other parts and so on. Fortunately I had my aspirator with me, since she died while we were examining her."

"That's the most horrible thing I've ever heard," said the woman. "What about her parents? Her fiancé?"

"They died in the crash. Burned to death in front of her. I'm not sure their bodies were ever recovered. The gators—"

"I don't believe you. Not a word. I don't believe a thing about this place. And I don't mind saying I think this is a pretty silly way to scam people out of their money."

"Now, dear—" said her husband.

"You will remember I charged you no admission," Alinger said. "This is a free exhibit."

"Oh, Dad, look!" the boy said, from across the room, reading a name on a card. "It's the man who wrote *James and the Giant Peach*!"

Alinger turned to him, ready to introduce the display in question, then saw the woman moving from the corner of his eye, and swiveled back to her.

"I would listen to one of the others first," Alinger said. She was lifting the earpieces to her head. "Some people don't care much for what they can't hear in the Carrie Mayfield jar."

She ignored him, put the earpieces on, and listened, her mouth pursed. Alinger clasped his hands together and leaned toward her, watching her expression.

Then, without warning, she took a quick step back. She still had the earpieces on, and the abrupt movement scraped the jar a short distance across the table, which gave Alinger a bad moment. He reached out quickly to keep it from sliding off onto the floor. She twisted the earpieces off her head, suddenly clumsy.

"Roald Dahl," the father said, putting his hand on his son's shoulder and admiring the jar the boy had discovered. "No kidding. Say, you went in big for the literary guys, huh?"

"I don't like it here," the woman said.

Her eyes were unfocused. She stared at the jar that contained Carrie Mayfield's last breath, but without seeing it. She swallowed noisily, a hand at her throat.

"Honey?" her husband said. He crossed the room to her, frowning, concerned. "You want to go? We just got here."

"I don't care," she said. "I want to leave."

"Oh, Mom," the boy complained.

"I hope you'll sign my guest book," Alinger said.

He trailed them to the coatroom.

The father was solicitous, touching his wife's elbow, regarding her with dewy, worried eyes. "Couldn't you wait in the car by yourself? Tom and I wanted to look around a while longer."

"I want to go right now," she said, her voice toneless, distant. "All of us."

The father helped her into her coat. The boy shoved his fists in his pockets and sullenly kicked at an old, worn doctor's bag, sitting beside the umbrella stand. Then he realized what he was kicking. He crouched, and without the slightest show of shame, unbuckled it to look at the aspirator.

The woman drew on her kidskin gloves, very carefully, pulling them tight against her fingers. She seemed a long way off in her own thoughts, so it was a surprise when all at once she roused herself, to turn on her heel and fix her gaze on Alinger.

"You're awful," she said. "Like some kind of graverobber."

Alinger folded his hands before him, and regarded her sympathetically. He had been showing his collection for years. He was used to every kind of reaction.

"Oh, honey," her husband said. "Have some perspective."

"I'm going to the car now," she said, lowering her head, drawing back into herself. "Catch up."

"Wait," the father said. "Wait for us."

He didn't have his coat on. Neither did the boy, who was on his knees, with the bag open, his fingertips moving slowly over the aspirator, a device that resembled a chrome thermos, with rubber tubes and a plastic face mask attached to one end.

She didn't hear her husband's voice, but turned away and went out, left the door open behind her. She went down the steep granite steps to the sidewalk, her eyes pointed at the ground the whole way. She was swaying when she did her sleepwalker's stroll into the street. She didn't look up, but started straight across for their car on the other side of the road.

Alinger was turning to get the guest book—he thought perhaps the man would still sign—when he heard the shriek of brakes, and a metallic crunch, as if a car had rushed headlong into a tree, only even before he looked he knew it wasn't a tree.

The father screamed and then screamed again. Alinger pivoted back in time to see him falling down the steps. A black Cadillac was turned at an unlikely angle in the street, steam coming up around the edges of the crumpled hood. The driver's side door was open, and the driver stood in the road, a porkpie hat tipped back on his head.

Even over the ringing in his ears, Alinger heard the driver saying, "She didn't even look. Right into traffic. Jesus Christ. What was I supposed to do?"

The father wasn't listening. He was in the street, on his knees, holding her. The boy stood in the coatroom, his jacket half on, staring out. A swollen vein beat in the child's forehead.

"Doctor!" the father screamed. "Please! Doctor!" He was looking back at Alinger.

Alinger paused to pick his overcoat off a hook. It was March, and windy, and he didn't want to get a chill. He hadn't reached the age of eighty by being careless or doing things in haste. He patted the boy on the head as he went by. He had not gone halfway down the steps, though, when the child called out to him.

"Doctor," the boy stammered, and Alinger looked back.

The boy held his bag out to him, still unbuckled.

"Your bag," the boy said. "You might need something in it."

Alinger smiled fondly, went back up the steps, took it from the boy's cold fingers.

"Thank you," he said. "I just might."

DEAD-WOOD

I t has been argued even trees may appear as ghosts. Reports of such manifestations are common in the literature of parapsychology. There is the famous white pine of West Belfry, Maine. It was chopped down in 1842, a towering fir with a white smooth bark like none anyone had ever seen, and with pine needles the color of brushed steel. A tea house and inn was built on the hill where it had stood. A cold spot existed in a corner of the yellow dining room, a zone of penetrating chill, the exact diameter of the white pine's trunk. Directly above the dining room was a small bedroom, but no guest would stay the night there. Those who tried said their sleep was disturbed by the keening rush of a phantom wind, the low soft roar of air in high branches; the gusts blew papers around the room and pulled curtains down. In March, the walls bled sap.

An entire phantom wood appeared in Canaanville, Pennsylvania, for a period of twenty minutes one day, in 1959. There are photographs. It was in a new development, a neighborhood of winding roads and small, modern bungalows. Residents woke on a Sunday morning and found themselves sleeping in stands of birch that seemed to grow right from the floor of their bedrooms. Underwater hemlocks swayed and drifted in backyard swimming pools. The phenomenon extended to a nearby shopping mall. The ground floor of Sears was filled with brambles, half-price skirts hanging from the branches of Norway maples, a flock of sparrows settled on the jewelry counter, picking at pearls and gold chains.

Somehow it's easier to imagine the ghost of a tree than it is the ghost of a man. Just think how a tree will stand for a hundred years, gorging itself on sunlight and pulling moisture from the earth, tirelessly hauling its life up out of the soil, like someone hauling a bucket up from a bottomless well. The roots of a shattered tree still drink for months after death, so used to the habit of life they can't give it up. Something that doesn't know it's alive obviously can't be expected to know when it's dead.

After you left—not right away, but after a summer had passed—I took down the alder we used to read under, sitting together on your mother's picnic blanket; the alder we fell asleep under that time, listening to the hum of the bees. It was old, and rotten, it had bugs in it, although new shoots still appeared on its boughs in the spring. I told myself I didn't want it to blow down and fall into the house, even though it wasn't leaning toward the house. But now, sometimes when I'm out there, in the wide-open of the yard, the wind will rise and shriek, tearing at my clothes. What else shrieks with it, I wonder?

THE WIDOW'S BREAKFAST

Killian left the blanket on Gage—didn't want it—and left Gage where he lay on a rise above a little creekbed somewhere in eastern Ohio. He didn't stop moving for the better part of a month after that, spent most of the summer of 1935 riding the freights north and east, as if he was still headed to see Gage's best cousin in New Hampshire. He wasn't, though. Killian would never meet her now. He didn't know where he was headed.

He was in New Haven for a while but didn't stay. One morning, in the early dark, he went to a place he had heard about, where the tracks swept out in a wide arc, and the trains had to slow down almost to nothing going around it. There he waited. A boy in an ill-fitting and dirty suit jacket crouched beside him, at the base of the embankment. When the northeastern came, Killian jumped up and ran alongside the train, and hauled himself up into a loaded freight car. The boy pulled himself into the car right behind him.

They rode together for a while, in the dark, the cars jolting from side to side and the wheels banging and clattering on the tracks. Killian dozed, came awake with the boy tugging on his belt buckle. The kid said for a quarter, but Killian didn't have a quarter and if he did, he wouldn't have spent it that way.

He grabbed the boy by the arms, and yanked his hands away with some effort, digging his fingernails into the soft undersides of the boy's wrists, and hurting him on purpose. Killian told him to leave be, and shoved him away. He told the boy that he looked like a nice kid and why did he want to be that way. Killian said to the boy to just wake him when the train stopped in Westfield. The kid sat on the other side of the car, one knee drawn up against his chest, and his arms wrapped around the knee, and didn't speak. Sometimes a thin line of gray morning light fell through one of the slats in the boxcar wall, and glided slowly up the boy's face, and across his hating and feverish eyes. Killian fell asleep again with the kid still glaring at him.

When he woke, the boy was gone. It was full light by then, but still early enough and cold enough so when Killian stood in the half-open boxcar door his breath was ripped away from him in clouds of frozen vapor. He held the edge of the door with one hand, and the fingers that were outside were soon burned raw by the sharp and icy current of the air. There was a tear in the armpit of his shirt, and the cold wind blew through that, too. He didn't know if Westfield was still ahead of him or not, but he felt he had slept for a long time—it was probably behind. Probably that was where the boy had jumped out. After Westfield there wouldn't be any other stops until the train dead-ended in Northampton, and Killian didn't want to go there. He stood in the door with the cold wind blasting at him. Sometimes he imagined he had died with Gage, and had wandered since as a ghost. It wasn't true, though. Things kept reminding him it wasn't true, like his neck stiff and achy from how he slept, or the cold air coming through the holes in his shirt.

At a trainyard in Lima, a railroad bull had caught Killian and Gage dozing together under their shared blanket, where they were hid in a shed. He had kicked them awake and told them to get. When they hadn't got fast enough, the bull struck Gage in the back of the head with his billy, driving him to his knees.

The next couple days, when Gage came awake in the mornings, he would say to Killian he was seeing double. Gage thought it was funny. He would sit for a while just where he was, turning his head from side to side, and laugh at the sight of the world multiplied. He had to blink a lot and rub at his eyes before his vision would clear. Then, three days after what happened in Lima, Gage started falling down. They would be walking together, and then Killian would notice all of a sudden that he was walking alone, and he would look back, and see Gage sitting on the ground, his face waxy and frightened. They stopped in a place where there was nothing, to rest for a day, but they shouldn't have stopped, Killian shouldn't have let them stop. They should have gone where there was a doctor. Killian knew that now. The very next morning Gage was dead with his eyes open and surprised by the creekbed.

Later Killian heard talk at campfires, heard other men tell about a railroad cop named Lima Slim. From their descriptions he guessed that this was the man who had struck Gage. Lima Slim had often shot at trespassers; once he had forced some men at gunpoint to jump off a train moving fifty miles an hour. Lima Slim was famous for the things he had done. Famous to bums anyway.

There was a bull at the Northampton yard named Arnold Choke some said was as bad as Lima Slim, which was why Killian didn't want to go there. After a long time of standing in the half-open doorway, he felt the train slowing down. Killian didn't know why; there wasn't a town ahead he could see. Maybe they were approaching a switch. He wondered if the train would come to a complete stop, but it didn't stop, and after a few seconds of losing speed, in a series of quick violent jerks, it began to accelerate again. Killian jumped. It wasn't really going that slow, and he hit hard on his left foot, and the gravel slid away under his heel. The foot twisted underneath him, and a sharp pain stabbed through his ankle. He did not shout when he pitched face-first into the wet brush.

It was October or November maybe, Killian didn't know, and in the woods by the train tracks was a carpet of dead leaves in colors of rust and butter. Killian limped across them. The leaves were not all gone from the trees. Here and there was a flare of crimson, streaks of ember-orange. A cold white smoke lay low to the ground in among the trunks of the birch and the spruce. On a wet stump Killian sat for a while, and held his ankle gently in his hands, while the sun rose higher, and the morning mist burned away. His shoes were burst and held together by dirt-caked strips of burlap, and his toes were so cold they were almost numb. Gage had had better shoes, but Killian had left them, just as he left the blanket. He had tried to pray over Gage's body, but had not been able to remember any of the Bible, except a sentence that went *Mary kept all these things, pondering them in her heart,* and that was from the birth of Jesus and no thing to say over a dead man.

It would be a warm day, although when Killian at last stood, it was still cool in under the shadows of the pines. He followed the tracks until his ankle was throbbing too badly to go on and he had to sit on the embankment and rest again. It was swelling badly now, and when he put weight on it, he felt a bitter, electric pain shoot through the bone. He had always trusted Gage to know when to jump. He had trusted Gage to know everything.

There was a white cottage away through the trees. Killian only glanced at it, and looked back at his ankle, but then he lifted his head and looked into the trees again. On the trunk of a nearby pine, someone had snapped away some bark, and carved an X in the wood, and rubbed coal in the X so it would stand out black. There were no secret hobo marks like some said, or if there were, Killian didn't know what they were and neither had Gage. An X like that, though, sometimes meant you could get something to eat at a place. Killian was strongly aware of the tight emptiness in his stomach.

He walked unsteadily through the trees to the yard behind the cottage and then hesitated at the edge of the woods. The paint was peeling and the windows were obscured by grime. Close against the back of the house was a garden bed, a long rectangle of earth with the rough dimensions of a grave. Nothing was growing in it.

Killian was standing there looking at the house when he noticed the girls. He had not seen them at first because they were so still and quiet. He had come at the cottage from the rear, but the forest extended up and around the side of the house, and the girls were there, kneeling in some ferns with their backs to him. He could not see what they were doing, but they were almost perfectly motionless. There were two of them, kneeling in their Sunday dresses. Each of them had white-blond hair, long and brushed and clean, and each had in her hair an arrangement of little brassy combs.

He stood and watched them and they knelt and were very still. One of them turned her head and looked back at him. She had a heart-shaped face and her eyes were a glacial shade of blue. She regarded him with no expression. In another moment the other girl turned her head to look at him as well. This other smiling a little. The smiling one was possibly seven. Her expressionless sister was perhaps ten. He lifted his hand in greeting. The unsmiling girl watched him for a moment longer, then turned her head away. He could not see what she was kneeling in front of, but whatever it was held her interest completely. The younger girl did not wave either, but seemed to nod at him before she too went back to looking at whatever was on the ground before them. Their silence and stillness unsettled him.

He crossed the yard to the back door. The screen door was orange with rust, and bellied outwards, pulling free from the frame in places. He took off his hat and was going to climb the steps to knock, but the inner door opened first and a woman appeared behind the screen. Killian stopped with his hat in his hands and put his begging face on.

The woman could have been thirty or forty or fifty. Her face was so drawn it seemed almost starved and her lips were thin and colorless. A dishrag hung from the waist strap of her apron.

"Hello, ma'am," Killian said. "I'm hungry. I was wonderin if I could have somethin to eat. A bite of toast maybe."

"You haven't had any breakfast anywhere?"

"No, ma'am."

"They give away a breakfast at Blessed Heart. Don't you know that?"

"Ma'am, I don't even know where that is."

She nodded briefly. "I'll make you toast. You can have eggs too if you want them. Do you want them?"

"Well. I guess if you made 'em, I wouldn't throw 'em in the road."

That was what Gage always said when he was offered more than he asked for, and it made the housewives laugh, but she didn't laugh, perhaps because he wasn't Gage and it didn't sound the same coming from him. Instead she only nodded once more and said, "All right. Scrape your feet on the—" She looked at his shoes and stopped speaking for a moment. "Look at those shoes. When you come in just take those shoes off and leave them by the door."

"Yes, ma'am."

He looked again at the girls before he climbed the steps, but their backs were to him and they paid him no mind. He entered and removed his shoes and walked across the chilled linoleum in his dirty bare feet. There was an odd stinging sensation in his ankle whenever he stepped on the left foot. By the time he sat there were already eggs sputtering in the pan.

"I know how you wound up at my back door. I know why you stopped at my house. Same reason all the other men stop here," she said, and he thought she was going to say something about the tree with the X on it, but she didn't. "It's because the train runs a little slower going into that switch, quarter a mile back, and all of you jump off so you won't have to see Arnold Choke in Northampton. Isn't that about it? Did you jump off at the switch?"

"Yes, ma'am."

" 'Cause of Arnold Choke?"

"Yes, ma'am. I've heard he's one you want to avoid."

"He's just got the reputation he does because of his last name. Arnold Choke isn't a danger to anyone. He's old and he's fat and if any of you ran from him he'd probably pass out trying to get you. Not that he'd ever run. He might run somewhere if he heard they were selling burgers two for a dime," she said. "You listen now. That train is going thirty miles an hour when it hits that switch. It doesn't slow hardly at all. Jumping off there is a lot more dangerous than going into the yard at Northampton."

"Yes, ma'am," he said, and rubbed his left leg.

"There's a pregnant girl tried to get off there last year who jumped into a tree and broke her neck. Do you hear me?"

"Yes, ma'am."

"A pregnant girl. Traveling with her husband. You ought to pass that around. Let other people know they're better off to stay on the train until she's good and stopped. Here's your eggs. You like some jam on this toast?"

"If it's no trouble, ma'am. Thank you, ma'am. I can't tell you how good this smells."

She leaned against the kitchen counter holding her spatula and watched him eat. He did not speak, but ate quickly, and in all that time she stared at him and said nothing.

"Well," she said when he was done. "I'll put a couple more in the pan for you."

"That's all right. This was plenty."

"You don't want them?"

He hesitated, unsure how to answer. It was a difficult question. "He wants them," she said, and cracked two eggs into her pan.

"Do I look that hungry?"

"Hungry isn't the word. You got a look like a stray dog ready to knock over trash cans for something to eat."

When she set the plate in front of him he said, "If there's somethin I can do to work this off, ma'am, I'd be glad to do it."

"Thank you. But there isn't anything."

"I wish you'd think of somethin. I appreciate you openin your kitchen to me this way. I'm not a no-account. I don't have no fear to work."

"Where are you from?"

"Missouri."

"I thought you were southern. You got a funny way of sounding. Where are you going to?"

"I don't know," he said.

She didn't ask him anything else, and stood against the counter with her spatula and again watched him eat. Then she went out and left him by himself in the kitchen.

When he was finished, he sat at the table unsure of what to do, or if he should go. While he was trying to decide, she came back, holding a pair of low black boots in one hand, a pair of black socks in the other.

"Put these on and see if they fit," she said.

"No, ma'am. I can't."

"You can and you will. Put them on. Your feet look about the right size for them."

He put on the socks and pulled the boots on over them. He was tender about sliding his left foot in, but still there was a sharp stab of pain through the ankle. He sucked in a harsh breath.

"Is there something wrong with that foot?" she asked.

"I twisted it."

"Getting off that train at the switch?"

"Yes, ma'am."

She shook her head at him. "Others will die. All for fear of a fat old man with six teeth in his head."

The boots were a little loose, perhaps a size too big. A zipper ran up the inside of each boot. The leather was black and clean and only a little scuffed at the tips. They looked as if they had hardly been worn.

"How do they fit you?"

"Good. I can't have them, though. These are just new."

"Well. They aren't doing me any good and my husband doesn't need them. He died in July."

"I'm sorry."

"So am I," she said with no change in her face. "Would you like some coffee? I didn't offer you coffee."

He did not answer so she poured him a cup, and herself a cup, and she sat down at the table.

"He died in a truck accident," she said. "It was a WPA truck. It rolled over. He wasn't the only one who died. Five other men were killed with him. Maybe you read about it. It was in lots of papers."

He didn't reply. He hadn't heard of it.

"He was driving—my husband. Some say it was his fault, that he was careless at the wheel. They investigated it. I guess maybe it was his fault." She was quiet for a while and then said, "The only good thing about his death is he doesn't have to walk around with that guilt on him. Living with having it his fault. That would have spoiled him inside."

Killian wished he was Gage. Gage would have known what to say. Gage would have reached across the table then and touched her hand. Killian sat in the dead man's boots and struggled for something. At last he blurted: "The most terrible things happen to the best people. The kindest people. Most of the time it isn't for any reason at all. It's just stupid luck. If you don't know for sure it was his fault, why make yourself feel sick thinkin it was? It's hard enough just to lose someone that means to you, without all that."

"Well. I try not to think about it," she said. "I do miss him. But I thank God every night for the twelve years we got to have together. I thank God for his daughters. I see his eyes in theirs."

"Yes," he said.

"They don't know what to do. They've never been so confused."

"Yes," he said.

They sat at the table for a little while, and then the woman said, "You look about his size all around. I can let you have one of his shirts and a pair of trousers as well as the boots."

"No, ma'am. I wouldn't feel right. Takin things from you I can't pay for."

"Stop that now. We won't talk about pay. I look for every small bit of good that can come out of such a bad thing. I'd like to give them to you. That would make me feel better," she said and smiled. He had took her hair for gray, wrapped up in a bun behind her head, but where she sat now she was in some watery sunlight from one of the windows, and he saw for the first time that her hair was blond-white just like her daughters'.

She got up and went out again. While she was away, he cleaned the dishes. The woman returned in a short time with a pair of khaki trousers and suspenders, a heavy plaid shirt, an undershirt. She directed him to a back bedroom off the kitchen, and left him while he dressed. The shirt was big and loose and had a faint male smell on it, not disagreeable; also a pipe-smoke smell. Killian had seen a corncob pipe on the mantel over the stove.

He came out with his dirty and ripped clothes under his arm, feeling clean and fresh and ordinary, a pleasant fullness in his stomach. She sat at the table holding one of his old shoes. She was smiling faintly, and peeling off the mud-caked wrap of burlap around it.

"Them shoes have earned their rest," Killian said. "I'm almost ashamed of the way I've treated 'em."

She lifted her head and contemplated him quietly. Looked at his trousers. He had rolled the trouser cuffs up over his ankles.

"I wasn't sure if he was your size or not," she said. "I thought he was bigger, but I didn't know. I thought it might only be my memory making him bigger."

"Well. He was just as big as you recall."

"He gets to seeming bigger," she said. "The further I get away from him."

There was nothing he could do for her to pay back what he owed for the clothes and the food. She told him Northampton was three miles and he ought to go now, because he would probably be hungry again by the time he got there, and there was a lunch at the Blessed Heart of the Virgin Mary where he could get a bowl of beans and a slice of bread. She told him there was a Hooverville on the east side of the Connecticut River, but if he went she advised him not to stay long, because it was often raided and men frequently arrested for squatting. At the door, she said it was better to get arrested at the trainyard than try to jump off early of the yard on a freight that was going too fast. She said she didn't want him to jump off any more trains, except ones that were stopped, or just inching along; it might be worse than a twisted ankle next time. He nodded and asked again if there was anything he could do for her. She said she had just told him something he could do for her.

He wanted to take her hand. Gage would have taken her hand and promised to pray for her and the husband she had lost. He wished he could tell her about Gage. Killian found, though, that he could not reach to touch her hand, or lift his arms in any way, and he didn't trust his voice to speak. He was often crushed by the decency of other people who had almost nothing themselves; at times he felt their kindnesses so powerfully he thought it would destroy some delicate inner part of him.

As he was crossing the yard to the road, in his new outfit, he glanced into the trees and saw the two girls in amongst the ferns. They were standing now, and each of them held a bouquet of wilty-looking old flowers, and they were staring at the ground. He stopped and watched them, wondering what they were doing, what was on the ground beyond the ferns that he couldn't see. As he stood there, both turned their heads—first the oldest girl, and then her younger sister, just as before—and looked back at him.

Killian smiled uncertainly and walked limping across the yard to them. He waded through the dew damp ferns to stand behind them. Just past where the girls stood was a patch of cleared ground, and on the ground a piece of black sacking. On the sack lay a third girl, the youngest yet, in a white dress with lace stitching at the collar and sleeves. Her bone-china white hands were folded across her breastbone, and a small bouquet was beneath them. Her eyes were closed. The muscles in her face trembled as she struggled not to smile. She was no more than five. A wreath of dried daisies around her blond hair. A heap of dead wilted flowers at her feet. A Bible opened at her side.

"Our sister Kate is dead," said the oldest girl.

"This is where we're having the wake," said the middle daughter.

Kate lay very still on top of the sacking. Her eyes remained shut, but she had to bite her lips not to grin.

"Do you want to play?" asked the middle daughter. "Do you want to play the game? You could lie down. You could be the dead person and we could cover you with flowers and read out of the Bible and sing 'Nearer My God to Thee.' "

"I'll cry," said the oldest girl. "I can make myself cry whenever I want."

Killian stood there. He looked at the girl on the ground, and then at the two mourners. He said at last, "I don't believe this is my kind of game. I don't want to be the dead person."

The oldest girl flicked her gaze across him, then stared into his face.

"Why not?" she asked. "You're dressed the part."

BOBBY CONROY COMES
BACK FROM THE DEAD

Bobby didn't know her at first. She was wounded, like him. The first thirty to arrive all got wounds. Tom Savini put them on himself.

Her face was a silvery blue, her eyes sunken into darkened hollows, and where her right ear had been was a ragged-edged hole, a gaping place that revealed a lump of wet, red bone. They sat a yard apart on the stone wall around the fountain, which was switched off. She had her pages balanced on one knee—three pages in all, stapled together—and was looking them over, frowning with concentration. Bobby had read his while he was waiting in line to go into makeup.

Her jeans reminded him of Harriet Rutherford. There were patches all over them, patches that looked as if they had been made out of kerchiefs; squares of red and dark blue, with paisley patterns printed on them. Harriet was always wearing jeans like that. Patches sewn into the butt of a girl's Levi's still turned Bobby on.

His gaze followed the bend of her legs down to where her blue jeans flared at the ankle, then on to her bare feet. She had kicked her sandals off, and was twisting the toes of one foot into the toes of the other. When he saw this he felt his heart lunge with a kind of painful-sweet shock.

"Harriet?" he said. "Is that little Harriet Rutherford who I used to write love poems to in high school?"

She peered at him sideways, over her shoulder. She didn't need to answer; he knew it was her. She stared for a long, measuring time, and then her eyes opened a little wider. They were a vivid, very undead green, and for an instant he saw them brighten with recognition and unmistakable excitement. But she turned her head away, went back to perusing her pages.

"No one ever wrote me love poems in high school," she said. "I'd remember. I would've died of happiness."

"In detention. Remember we got two weeks after the cooking show skit? You had a cucumber carved like a dick. You said it needed to stew for an hour and stuck it in your pants. It was the finest moment in the history of the Die Laughing Comedy Collective."

"No. I have a good memory and I don't recall this comedy troupe." She looked back down at the pages balanced on her knee. "Do you remember any details about these supposed poems?"

"How do you mean?"

"A line. Maybe if you could remember something about one of these poems—one line of heartrending verse—it would all come flooding back to me."

He didn't know if he could at first; he stared at her blankly, his tongue pressed to his lower lip, trying to call something back and his mind stubbornly blank.

Then he opened his mouth and began to speak, remembering as he went along: *"I love to watch you in the shower. I hope that's not obscene."*

"But when I see you soap your boobs, I get sticky in my jeans!" Harriet cried, turning her body toward him. "Bobby Conroy, *goddamn*, come here and hug me without screwing up my makeup."

He leaned into her and put his arms around her narrow back. He shut his eyes and squeezed, feeling absurdly happy, maybe the happiest he had felt since moving back in with his parents. He had not spent a day in Monroeville when he didn't think about seeing her. He was depressed, he daydreamed about her, stories that began with exactly this moment—or not exactly *this* moment, he had not imagined them both made up like partially decomposed corpses, but close enough.

When he woke every morning, in his bedroom over his parents' garage, he felt flat and listless. He'd lie on his lumpy mattress and stare at the skylights overhead. The skylights were milky with dust, and through them every sky appeared the same, a bland, formless white. Nothing in him wanted to get up. What made it worse was he still remembered what it felt like to wake in that same bed with a teenager's sense of his own limitless possibilities, to wake charged with enthusiasm for the day. If he daydreamed about meeting Harriet again, and falling into their old friendship—and if these early morning daydreams sometimes turned explicitly sexual, if he remembered being with her in her father's shed, her back on the stained cement, her too-skinny legs pulled open, her socks still on—then at least it was something to stir his blood a little, get him going. All his other daydreams had thorns on them. Handling them always threatened a sudden sharp prick of pain.

They were still holding each other when a boy spoke, close by. "Mom, who are you hugging?"

Bobby Conroy opened his eyes, shifted his gaze to the right. A little blue-faced dead boy with limp black hair was staring at them. He wore a hooded sweatshirt, the hood pulled up.

Harriet's grip on Bobby relaxed. Then, slowly, her arms slid away. Bobby regarded the boy for an instant longer—the kid was no older than six—and then dropped his eyes to Harriet's hand, the wedding band on her ring finger.

Bobby looked back at the kid, forced a smile. Bobby had been to more than seven hundred auditions during his years in New York City, and he had a whole catalog of phony smiles.

"Hey, chumley," Bobby said. "I'm Bobby Conroy. Your mom and me are old buddies from way back when mastodons walked the earth."

"Bobby is my name too," the boy said. "Do you know a lot about dinosaurs? I'm a big dinosaur guy myself."

Bobby felt a sick pang that seemed to go right through the middle of him. He glanced at her face—didn't want to, couldn't help himself—and found Harriet watching him. Her smile was anxious and compressed.

"My husband picked it," she said. She was, for some reason, patting Bobby's leg. "After a Yankee. He's from Albany originally."

"I know about mastodons," Bobby said to the boy, surprised to find that his voice sounded just the same as it ever did. "Big hairy elephants the size of school buses. They once roamed the entire Pennsylvanian plateau, and left mountainous mastodon poops everywhere, one of which later became Pittsburgh."

The kid grinned, and threw a quick glance at his mother, perhaps to appraise what she made of this offhand reference to poop. She smiled indulgently.

Bobby saw the kid's hand and recoiled. "Ugh! Wow, that's the best wound I've seen all day. What is that, a fake hand?"

Three fingers were missing from the boy's left hand. Bobby grabbed it and yanked on it, expecting it to come off. But it was warm and fleshy under the blue makeup, and the kid pulled it out of Bobby's grip.

"No," he said. "It's just my hand. That's the way it is."

Bobby blushed so intensely his ears stung, and was grateful for his makeup. Harriet touched Bobby's wrist.

"He really doesn't have those fingers," she said.

Bobby looked at her, struggling to frame an apology. Her smile was a little fretful now, but she wasn't visibly angry with him, and the hand on his arm was a good sign.

"I stuck them into the table saw, but I don't remember because I was so little," the boy explained.

"Dean is in lumber," Harriet said.

"Is Dean staggering around here somewhere?" Bobby asked, craning his head and making a show of looking around, although of course he had no idea what Harriet's Dean might look like. Both floors of the atrium at the center of the mall were crowded with other people like them, made up to look like the recent dead. They sat together on benches, or stood together in groups, chatting, laughing at one another's wounds, or looking over the mimeographed pages they had been given of the screenplay. The mall was closed—steel gates pulled down in front of the entrances to the stores—no one in the place but the film crew and the undead.

"No, he dropped us off and went in to work."

"On a Sunday?"

"He owns his own yard."

It was as good a setup for a punch line as he had ever heard, and he paused, searching for just the right one . . . and then it came to him that making wisecracks about Dean's choice of work to Dean's wife in front of Dean's five-year-old might be ill-advised, and never mind that he and Harriet had once been best friends and the royal couple of the Die Laughing Comedy Collective their senior year in high school. Bobby said, "He does? Good for him."

"I like the big gross tear in your face," the little kid said, pointing at Bobby's brow. Bobby had a nasty scalp wound, the skin laid open to the lumpy bone. "Didn't you think the guy who made us into dead people was cool?"

Bobby had actually been a little creeped out by Tom Savini, who kept referring to an open book of autopsy photographs while applying Bobby's makeup. The people in those pictures, with their maimed flesh and slack, unhappy faces, were really dead, not getting up later to have a cup of coffee at the craft services table. Savini studied their wounds with a quiet appreciation, the same as any painter surveying the subject of his art.

But Bobby could see what the kid meant about how he was cool. With his black leather jacket, motorcycle boots, black beard, and memorable eyebrows—thick black eyebrows that arched sharply upward, like Dr. Spock or Bela Lugosi—he looked like a death-metal rock god.

Someone was clapping their hands. Bobby glanced around. The director, George Romero, stood close to the bottom of the escalators, a bearish man well over six feet tall, with a thick brown beard. Bobby had noticed that many of the men working on the crew had beards. A lot of them had shoulder-length hair too, and wore army-navy castoffs and motorcycle boots like Savini, so that they resembled a band of counterculture revolutionaries.

Bobby and Harriet and little Bob gathered with the other extras to hear what Romero had to say. He had a booming, confident voice and when he grinned, his cheeks dimpled, visible in spite of the beard. He asked if anyone present knew anything about making movies. A few people, Bobby included, raised their hands. Romero said thank God someone in this place does, and everyone laughed. He said he wanted to welcome them all to the world of big-budget Hollywood filmmaking, and everyone laughed at that too, because George Romero made pictures only in Pennsylvania, and everyone knew *Dawn of the Dead* was lower than low-budget, it was a half step above no-budget. He said he was grateful to them all for coming out today, and that for ten hours of grueling work, which would test them body and soul, they would be paid *in cash*, a sum so colossal he dare not say the number aloud, he could only show it. He held aloft a dollar bill, and there was more laughter. Then Tom Savini, up on the second floor, leaned over the railing, and shouted, "Don't laugh, that's more than most of us are getting paid to work on this turkey."

"Lots of people are in this film as a labor of love," George Romero said. "Tom is in it because he likes squirting pus on people." Some in the crowd moaned. "Fake pus! Fake pus!" Romero cried.

"You *hope* it was fake pus," Savini intoned from somewhere above, but he was already moving away from the railing, out of sight.

More laughter. Bobby knew a thing or two about comic patter, and had a suspicion that this bit of the speech was rehearsed, and had been issued just this way, more than once.

Romero talked for a while about the plot. The recently dead were coming back to life; they liked to eat people; in the face of the crisis, the government had collapsed; four young heroes had sought shelter in this mall. Bobby's attention wandered, and he found himself looking down at the other Bobby, at Harriet's boy. Little Bob had a long, solemn face, dark chocolate eyes, and lots of thick black hair, limp and disheveled. In fact, the kid bore a passing resemblance to Bobby himself, who also had brown eyes, a slim face, and a thick untidy mass of black hair on his head.

Bobby wondered if Dean looked like him. The thought made his blood race strangely. What if Dean dropped in to see how Harriet and little Bobby were doing, and the man turned out to be his exact twin? The thought was so alarming it made him feel briefly weak—but then he remembered he was made up like a corpse, blue face, scalp wound. Even if they looked exactly alike they wouldn't look anything alike.

Romero delivered some final instructions on how to walk like a zombie—he demonstrated by allowing his eyes to roll back in their sockets and his face to go slack—and then promised they'd be ready to begin filming the first shot in a few minutes.

Harriet pivoted on her heel, turned to face him, her fist on her hip, eyelids fluttering theatrically. He turned at the same time, and they almost bumped into each other. She opened her mouth to speak but nothing came out. They were standing too close to each other, and the unexpected physical proximity seemed to throw her. He didn't know what to say either, all thought suddenly wiped from his mind. She laughed, and shook her head, a reaction that struck him as artificial, an expression of anxiety, not happiness.

"Let's set, pardner," she said. He remembered that when a skit wasn't going well, and she got rattled, she sometimes slipped into a big, drawling John Wayne impersonation on stage, a nervous habit he had hated then and that he found, in this moment, endearing.

"Are we going to have something to do soon?" little Bob asked.

"Soon," she said. "Why don't you practice being a zombie? Go on, lurch around for a while."

Bobby and Harriet sat down at the edge of the fountain again. Her hands were small, bony fists on her thighs. She stared into her lap, her eyes blank, gaze directed inward. She was digging the toes of one bare foot into the toes of the other again.

He spoke. One of them had to say something.

"I can't believe you're married and you have a kid!" he said, in the same tone of happy astonishment he reserved for friends who had just told him they had been cast in a part he himself had auditioned for. "I love this kid you're dragging around with you. He's so cute. But then, who can resist a little kid who looks half rotted?"

She seemed to come back from wherever she had been, smiled at him—almost shyly.

He went on, "And you better be ready to tell me everything about this Dean guy."

"He's coming by later. He's going to take us out to lunch. You should come."

"That could be fun!" Bobby cried, and made a mental note to take his enthusiasm down a notch.

"He can be really shy the first time he meets someone, so don't expect too much."

Bobby waved a hand in the air: *pish-posh*. "It's going to be great. We'll have lots to talk about. I've always been fascinated with lumberyards and—plywood."

This was taking a chance, joshing her about the husband he didn't know. But she smirked and said: "Everything you ever wanted to know about two-by-fours but were afraid to ask."

And for a moment they were both smiling, a little foolishly, knees almost touching. They had never really figured out how to talk to each other. They were always half on stage, trying to use whatever the other person said to set up the next punch line. That much, anyway, hadn't changed.

"God, I can't believe running into you here," she said. "I've wondered about you. I've thought about you a lot."

"You have?"

"I figured you'd be famous by now," she said.

"Hey, that makes two of us," Bobby said and winked. Immediately he wished he could take the wink back. It was fake and he didn't want to be fake with her. He hurried on, answering a question she hadn't asked. "I'm settling in. Been back for three months. I'm staying with my parents for a while, kind of readapting to Monroeville."

She nodded, still regarding him steadily, with a seriousness that made him uncomfortable. "How's it going?"

"I'm making a life," Bobby lied.

IN BETWEEN SETUPS, Bobby and Harriet and little Bob told stories about how they had died.

"I was a comedian in New York City," Bobby said, fingering his scalp wound. "Something tragic happened when I went on stage."

"Yeah," Harriet said. "Your act."

"Something that had never happened before."

"What, people laughed?"

"I was my usual brilliant self. People were rolling on the floor."

"Convulsions of agony."

"And then as I was taking my final bow—a terrible accident. A stagehand up in the rafters dropped a forty-pound sandbag right on my head. But at least I died to the sound of applause."

"They were applauding the stagehand," Harriet said.

The little boy looked seriously up into Bobby's face, and took his hand. "I'm sorry you got hit in the head." His lips grazed Bobby's knuckles with a dry kiss.

Bobby stared down at him. His hand tingled where little Bob's mouth had touched it.

"He's always been the kissiest, huggiest kid you ever met," Harriet said. "He's got all this pent-up affection. At the slightest sign of weakness he's ready to slobber on you." As she said this she ruffled little Bobby's hair. "What killed you, squirt?"

He held up his hand, waggled his stumps. "My fingers got cut off on Dad's table saw and I bled to death."

Harriet went on smiling but her eyes seemed to film over slightly. She fished around in her pocket and found a quarter. "Go get a gumball, bud."

He snatched it and ran.

"People must think we're the most careless parents," she said, staring expressionlessly after her son. "But it was no one's fault about his fingers."

"I'm sure."

"The table saw was unplugged and he wasn't even two. He never plugged anything in before. We didn't know he knew how. Dean was right there with him. It just happened so fast. Do you know how many things had to go wrong, all at the same time, for that to happen? Dean thinks the sound of the saw coming on scared him and he reached up to try and shut it off. He thought he'd be in trouble." She was briefly silent, watching her son work the gumball machine, then said, "I always thought about my kid—this is the one part of my life

I'm going to get right. No indiscriminate fuck-ups about this. I was planning how when he was fifteen he'd make love to the most beautiful girl in school. How he'd be able to play five instruments and he'd blow everyone away with all his talent. How he'd be the funny kid who seems to know everyone." She paused again, and then added, "He'll be the funny kid now. The funny kid always has something wrong with him. That's why he's funny—to shift people's attention to something else."

In the silence that followed this statement, Bobby had several thoughts in rapid succession. The first was that *he* had been the funny kid when he was in school; did Harriet think there had been something wrong with *him* he had been covering for? Then he remembered they were *both* the funny kids, and thought: *What was wrong with us?*

It had to be something, otherwise they'd be together now and the boy at the gumball machine would be theirs. The thought that crossed his mind next was that, if little Bobby was *their* little Bobby, he'd still have ten fingers. He felt a seething dislike of Dean the lumberman, an ignorant squarehead whose idea of spending together-time with his kid probably meant taking him to the fair to watch a truck-pull.

An assistant director started clapping her hands and hollering down for the undead to get into their positions. Little Bob trotted back to them.

"Mom," he said, the gumball in his cheek. "You didn't say how you died." He was looking at her torn-off ear.

"I know," Bobby said. "She ran into this old friend at the mall and they got talking. You know, and I mean they *really* got talking. *Hours* of blab. Finally, her old friend said, 'Hey, I don't want to chew your ear off here.' And your mom said, 'Aw, don't worry about it . . .' "

"A great man once said, 'lend me your ears,' " Harriet said. She smacked the palm of her hand hard against her forehead. "Why did I listen to him?"

EXCEPT FOR THE dark hair, Dean didn't look anything like him. Dean was *short*. Bobby wasn't prepared for how short. He was shorter than Harriet, who was herself not much over five-and-a-half feet tall. When they kissed, Dean had to stretch his neck. He was compact, and solidly built, broad at the shoulders, deep through the chest, narrow at the hips. He wore thick glasses with gray plastic frames, the eyes behind them the color of unpolished pewter. They were shy eyes—his gaze met Bobby's when Harriet introduced them, darted away, returned, and darted away again—not to mention old; at the corners of them the skin was creased in a web of finely etched laugh lines. He was older than Harriet, maybe by as many as ten years.

They had only just been introduced when Dean cried suddenly, "Oh, you're *that* Bobby! You're *funny* Bobby. You know, we almost didn't name our *kid* Bobby because of you. I've had it drilled into me, if I ever run into you, I'm supposed to reassure you that naming him Bobby was my idea. 'Cause of Bobby Murcer. Ever since I was old enough to imagine having kids of my own I always thought—"

"I'm funny!" Harriet's son interrupted.

Dean caught him under the armpits and lofted him into the air. "You sure are!"

Bobby wasn't positive he wanted to have lunch with them, but Harriet looped her arm through his and marched him toward the doors out to the parking lot, and her shoulder—warm and bare—was leaning against his, so there was really no choice.

Bobby didn't notice the other people in the diner staring at them, and forgot they were in makeup until the waitress approached. She was hardly out of her teens, with a head of frizzy yellow hair that bounced as she walked.

"We're dead," little Bobby announced.

"Gotcha," the girl said, nodding and pointing her ball-point pen at them. "I'm guessing you either all work on the horror movie, or you already tried the special, which is it?"

Dean laughed, dry, bawling laughter. Dean was as easy a laugh as Bobby had ever met. Dean laughed at almost everything Harriet said, and most of what Bobby himself said. Sometimes he laughed so hard the people at the other tables started in alarm. Once he had control of himself, he would apologize with unmistakable earnestness, his face flushed a delicate shade of rose, eyes gleaming and wet. That was when Bobby began to see at least one possible answer to the question that had been on his mind ever since learning she was married to Dean-who-owned-his-own-lumberyard: *Why him?* Well—he was a willing audience, there was that.

"So I thought you were acting in New York City," Dean said at last. "What brings you back?"

"Failure," Bobby said.

"Oh—I'm sorry to hear that. What are you up to now? Are you doing some comedy locally?"

"You could say that. Only around here they call it substitute teaching."

"Oh! You're teaching! How do you like it?"

"It's great. I always planned to work either in film or television or junior high. That I should finally make it so big subbing eighth-grade gym—it's a dream come true."

Dean laughed, and chunks of pulverized chicken-fried steak flew out of his mouth.

"I'm sorry. This is awful," he said. "Food everywhere. You must think I'm a total pig."

"No, it's okay. Can I have the waitress bring you something? A glass of water? A trough?"

Dean bent so his forehead was almost touching his plate, his laughter wheezy, asthmatic. "Stop. Really."

Bobby stopped, but not because Dean said. For the first time he had noticed that Harriet's knee was knocking his under the table. He wondered if this was intentional, and the first chance he got he leaned back and looked. No, not intentional. She had kicked her sandals off and was digging the toes of one foot into the other, so fiercely that sometimes her right knee swung out and banged his.

"Wow, I would've loved to have a teacher like you. Someone who can make kids laugh," Dean said.

Bobby chewed and chewed, but couldn't tell what he was eating. It didn't have any taste.

Dean let out a shaky sigh, wiped the corners of his eyes again. "Of course, I'm not funny. I can't even remember knock-knock jokes. I'm not good for much else except working. And Harriet is *so* funny. Sometimes she puts on shows for Bobby and me, with these dirty socks on her hands. We get laughing so hard we can't breathe. She calls it the trailer-park Muppet show. Sponsored by Pabst Blue Ribbon." He started laughing and thumping the table again. Harriet stared intently into her lap. Dean said, "I'd love to see her do that on Carson. This is—what do you call them, routines?—this could be a classic routine."

"Sure sounds it," Bobby said. "I'm surprised Ed McMahon hasn't already called to see if she's available."

WHEN DEAN DROPPED them back at the mall and left for the lumberyard, the mood was different. Harriet seemed distant; it was hard to draw her into any kind of conversation—not that Bobby felt like trying very hard. He was suddenly irritable. All the fun seemed to have gone out of playing a dead person for the day. It was mostly waiting—waiting for the gaffers to get the lights just so, for Tom Savini to touch up a wound that was starting to look a little too much like latex, not enough like ragged flesh—and Bobby was sick of it. The sight of other people having a good time annoyed him. Several zombies stood in a group, playing Hacky Sack with a quivering red spleen, and laughing. It made a juicy splat every time it hit the floor. Bobby wanted to snarl at them for being so merry. Hadn't any of them heard of method acting, Stanislavsky? They should all be sitting apart from one another, moaning unhappily and fondling giblets. He heard *himself* moan aloud, an angry, frustrated sound, and little Bobby asked what was wrong. He said he was just practicing. Little Bob went to watch the Hacky Sack game.

Harriet said, without looking at him, "That was a good lunch, wasn't it?"

"*Sen*-sational," Bobby said, thinking, *Better be careful.* He was restless, charged with an energy he didn't know how to displace. "I feel like I really hit it off with Dean. He reminds me of my grandfather. I had this great grandfather who could wiggle his ears and who thought my name was Evan. He'd give me a quarter to stack wood for him, fifty cents if I'd do it with my shirt off. Say, how old *is* Dean?"

They had been walking together. Now Harriet stiffened, stopped. Her head swiveled in his direction, but her hair was in front of her eyes, making it hard to read the expression in them. "He's nine years older than me. So what?"

"So nothing. I'm just glad you're happy."

"I *am* happy," Harriet said, her voice a half octave too high.

"Did he get down on one knee when he proposed?"

Harriet nodded, her mouth crimped, suspicious.

"Did you have to help him up afterward?" Bobby asked. His own voice was sounding a little off-key, too, and he thought, *Stop now.* It was like a cartoon; he saw Wile E. Coyote strapped to the front of a steam engine, jamming his feet down on the rails to try to brake the train, smoke boiling up from his heels, feet swelling, glowing red.

"Oh, you prick," she said.

"I'm sorry!" He grinned, holding his hands palms up in front of him. "Kidding, kidding. Funny Bobby, you know. I can't help myself." She hesitated—had been about to turn away—not sure whether she should believe him or not. Bobby wiped his mouth with his hand. "So we know what you do to make Dean laugh. What's he do to make you laugh? Oh, that's right, he isn't *funny*. Well, what's he do to make your heart race? Besides kiss you with his dentures out?"

"Leave me alone, Bobby," she said. She turned away, but he came around to get back in front of her, keep her from walking off.

"No."

"Stop."

"Can't," he said, and suddenly he understood he was angry with her. "If he isn't funny, he must be something. I need to know what."

"*Patient,*" she said.

"Patient," Bobby repeated. It stunned him—that this could be her answer.

"With me."

"With you," he said.

"With Robert."

"Patient," Bobby said. Then he couldn't say anything more for a moment because he was out of breath. He felt suddenly that his makeup was itching his face. He wished that when he started to press she had just walked away from him, or told him to fuck off, or hit him even, wished she had responded with anything but *patient*. He swallowed. "That's not good enough." Knowing he couldn't stop now, the train was going into the canyon, Wile E. Coyote's eyes bugging three feet out of his head in terror. "I wanted to meet whoever you were with and feel sick with jealousy, but instead I just feel sick. I wanted you to fall in love with someone good-looking and creative and brilliant, a novelist, a playwright, someone with a sense of humor and a fourteen-inch dong. Not a guy with a buzz cut and a lumberyard, who thinks erotic massage involves a tube of Ben-Gay."

She smeared at the tears dribbling down her face with the backs of her hands. "I knew you'd hate him, but I didn't think you'd be mean."

"It's not that I hate him. What's to hate? He's not doing anything any other guy in his position wouldn't do. If I was two feet tall and geriatric, I'd *leap* at the chance to have a piece of ass like you. You bet he's patient. He better be. He ought to be down on his fucking knees every night, bathing your feet in sacramental oils, that you'd give him the time of day."

"You had your chance," she said. She was struggling not to let her crying slip out of control. The muscles in her face quivered with the effort, pulling her expression into a grimace.

"It's not about what chances I had. It's about what chances you had."

This time when she pivoted away from him, he let her go. She put her hands over her face. Her shoulders were jerking and she was making choked little sounds as she went. He watched her walk to the wall around the fountain where they had met earlier in the day. Then he remembered the boy and turned to look, his heart drumming hard, wondering what little Bobby might've seen or heard. But the kid was running down the broad concourse, kicking the spleen in front of him, which had now collected a mass of dust bunnies around it. Two other dead children were trying to kick it away from him.

Bobby watched them play for a while. A pass went wide, and the spleen skidded past him. He put a foot on it to stop it. It flexed unpleasantly beneath the sole of his shoe. The boys stopped three yards off, stood there breathing hard, awaiting him. He scooped it up.

"Go out," he said, and lobbed it to little Bobby, who made a basket catch and hauled away with his head down and the other kids in pursuit.

When he turned to peek at Harriet he saw her watching him, her palms pressed hard against her knees. He waited for her to look away, but she didn't, and finally he took her steady gaze as an invitation to approach.

He crossed to the fountain, sat down beside her. He was still working out how to begin his apology when she spoke.

"I wrote you. You stopped writing back," she said. Her bare feet were wrestling with each other again.

"I hate how overbearing your right foot is," he said. "Why can't it give the left foot a little space?" But she wasn't listening to him.

"It didn't matter," she said. Her voice was congested and hoarse. The makeup was oil-based, and in spite of her tears, hadn't streaked. "I wasn't mad. I knew we couldn't have a relationship, just seeing each other when you came home for Christmas." She swallowed thickly. "I really thought some-one would put you in their sitcom. Every time I thought about that—about seeing you on TV, and hearing people laugh when you said things—I'd get this big, stupid smile on my face. I could float through a whole afternoon thinking about it. I don't understand what in the world could've made you come back to Monroeville."

But he had already said what in the world drew him back to his parents and his bedroom over the garage. Dean had asked in the diner, and Bobby had answered him truthfully.

One Thursday night, only last spring, he had gone on early in a club in the Village. He did his twenty minutes, earned a steady if-not-precisely-overwhelming murmur of laughter, and a spatter of applause when he came off. He found a place at the bar to hear some of the other acts. He was just about to slide off his stool and go home when Robin Williams leaped on stage. He was in town, cruising the clubs, testing material. Bobby quickly shifted his weight back onto his stool and sat listening, his pulse thudding heavily in his throat.

He couldn't explain to Harriet the import of what he had seen then. Bobby saw a man clutching the edge of a table with one hand, his date's thigh with the other, grabbing both so hard his knuckles were drained of all color. He was bent over with tears dripping off his face, and his laughter was high and shrill and convulsive, more animal than human, the sound of a dingo or something. He was shaking his head from side to side and waving a hand in the air, *Stop, please, don't do this to me.* It was hilarity to the point of distress.

Robin Williams saw the desperate man, broke away from a discourse on jerking off, pointed at him and shouted, "*You!* Yes, *you,* frantic hyena-man! You get a free pass to every show I do for the rest of my motherfucking life!" And then there was a sound rising in the crowd, more than laughter or applause, although it included both. It was a low, thunderous rumble of uncontained delight, a sound so immense it was felt as much as heard, a thing that caused the bones in Bobby's chest to hum.

Bobby himself didn't laugh once, and when he left, his stomach was churning. His feet fell strangely, heavily against the sidewalk, and for some time he did not know his way home. When at last he was in his apartment, he sat on the edge of his bed, his suspenders pulled off and his shirt unbuttoned, and for the first time felt things were hopeless.

He saw something flash in Harriet's hand. She was jiggling some quarters.

"Going to call someone?" he asked.

"Dean," she said. "For a ride."

"Don't."

"I'm not staying. I can't stay."

He watched her tormented feet, toes struggling together, and finally nodded. They stood at the same time. They were, once again, standing uncomfortably close.

"See you, then," she said.

"See you," he said. He wanted to reach for her hand, but didn't, wanted to say something, but couldn't think what.

"Are there a couple people around here who want to volunteer to get shot?" George Romero asked from less than three feet away. "It's a guaranteed close-up in the finished film."

Bobby and Harriet put their hands up at the same time.

"Me," Bobby said.

"Me," said Harriet, stepping on Bobby's foot as she moved to get George Romero's attention. "Me!"

"IT'S GOING TO be a great picture, Mr. Romero," Bobby said. They were standing shoulder to shoulder, making small talk, waiting for Savini to finish wiring Harriet with her squib—a condom partially filled with cane syrup and food coloring that would explode to look like a bullet hit. Bobby was already wired . . . in more than one sense of the word. "Someday everyone in Pittsburgh is going to claim they walked dead in this movie."

"You kiss ass like a pro," Romero said. "Do you have a show-biz background?"

"Six years off-Broadway," Bobby said. "Plus I played most of the comedy clubs."

"Ah, but now you're back in greater Pittsburgh. Good career move, kid. Stick around here, you'll be a star in no time."

Harriet skipped over to Bobby, her hair flouncing. "I'm going to get my tit blown off!"

"Magnificent," Bobby said. "People just have to keep on going, because you never know when something wonderful is going to happen."

George Romero led them to their marks, and walked them through what he wanted from them. Lights pointed into silver, spangly umbrellas, casting an even white glow and a dry heat over a ten-foot stretch of floor. A lumpy striped mattress rested on the tiles, just to one side of a square pillar.

Harriet would get hit first, in the chest. She was supposed to jerk back, then keep coming forward, showing as little reaction to the shot as she could muster. Bobby would take the next bullet in the head and it would bring him down. The squib was hidden under one latex fold of his scalp wound. The wires that would cause the Trojan to explode were threaded through his hair.

"You can slump first, and slide down and to the side," George Romero said. "Drop to one knee if you want, and then spill yourself out of the frame. If you're feeling a bit more acrobatic you can fall straight back—just be sure you hit the mattress. No one needs to get hurt."

It was just Bobby and Harriet in the shot, which would picture them from the waist up. The other extras lined the walls of the shopping-mall corridor, watching them. Their stares, their steady murmuring, induced in Bobby a pleasurable burst of adrenaline. Tom Savini knelt on the floor, just outside the framed shot, with a metal box in hand, wires snaking across the floor toward Bobby and Harriet. Little Bob sat next to him, his hands cupped under his chin, squeezing the spleen, his eyes shiny with anticipation. Savini had told little Bob all about what was going to happen, preparing the kid for the sight of blood bursting from his mother's chest, but little Bob wasn't worried. "I've been seeing gross stuff all day. It isn't scary. I like it." Savini was letting him keep the spleen as a souvenir.

"Roll," Romero said. Bobby twitched—what, they were rolling? Already? He only just gave them their marks! Christ, Romero was still standing in front of the camera!—and for an instant Bobby grabbed Harriet's hand. She squeezed his fingers, let go. Romero eased himself out of the shot. "Action."

Bobby rolled his eyes back in his head, rolled them back so far he couldn't see where he was going. He let his face hang slack. He took a plodding step forward.

"Shoot the girl," Romero said.

Bobby didn't see her squib go off because he was a step ahead of her. But he heard it, a loud, ringing crack that echoed; and he smelled it, a sudden pungent whiff of gunpowder. Harriet grunted softly.

"Annnd," Romero said. "Now the other one."

It was like a gunshot going off next to his head. The bang of the blasting cap was so loud it immediately deafened his eardrums. He snapped backward, spinning on his heel. His shoulder slammed into something just behind him, he didn't see what. He caught a blurred glimpse of the square pillar next to the mattress, and in that instant was seized with a jolt of inspiration. He smashed his forehead into it on his way down, and as he reeled away, saw he had left a crimson flower on the white plaster.

He hit the mattress, the cushion springy enough to provide

a little bounce. He blinked. His eyes were watering, creating a visual distortion, a subtle warping of things. The air above him was filled with blue smoke. The center of his head stung. His face was splattered with cool, sticky fluid. As the ringing in his ears faded, he simultaneously became aware of two things. The first was the sound, a low, subterranean bellow, a distant, steady rumble of applause. The sound filled him like breath. George Romero was moving toward him, also clapping, smiling in that way that made dimples in his beard. The second thing he noticed was Harriet curled against him, her hand on his chest.

"Did I knock you down?" he asked.

" 'Fraid so," she said.

"I knew it was only a matter of time before I got you in bed with me," he said.

Harriet smiled, an easy contented smile like he hadn't seen at any other time the whole day. Her blood-drenched bosom rose and fell against his side.

Little Bob ran to the edge of the mattress and leaped onto it with them. Harriet got her arm underneath him, scooped him up, and rolled him into the narrow space between her and Bobby. Little Bob grinned and put his thumb in his mouth. Bobby's face was close to the boy's head, and suddenly he was aware of the smell of little Bob's shampoo, a melon-flavored scent.

Harriet watched him steadily across her son, still with that same smile on her face. His gaze drifted toward the ceiling, the banks of skylights, the crisp, blue sky beyond. Nothing in him wanted to get up, wanted to move past the next few moments. He wondered what Harriet did with herself when Dean was at work and little Bobby was at school. Tomorrow was a Monday; he didn't know if he would be teaching or free. He hoped free. The workweek stretched ahead of him, empty of responsibilities or concerns, limitless in its possibilities. The three of them, Bobby, and the boy, and Harriet, lay on the mattress, their bodies pressed close together and there was no movement but for their breathing.

George Romero turned back to them, shaking his head. "That was great, when you hit the pillar, and you left that big streak of gore. We should do it again, just the same way. This time you could leave some brains behind. What do you two kids say? Either one of you feel like a do-over?"

"Me," Bobby said.

"Me," said Harriet. "Me."

"Yes, please," said little Bobby, around the thumb in his mouth.

"I guess it's unanimous," Bobby said. "Everyone wants a do-over."

MY FATHER'S MASK

On the drive to Big Cat Lake, we played a game. It was my mother's idea. It was dusk by the time we reached the state highway, and when there was no light left in the sky, except for a splash of cold, pale brilliance in the west, she told me they were looking for me.

"They're playing-card people," she said. "Queens and kings. They're so flat they can slip themselves under doors. They'll be coming from the other direction, from the lake. Searching for us. Trying to head us off. Get out of sight whenever someone comes the other way. We can't protect you from them—not on the road. Quick, get down. Here comes one of them now."

I stretched out across the backseat and watched the headlights of an approaching car race across the ceiling. Whether I was playing along or just stretching out to get comfortable, I wasn't sure. I was in a funk. I had been hoping for a sleepover at my friend Luke Redhill's, Ping-Pong and late-night TV with Luke (and Luke's leggy older sister Jane, and her lush-haired friend Melinda), but had come home from school to find suitcases in the driveway and my father loading the car. That was the first I heard we were spending the night at my grandfather's cabin on Big Cat Lake. I couldn't be angry at my parents for not letting me in on their plans in advance, because they probably hadn't made plans in advance. It was very likely they had decided to go up to Big Cat Lake over lunch. My parents didn't have plans. They had impulses and a thirteen-year-old son and they saw no reason to ever let the latter upset the former.

"Why can't you protect me?" I asked.

My mother said, "Because there are some things a mother's love and a father's courage can't keep you safe from. Besides, who could fight them? You know about playing-card people. How they all go around with little golden hatchets and little silver swords. Have you ever noticed how well armed most good hands of poker are?"

"No accident the first card game everyone learns is War," my father said, driving with one wrist slung across the wheel. "They're all variations on the same plot. Metaphorical kings fighting over the world's limited supplies of wenches and money."

My mother regarded me seriously over the back of her seat, her eyes luminous in the dark.

"We're in trouble, Jack," she said. "We're in terrible trouble."

"Okay," I said.

"It's been building for a while. We kept it from you at first, because we didn't want to scare you. But you have to know. It's right for you to know. We're—well, you see—we don't have any money anymore. It's the playing-card people. They've been working against us, poisoning investments, tying assets up in red tape. They've been spreading the most awful rumors about your father at work. I don't want to upset you with the crude details. They make menacing phone calls. They call me up in the middle of the day and talk about the awful things they're going to do to me. To you. To all of us."

"They put something in the clam sauce the other night, and gave me wicked runs," my father said. "I thought I was going to die. And our dry cleaning came back with funny white stains on it. That was them too."

My mother laughed. I've heard that dogs have six kinds of barks, each with a specific meaning: *intruder, let's play, I need to pee.* My mother had a certain number of laughs, each with an unmistakable meaning and identity, all of them wonderful. This laugh, convulsive and unpolished, was the way she responded to dirty jokes; also to accusations, to being caught making mischief.

I laughed with her, sitting up, my stomach unknotting. She had been so wide-eyed and solemn, for a moment I had started to forget she was making it all up.

My mother leaned toward my father and ran her finger over his lips, miming the closing of a zipper.

"You let me tell it," she said. "I forbid you to talk anymore."

"If we're in so much financial trouble, I could go and live with Luke for a while," I said. *And Jane*, I thought. "I wouldn't want to be a burden on the family."

She looked back at me again. "The money I'm not worried about. There's an appraiser coming by tomorrow. There are some wonderful old things in that house, things your grandfather left us. We're going to see about selling them."

My grandfather, Upton, had died the year before, in a way no one liked to discuss, a death that had no place in his life, a horror-movie conclusion tacked on to a blowsy, Capra-esque comedy. He was in New York, where he kept a condo on the fifth floor of a brownstone on the Upper East Side, one of many places he owned. He called the elevator and stepped through the doors when they opened—but there was no elevator there, and he fell four stories. The fall did not kill him. He lived for another day, at the bottom of the elevator shaft. The elevator was old and slow and complained loudly whenever it had to move, not unlike most of the building's residents. No one heard him screaming.

"Why don't we sell the Big Cat Lake house?" I asked. "Then we'd be rolling in the loot."

"Oh, we couldn't do that. It isn't ours. It's held in trust for all of us, me, you, Aunt Blake, the Greenly twins. And even if it did belong to us, we couldn't sell it. It's always been in our family."

For the first time since getting into the car, I thought I understood why we were *really* going to Big Cat Lake. I saw at last that my weekend plans had been sacrificed on the altar of interior decoration. My mother loved to decorate. She loved picking out curtains, stained-glass lamp-shades, unique iron knobs for the cabinets. Someone had put her in charge of re-decorating the cabin on Big Cat Lake—or, more likely, she had put herself in charge—and she meant to begin by getting rid of all the clutter.

I felt like a chump for letting her distract me from my bad mood with one of her games.

"I wanted to spend the night with Luke," I said.

My mother directed a sly, knowing look at me from beneath half-lowered eyelids, and I felt a sudden scalp-prickle of unease. It was a look that made me wonder what she knew and if she had guessed the true reasons for my friendship with Luke Redhill, a rude but good-natured nose-picker I considered intellectually beneath me.

"You wouldn't be safe there. The playing-card people would've got you," she said, her tone both gleeful and rather too coy.

I looked at the ceiling of the car. "Okay."

We rode for a while in silence.

"Why are they after me?" I asked, even though by then I was sick of it, wanted done with the game.

"It's all because we're so incredibly superlucky. No one ought to be as lucky as us. They hate the idea that anyone is getting a free ride. But it would all even out if they got ahold of you. I don't care how lucky you've been, if you lose a kid, the good times are over."

We were lucky, of course, maybe even superlucky, and it wasn't just that we were well off, like everyone in our extended family of trust-fund ne'er-do-wells. My father had more time for me than other fathers had for their boys. He went to work after I left for school, and was usually home by the time I got back, and if I didn't have anything else going on, we'd drive to the golf course to whack a few. My mother was beautiful, still young, just thirty-five, with a natural instinct for mischief that had made her a hit with my friends. I suspected that several of the kids I hung out with, Luke Redhill included, had cast her in a variety of masturbatory fantasies, and that indeed their attraction to her explained most of their fondness for me.

"And why is Big Cat Lake so safe?" I said.

"Who said it's safe?"

"Then why are we going there?"

She turned away from me. "So we can have a nice cozy fire

in the fireplace, and sleep late, and eat egg pancakes, and spend the morning in our pajamas. Even if we are in fear for our lives, that's no reason to be miserable all weekend."

She put her hand on the back of my father's neck and played with his hair. Then she stiffened, and her fingernails sank into the skin just below his hairline.

"Jack," she said to me. She was looking past my father, through the driver's-side window, at something out in the dark. "Get down, Jack, get down."

We were on Route 16, a long straight highway, with a narrow grass median between the two lanes. A car was parked on a turnaround between the lanes, and as we went by it, its headlights snapped on. I turned my head and stared into them for a moment before sinking down out of sight. The car—a sleek silver Jaguar—turned onto the road and accelerated after us.

"I told you not to let them see you," my mother said. "Go faster, Henry. Get away from them."

Our car picked up speed, rushing through the darkness. I squeezed my fingers into the seat, sitting up on my knees to peek out the rear window. The other car stayed exactly the same distance behind us no matter how fast we went, clutching the curves of the road with a quiet, menacing assurance. Sometimes my breath would catch in my throat for a few moments before I remembered to breathe. Road signs whipped past, gone too quickly to be read.

The Jag followed for three miles before it swung into the parking lot of a roadside diner. When I turned around in my seat my mother was lighting a cigarette with the pulsing orange ring of the dashboard lighter. My father hummed softly to himself, easing up on the gas. He swung his head a little from side to side, keeping time to a melody I didn't recognize.

I RAN THROUGH the dark, with the wind knifing at me and my head down, not looking where I was going. My mother was right behind me, the both of us rushing for the porch. No light lit the front of the cottage by the water. My father had switched car and headlights off, and the house was in the woods, at the end of a rutted dirt road where there were no streetlamps. Just beyond the house I caught a glimpse of the lake, a hole in the world, filled with a heaving darkness.

My mother let us in and went about switching on lights. The cabin was built around a single great room with a lodge-house ceiling, bare rafters showing, log walls with red bark peeling off them. To the left of the door was a dresser, the mirror on the back hidden behind a pair of black veils. Wandering, my hands pulled into the sleeves of my jacket for warmth, I approached the dresser. Through the semitransparent curtains I saw a dim, roughly formed figure, my own obscured reflection, coming to meet me in the mirror. I felt a tickle of unease at the sight of the reflected me, a featureless shadow skulking behind black silk, someone I didn't know. I pushed the curtain back, but saw only myself, cheeks stung into redness by the wind.

I was about to step away when I noticed the masks. The mirror was supported by two delicate posts, and a few masks hung from the top of each, the sort, like the Lone Ranger's, that only cover the eyes and a little of the nose. One had whiskers and glittery spackle on it and would make the wearer look like a jeweled mouse. Another was of rich black velvet and would have been appropriate dress for a courtesan on her way to an Edwardian masquerade.

The whole cottage had been artfully decorated in masks. They dangled from doorknobs and the backs of chairs. A great crimson mask glared furiously down from the mantel above the hearth, a surreal demon made out of lacquered papier-mâché, with a hooked beak and feathers around the eyes—just the thing to wear if you had been cast as the Red Death in an Edgar Allan Poe revival.

The most unsettling of them hung from a lock on one of the windows. It was made of some distorted but clear plastic, and looked like a man's face molded out of an impossibly thin piece of ice. It was hard to see, dangling in front of the glass, and I twitched nervously when I spotted it from the corner of my eye. For an instant I thought there was a man, spectral and barely there, hovering on the porch, gaping in at me.

The front door crashed open and my father came in dragging luggage. At the same time, my mother spoke from behind me.

"When we were young, just kids, your father and I used to sneak off to this place to get away from everyone. *Wait*. Wait, I know. Let's play a game. You have until we leave to guess which room you were conceived in."

She liked to try and disgust me now and then with intimate, unasked-for revelations about herself and my father. I frowned and gave what I hoped was a scolding look, and she laughed again, and we were both satisfied, having played ourselves perfectly.

"Why are there curtains over all the mirrors?"

"I don't know," she said. "Maybe whoever stayed here last hung them up as a way to remember your grandfather. In Jewish tradition, after someone dies, the mourners cover the mirrors, as a warning against vanity."

"But we aren't Jewish," I said.

"It's a nice tradition, though. All of us could stand to spend less time thinking about ourselves."

"What's with all the masks?"

"Every vacation home ought to have a few masks lying around. What if you want a vacation from your own face? I get awfully sick of being the same person day in, day out. What do you think of that one, do you like it?"

I was absentmindedly fingering the glassy, blank-featured mask hanging from the window. When she brought my attention to what I was doing, I pulled my hand back. A chill crawled along the thickening flesh of my forearms.

"You should put it on," she said, her voice breathy and eager. "You should see how you look in it."

"It's awful," I said.

"Are you going to be okay sleeping in your own room? You could sleep in bed with us. That's what you did the last time you were here. Although you were much younger then."

"That's all right. I wouldn't want to get in the way, in case you feel like conceiving someone else."

"Be careful what you wish for," she said. "History repeats."

THE ONLY FURNITURE in my small room was a camp cot dressed in sheets that smelled of mothballs and a wardrobe against one wall, with paisley drapes pulled across the mirror on the back. A half-face mask hung from the curtain rod. It was made of green silk leaves, sewn together and ornamented with emerald sequins, and I liked it until I turned the light off. In the gloom, the leaves looked like the horny scales of some lizard-faced thing, with dark gaping sockets where the eyes belonged. I switched the light back on and got up long enough to turn it face to the wall.

Trees grew against the house and sometimes a limb batted the side of the cottage, making a knocking sound that always brought me awake with the idea someone was at the bedroom door. I woke, dozed, and woke again. The wind built to a thin shriek and from somewhere outside came a steady, metallic ping-ping-ping, as if a wheel were turning in the gale. I went to the window to look, not expecting to see anything. The moon was up, though, and as the trees blew, moonlight raced across the ground, through the darkness, like schools of those little silver fish that live in deep water and glow in the dark.

A bicycle leaned against a tree, an antique with a giant front wheel and a rear wheel almost comically too small. The front wheel turned continuously, ping-ping-ping. A boy came across the grass toward it, a chubby boy with fair hair, in a white nightgown, and at the sight of him I felt an instinctive rush of dread. He took the handlebars of the bike, then cocked his head as if at a sound, and I mewed, shrank back from the glass. He turned and stared at me with silver eyes and silver teeth, dimples in his fat cupid cheeks, and I sprang awake in my mothball-smelling bed, making unhappy sounds of fear in my throat.

When morning came, and I finally struggled up out of sleep for the last time, I found myself in the master bedroom, under heaped quilts, with the sun slanting across my face. The impression of my mother's head still dented the pillow beside me. I didn't remember rushing there in the dark and was glad. At thirteen, I was still a little kid, but I had my pride.

I lay like a salamander on a rock—sun-dazed and awake without being conscious—until I heard someone pull a zipper on the other side of the room. I peered around and saw my father, opening the suitcase on top of the bureau. Some subtle rustling of the quilts caught his attention, and he turned his head to look at me.

He was naked. The morning sunshine bronzed his short, compact body. He wore the clear plastic mask that had been hanging in the window of the great room the night before. It squashed the features beneath, flattening them out of their recognizable shapes. He stared at me blankly, as if he hadn't known I was lying there in the bed, or perhaps as if he didn't know me at all. The thick length of his penis rested on a cushion of gingery hair. I had seen him naked often enough before, but with the mask on he was someone different, and his nakedness was disconcerting. He looked at me and did not speak—and that was disconcerting too.

I opened my mouth to say hello and good morning, but there was a wheeze in my chest. The thought crossed my mind that he was, really and not metaphorically, a person I didn't know. I couldn't hold his stare, looked away, then slipped from under the quilts and went into the great room, willing myself not to run.

A pot clanked in the kitchen. Water hissed from a faucet. I followed the sounds to my mother, who was at the sink, filling a tea kettle. She heard the pad of my feet, and glanced back over her shoulder. The sight of her stopped me in my tracks. She had on a black kitten mask, edged in rhinestones, and with glistening whiskers. She was not naked, but wore a MILLER LITE T-shirt that came to her hips. Her legs, though, were bare, and when she leaned over the sink to shut off the water I saw a flash of strappy black panties. I was reassured by the fact that she had grinned to see me, and not just stared at me as if we had never met.

"Egg pancakes in the oven," she said.

"Why are you and Dad wearing masks?"

"It's Halloween, isn't it?"

"No," I said. "Try next Thursday."

"Any law against starting early?" she asked. Then she paused by the stove, an oven mitt on one hand, and shot another look at me. "Actually. *Actually*."

"Here it comes. The truck is backing up. The back end is rising. The bullshit is about to come sliding out."

"In this place it's always Halloween. It's called Masquerade House. That's our secret name for it. It's one of the rules of the cottage: While you're staying here you have to wear a mask. It's always been that way."

"I can wait until Halloween."

She pulled a pan out of the oven and cut me a piece of egg pancake, poured me a cup of tea. Then she sat down across from me to watch me eat.

"You have to wear a mask. The playing-card people saw you last night. They'll be coming now. You have to put a mask on so they won't recognize you."

"Why wouldn't they recognize me? I recognize you."

"You think you do," she said, her long-lashed eyes vivid and humorous. "Playing-card people wouldn't know you behind a mask. It's their Achilles heel. They take everything at face value. They're very one-dimensional thinkers."

"Ha ha," I said. "When's the appraiser coming?"

"Sometime. Later. I don't really know. I'm not sure there even is an appraiser. I might've made that up."

"I've only been awake twenty minutes and I'm already bored. Couldn't you guys have found a babysitter for me and come up here for your weird mask-wearing, baby-making weekend by yourselves?" As soon as I said it, I felt myself starting to blush, but I was pleased that I had it in me to needle her about their masks and her black underwear and the burlesque game they had going that they thought I was too young to understand.

She said, "I'd rather have you along. Now you won't be getting into trouble with that girl."

The heat in my cheeks deepened, the way coals will when someone sighs over them. "What girl?"

"I'm not sure which girl. It's either Jane Redhill or her friend. Probably her friend. The person you always go over to Luke's house hoping to see."

Luke was the one who liked her friend, Melinda; I liked Jane. Still, my mother had guessed close enough to unsettle me. Her smile broadened at my stricken silence.

"She is a pert little cutie, isn't she? Jane's friend? I guess they both are. The friend, though, seems more your type. What's her name? Melinda? The way she goes around in her baggy farmer overalls. I bet she spends her afternoons reading in a treehouse she built with her father. I bet she baits her own worms and plays football with the boys."

"Luke is hot for her."

"So it's Jane."

"Who said it has to be either of them?"

"There must be some reason you hang around with Luke. Besides Luke." Then she said, "Jane came by selling magazine subscriptions to benefit her church a few days ago. She seems like a very wholesome young thing. Very community minded. I wish I thought she had a sense of humor. When you're a little older, you should cold-cock Luke Redhill and drop him in the old quarry. That Melinda will fall right into your arms. The two of you can mourn for him together. Grief can be very romantic." She took my empty plate and got up. "Find a mask. Play along."

She put my plate in the sink and went out. I finished a glass of juice and meandered into the great room after her. I glanced at the master bedroom, just as she was pushing the door shut behind her. The man who I took for my father still wore his disfiguring mask of ice, and had pulled on a pair of jeans. For a moment our eyes met, his gaze dispassionate and unfamiliar. He put a possessive hand on my mother's hip. The door closed and they were gone.

In the other bedroom, I sat on the edge of my bed and stuck my feet into my sneakers. The wind whined under the eaves. I felt glum and out of sorts, wanted to be home, had no idea what to do with myself. As I stood, I happened to glance at the green mask made of sewn silk leaves, turned once again to face the room. I pulled it down, rubbed it between thumb and forefinger, trying out the slippery smoothness of it. Almost as an afterthought, I put it on.

MY MOTHER WAS in the living room, fresh from the shower.

"It's you," she said. "Very Dionysian. Very Pan. We should get a towel. You could walk around in a little toga."

"That would be fun. Until hypothermia set in."

"It is drafty in here, isn't it? We need a fire. One of us has to go into the forest and collect an armful of dead wood."

"Boy, I wonder who that's going to be."

"Wait. We'll make it into a game. It'll be exciting."

"I'm sure. Nothing livens up a morning like tramping around in the cold foraging for sticks."

"Listen. Don't wander from the forest path. Out there in the woods, nothing is real except for the path. Children who drift away from it never find their way back. Also—this is the most important thing—don't let anyone see you, unless they come masked. Anyone in a mask is hiding out from the playing-card people, just like us."

"If the woods are so dangerous for children, maybe I ought to stay here and you or Dad can go play pick-up sticks. Is he ever coming out of the bedroom?"

But she was shaking her head. "Grown-ups can't go into the forest at all. Not even the trail is safe for someone my age. I can't even see the trail. Once you get as old as me it disappears from sight. I only know about it because your father and I used to take walks on it, when we came up here as teenagers. Only the young can find their way through all the wonders and illusions in the deep dark woods."

Outside was drab and cold beneath the pigeon-colored sky. I went around the back of the house, to see if there was a wood-pile. On my way past the master bedroom, my father thumped on the glass. I went to the window to see what he wanted, and was surprised by my own reflection, superimposed over his face. I was still wearing the mask of silk leaves, had for a moment forgotten about it.

He pulled the top half of the window down and leaned out, his own face squashed by its shell of clear plastic, his wintry blue eyes a little blank. "Where are you going?"

"I'm going to check out the woods, I guess. Mom wants me to collect sticks for a fire."

He hung his arms over the top of the window and stared across the yard. He watched some rust-colored leaves trip end-over-end across the grass. "I wish I was going."

"Then come."

He glanced up at me, and smiled, for the first time all day. "No. Not right now. Tell you what. You go on, and maybe I'll meet you out there in a while."

"Okay."

"It's funny. As soon as you leave this place, you forget how—pure it is. What the air smells like." He stared at the grass and the lake for another moment, then turned his head, caught my eye. "You forget other things too. Jack, listen, I don't want you to forget about—"

The door opened behind him, on the far side of the room. My father fell silent. My mother stood in the doorway. She was in her jeans and sweater, playing with the wide buckle of her belt.

"Boys," she said. "What are we talking about?"

My father didn't glance back at her, but went on staring at me, and beneath his new face of melted crystal, I thought I saw a look of chagrin, as if he'd been caught doing something faintly embarrassing; cheating at solitaire maybe. I remembered, then, her drawing her fingers across his lips, closing an imaginary zipper, the night before. My head went queer and light. I had the sudden idea I was seeing another part of some unwholesome game playing out between them, the less of which I knew, the happier I'd be.

"Nothing," I said. "I was just telling Dad I was going for a walk. And now I'm going. For my walk." Backing away from the window as I spoke.

My mother coughed. My father slowly pushed the top half of the window shut, his gaze still level with mine. He turned the lock—then pressed his palm to the glass, in a gesture of goodbye. When he lowered his hand, a steamy imprint of it remained, a ghost hand that shrank in on itself and vanished. My father drew down the shade.

I FORGOT ABOUT gathering sticks almost as soon as I set out. I had by then decided that my parents only wanted me out of the house so they could have the place to themselves, a thought that made me peevish. At the head of the trail I pulled off my mask of silk leaves and hung it on a branch.

I walked with my head down and my hands shoved into the pockets of my coat. For a while the path ran parallel to the lake, visible beyond the hemlocks in slivers of frigid-looking blue. I was too busy thinking that if they wanted to be perverted and un-parent-like, they should've figured a way to come up to Big Cat Lake without me, to notice the path turning and leading away from the water. I didn't look up until I heard the sound coming toward me along the trail: a steely whirring, the creak of a metal frame under stress. Directly ahead the path divided to go around a boulder, the size and rough shape of a half-buried coffin stood on end. Beyond the boulder, the path came back together and wound away into the pines.

I was alarmed, I don't know why. It was something about the way the wind rose just then, so the trees flailed at the sky. It was the frantic way the leaves scurried about my ankles, as if in a sudden hurry to get off the trail. Without thinking, I sat down behind the boulder, back to the stone, hugging my knees to my chest.

A moment later the boy on the antique bike—the boy I thought I had dreamed—rode past on my left, without so much as a glance my way. He was dressed in the nightgown he had been wearing the night before. A harness of white straps held a pair of modest white-feathered wings to his back. Maybe he had had them on the first time I saw him and I hadn't noticed them in the dark. As he rattled past, I had a brief look at his dimpled cheeks and blond bangs, features set in an expression of serene confidence. His gaze was cool, distant. Seeking. I watched him expertly guide his Charlie Chaplin cycle between stones and roots, around a curve, and out of sight.

If I hadn't seen him in the night, I might have thought he was a boy on his way to a costume party, although it was too cold to be out gallivanting in a nightgown. I wanted to be back at the cabin, out of the wind, safe with my parents. I was in dread of the trees, waving and shushing around me.

But when I moved, it was to continue in the direction I had been heading, glancing often over my shoulder to make sure the bicyclist wasn't coming up behind me. I didn't have the nerve to walk back along the trail, knowing that the boy on the antique bike was somewhere out there, between myself and the cabin.

I hurried along, hoping to find a road, or one of the other summer houses along the lake, eager to be anywhere but in the woods. Anywhere turned out to be less than a ten-minute walk from the coffin-shaped rock. It was clearly marked—a weathered plank, with the words "ANY-WHERE" painted on it, was nailed to the trunk of a pine—a bare patch in the woods where people had once camped. A few charred sticks sat in the bottom of a blackened firepit. Someone, children maybe, had built a lean-to between a pair of boulders. The boulders were about the same height, tilting in toward one another, and a sheet of plywood had been set across the top of them. A log had been pulled across the opening that faced the clearing, providing both a place for people to sit by a fire and a barrier that had to be climbed over to enter the shelter.

I stood at the ruin of the ancient campfire, trying to get my bearings. Two trails on the far side of the camp led away. There was little difference between them, both narrow ruts gouged out in the brush, and no clue as to where either of them might lead.

"Where are you trying to go?" said a girl on my left, her voice pitched to a good-humored hush.

I leaped, took a half-step away, looked around. She was leaning out of the shelter, hands on the log. I hadn't seen her in the shadows of the lean-to. She was black-haired, a little older than myself—sixteen maybe—and I had a sense she was pretty. It was hard to be sure. She wore a black sequined mask, with a fan of ostrich feathers standing up from one side. Just behind her, further back in the dark, was a boy, the upper half of his face hidden behind a smooth plastic mask the color of milk.

"I'm looking for my way back," I said.

"Back where?" asked the girl.

The boy kneeling behind her took a measured look at her outthrust bottom in her faded jeans. She was, consciously or not, wiggling her hips a little from side to side.

"My family has a summer place near here. I was wondering if one of those two trails would take me there."

"You could go back the way you came," she said, but mischievously, as if she already knew I was afraid to double back.

"I'd rather not," I said.

"What brought you all the way out here?" asked the boy.

"My mother sent me to collect wood for the fire."

He snorted. "Sounds like the beginning of a fairy tale." The girl cast a disapproving look back at him, which he ignored. "One of the bad ones. Your parents can't feed you anymore, so they send you off to get lost in the woods. Eventually someone gets eaten by a witch for dinner. Baked into a pie. Be careful it's not you."

"Do you want to play cards with us?" the girl asked, and held up a deck.

"I just want to get home. I don't want my parents worried."

"Sit and play with us," she said. "We'll play a hand for answers. The winner gets to ask each of the losers a question, and no matter what, they have to tell the truth. So if you beat me, you could ask me how to get home without seeing the boy on the old bicycle, and I'd have to tell you."

Which meant she had seen him and somehow guessed the rest. She looked pleased with herself, enjoyed letting me know I was easy to figure out. I considered for a moment, then nodded.

"What are you playing?" I asked.

"It's a kind of poker. It's called Cold Hands, because it's the only card game you can play when it's this cold."

The boy shook his head. "This is one of these games where she makes up the rules as she goes along." His voice, which had an adolescent crack in it, was nevertheless familiar to me.

I crossed to the log and she retreated on her knees, sliding back into the dark space under the plywood roof to make room for me. She was talking all the time, shuffling her worn deck of cards.

"It isn't hard. I deal five cards to each player, face-up. When I'm done, whoever has the best poker hand wins. That probably sounds too simple, but then there are a lot of funny little house rules. If you smile during the game, the player sitting to your left can swap one of his cards for one of yours. If you can build a house with the first three cards you get dealt, and if the other players can't blow it down in one breath, you get to look through the deck and pick out whatever you want for your fourth card. If you draw a black forfeit, the other players throw stones at you until you're dead. If you have any questions, keep them to yourself. Only the winner gets to ask questions. Anyone who asks a question while the game is in play loses instantly. Okay? Let's start."

My first card was a Lazy Jack. I knew because it said so across the bottom, and because it showed a picture of a golden-haired jack lounging on silk pillows, while a harem girl filed his toenails. It wasn't until the girl handed me my second card—the three of rings—that I mentally registered the thing she had said about the black forfeit.

"Excuse me," I started. "But what's a—"

She raised her eyebrows, looked at me seriously.

"Never mind," I said.

The boy made a little sound in his throat. The girl cried out, "He smiled! Now you can trade one of your cards for one of his!"

"I did not!"

"You did," she said. "I saw it. Take his queen and give him your jack."

I gave him the Lazy Jack and took the Queen of Sheets away from him. It showed a nude girl asleep on a carved four-poster, amid the tangle of her bedclothes. She had straight brown hair, and strong, handsome features, and bore a resemblance to Jane's friend, Melinda. After that I was dealt the King of Penny-farthings, a red-bearded fellow carrying a sack of coins that was splitting and beginning to spill. I was pretty sure the girl in the black mask had dealt him to me from the bottom of the deck. She saw I saw and shot me a cool, challenging look.

When we each had three cards, we took a break and tried to build houses the others couldn't blow down, but none of them would stand. Afterward I was dealt the Queen of Chains and a card with the rules of cribbage printed on it. I almost asked if it was in the deck by accident, then thought better of it. No one drew a black forfeit. I didn't even know what one was.

"Jack wins!" shouted the girl, which unnerved me a little, since I had never introduced myself. "Jack is the winner!" She flung herself against me and hugged me fiercely. When she straightened up, she was pushing my winning cards into the pocket of my jacket. "Here, you should keep your winning hand. To remember the fun we had. It doesn't matter. This old deck is missing a bunch of cards anyway. I just knew you'd win!"

"Sure she did," said the boy. "First she makes up a game with rules only she can understand, then she cheats so it comes out how she likes."

She laughed, unpolished, convulsive laughter, and I felt cold on the nape of my neck. But really, I think I already knew by then, even before she laughed, who I was playing cards with.

"The secret to avoiding unhappy losses is to only play games you make up yourself," she said. "Now. Go ahead, Jack. Ask anything you like. It's your right."

"How do I get home without going back the way I came?"

"That's easy. Take the path closest to the 'any-where' sign, which will take you anywhere you want to go. That's why it says anywhere. Just be sure the cabin is really where you want to go, or you might not get there."

"Right. Thank you. It was a good game. I didn't understand it, but I had fun playing." And I scrambled out over the log.

I hadn't gone far before she called out to me. When I looked back, she and the boy were side-by-side, leaning over the log and staring out at me.

"Don't forget," she said. "You get to ask him a question too."

"Do I know you?" I said, making a gesture to include both of them.

"No," he said. "You don't really know either of us."

THERE WAS A JAG parked in the driveway behind my parents' car. The interior was polished cherry, and the seats looked as if they had never been sat on. It might have just rolled off the dealership floor. By then it was late in the day, the light slanting in from the west, cutting through the tops of the trees. It didn't seem like it could be so late.

I thumped up the stairs, but before I could reach the door to go in, it opened, and my mother stepped out, still wearing the black sex-kitten mask.

"Your mask," she said. "What'd you do with it?"

"Ditched it," I said. I didn't tell her I hung it on a tree branch because I was embarrassed to be seen in it. I wished I had it now, although I couldn't have said why.

She threw an anxious look back at the door, then crouched in front of me.

"I knew. I was watching for you. Put this on." She offered me my father's mask of clear plastic.

I stared at it a moment, remembering the way I recoiled from it when I first saw it, and how it had squashed my father's features into something cold and menacing. But when I slipped it on my face, it fit well enough. It carried a faint fragrance of my father, coffee and the sea-spray odor of his aftershave. I found it reassuring to have him so close to me.

My mother said, "We're getting out of here in a few minutes. Going home. Just as soon as the appraiser is done looking around. Come on. Come in. It's almost over."

I followed her inside, then stopped just through the door. My father sat on the couch, shirtless and barefoot. His body looked as if it had been marked up by a surgeon for an operation. Dotted lines and arrows showed the location of liver, spleen, and bowels. His eyes were pointed toward the floor, his face blank.

"Dad?" I asked.

His gaze rose, flitted from my mother to me and back. His expression remained bland and unrevealing.

"Shh," my mother said. "Daddy's busy."

I heard heels cracking across the bare planks to my right and glanced across the room, as the appraiser came out of the master bedroom. I had assumed the appraiser would be a man, but it was a middle-aged woman in a tweed jacket, with some white showing in her wavy yellow hair. She had austere, imperial features, the high cheekbones and expressive, arching eyebrows of English nobility.

"See anything you like?" my mother asked.

"You have some wonderful pieces," the appraiser said. Her gaze drifted to my father's bare shoulders.

"Well," my mother said. "Don't mind me." She gave the back of my arm a soft pinch and slipped around me, whispered out of the side of her mouth, "Hold the fort, kiddo. I'll be right back."

My mother showed the appraiser a small, strictly polite smile, before easing into the master bedroom and out of sight, leaving the three of us alone.

"I was sorry when I heard Upton died," the appraiser said. "Do you miss him?"

The question was so unexpected and direct it startled me; or maybe it was her tone, which was not sympathetic, but sounded to my ears too curious, eager for a little grief.

"I guess. We weren't so close," I said. "I think he had a pretty good life, though."

"Of course he did," she said.

"I'd be happy if things worked out half as well for me."

"Of course they will," she said, and put a hand on the back of my father's neck and began rubbing it fondly.

It was such a casually, obscenely intimate gesture, I felt a sick intestinal pang at the sight. I let my gaze drift away—had to look away—and happened to glance at the mirror on the back of the dresser. The curtains were parted slightly, and in the reflection I saw a playing-card woman standing behind my father, the queen of spades, her eyes of ink haughty and distant, her black robes painted onto her body. I wrenched my gaze from the looking-glass in alarm, and glanced back at the couch. My father was smiling in a dreamy kind of way, leaning back into the hands now massaging his shoulders. The appraiser regarded me from beneath half-lowered eyelids.

"That isn't your face," she said to me. "No one has a face like that. A face made out of ice. What are you hiding?"

My father stiffened, and his smile faded. He sat up and forward, slipping his shoulders out of her grip.

"You've seen everything," my father said to the woman behind him. "Do you know what you want?"

"I'd start with everything in this room," she said, putting her hand gently on his shoulder again. She toyed with a curl of his hair for a moment. "I can have everything, can't I?"

My mother came out of the bedroom, lugging a pair of suitcases, one in each hand. She glanced at the appraiser with her hand on my father's neck, and huffed a bemused little laugh—a laugh that went *huh* and which seemed to mean more or less just that—and picked up the suitcases again, marched with them toward the door.

"It's all up for grabs," my father said. "We're ready to deal."

"Who isn't?" said the appraiser.

My mother set one of the suitcases in front of me, and nodded that I should take it. I followed her onto the porch, and then looked back. The appraiser was leaning over the couch, and my father's head was tipped back, and her mouth was on his. My mother reached past me and closed the door.

We walked through the gathering twilight to the car. The boy in the white gown sat on the lawn, his bicycle on the grass beside him. He was skinning a dead rabbit with a piece of horn, its stomach open and steaming. He glanced at us as we went by and grinned, showing teeth pink with blood. My mother put a motherly arm around my shoulders.

After she was in the car, she took off her mask and threw it on the backseat. I left mine on. When I inhaled deeply I could smell my father.

"What are we doing?" I asked. "Isn't he coming?"

"No," she said, and started the car. "He's staying here."

"How will he get home?"

She turned a sideways look upon me, and smiled sympathetically. Outside, the sky was a blue-almost-black, and the clouds were a scalding shade of crimson, but in the car it was already night. I turned in my seat, sat up on my knees, to watch the cottage disappear through the trees.

"Let's play a game," my mother said. "Let's pretend you never really knew your father. He went away before you were born. We can make up fun little stories about him. He has a Semper Fi tattoo from his days in the marines, and another one, a blue anchor, that's from—" Her voice faltered, as she came up suddenly short on inspiration.

"From when he worked on a deep-sea oil rig."

She laughed. "Right. And we'll pretend the road is magic. The Amnesia Highway. By the time we're home, we'll both believe the story is true, that he really did leave before you were born. Everything else will seem like a dream, those dreams as real as memories. The made-up story will probably be better than the real thing anyway. I mean, he loved your bones, and he wanted everything for you, but can you remember one interesting thing he ever did?"

I had to admit I couldn't.

"Can you even remember what he did for a living?"

I had to admit I didn't. Insurance?

"Isn't this a good game?" she asked. "Speaking of games. Do you still have your deal?"

"My deal?" I asked, then remembered, and touched the pocket of my jacket.

"You want to hold onto it. That's some winning hand. King of Pennyfarthings. Queen of Sheets. You got it all, boy. I'm telling you, when we get home, you give that Melinda a call." She laughed again, and then affectionately patted her tummy. "Good days ahead, kid. For both of us."

I shrugged.

"You can take the mask off, you know," my mother said. "Unless you like wearing it. Do you like wearing it?"

I reached up for the sun visor, turned it down, and opened the mirror. The lights around the mirror switched on. I studied my new face of ice, and the face beneath, a malformed, human blank.

"Sure," I said. "It's me."

VOLUNTARY COMMITTAL

I don't know who I'm writing this for, can't say who I expect to read it. Not the police, anyway. I don't know what happened to my brother, and I can't tell them where he is. Nothing I could put down here would help them find him.

And anyway, this isn't really about his disappearance . . . although it *does* concern a missing person, and I'd be lying if I said I didn't think the two things had anything to do with each other. I have never told anyone what I know about Edward Prior, who left school one October day in 1977, and never arrived home for chili and baked potatoes with Mom. For a long time, the first year or two after he vanished, I didn't want to think about my friend Eddie. I would do anything not to think about him. If I passed some people talking about him in the halls of my high school—*I heard he stole his momma's weed and some money and ran away to fuckin California!*—I'd fix my eyes on some point in the distance and pretend I was deaf. And if someone actually approached and asked me straight out what I thought had happened to him—now and then someone would, since we were known *compañeros*—I'd set my face into a rigid blank and shrug. "I almost think I care sometimes," I said.

Later, I didn't think about Eddie out of studiously formed habit. If anything happened by chance to remind me of him—if I saw a boy who looked like him, or read something in the news about a missing teen—I would instantly begin to think of something else, hardly aware I was even doing it.

In the last three weeks, though, ever since my little brother Morris went missing, I find myself thinking about Ed Prior more and more; can't seem, through any effort of will, to turn thoughts of him aside. The urge to talk to someone about what I know is really almost more than I can bear. But this isn't a story for the police. Believe me, it wouldn't do them any good, and it might do myself a fair amount of bad. I can't tell them where to look for Edward Prior any more than I can tell them where to look for Morris—can't tell what I don't know—but if I were to share this story with a detective, I think I might be asked some harsh questions, and some people (Eddie's mother, for example, still alive and on her third marriage) would be put through a lot of unnecessary emotional strain.

And it's just possible I could wind up with a one-way ticket to the same place where my brother spent the last two years of his life: the Wellbrook Progressive Mental Health Center. My brother was there voluntarily, but Wellbrook includes a wing just for people who had to be committed. Morris was part of the clinic's work program, pushed a mop for them four days out of the week, and on Friday mornings he went into the Governor's Wing, as it's known, to wash their shit off the walls. And their blood.

Was I just talking about Morris in the past tense? I guess I was. I don't hope anymore that the phone will ring, and it will be Betty Millhauser from Wellbrook, her voice rushed and winded, telling me they've found him in a homeless shelter somewhere, and they're bringing him back. I don't think anyone will be calling to tell me they found him floating in the Charles, either. I don't think anyone will be calling at all, except maybe to say nothing is known. Which could almost be the epitaph on Morris's grave. And maybe I have to admit that I'm writing this, not to show it to anyone, but because I can't help myself, and a blank page is the only safe audience for this story I can imagine.

MY LITTLE BROTHER didn't start to talk until he was four. A lot of people thought he was retarded. A lot of people around my old hometown, Pallow, *still* think he was mentally retarded, or autistic. For the record, when I was a kid I half-thought he was retarded myself, even though my parents told me he wasn't.

When he was eleven, he was diagnosed with juvenile schizophrenia. Later came other diagnoses: depression, obsessive-compulsive personality disorder, acute depressive schizophrenia. I don't know if any of those words really capture the sense of who he was, and what he struggled with. I know that even when he found his words, he didn't use them that much. That he was always too small for his age, a boy with delicate bones, slender long-fingered hands, and an elfin face. He was always curiously affectless, his feelings submerged too deeply to create a stir on his face. He never seemed to blink. At times, my brother made me think of one of those tapered, horned conch shells, with a glossy pink interior curving away and out of sight into some tightly wound inner mystery. You could hold your ear to such a shell and imagine you heard the depths of a vast roaring ocean—but it was really just a trick of acoustics. The sound you were hearing was the soft, rushing thunder of nothing there. The doctors had their diagnoses, and when I was fourteen years old, that was mine.

Because he was susceptible to agonizing ear infections, Morris wasn't let out in the winter . . . which by my mother's definition began when the World Series ended and ended when the baseball season began. Anyone who has ever had small children themselves can tell you how hard it is to keep them happily occupied for any real length of time when you can't just send them outside. My own son is twelve now and lives with my ex in Boca Raton, but we all lived together as a family until he was seven, and I remember just how draining a cold and rainy day, all of us stuck inside, could be. For my little brother, every day was a cold and rainy day, but unlike with other children, it wasn't hard to keep him busy. He occupied *himself*, descending into the cellar as soon as he came home from school, to work with quiet industry, for the rest of the afternoon, on one of his immense, sprawling, technically complicated and fundamentally worthless construction projects.

His first fascination was the towers and elaborate temples he would build out of Dixie cups. I have a memory of what might have been the first time he ever made something out of them. It was evening, and all of us, my parents, Morris and I, were gathered in the television room for one of our rare family rituals, the nightly watching of *M*A*S*H*. By the time the show faded into its second commercial break, however, we had all pretty much quit paying attention to the antics of Alan Alda and company, and were staring at my brother.

My father sat on the floor beside him. I think initially he might've been helping him build. My father was a bit of an autistic person himself, a shy, clumsy man who didn't get out of his pajamas on weekends, and who had almost no social truck with the world whatsoever beyond my mother. He never showed any sign of disappointment in Morris, and he often seemed most content when he was stretched out beside my brother, painting sunshine-filled stick-figure worlds on construction paper with him. This time, though, he sat back and let Morris work alone, as curious as the rest of us to see how it would come out. Morris built and stacked and arranged, his long, slender fingers darting here and there, placing the cups so quickly it almost looked like a magic trick, or the work of a robot on an assembly line . . . without hesitation, seemingly without thought, never accidentally knocking another cup down. Sometimes he wasn't even looking at what his hands were doing, was staring instead into the box of Dixie Cups, as if to see how many were left. The tower climbed higher and higher, cups flying onto it so quickly I found myself sometimes holding my breath in actual disbelief.

A second box of Dixie Cups was opened and used up. By the time he was finished—which happened when he had gone through all the wax cups my father could find for him—the tower was as tall as Morris himself, and surrounded by a defensive wall with an open gate. Because of the spaces between the cups, there seemed to be narrow archer's windows in the sides of the tower, and the top of both tower and wall appeared crenellated. It had startled us all a little, watching Morris build the thing with such speed and self-assurance, but it wasn't an inherently fabulous structure. Any other five-year-old might've built the same thing. It was only remarkable in that it suggested larger underlying ambitions. One sensed Morris easily could've gone on building, adding smaller watch towers, out-buildings, a whole rustic Dixie cup village. And when the cups were gone, Morris glanced around and *laughed,* a sound I think I had never heard before then—a high, almost piercing noise, unpracticed and more alarming than pleasant. He laughed, and he clapped for himself, just once, the way a maharajah might clap to send away a servant.

The other way the tower was obviously different from the work of some other child his age was that any normal five-year-old would've constructed such a thing for one purpose—to give it a swift kick and watch the cups come down in a dry, rattling collapse. I know that's what I wanted to do with his tower, and I was three years older: march along it, bashing with both feet, for the sheer joy of knocking down something big and carefully built, a Little League Godzilla.

Every emotionally normal child has a streak of that in them. I suppose, if I am honest, that streak was a little broader in myself than it was in others. My compulsion to knock things down continued into adulthood, and ultimately included my wife, who disliked the habit, and expressed her displeasure with divorce papers and a jaundiced-looking lawyer who possessed all the personal warmth of a wood-chipper, and who operated with just such grinding mechanical efficiency in the courtroom.

Morris, though, soon lost interest in his finished work, and wanted juice. My father led him away into the kitchen, murmuring that he would bring home a huge box of cups for Morris to play with tomorrow, so he could build an even bigger castle in the basement. I couldn't believe that Morris had left his tower just standing there. It was a tease I couldn't bear. I shoved myself up off the couch, took a crooked step towards it—and then my mother caught my arm and held it. Her gaze latched into mine, and it carried a dark warning: *Don't even think.* Neither of us spoke, and in another instant I pulled my arm out of her hand and drifted out of the room myself.

My mother did love me, but rarely said so, and often seemed to hold me at an emotional arm's length. She understood me in a way my father didn't. Once, horsing around in the shallows of Walden Pond, I skipped a stone at a smaller boy who had splashed me. It hit his upper arm with a meaty *thwack* and raised an ugly purple welt. My mother saw to it that I didn't swim the rest of the summer, although we continued to visit Walden every Saturday afternoon, so Morris could paddle clumsily around; someone had persuaded my parents that swimming was therapeutic for him, and so she was as firm that he should swim as she was that I shouldn't. I was required to sit on the sand with her, and was not allowed to stray out of sight of her beach towel. I could read, but was not allowed to play with, or even talk to, other children. Looking back, it's hard to resent her if she was overly severe with me then, and on other occasions. She saw, more plainly than others, a lot of what was worst in me, and it worried her. She had some sense of my potential, and instead of filling her with hope and excitement, it made her harsh with me.

What Morris had done in the living room, in the space of a half hour, was just a hint of what he would do with three times the area to work in, and as many Dixie cups as he wanted. In the next year he painstakingly built an elevated superhighway—it meandered all around our spacious, well-lit basement, but if stretched out straight it would've measured nearly a quarter mile—a giant Sphinx, and a great circular igloo, large enough for both of us to sit inside, with a low entrance I could just squirm through.

From there it was no great stretch to designing towering, if impersonal, LEGO metropolises, patterned after the skylines of actual cities. A year after that, he graduated to dominoes, building delicate cathedrals with dozens of perfectly balanced ivory spires, reaching halfway to the ceiling. When Morris was nine, he became briefly famous, at least in Pallow, when Boston's *Chronicle* ran a short feature on him. Morris had set up over eighteen thousand dominoes in the gym of his school for the developmentally challenged. He arranged them in the shape of a giant griffin battling a column of knights, and Channel Five shot him setting them off, filmed the whole great roaring tumble. His dominoes fell in such a way that arrows appeared to fly, and the griffin seemed to slash at one of the gasping chain-mailed knights; three lines of crimson dominoes fell over, looking for all the world like gashes. For a week I suffered fits of black, poisonous jealousy, left the room when he came into it, couldn't stand that there should be so much attention focused on him; but my resentment made as little impression on him as his own celebrity. Morris was equally indifferent to both. I gave up my anger when I saw it made as much sense as screaming into a well, and eventually the rest of the world forgot that for a moment, Morris had been someone interesting.

By the time I entered my freshman year in high school and started chumming around with Eddie Prior, Morris had moved on to building fortresses out of cardboard boxes that my father brought home for him from the warehouse where he worked as a shipping agent. Almost from the start, it was different with his cardboard hideouts than it had been with the things he built out of dominoes or Dixie cups. While his other construction projects had clear beginnings and endings, he never really seemed to finish any one particular design with his cardboard boxes. One scheme flowed into another, a shelter becoming a castle becoming a series of catacombs. He painted exteriors, decorated interiors, laid carpet, cut windows, doors that would flap open and shut. Then one day, without any warning or explanation, Morris would disassemble large sections of what he had built, and begin reorganizing the whole structure along completely different architectural lines.

Also, though, his work with Dixie cups or LEGOS had always calmed him, while the things he built with cardboard boxes left him restless and dissatisfied. The ultimate cardboard hang-out was always just a few boxes away from being done, and until he got it right, the great looming *thing* he was building in the basement had a curious and unhappy power over him.

I remember coming into the house late on a Sunday afternoon, clomping across the kitchen in my snow boots to get something out of the fridge, glancing through the open basement door and down the steps . . . and then sticking in place, breath catching in my throat. Morris sat turned sideways on the bottom step, his shoulders hitched up to his ears, his face a pasty, unnatural white, twisted in a grimace. He held one palm pressed hard to his forehead, as if he had been struck there. But the thing that alarmed me the most, the thing I noticed as I came slowly down the steps towards him, was that while it was almost too cold in the basement to be comfortable, Morris's cheeks were slicked with sweat, the front of his plain white T-shirt soaked through in a V-shaped stain. When I was three steps above him, just as I was about to call his name, his eyes popped open. An instant later that expression of cringing pain began to fade away, his face relaxing, going slack.

"What's happening?" I asked. "You all right?"

"Yes," he said without inflection. "Just—got lost for a minute."

"Lost track of time?"

He seemed to need a moment to process this. His eyes narrowed; the look in them sharpened. He stared dimly at his fortress, which was, at that time, a series of twenty boxes arranged in a large square. About half of the boxes were painted a fluorescent yellow, with circular porthole windows cut in their sides. The portholes had sheets of Saran Wrap taped into them. Morris had gone over them with a hair dryer, so the plastic was stretched tight and smooth. This part of the fort was a holdover from a yellow submarine Morris had attempted to build. A periscope made out of a cardboard poster tube stuck out of the top of one very large box. The rest of the boxes, though, were painted in bold reds and blacks, with a flowing scrim of golden Arabian-style writing running along their sides. The windows of these boxes were cut in bell shapes that instantly brought to mind the palaces of Mideastern despots, harem girls, Aladdin.

Morris frowned and slowly shook his head. "I went in and I couldn't find my way out. Nothing looked right."

I glanced at the fort, which had an entrance at every corner and windows cut into every other box. Whatever my brother's handicaps, I couldn't imagine him getting so confused inside his fortress that he couldn't figure out where he was.

"Why didn't you just crawl to a window and see where you were?"

"There weren't any windows where I got lost. I heard someone talking and tried to get out following his voice but it was a long way off and I couldn't figure out where it was coming from. It wasn't you, was it? It didn't sound like your voice, Nolan."

"No!" I said. "What voice?" Glancing around as I said this, wondering if we were alone in the basement. "What did it say?"

"I couldn't always hear. Sometimes my name. Sometimes he said to keep going. And once he said there was a window ahead. He said I'd see sunflowers on the other side." Morris paused, then let out a weak sigh. "I might've seen it at the end of a tunnel—the window and the sunflowers—but I was scared to go too close, so I turned around and that's when my head started to hurt. And pretty soon I found one of the doors out."

I thought there was a good chance, then, that Morris had suffered a minor break with reality while crawling around inside his fort, a not impossible circumstance. Only a year before, he had taken to painting his hands red, because he said it helped him to *feel* sounds. When he was in a room with music playing he would shut his eyes, hold his crimson hands above his head like antennae, and wiggle his whole body in a sort of spastic belly dance.

I was also unnerved by the much more unlikely possibility that there really *was* someone in the basement, a chanting psychopath who was perhaps at this very moment hunched in one of the tight spaces of Morris's fort. Either way, I was creeped out. I took Morris's hand and told him to come upstairs with me, so he could tell our mother what had happened.

When this story was repeated to her, she looked stricken. She put a hand on Morris's forehead. "You're all clammy! Let's go upstairs, Morris. Let's get you some aspirin. I want you to lie down. We can talk about this after you've had a minute to rest."

I was all for searching the basement right away, to see if anyone was down there, but my mother shooed me aside, making a face whenever I spoke. The two of them disappeared upstairs, and I sat at the kitchen counter, eyeing the basement door, in a state of fidgety unease, for most of the next hour. That door was the cellar's only exit. If I had heard the sound of feet climbing the steps, I would have leapt up screaming. But no one came up, and when my father arrived home, we went down to search the basement together. No one was hiding behind the boiler or the oil tank. In fact, our cellar was tidy and well lit, with few good hiding spots. The only place an intruder might conceal himself was Morris's fort. I walked around it, kicking it and peeking in through the windows. My dad said I ought to climb in for a look around, and then laughed at the expression on my face. When he went upstairs I ran after him. I didn't want to be anywhere near the bottom of the basement stairs when he clicked the lights off.

ONE MORNING, I was throwing my books into my gym bag before leaving for school and two folded sheets of paper fell out of *Visions of American History*. I picked them up and stared at them, at first without recognition—two mimeographed sheets, typewritten questions, large blocks of white space where a person could fill in answers. When I realized what I was staring at, I almost cursed the ugliest curse I knew, with my mother only a few feet away from me . . . an error which would've got my ear bent the wrong way, and which would've led to an interrogation I was better off avoiding. It was a take-home exam, handed out last Friday, due back that morning.

I had been spacing out in history over the course of the last week. There was a girl, something of a punk, who wore tattery denim skirts and lurid red fishnet stockings, and who sat beside me. She would flap her legs open and shut in boredom, and I remember when I leaned forward I could sometimes catch a flash of her surprisingly plain white panties from out of my peripheral vision. If we had been reminded in class about the take-home test, I hadn't heard.

My mother dropped me at school. I stalked the frozen asphalt out back, stomach cramping. American history. Second period. I had no time. I hadn't even read the two most recently assigned chapters. I knew I should sit down somewhere, and try to get a little bit of it done, skim the reading, scribble out a few half-assed answers. I couldn't sit down, couldn't bear to look at my take-home again. I felt overcome with a paralyzing helplessness, the dreadful, sickening sensation of no way out, my fate settled.

At the border between the asphalt lot and the frozen, tramped-down fields beyond, there was a row of thick wooden posts that had once supported a fence, long since cleared away. A boy named Cameron Hodges from my American history class sat on one of these posts, a couple of his friends around him. Cameron was a pale-haired boy, who wore large glasses in round frames, behind which loomed inquisitive and perpetually moist blue eyes. He was on the honors list and a member of the student council, but in spite of these significant handicaps, he was almost popular, liked without really trying to be liked. This was in part because he didn't make a big show out of how much he knew, wasn't the sort to always be sticking his hand in the air whenever he knew the answer to a particularly hard problem. He had something else, though, too—a quality of reasonableness, a mixture of calm and an almost princely sense of fair play, that had the effect of making him seem more mature and experienced than the rest of us.

I liked him—had even cast my vote for him in the student elections—but we didn't ever have much to do with each other. I couldn't see myself with a friend like him . . . by which I mean, I couldn't imagine someone like him being interested in someone like me. I was a hard boy to know, uncommunicative, suspicious of other people's intentions, hostile almost by reflex. In those days, if someone happened to laugh as they walked by me, I always glared at them, just in case what was amusing them was me.

As I wandered close to him, I saw that he had his exam out. His friends were checking their answers against his: "introduction of the cotton gin to the South, right, that's what I said too." I was passing directly behind Cameron. I didn't think. I leaned past him and jerked his take-home out of his hands.

"Hey," Cameron said, reached to get it back.

"I need to copy," I said, my voice hoarse. I turned my body away, so he couldn't grab his exam back. I was flushed, breathing hard, appalled to be doing what I was doing but doing it anyway. "I'll give it back at history."

Cameron slid off the post. He came towards me, his palms turned up, his eyes shocked and beseeching, magnified unnaturally by the lenses of his glasses. "Nolan. Don't." It surprised me—I don't know why—to hear him say my name. I wasn't sure until then that he knew it. "If your answers are just like

273

mine, Mr. Sarducchi will know you copied. We'll both get Fs."
There was an audible tremor in his voice.

"Don't cry," I said. It came out harsher than I wanted it
to—I think I was really worried he might cry—so it sounded
like a taunt. Other kids laughed.

"Yeah," said Eddie Prior, who suddenly appeared between
Cameron and me. He planted his hand in the center of Cameron's forehead and shoved. Cameron went down on his ass,
hard, with a yelp. His glasses fell off and skidded away across
a puddle of ice. "Don't be a faggot. No one's going to know.
You'll get it back."

Then Eddie threw an arm over my shoulders and we were
walking away together. He spoke out of the side of his mouth,
as if we were two convicts in a movie talking in a prison yard
about the big breakout.

"Lerner," he said, referring to me by my last name. He called
everyone by their last names. "Lemmie have that after you're
done with it. Due to unforeseen circumstances beyond my
control, namely my mom's boyfriend is a loudmouthed cunt, I
had to get out of the house last night, and I wound up playing
foosball with my cousin till all hours. Upshot: I didn't get past
answering the first two questions of this friggin thing."

Although Eddie Prior pulled down Cs and Ds in everything
except shop, and found his way to detention almost weekly, he
was as charismatic in his own way as Cameron Hodges was in
his. He seemed impossible to rattle, a trait which powerfully
impressed others. Furthermore, he was so relentlessly good-
humored, so game for fun, no one could stay mad at him. If
a teacher told him to get out of class for making one ignorant
remark or another, Eddie would raise his shoulders in a slow,
who-can-figure-anything-in-this-crazy-old-world shrug, carefully collect his books, and slink out—shooting one last sly
look at the other students in a way that always set off a chain-
reaction of titters. The next morning, the same teacher who had
kicked him out of class would be tossing a football around with
him in the faculty parking lot, while the two bullshitted about
the Celtics.

It seems to me the quality that separates the popular from
the unpopular—the one and only quality that Eddie Prior and

Cameron Hodges had in common—is a strong sense of self. Eddie knew who he was. He accepted himself. His failings had ceased to trouble him. Every word he spoke was a thoughtless, pure expression of his true personality. Whereas I had no clear picture of myself, and was always looking to others, watching them intently, both hoping and fearing that I would catch some clear sign of who they saw when they looked at me.

So in the next moment, as Eddie and I moved away from Cameron, I experienced the kind of abrupt, unlikely psychological shift that is the adolescent's stock-in-trade. I had only just ripped Cameron's test from his hands, desperate to find a way out of the trap I had made for myself, and more than a little horrified at what I was willing to do to save myself. Theoretically I was still desperate and horrified—but it delighted me to find myself reeling along with Ed Prior's arm over my shoulders, as if we were lifelong friends coming out of the White Barrel Tavern at two in the morning. It gave me a delightful shock of surprise to hear him casually refer to his mother's boyfriend as a loudmouthed cunt; it seemed as smooth a witticism as anything that had ever fallen out of the mouth of Steve Martin. What I did next, I would've thought impossible just five minutes before. I handed him Cameron's exam.

"You already got two questions done? Take it. Doesn't sound like you need it for long. I'll look at it when you're finished," I said.

He grinned at me, and two deep comma-shaped dimples appeared in the baby fat of his cheeks. "How'd you get yourself into this fix, Lerner?"

"I forgot we had a take-home. I can't pay attention in that class. Don't you know Gwen Frasier?"

"Yeah. She's a fuckin skag. What about her?"

"She's a fuckin skag who doesn't wear any panties," I said. "She sits right next to me and she's always opening and closing her legs. I got her one-eyed beaver staring me in the face half of class, how am I supposed to think about history?"

He boomed with laughter, in a voice so loud, people all over the lot stared. "She's probably givin it some air to dry out her herpes sores. You want to watch out for her, partner." And then he laughed some more, laughed until he was wiping at the water brimming in his eyes. I laughed too, something I never did easily, and I felt a shiver in the nerve endings. He had called me partner.

I SEEM TO remember he never did get Cameron's take-home back to me, and I wound up handing in my test completely blank anyway—on this point my memory is a little hazy. After that morning, though, I followed him around a lot. He liked to talk about his older brother, Wayne, who had spent four weeks of a three-month sentence in the juvenile detention hall, for the crime of firebombing someone's Oldsmobile, and who had then busted out and was now living on the road. Eddie said Wayne called sometimes to brag on all the barhouse gash he was getting, and all the heads he was busting. He was vague about what his older brother was doing to get by, though. Helping on farms out in Illinois, Eddie said once. Boosting cars for Detroit niggers, he said another time.

We hung out a lot with a fifteen-year-old named Mindy Ackers, who babysat an infant in a basement apartment across the street from Eddie's duplex. The place smelled of mold and urine, but we'd blow whole afternoons there, smoking cigarettes with her, and gambling on games of checkers, while the baby crawled around bare-assed under our feet. Other days, Eddie and I took the footpath through the woods behind Christobel Park, out to the concrete pedestrian overpass that ran above Route 111. Eddie always brought a brown paper bag full of garbage with him, heisted from the apartment where Mindy did her babysitting, a sack containing shit-filled diapers and sopping cartons of rancid Chinese. He dropped bombs of garbage at trucks passing below. Once, he aimed a diaper at an enormous semi with red flames airbrushed across the hood and steer horns fixed in the spot where the hood ornament belonged. The diaper burst on the passenger side of the windshield, and a splash of dill yellow diarrhea sprayed across the glass. The air brakes shrieked, smoke boiling off the tires. The driver yanked his air horn at us, a tremendous yelp of sound that caused my heart to surge in alarm. We grabbed each other, and ran laughing.

"Book it, fat ass, I think he's coming after us!" Eddie shrieked, and I ran for the sheer excitement of running. I didn't really think anyone would go to the trouble to get out of their truck and gallop after us, but it was a thrill to pretend.

Later, when we had slowed down, and were walking through Christobel Park, both of us gasping for breath, Eddie said, "There isn't any form of human life more foul than truckers. I never met one that didn't smell like a bucket of piss after a long haul." I wasn't completely surprised to learn later that Eddie's mother's boyfriend—the loudmouthed cunt—was himself a long-haul trucker.

Sometimes Ed came to my house, mostly to watch TV. We had good reception. He was curious about my brother, wanted to know all about whatever was wrong with him, was interested to see what he was working on in the basement. Eddie remembered seeing Morris knock over his griffin domino chain on TV, even though that had happened a couple years before. This was never said, but I think he was enraptured by the idea of knowing an idiot-savant. He would've been just as excited to meet my brother if he was a double-amputee, or a dwarf. Eddie wanted a little Ripley's Believe-It-or-Not in his life. In the end, people usually get a bit more of what they want than they can really handle, don't they?

On one of his first visits to my house, we went down for a look at the latest incarnation of Morris's fort. Morris had about forty boxes strapped together to make a network of tunnels laid out in the shape of a monstrous octopus, with eight long passageways winding back to an enormous central box that had once held a projection-screen television. It would've made sense to paint it so it *looked* like an octopus—a leering kraken—and indeed, several of the thick trunk-like "arms" had been painted a lime green, with red discs on them to indicate suction cups. But other arms were leftovers from older forts—one arm was built out of the remnants of the yellow submarine, another had been part of a rocketship design, and was white, with fins and lots of American flag decals. And the huge box at the center of the octopus was completely unpainted, but encased in a shell of chicken-wire mesh, which was shaped to look like a pair of lopsided horns. All the rest of the fortress had the appearance of a child's homemade playset . . . spectacular looking, but just a playset nonetheless, something maybe Dad had helped to build. It was this last detail, the unexplained, *unexplainable* chicken-wire horns, that marked it out as the work of someone who was seriously bullshit crazy.

"Awesome," Eddie said, standing at the bottom of the stairs and looking out upon it, but I could see by a certain dimming in his eyes that he wasn't all that impressed, had been hoping for more.

I hated to see him let down, for any reason. If he wanted my brother to be a savant, so did I. I dropped to all fours, at one of the entrances. "You got to crawl in to get the full effect. They're always cooler inside than they are outside."

And without looking to see if he'd follow, I climbed in.

I was a big fourteen-year-old, clumsy, broad-shouldered, maybe a hundred and twenty pounds . . . but still a kid, not an adult, with a kid's proportions and a kid's flexibility, able to squeeze my way through even the narrowest tunnel. But I didn't usually make a habit out of climbing through Morris's forts. I had discovered early on, scrambling through one of his first designs, that I didn't like being in them much, had a touch of claustrophobia inside me. Now, though, with Eddie following behind me, I heaved myself in, as if worming around inside one of Morris's cardboard hideouts was my idea of high good times.

I climbed through one linked snaking tunnel after another. In one of the boxes there was a cardboard shelf with a jelly jar on it; flies buzzed inside of it, bumping softly and a little frantically against the glass. The close acoustics of the box amplified and distorted the sound of them, so at times the buzzing almost seemed to be inside my own head. I studied them for a moment, frowning, a little disturbed by the sight of them—was Morris going to let them die in there?—then crawled on. I wormed through a wide passageway in which the walls had been covered with glow-in-the-dark stars and moons and Cheshire cats—a whole neon galaxy swarmed around me. The walls themselves had been painted black, and at first I couldn't see them. For one brief, sickening instant, I had an impression that there weren't any walls at all, as if I were crawling through empty space on some narrow invisible ramp, nothing above me or below me for who knew how far; and if I went off the ramp there would be nothing to stop my fall. I could still hear the flies buzzing in their jelly jar, although I had left them somewhere far behind me. I was dizzy, I reached out with one hand, and my fingertips pressed against the side of the box. Like that, the impression of crawling through gaping empty space passed, although I still felt a little swimmy in the head. The next box was the smallest and darkest of them all, and as I was squeezing through it, my back brushed a series of small tin bells hanging from the ceiling. The sound of their soft, tinny clashing startled me so badly I almost shrieked.

But I could see a circular opening ahead, looking into a space lit by drifting pastel lights. I pulled myself into it.

The box at the center of Morris's cardboard kraken was roomy enough to provide shelter for a family of five and their dog. A battery-operated lava lamp bubbled in one corner, red globs of plasma rising and sinking through viscous amber fluid. Morris had papered the inside of the enormous box with silver foil Christmas wrap. Sparks and filaments of light raced here and there in trembling waves, sheets of gold and raspberry and lime, crashing into each other and vanishing. It was as if in the course of my long crawl to the center of the fort, I had gradually been shrinking, until at last I was no larger than a field mouse, and had arrived in a little room suspended inside a disco ball. The sight gave me a weak shiver of wonder. My temples throbbed dully, the strange, wandering lights beginning to bother my eyes.

I hadn't seen Morris since getting home, had assumed he was out with our mother on an errand. But he was waiting there in the large central box, sitting on his knees with his back to me. To one side of him was a comic book and a pair of scissors. He had cut the back cover off and inserted it into a white cardboard frame, and now he was sticking it to the wall with pieces of Scotch tape. He heard me enter, and glanced back at me, but didn't say hello, and returned straightaway to hanging his picture.

I heard scuffling noises in the passageway behind me, and slid to one side to make room. An instant later Eddie poked his head through the circular hatch and peered up into the foil-lined box. His face was flushed and he was grinning in that way that made dimples in his cheeks.

"Holy shit," Eddie said. "Look at this place. I want to bang a chick in here."

He pulled himself the rest of the way out of the tunnel, and sat on his knees.

"Bitchin fort," Eddie said to Morris's back. "I would've killed to have a fort like this when I was your age." Ignoring the fact that at eleven, Morris was actually too old to be playing in cardboard forts himself.

Morris didn't reply. Eddie shot me a sideways look and I shrugged. Eddie cast his gaze around, taking it all in, mouth hanging open in an expression of obvious pleasure, while a storm of brilliant lights, gold and silver, billowed silently around us.

"Crawling in here was wild," Eddie went on. "What'd you think of the tunnel that was lined with black fur? I felt like when I got to the end I was going to pop out of a gorilla's snatch."

I laughed, but gave him a questioning, puzzled look. I didn't remember a fur-lined tunnel—and he had, after all, been right behind me, had followed the same path I followed.

"Also the wind-chimes," Eddie said.

"They were bells," I corrected.

"Oh, were they?"

Morris finished hanging his picture and, without speaking to us, crawled to a triangular exit. Before he went through, though, he looked back at us one last time. When he spoke, he spoke to me: "Don't follow me this way. Go back the way you came." Then: "This way won't do what it's supposed to. I need to work on it some more. It isn't right yet."

With that, he ducked through the hatch and disappeared.

I looked at Eddie, to offer an apology, was preparing a statement along the lines of, *Sorry my brother's such an absolute fruitcake.* But Eddie had crawled around me and was studying the picture Morris had hung on the wall. It showed a family of Sea Monkeys, standing together in a close group—nude, pot-bellied creatures with waving flesh-colored antennae and human faces.

"Look," Eddie said. "He hung up a picture of his real family."

I laughed. Eddie wasn't much in the personal ethics department, but it was never any trouble for him to make me laugh.

I WAS ON my way out of the house—it was a Friday, in the first couple weeks of February—when Eddie called and said not to come to his place, but to meet me on the footbridge over 111. Something in his tone, a hoarseness, a strained quality, caught my attention. Nothing he said was out of the ordinary, but sometimes his voice seemed about to crack, and I had an impression of him struggling to clamp down on a surge of unhappiness.

The footbridge was a twenty-minute hike from my house, down Christobel Avenue, through the park, and then up the nature trail into the woods. The nature trail was a groomed path of crushed blue stones, which climbed the rising hills under bare stands of birch and moose maple. In about a third of a mile the path came out onto the footbridge. Eddie was leaning over the railing, watching the cars in the eastbound lane rush by below.

He didn't look at me as I came towards him. Lined on the belly-high wall in front of him were three crumbly bricks, and just as I came up beside him, he nudged one off. I felt an instant of nervous shock, but the brick fell onto the back end of an eighteen-wheeler rolling by below, without damaging anything. The truck was hauling a trailer loaded with steel pipes. The brick hit the top pipe with a clash and a bang, then tumbled down the side of the pile, setting off a series of tuneful clangs and ringing gongs, a hammer thrown at the metal tubes of some enormous pipe organ. Eddie opened his mouth in his broad, homely, impossibly likable grin, showing the gaps in his teeth. He glanced at me, to see if I appreciated the unexpected musicality produced by his latest truck bombing. That was when I saw his left eye. It was surrounded by a ring of bruised flesh, ugly purple, with faint highlights of yellow.

When I spoke, I barely recognized my voice as my own. My tone was winded and faint. "What happened?"

"Lookit," he said, and dug a Polaroid out of the pocket of his jacket. He was grinning still, but when he passed the picture to me he wouldn't meet my gaze. "Feast your eyes." It was as if I hadn't said anything.

The picture showed two fingers, belonging to a girl, her fingernails painted a creamy silver. They were pressing into a triangle of red-and-black striped fabric, caught in the cleft of skin between her legs. I could see her thighs at the edges of the photo, blurred, too-pale flesh.

"I beat Ackers ten games in a row," he said. "We bet if she lost the tenth game she had to take a picture of herself fingerin her clit. She went in the bedroom so I didn't actually see her take the picture. But she wants to go again sometime and try and win the photo back. If I beat her another ten games in a row I'm going to make her finger herself right in front of me."

I turned, so that we were standing side-by-side, leaning against the railing, facing oncoming traffic. I gazed blankly at the photo for another moment, not thinking much of anything, unsure how to act, what to say. Mindy Ackers was a plain girl with frizzy red hair, devastating acne and a throbbing crush on Eddie. If she lost the next ten games of checkers to him, it would be on purpose.

At the moment, though, what she had or hadn't done to entertain him was a lot less interesting than how Eddie had wound up with that freshly minted shiner on his left eye . . . a thing, apparently, he didn't want to discuss.

"Fuckin wild," I said, finally, and set the photo on the cement wall below the railing. Without thinking, I put my hand down on one of the bricks.

A tractor-trailer thundered past below us, engine barking as the driver shifted into a lower, noisier gear. Black diesel-smelling smoke swirled up through the snow, which was falling in big, curling flakes. When had it started to snow? I wasn't sure.

"How'd you do that to your eye?" I tried again, surprised at my own nerve.

He wiped his nose with the back of his hand. He was still grinning. "Fuckin bag of shit my mom is going out with caught me lookin in his wallet. Like I was going to steal his food stamps or something. He's going to bed early, he's got to leave for Kentucky before sunup, so I'm just staying out of the house until—oh wait. Look. Oil tanker comin."

I glanced down and saw another big semi booming towards us, pulling a long steel tank behind it.

"We got one chance to blow it up," Eddie said. "Four ounces of C-4. We hit this motherfucker just right we'll take out the whole road."

There was a brick on the wall, right in front of him, and I waited for him to put his hand on it and shove it off onto the oil tanker as it passed below. Instead, though, he put his hand on top of mine, which was still resting on the other brick. I felt a little pulse of alarm, but made no effort to pull my hand free. That's probably a fact worth underlining. What happened next I let happen.

"Wait for it," he said. "Steady. Don't miss. *Now.*"

Just as the oil truck started in under the footbridge, he gave my hand a shove. The brick struck the side of the oil tank below with a ringing *ke-rang!* It took a hard bounce and flipped sideways, away from the truck and out across the passing lane, where at that moment, a red Volvo was just pulling abreast of the rolling tanker. The brick crunched into the windshield—I had time to see a pattern of spiderweb fracture lines shooting out across the glass—and then the car disappeared under the footbridge.

We both spun around and jumped to the opposite railing. My lungs seized up, for a moment I couldn't force any air up out of my chest. When the Volvo came out from under the footbridge, it was already veering to the left, across the shoulder of the road. It left the highway a moment later and went down the snowy embankment at around thirty miles an hour. In the shallow valley at the bottom of the embankment were a few whippy maple saplings. The Volvo hit one with a brittle crack. The whole shattered windshield fell out in one glittering piece and slid across the hood, then dropped into the snow.

I was still struggling to inhale when the passenger side front door sprang open. A blond, matronly woman in a red overcoat, belted at the waist, clambered out. She was holding a mittened hand over one eye. She was screaming, yanking at the back door.

"Amy!" she screamed. "Oh God, Amy!"

Then Eddie had me by the elbow. He turned me around, shoved me at the path. He yelled, "Fuck outta here!"

He shoved me again as we came off the footbridge and onto the trail into the park, shoved me so hard I fell to one knee on the crushed blue stones—sharp darts of pain shot into my kneecap—but then he was wrenching me up by the elbow again and rushing me on. I didn't think. I ran. With blood thudding in my temples, and my face burning in the cold air, I ran.

I DIDN'T START to think until we reached the park, and slowed to a walk. We were moving, without discussing it, in the direction of my house. My lungs hurt from the effort of running in snow boots, and from hauling in chestfuls of frozen air.

She went around to the back door, shouting *Oh God, Amy!* Someone in the backseat, then, a little girl. The tall, heavyset blonde was holding a mitten over her eye. Did she get a shard of glass in it? Had we blinded her? Also: the blonde spilled out of the passenger seat. Why didn't the driver get out? Was he conscious? Was he *dead?* My legs wouldn't stop shaking. I remembered Eddie pushing my hand, remembered the brick slipping out from under my palm, tumbling end over end, and then the way it banged off the side of the oil tanker and flipped into the windshield of the Volvo. I couldn't take it back. I saw that then, the thought struck me like a revelation. I looked down at the hand that had shoved the brick, and saw a photo in it, Mindy Ackers probing the triangle of cotton between her legs. I didn't remember picking it up. I showed it to Eddie, wordlessly. He looked at it, his eyes foggy, baffled.

"Keep it," he said. It was the first either of us had spoken since he yelled *Fuck outta here.*

We passed my mother on the way into my house. She was standing next to the mailbox, making small talk with our next-door neighbor, and she absentmindedly touched the back of my neck as I went by her, a flitting, intimate brush of the fingers that caused me to shudder.

I didn't say anything until we were inside, taking our boots and coats off in the mudroom. My father was at work, I didn't know where Morris was and didn't care. The house was darkened and silent, had about it the stillness of an empty place.

As I unbuttoned my corduroy jacket, I said, "We should call someone." My voice seemed to come from somewhere else, not from in my chest and throat, but from the corner of the room, under the pile of hats that were laying there.

"Call who?"

"The police. To see if they're all right."

He stopped pulling off his denim jacket and stared at me. In the poor light, his black eye looked like a tragic accident with mascara.

I went on talking for some reason. "We could just say we were standing on the footbridge and we saw the accident. We don't need to say we were the ones who caused it."

"We *didn't* cause it."

"Well—" I started, and then didn't know what to say next. It was such a baldly false statement, I couldn't think of any way to respond that wouldn't come off like a provocation.

"The brick took a bad spin," he said. "How could that be our fault?"

"I just want to make sure everyone is all right," I said. "There was a little kid in the back—"

"Fuck there was."

"Well—" I faltered again, then forced myself to continue. "There *was*, Eddie. Her mom was calling for her."

He stopped moving for an instant, studying me carefully, a look of unhappy, truculent calculation on his face. Then he lifted his shoulders in a stiff shrug, and went back to kicking off his boots.

"If you call the police I'll kill myself," he said. "Then you can have that on your head, too."

It felt as if there was a great pressure weighing down on my chest, compressing my lungs. I tried to speak. My voice came out in a whistling whisper. "Come on."

"I mean it," he said. "I would." He paused again, then said, "You know how I said my brother called me that time about all the money he was making ripping off cars in Detroit?"

I nodded.

"That was bullshit. Remember how I said he called to tell me about fucking redheaded twins while he was out in Minnesota?"

After a moment I nodded again.

"That was bullshit too. It was always bullshit. He never called." Eddie took a long breath, which shuddered just slightly on the inhale. "I don't know where he's at, or what he's doing. He only called me once, while he was still in the Juvie. Two days before he broke out. He didn't sound right. He was trying not to cry. He said never do anything that will get you in here. He made me promise. He said they try and make you faggot in there. There's all these Boston niggers who act faggot, and they gang up on you. And then he disappeared and no one knows what happened to him. But I think if he was okay somewhere he would've called by now. Me and him were tight. He wouldn't just make me wonder. And I know my brother, and he wouldn't want to be someone's faggot." He was crying by now, soundlessly. He swiped at his cheeks with the sleeve of his sweatshirt, and then fixed his fierce, watery stare on me. He said, "And I'm not going to Juvie over some stupid accident that wasn't even my fault. No one's going to turn me homo. I already had something like that happen to me once. That fucking smelly shit, my mother's fucking Tennessee shithead—" He broke off, tore his gaze away, gasping slightly.

I didn't say anything. The sight of Eddie Prior with tears soaking his face took away any arguments I might've made for going to the police, silenced me completely.

In a low, shaky voice, he went on, "We can't undo it. It happened. It was a stupid accident. A bad ricochet. It's no one's fault. Whoever got hurt we just have to live with it now. We just have to sit tight. No one's ever going to figure out we had anything to do with it. I got the bricks from under the footbridge. There's a bunch of them coming loose. Unless someone saw us, no one will ever know it didn't just fall. But if you really got to call someone, just let me know first, because I won't let them do to me what they did to my brother."

It was several moments before I could collect the air to speak.

"Forget it," I said. "Let's just watch some TV and cool out."

We finished pulling off our winter clothes, and stepped into the kitchen . . . and I almost walked into Morris, who was standing at the open door to the basement, with a reel of brown packing tape in one hand. His head was tilted to the side, in a listening-to-the-spheres pose, his eyes wide with their usual empty-headed curiosity.

Eddie bumped me aside with his elbow, grabbed the front of Morris's black cord turtleneck, and slammed him into the wall. Morris's already wide eyes flew open even wider. He stared with blank, dumb confusion into Eddie's flushed face. I grabbed Eddie's wrist, tried to pry his fingers free, couldn't break his grip.

"Were you eavesdropping on us you little retard?" Eddie asked.

"Eddie—Eddie—it doesn't matter what he heard. Forget it. He won't tell. Let him go," I said.

And just like that Eddie released him. Morris gazed into his face, blinking, mouth hanging open and slack. He took a brief sideways peek at me—what was that all about?—then moved his shoulders in a little shrug.

"I had to pull apart the octopus," Morris said. "I liked all those arms streaming to the center. How they were like spokes on a wheel. But no matter where you climb in, you always know where you're going and not-knowing is better. Not so easy to do but better. I have new ideas now. This time I'm going to start from the center and work out, same as spiders do."

"Wicked," I said. "Go for it."

"My new design will use the most boxes ever. Wait'll you see."

"We'll be counting the minutes, won't we, Eddie?"

"Yeah," he said.

"I'll be downstairs working on it if anyone needs me," Morris said, and he slipped through the narrow gap between Eddie and myself, clunked off down the basement steps.

We made our way into the living room. I put on the TV, but I couldn't focus on what we were watching. I felt removed from myself, felt as if I were standing at the end of a long corridor, and at the far end I could see Eddie and me sitting together on the couch, only it wasn't me, it was a hollow wax figure cast in my image.

Eddie said, "Sorry I freaked out on your brother."

I wanted Eddie to go away, wanted to be by myself, curled up on my bed in the quiet, restful dark of my bedroom. I didn't know how to ask him to go.

Instead, I said, through just slightly numb lips, "If Morris *did* tell—and he won't, I swear—even if he heard us, he wouldn't understand what we were talking about—but if he did tell someone—you wouldn't—you—"

"Kill myself?" Eddie asked. He made a rough, derisive sound in his throat. "Fuck no. I'd kill *him*. But he won't tell, right?"

"No," I said. My stomach hurt.

"And you won't tell," he said, a few minutes later. The day was growing late, the light draining away all around us.

"No," I said.

He pushed himself to his feet, swatted my leg on the way out of the room. "Got to go. I'm eating dinner with my cousin. I'll see you tomorrow."

I waited until I heard the door close in the mudroom as he went out. Then I came to my feet myself, light-headed and woozy. I reeled into the front hall and started upstairs. I almost fell over Morris. He was sitting six steps up from the bottom, his hands on his knees, his face a tranquilized blank. In his dark clothes, only his waxy pale face was visible in the dim of the front hall. My heart lurched when I saw him there. For a moment I stood over him, staring down at him. He stared back, his expression as alien and unreadable as ever.

So he had heard the rest of it, including what Eddie said about killing him if he told. But I really didn't think he could've understood us.

I stepped around him, and went up to my room. I shut the door behind me and crawled under the blankets, still dressed in my clothes, just as I had imagined doing. The room tilted and swayed around me until I was almost overcome with seasickness, and had to pull the covers over my head to block out the senseless, disorientating motion of the world.

I LOOKED IN the paper the next morning for some information about the accident—*little girl left in coma after overpass ambush*—but there was nothing.

*　　　*　　　*

I CALLED A hospital that afternoon, and said I was wondering about the accident on 111 the other day, the car that went off the road, the windshield fell out and some people were hurt. My voice was unsteady and nervous, and the receptionist on the other end began to interrogate me—why did I need to know? who was I?—and I hung up.

I WAS IN my room a few days later, feeling through the pockets of my winter coat for a pack of gum, when I came across a sharp-edged square of some slippery, plastic-like material. I pulled it out and stared at the Polaroid of Mindy Ackers fingering her crotch. The sight turned my stomach. I pulled open the top drawer, flung it in, and slammed the drawer behind it. It made me feel short of breath, just to look at it; remembering the Volvo crashed into the tree, the woman spilling out, mitten over her eye, *Oh God, Amy!* My memories of the accident were growing uncertain by then. Sometimes I imagined there had been blood on the side of the blonde's face. Sometimes I imagined there had been blood dappling the broken glass of the windshield in the snow. And sometimes I imagined I had heard the teakettle shrieking of a child crying out in pain. This was an especially hard conviction to shake; someone had been screaming, I was sure of it, someone besides the woman. Maybe me.

I DIDN'T WANT to have anything to do with Eddie after that, but he couldn't be avoided. He sat next to me in classes and passed me notes. I had to pass notes back to him so he wouldn't think I was brushing him off. He showed up at my house after school, without warning, and we sat in front of the TV together. He brought his checkerboard and would set it up while we watched *Hogan's Heroes*. I see now—and maybe I saw then— that he was consciously sticking close to me, watching over me. He knew he couldn't allow me to put a distance between us, that if we weren't partners anymore, I might do anything, even confess. And he knew too that I didn't have the spine for ending a friendship, that I couldn't not open the door to him when he rang the bell. That it was in me to just go along with the situation, no matter how uncomfortable, rather than try and change things and risk an upsetting confrontation.

Then, one afternoon, about three weeks after the accident out on Route 111, I discovered Morris in my room, standing at my dresser. The top drawer was open. In one hand he had a box of X-acto knife blades; there was a whole pile of junk like that in there, twine, staples, a roll of duct tape, and sometimes if Morris needed something for his never-ending fort, he would raid my supplies. In his other hand was the Polaroid of Mindy Ackers's crotch. He held it almost to his nose, stared at it with round, uncomprehending eyes.

"Don't go through my stuff," I said.

"Isn't it sad you can't see her face?" he said.

I snapped the picture out of his hand and tossed it in the dresser. "Go through my stuff again and I'll kill you."

"You sound like Eddie," Morris said, and he turned his head and stared at me. I hadn't seen a lot of him the last few days. He had been in the basement even more than usual. His lean, delicate-boned face was thinner than I remembered, and I was uniquely conscious in that moment of how slight and fragile, how childlike his build was. He was almost twelve, but could've easily passed for eight. "Are you and him still friends?"

I was ragged from being worried all the time, spoke without thinking. "I don't know."

"Why don't you tell him to go? Why don't you make him go away?" He stood almost too close to me, staring up into my face with his unblinking saucer-plate eyes.

"I can't," I said, and turned away, because I couldn't bear to meet his worried, mystified gaze. I felt stretched to the limit of what I could take, my nerves worn raw. "I wish I could. But no one can make him go away." I leaned against the dresser, rested my forehead against the edge of it for a moment. In a rough whisper that I hardly heard myself, I said, "He can't let me get away."

"Because of what happened?"

I shot him a look then. He was hovering at my elbow, his hands curled against his chest, his fingertips fluttering nervously.

So he understood . . . maybe not all of it, but some. Enough. He knew we had done something terrible. He knew the strain of it was pulling me apart.

"You forget about what happened," I said, my voice stronger now, edged almost with threat. "You forget about what you heard. If anyone finds out—Morris, you can't tell anyone. Not ever."

"I want to help."

"I can't be helped," I said and the truth of this statement, said just in this way, hit me hard. In a lame, unhappy tone, I finally added, "Go away. Please."

Morris frowned slightly, and bowed his head, seemed briefly hurt. Then he said, "I'm almost finished with the new fort. I see it all now. How it will be." Then he fixed his arresting, wide-eyed stare on me once again. "I'm building it for you, Nolan. Because I want you to feel better."

I let out a soft breath that was almost a laugh. For a moment we had almost been talking like any pair of brothers who loved and worried about each other, talking like near-equals; for a few seconds I had forgotten Morris's delusions and fantasies. Had forgotten that reality, for him, was a thing he only glimpsed now and then through the drifting vapors of his waking daydreams. To Morris, the only sensible response to unhappiness was to build a skyscraper out of egg cartons.

"Thanks, Morris," I said. "You're a good kid. You just need to stay out of my room."

He nodded, but he was still frowning to himself when he slipped around me and went out into the hall. I watched him walk away from me down the stairs, his scarecrow's shadow lunging and swaying across the wall, growing larger with every step he took towards the light below and some future that would be built one box at a time.

MORRIS WAS IN the basement until dinner—mother had to yell for him three times before he came upstairs—and when he sat at the table his hands had a white, plaster-like powder on them. He returned to the basement as soon as our dinner plates were parked in the soapy water filling the sink. He stayed down there until it was almost nine in the evening, and only quit when my mother hollered that it was time for bed.

I went by the open door to the cellar once, not long before I went to bed myself, and paused there. I had caught a whiff of something that at first I couldn't identify—it was like glue, or fresh paint, or plaster, or some combination of the three.

My father came into the mudroom, stamping his feet. There had been a little dusting of snow, and he had been outside, sweeping it off the steps.

"What's that?" I asked, wrinkling my nose.

He came to the top of the basement stairs, and sniffed.

"Oh," my father said. "Morris mentioned he was going to do some work with papier-mâché. There's no telling what that kid will play with to get his kicks, is there?"

MY MOTHER VOLUNTEERED at an old folks' home every Thursday, where she read letters to people with bad eyes and played piano in the rec room, banging on the keys so the half-deaf could hear her, and on those afternoons, I was left in sole charge of the house and my little brother. When the next Thursday rolled around, she wasn't out of the house more than ten minutes when Eddie banged his fist on the side door.

"Hey, partner," Eddie said. "Guess what? Mindy Ackers just fed me my ass in five straight games. I have to give her back that picture. You have it, don't you? I hope you been taking good care of it for me."

"You're welcome to the nasty fucking thing," I said, a little relieved that he was obviously only stopping by for a minute. It was rare to be able to get rid of him so quickly. He kicked off his boots and followed me into the kitchen. "Let me go get it. It's in my room."

"Probably on your night-table, you sick fuck," Eddie said, and laughed.

"Are you talking about Eddie's photograph?" Morris asked, his voice floating up from the bottom of the basement stairs. "I've got it. I was looking at it. It's down here."

I was probably quite a bit more surprised by this statement than Eddie was. I had made it clear to Morris that I wanted him to leave it alone, and it was unlike him to disregard a direct order.

"Morris, I told you to stay out of my stuff," I yelled.

Eddie stood at the top of the steps, leering down into the basement.

"What are you doin with it, you little masturbator?" he called down to Morris.

Morris didn't reply and Eddie tromped down the staircase, with me right behind him.

Eddie stopped three steps from the bottom and put his fists on his hips, stared out across the expanse of the basement.

"Whoa," he said. "Cool."

The cellar was filled, from end to end, with a great labyrinth of cardboard boxes. Morris had repainted them, *all* of them. The boxes closest to the foot of the stairs were the creamy white of whole milk, but as the network of tunnels spread out into the rest of the room, the boxes darkened to a shade of pale blue, then to violet, then to cobalt. The boxes at the furthest edge of the room were entirely black, limning a horizon of artificial night.

I saw crate-size boxes with passageways leading from every side. I saw windows, cut in the shapes of stars and stylized suns. At first I thought these windows had sheets of weirdly shining orange plastic taped into them. But then I saw how they pulsed and flickered softly, and realized that they were actually sheets of clear plastic, lit from within by some unsteady source of orange light—Morris's lava lamp, no doubt. But most of the boxes didn't have windows at all, especially as you got out away from the bottom of the staircase and moved towards the far walls of the basement. It would be dark in there.

In the northwestern corner of the basement, rising above all the other boxes, was an enormous crescent moon, made out of papier-mâché and painted a waxy, faintly luminescent white. The moon had thin pinched lips and a single sad, drooping eye that seemed to regard us with an expression of unfocused disappointment. I was so unprepared for the sight of it, so stunned—it was truly immense—that it took me a minute to realize I was looking at the giant box that had once been at the center of Morris's octopus. Back then, it had been encased in a mesh of chicken-wire, shaped into two points like lopsided horns. I remembered thinking that Morris's massive, misshapen chicken-wire sculpture was irrefutable proof that my brother's already soft brains were deteriorating. Now I saw that it had always been a moon; anyone with eyes could've seen it for what it was . . . just not me. I think this was always one of my critical failings. If something didn't make sense to me right away, I could never manage to look past what confused me to see a larger design or pattern, either in a structure or in the shape of my own life.

At the very foot of the stairs was an entrance to Morris's cardboard catacombs. It was a tall box, about four feet high, stood on its side, with two flaps pulled open like a pair of double doors. A black sheet of muslin had been stapled up inside, blocking my view of the tunnel leading out of the box and into the maze. I heard distant, echoing music from somewhere, a low, reverberating, trance-inducing melody. A deep baritone sang, *"The ants go marching one-by-one, hurrah! Hurrah!"* It took me a moment to realize that the music was coming from somewhere within the system of tunnels.

I was so astonished I couldn't stay angry with Morris for swiping the picture of Mindy Ackers. I was so astonished I couldn't even speak. It was Eddie who spoke first.

"I don't believe that moon," he said, to no one in particular. He sounded like I felt—a little winded by surprise. "Morris, you're a fucking genius."

Morris stood to the right, his face bland, his gaze directed out across the vast sprawl. "I stuck your picture up inside my new fort. I hung it in the gallery. I didn't know you'd want it back. You can go get it if you want."

Eddie flicked a sideways look at Morris, and his grin broadened. "You hid it in there and you want me to find it. Boy, you are a weird shit, you know that, Morrie?" He bounded down the last three steps, almost did a Gene Kelly dance down them. "Where's the gallery? Way out there, inside that moon?"

"No," Morris said. "Don't head that way."

"Yeah," Eddie said, and laughed. "*Right*. What other pictures do you have hanging up in there? Bunch of centerfolds? You got your own little private room in there for spankin it?"

"I don't want to say anything more. I don't want to ruin the surprise. You should just go in and see."

Eddie shot me a look. I didn't know what to say, but I was surprised to feel a tremulous kind of anticipation, with a white thread of unease stitched through it. I both wanted and dreaded to see him disappear into Morris's confused, brilliant fortress. Eddie shook his head—*Do you believe this shit?*—and got down on all fours. He started to crawl into the entrance, then glanced back at me once again. I was surprised to see a flush of almost childlike eagerness on his face. It was a look that unsettled me for some reason. I myself felt no eagerness whatsoever to squirm around in the dark, cramped interior of Morris's immense maze.

"You ought to come," Eddie said. "We ought to check this out together."

I nodded, feeling a little weak—there were no words in the language of our friendship for saying *no*—and started down the last few basement stairs. Eddie pushed aside the flap of black muslin, and the music echoed out from within a large circular tunnel, a cardboard pipe almost three feet in diameter. *"The ants go marching three-by-three, hurrah! Hurrah!"* I came down off the last step, started to duck down to climb in after Eddie—and Morris came up beside me and seized my arm, his grip unaccountably tight.

Eddie didn't glance back, didn't see us standing together that way. He said, *"Ke-rist.* Any hints?"

"Go towards the music," Morris said.

Eddie's head moved up and down in a slow nod, as if this should've been obvious. He stared into the long, dark, circular tunnel ahead of him.

In a perfectly normal tone of voice, Morris said to me, "Don't go. Don't follow him."

Eddie started worming his way into the tunnel.

"Eddie!" I said, feeling a sudden, inexplicable burst of alarm. "Eddie, wait a minute! Come back out."

"Holy shit, it's dark in here," Eddie said, as if he hadn't heard me. In fact, I'm sure he *didn't* hear me—had stopped being able to hear me almost as soon as he entered Morris's labyrinth.

"Eddie!" I shouted. "Don't go in there!"

"There better be some windows up ahead," Eddie murmured . . . talking to himself. "If I start getting claustrophobic, I'll just stand up and tear this motherfucker apart." He inhaled deeply, let it out. "Okay. Let's go."

The curtain flapped down across his feet and Eddie disappeared.

Morris let go of my arm. I looked over at him, but his stare was directed towards his sprawling fortress, towards the cardboard tube into which Eddie had climbed. I could hear Eddie clunking through it, away from us; I heard him come out the other end, into a large box, about four feet tall and a couple feet across. He bumped into it—knocked one of the walls with a shoulder maybe—and it shifted slightly. A cardboard tunnel led to the right, another to the left. He picked the one that pointed in the general direction of the moon. From the bottom of the basement steps I could follow his progress, could see boxes shaking slightly as he passed through them, could hear the muffled thump of his body striking the walls now and then. Then I lost track of him for a moment or two, couldn't locate him until I heard his voice.

"I *see* you guys," he crooned, and I heard him tapping against thick plastic.

I looked around and saw his face behind a star-shaped window. He was grinning in a way that showed the David Letterman gap between his front teeth. He gave me the finger. The red furnace light of Morris's lava lamp surged and faded around him. Then he crawled on. I never saw him again.

But I heard him. For a while longer I could hear him making his way along, moving in the rough direction of the moon, away into the far reaches of our basement. Over the muffled warble of the music—"*down, in the ground, to get out of the rain*"—I could still hear him bumping into the walls of the maze. I saw a box tremble. Once I heard him pass over a strip of bubble wrap that must've been stapled to the floor in one of the tunnels. A cluster of plastic blisters popped with sharp, flat reports, like a string of penny firecrackers going off, and I heard him say, "Fuck!"

After that I lost track of him again. Then his voice came once more—off to my right, all the way across the room from where I had heard him last.

"Shit," was all he said. For the first time I thought I heard in his tone an undercurrent of irritation, a shortness of breath.

An instant later, he spoke again, and a flash of light-headed disorientation passed over me, left me weak in the knees. Now his voice seemed to come impossibly from the *left*, as if he had traveled a hundred feet in the space of a breath.

"Dead fucking end," he said, and a tunnel off to the left shook as he scrambled through it.

Then I wasn't sure where he was. Most of a minute ticked by, and I noticed that my hands were clenched in sweaty fists, and that I was almost holding my breath.

"Hey," Eddie said from somewhere, and I thought I heard a warble of unease in his voice. "Is someone else crawling around in here?" He was a good distance off from me. I thought the sound of his voice seemed to come from one of the boxes close to the moon.

A long silence followed. By now the music had wrapped all the way around and the song was playing again from the beginning. For the first time I found myself listening to it, really *listening*. The lyrics weren't like I remembered them from summer camp sing-a-longs. At one point, the low singing voice cried:

> "*The ants go marching two-by-two, Hurrah! Hurrah!*
> *The ants go marching two-by-two, Hurrah! Hurrah!*
> *The ants go marching two-by-two,*
> *They walked across the Leng plateau*
> *And they all went marching down!*"

Whereas in the version I remembered, it seemed to me there had been something about a little one stopping to pick a rock out of his shoe. Also it made me antsy, the way the song just kept looping around and around.

"What's up with this tape?" I said to Morris. "How come it only plays this one song?"

"I don't know," he said. "The music started playing this morning. It hasn't stopped since. It's been playing all day."

I turned my head and stared, a feeling of cool, tingling fright prickling through my chest.

"What do you mean, *it hasn't stopped?*"

"I don't even know where it's coming from," Morris said. "It isn't anything I did."

"Isn't there a tape deck?"

Morris shook his head, and for the first time I felt panic.

"Eddie!" I shouted.

There was no response.

"Eddie!" I called again, and started walking across the room, stepping over and around boxes, moving towards the moon and where I had last heard Eddie's voice. "Eddie, answer me!"

From an impossibly long distance off, I heard something, part of a sentence: "Trail of bread crumbs." It didn't even sound like Eddie's voice—the words were spoken in a clipped, supercilious tone, sounded almost like one of the overlapping voices you hear in that crazy nonsense song by the Beatles, *Revolution #9*—and I couldn't pinpoint where it came from, wasn't sure if its origin was ahead of or behind me. I turned around and around, trying to figure where the voice had come from, when the music abruptly switched off, with the ants marching nine. I cried out in surprise, and looked to Morris.

He held his X-acto knife—loaded with a blade swiped from my dresser, no doubt—and was on his knees, cutting the tape that attached the first box in the maze to the second.

"There. He's gone," Morris said. "All done." He pulled the entrance to the maze free, neatly flattened the box and set it aside.

"What are you talking about?"

He wasn't looking at me. He was methodically beginning to take it all apart, severing tape, pressing boxes flat, piling them next to the stairs. He went on, "I wanted to help. You said he wouldn't go away, so I *made* him go away." He lifted his gaze for a moment, and stared at me with those eyes that always seemed to look right through me. "He had to go away. He wasn't ever going to leave you alone."

"Jesus," I breathed. "I knew you were crazy, but I didn't know you were a total shithouse rat. What do you mean, he's gone? He's right here. He's got to be right here. He's still in the boxes. Eddie!" Shouting his name, my voice a little hysterical. "Eddie!"

But he *was* gone, and I knew it. Knew that he had gone into Morris's boxes and crawled right through them into someplace else, someplace not our basement. I started moving across the fort, looking into windows, kicking boxes. I began pulling the catacombs apart, ripping tape away with my hands, flipping boxes over to look inside them. I stumbled this way and that, tripping once, half-crushing a tunnel.

Inside one box, the walls were covered with a photo collage, pictures of the blind: old people with milky white eyes staring out of their carved-from-wood faces, a black man with a slide guitar across his knees and round black sunglasses pushed up the bridge of his nose, Cambodian children with scarves wrapped over their eyes. Since there were no windows cut into the box, the collage would've been invisible to anyone crawling through it. In another box, pink strips of flypaper—they looked like dusty strings of salt-water taffy—hung from the ceiling, but there weren't any flies stuck to them. Instead there were several lightning bugs, still alive, blinking yellow-green for an instant and then fading out. I did not think, at the time, that it was March, and lightning bugs impossible to come by. The interior of a third box had been painted a pale sky blue, with flocks of childish blackbirds drawn against it. In the corner of the box was what I at first took to be a cat's toy, a mass of faded dark feathers with dust bunnies clinging to it. When I tipped the box on its side, though, a dead bird slid out. The body was dried out and desiccated, and its eyes had fallen back into its head, leaving little black sockets that looked like cigarette burns. I almost screamed at the sight of it. My stomach rioted; I tasted bile in the back of my throat.

Then Morris had me by the elbow, and was steering me towards the steps.

"You won't find him like that," he said. "Please sit down, Nolan."

I sat on the bottom step. By then I was fighting not to cry. I kept waiting for Eddie to jump out laughing from somewhere— *Oh man, I fooled you*—and at the same time some part of me knew he never would.

It was a while before I realized Morris had lowered himself to his knees in front of me, like a man preparing to propose to his bride. He regarded me steadily.

"Maybe if I put it back together the music will start again. And you can go in and look for him," he said. "But I don't think you can come back out. There's doors in there that only swing one way. Do you understand, Nolan? It's bigger inside than it looks." He stared at me steadily, with his oddly bright, saucer eyes, and then said, in a tone of quiet force, "I don't want you to go in, but I'll put it back together if you tell me to."

I stared at him. He stared back, waiting, his head tilted to that curious, listening angle, like a chickadee on a branch considering the sound of raindrops falling through the trees. I imagined him carefully putting back together what we had pulled apart in the last ten minutes . . . then imagined the music blaring to life from somewhere inside the boxes, roaring this time: "*DOWN! IN THE GROUND! TO GET OUT! OF THE RAIN!*" If that music started up again, without any warning, I thought I would scream; I wouldn't be able to help myself.

I shook my head. Morris turned away and went back to disassembling his creation.

I sat at the bottom of the stairs for most of an hour, watching Morris carefully tear down his cardboard fortress. Eddie never came out of it. No other sound ever issued from within. I heard the back door open and my mother troop in, crossing the floorboards overhead. She shouted for me to come and help with the groceries. I went up, lugged in bags, put food in the fridge. Morris came up for supper, went down again. Taking a thing apart is always faster than putting something together. This is true of everything except marriage. When I glanced down the steps into the basement, at a quarter to eight, I could see three stacks of neatly flattened boxes, each about four feet high, and a vast expanse of bare concrete floor. Morris was at the bottom of the steps, sweeping. He stopped, and glanced up at me—giving me an impenetrable, alien stare—and I shivered. He went back to his work, moving the broom in short compact strokes across the floor, brush, brush, brush.

I lived in the house four more years, but never visited Morris in the basement after that, avoided the place entirely, as best

I could. By the time I left for college, Morris's bed was down there, and he rarely came up. He slept in a low hut he had made himself out of empty Coke bottles and carefully cut pieces of ice blue foam.

The moon was the only part of the fortress Morris didn't dismantle. A few weeks after Eddie vanished, my father drove the moon to Morris's school for the developmentally challenged, where it won third prize—fifty dollars and a medal—in an art show. I couldn't tell you what happened to it after that. Like Eddie Prior, it never returned.

I RECALL THREE things about the few weeks that followed Eddie's disappearance.

I remember my mother opening the door of my bedroom, just after twelve, on the night he went missing. I was curled on my side in bed, the sheet pulled over me. I wasn't sleeping. My mother wore a pink chenille robe, loosely belted at the waist. I squinted at her, framed against the light from the hallway.

"Nolan, Ed Prior's mother just called. She's been calling Eddie's friends. She doesn't know where he is. She hasn't seen him since he left for school. I said I'd ask if you knew anything about it. Did he come by here today?"

"I saw him at school," I said, and then went mute, didn't know where to go from there, what would be safe to admit.

My mother probably assumed she had just woken me from a full sleep, and I was too groggy to think. She said, "Did the two of you talk?"

"I don't know. I guess we said hello. I can't remember what else." I sat up in bed, blinking at the light. "Actually, we haven't been hanging out as much lately."

She nodded. "Well. Maybe that's for the best. Eddie is a good kid, but he's a little bit of a boss, don't you think? He doesn't give you much space to just be yourself."

When I spoke again, there was the slightest note of strain in my voice. "Did his mother call the police?"

"Don't you worry," my mother said, misunderstanding my tone, imagining I was anxious about Eddie's welfare, when in fact I was anxious about my own. "She just thinks he's laying low with one of his buds. I guess he's done it before. He's been fighting a lot with her boyfriend. Once, Eddie took off for a whole weekend, she said." She yawned, covered her mouth with the back of her hand. "It's just natural for her to be nervous, though, after what happened to her older boy. Him disappearing from the Juvie and just dropping off the face of the earth like that."

"Maybe it runs in the family," I said, my voice choked.

"Hm? What?"

"Disappearing," I said.

"Disappearing," she said, and then, after a moment, nodded once more. "I suppose anything can run in families. Even that. Good night, Nolan."

"Good night, Mom."

She was easing the door shut, and then paused, and leaned back into my room, and said, "I love you, kid," which she always said only when I least expected it and was least prepared for it. The backs of my eyeballs prickled painfully. I tried to reply, but when I opened my mouth, I found my throat too constricted to force any air up it. By the time I cleared my throat she was gone.

A FEW DAYS later I was called out of study hall and sent to the vice-principal's office. A detective named Carnahan had planted himself behind the vice-principal's desk. I can't recall much of what he asked me, or how I answered. I remember Carnahan's eyes were the color of thick ice—a whitish-blue—and that he didn't look at me once in the course of our five-minute discussion. I recall also that he got Eddie's last name wrong, twice, referring to him as Edward Peers instead of Edward Prior. I corrected him the first time, let it pass the second. During the entire interview, I was in a state of high, dizzying tension; my face felt numbed, as if by novocaine, and when I spoke I could hardly seem to move my lips. I was sure Carnahan would notice and find this peculiar, but he never did. Finally he told me to stay off drugs, and then looked down at some papers in front of him and went completely silent. For almost a whole minute I continued to sit across from him, not knowing what to do with myself. Then he glanced up, surprised to find me still hanging around. He made a shooing gesture with one hand, said I could go, and would I ask the next person to come in.

As I stood up, I said, "Do you have any idea what happened to him?"

"I wouldn't worry too much about it. Mr. Peers's older brother broke out of Juvenile Detention last summer and hasn't been seen since. I understand the two were close." Carnahan turned his gaze back upon his papers, began shuffling them around. "Or maybe your friend just decided to hit the road on his own. He's disappeared a couple times before. You know what they say. Practice makes perfect."

When I went out, Mindy Ackers was sitting on the bench against the wall in the receptionist's area. When she saw me, she sprang lightly to her feet, smiled, bit her lower lip. With her braces and bad complexion, Mindy didn't have many friends, and no doubt felt Eddie's absence keenly. I didn't know much about her, but I knew she always wanted more than anything for Eddie to like her, and was happy to be the butt of his jokes, if only because it gave her a chance to hear him laugh. I liked and pitied her. We had a lot in common.

"Hey, Nolan," she said, with a look that was both hopeful and pleading. "What'd the cop say? Do they think they know where he went?"

I felt a flash then of something almost like anger, not for her, but for Eddie; a harsh contempt for the way he chortled about her and made fun behind her back.

"No," I said. "I wouldn't worry about him. I guarantee you that wherever he is, he isn't worrying about you."

I saw her eyes flicker with hurt, and then I pulled my gaze away and went on, without looking back, already wishing I hadn't said anything, because what did it matter if she missed him? I never had another conversation with her after that. I don't know what happened to Mindy Ackers after high school. You know someone for a while and then one day a hole opens underneath them, and they fall out of your world.

THERE IS ONE other thing I remember, from the period that followed immediately after Eddie's disappearance. As I said,

I tried not to think about what had happened to him, and I avoided conversations about him. It wasn't as hard to do as you'd think. I'm sure those who cared were trying to give me a little distance, conscious that a close friend had skipped out on me without a word. By the end of the month, it was almost as if I really *didn't* know anything about what had happened to Edward Prior . . . or maybe even as if I hadn't known Eddie at all. I was already sealing up my memories of him—the overpass, checkers with Mindy, his stories about his older brother Wayne—behind a wall of carefully laid mental bricks. I was thinking about other things. I wanted a job, was considering putting in an application at the supermarket. I wanted spending money, I wanted to get out of the house more. AC/DC was coming to town in June and I wanted tickets. Brick after brick after brick.

Then, one Sunday afternoon at the very beginning of April, we were all of us, the whole family, on our way out to have roast and potatoes at my Aunt Neddy's house. I was upstairs, getting dressed for Sunday dinner, and my mother shouted to look in Morris's room for his good shoes. I slipped into his small room—bed neatly made, a clean sheet of paper clipped to his artist's easel, books on the shelf arranged in alphabetical order—and pulled open the closet door. At the very front of the closet was an ordered row of Morris's shoes, and at one end of them were Eddie's snow boots, the ones he had taken off in the mudroom, before going downstairs and disappearing forever into Morris's enormous fort. At the edges of my vision, the walls of the room seemed to swell and subside like a pair of lungs. I felt faint, thought if I let go of the doorknob I might lose my balance and topple over.

Then my mother was standing in the hallway. "I've been yelling for you. Did you find them?"

I turned my head and looked at her for a moment. Then I looked back into the closet. I bent over and got Morris's good loafers, and then pushed the closet door shut.

"Yes," I said. "Here. Sorry. Spaced out for a minute."

She shook her head. "The men in this family are all exactly the same. Your dad is in outer space half the time, you shuffle around in a trance, and your brother—I swear to God one of these days your brother is going to climb into one of his little forts and never come out."

MORRIS PASSED A high school equivalency test shortly before he turned twenty, and for a few years after proceeded through a long string of menial jobs, living for a while in my parents' basement, then in an apartment in New Hampshire. He shoveled burgers at McDonald's, stacked crates in a bottling plant, and mopped the floor at a shopping mall, before finally settling into a steady gig pumping gas.

When he missed three consecutive days of work at the Citgo, his boss gave my parents a call, and they went to visit Morris in his apartment. He had rid himself of all his furniture, and hung white sheets from the ceiling in every room, making a network of passageways with gently billowing walls. They found him at the end of one of these slowly rippling corridors, sitting naked on a bare mattress. He told them if you followed the right path through the maze of hanging sheets, you would come to a window that looked out upon an overgrown vineyard, and distant cliffs of white stone, and a dark ocean. He said there were butterflies, and an old worn fence, and that he wanted to go there. He said he had tried to open the window but it was sealed shut.

But there was only one window in his apartment, and it looked onto the parking lot out back. Three days later he signed some papers my mother brought him, and accepted voluntary committal to the Wellbrook Progressive Mental Health Center.

My father and I helped him move in. It was early September then, and it felt as if we were settling Morris into a dorm at a private college somewhere. Morris's room was on the third floor, and my father insisted on carrying Morris's heavy, brass-hinged trunk up the stairs alone. By the time he slammed it down at the foot of Morris's bed, his soft, round face was unpleasantly ashen, and he was lathered in sweat. He sat there holding his wrist for a while. When I asked about it, he said he had bent it funny carrying the trunk.

One week later, to the day, he sat up in bed, abruptly enough to wake my mother. She forced her eyes open, stared up at him. He was holding that same wrist, and hissing as if pretending to be a snake, his eyes protruding from his head and the veins straining in his temples. He died a good ten minutes before the ambulance arrived, of a massive coronary. My mother followed him the year after that. Uterine cancer. She declined aggressive treatment. A diseased heart, a poisoned womb.

I live in Boston, almost an hour away from Wellbrook. I fell into the habit of visiting my little brother on the third Saturday of every month. Morris liked order, routines, habits. It pleased him to know just when I would be coming. We took walks together. He made a wallet for me out of duct tape, and a hat glued all over with rare, hard-to-find bottle caps. I don't know what happened to the wallet. The hat sits on my file cabinet, in my office, here at the university. I pick it up and stick my face into it sometimes. It smells like Morris, which is, to be exact, the dusty-dry odor of the basement in my parents' house.

Morris took a job in the custodial department at Wellbrook, and the last time I saw him he was working. I was in the area, and popped in during a weekday, stepping outside of our routine for once. I was sent to look for him in the loading area, out behind the cafeteria.

He was in an alley off the employee parking lot, around behind a Dumpster. The kitchen staff had been throwing empty cardboard boxes back there, and now there was an enormous drift of them against one wall. Morris had been asked to flatten them and bundle them in twine for the recycling truck.

It was early fall, a little rust just beginning to show in the crowns of the giant oaks behind the building. I stood at the corner of the Dumpster, watching him for a moment. He didn't know I was there. He was holding a large white box, open at either end, in both hands, turning it this way and that, staring blankly through it. His pale brown hair stood up in back in a curling cowlick. He was crooning to himself, in a low, slightly off-key voice. When I heard what he was singing, I swayed on my heels, the world lurching around me. I grabbed the edge of the Dumpster to hold myself steady.

"The ants go marching . . . one-by-one . . ." he sang. He

turned the box around and around in his hands. "*Hurrah.
Hurrah.*"

"Stop that," I said.

He turned his head and stared at me—at first without recognition, I thought. Then something cleared from his eyes, and
the corners of his mouth turned up in a smile. "Oh, hello, Nolan. Do you want to help me flatten some boxes?"

I came forward on unsteady legs. I had not thought of Eddie Prior in I-don't-know-how-long. There was a bad sweat on
my face. I took a box, pressed it flat, added it to the small pile
Morris was making.

We chatted for a while, but I don't remember about what.
How it was going. How much money he had saved.

Then he said, "Do you remember those old forts I used to
build? The ones in the basement?"

I felt an icy sense of pressure, a kind of weight, pushing out
against the inside of my chest. "Sure. Why?"

He didn't reply for a time. Flattened another box. Then
Morris said, "Do you think I killed him?"

It was hard to breathe. "Eddie Prior?" The simple act of
saying his name made me dizzy; a terrible lightness spread out
from my temples, and back into my head.

Morris stared at me, without comprehension, and pursed
his lips. "No. Daddy." As if it should've been obvious. Then he
turned back, lifted up another long box, stared into it thoughtfully. "Dad always brought home boxes like this for me from
work. He knew. How exciting it is to hold a box and not be
sure what's in it. What it might contain. A whole world might
be closed in there. Who could tell from the outside? The featureless outside."

We had finished stacking most of the boxes into a single flat
pile. I wanted to be done, wanted us to go inside, play some
Ping-Pong in the rec room, put this place and this conversation
behind us. I said, "Aren't you supposed to tie these up into a
bundle?"

He glanced down at his stack of cardboard, said, "Forgot
the twine. Don't worry. Just leave all this here. I'll take care of
it later."

It was twilight when I left, the sky above Wellbrook a flat, cloudless surface colored a very pale violet. Morris stood in the bay windows of the recreation room and waved goodbye. I lifted my hand to him and drove away, and they called me three days later to say he was gone. The detective who visited me in Boston to see if I knew anything that might help the police to find him managed to get my brother's name right, but the long-term results of his investigation into my brother's disappearance have yielded no more success than Mr. Carnahan's search for Edward Prior.

Shortly after he was formally declared a missing person, Betty Millhauser, the care coordinator at the clinic in charge of Morris's case, called to say they were going to have to put his possessions into storage until "he came back"—a turn of phrase she delivered in a tone of shrill optimism that I found painful—and if I wanted to, I could come in and collect some of his things to take home with me. I said I'd stop in the first time I had a chance, which turned out to be Saturday, on the exact day I would've visited Morris had he still been there.

An orderly left me alone in Morris's small third-floor room. Whitewashed walls, a thin mattress on a metal frame. Four pairs of socks in the dresser; four pairs of sweat pants; two unopened plastic packages of Jockey underwear. A toothbrush. Magazines: *Popular Mechanics*, *Reader's Digest*, and a copy of *The High Plains Literary Review*, which had published an essay I had written about Edgar Allan Poe's comic verse. In his closet, I discovered a blue blazer Morris had modified, stringing it with the lights for a Christmas tree. An electrical cord was tucked into one pocket. He wore it at the annual Wellbrook Christmas party. It was the only thing in the room that wasn't completely anonymous, the only item that actually made me think of him. I put it in the laundry bag.

I stopped in the administration offices to thank Betty Millhauser for letting me go through Morris's room and to tell her I was leaving. She asked if I had looked in his locker down in the custodial department. I said I didn't even know he had a locker, and where was the custodial department located? The basement.

The basement was a large, high-ceilinged space, with a cement floor and beige brick walls. The single long room was divided in two by a wall of stiff chain-link, painted black. On one side was a small, tidy area for the custodial staff. A row of lockers, a card table, stools. A Coke machine buzzed against the wall. I couldn't see into the rest of the basement—the lights were switched off on the other side of the chain-link divider— but I heard a boiler roaring softly somewhere off in the darkness, heard water rushing in pipes. The sound reminded me of what you hear when you listen to a seashell.

At the foot of the stairs was a small cubicle. Windows looked in on a cluttered desk covered in drifts of paper. A stocky black man in green coveralls sat behind it, turning through the pages of the *Wall Street Journal*. He saw me standing by the lockers, and got up, came out, shook hands—his was callused and powerful. His name was George Prine, and he was the head custodian. He pointed me to Morris's locker, and stood a few steps behind me, arms crossed over his chest, watching me go through it.

"Your boy was an easy kid to get along with," Prine said, as if Morris had been my son instead of my brother. "He drifted off into his own private world now and then, but that's pretty much the order of things 'round this place. He was good about his work, though. Didn't clock in and then sit around tying his boots and yapping with the other guys like some do. When he punched his card he was ready to work."

There was next to nothing in Morris's locker. His jumpsuits, his boots, an umbrella, a slim creased paperback called *Flatland*.

" 'Course after he got off work, that was a different story. He'd hang around for hours. He'd get building something with his boxes and go so far away into himself, he'd forget dinner if I didn't tell him to get."

"What?" I asked.

Prine smiled, a little quizzically, as if I should've known what he was talking about. He walked past me to the wall of chain-link and flipped a switch. The lights came on in the other half of the basement. Beyond the chain-link divider was a bare expanse of floor under a ceiling crawling with ductwork and pipes. This wide, open area was filled with boxes, assembled into a sprawling, confused child's play fort, with at least four different entrances, tunnels and chutes and windows in strange deformed shapes. The outsides of the boxes had been painted with green ferns and waving flowers, with ladybugs the size of pie plates.

"I'd like to bring my kids here," Prine said. "Let them crawl around inside there for a while. They'd have a blast."

I turned and started walking for the stairs . . . shaken, cold all over, breathing harshly. But then, as I brushed past George Prine, an impulse came over me, and I grabbed his upper arm and squeezed, maybe harder than I meant to.

"Keep your children away from it," I said, my voice a strangled whisper.

He put his hand on my wrist and gently, but firmly, pulled my hand off his arm. His eyes held me at a distance; he regarded me with an air of calm, wary consideration, the way a man might look at a snake he's snatched out of the weeds, holding it just behind the head so it won't bite.

"You're as crazy as he was," he said. "You ever think of moving in?"

I HAVE TOLD this story as completely as I can, and now I will wait and see if, with this act of confession behind me, I can drive Eddie Prior back into my unconscious. I will learn if I can settle once more into my days of safe habit and thoughtless repetition: classes, papers, readings, English Department functions. Building the wall back up again, brick by brick.

But I am not sure what has been pulled down can be repaired. The mortar is too old, the wall too poorly constructed. I was never the builder my brother was. I have been visiting the library in my old hometown of Pallow a lot lately, reading over old newspapers in microfiche. I've been searching for an article, some small report, of an accident on Route 111, a brick dropped into a windshield, a Volvo off the road. I've been trying to find out if anyone was badly hurt. If anyone was killed. Not-knowing was once my refuge. Now I find it impossible to bear.

And so maybe it will turn out I have been writing this for

someone else after all. The thought has crossed my mind that maybe George Prine was right. Maybe the person I should show this story to is Betty Millhauser, Morris's ex–care coordinator.

At least if I was living at Wellbrook, I'd be in a place where I might feel some connection to Morris. I'd like to feel a connection to someone or something. I could have his old room. I could have his old job—his old locker.

And if that isn't enough—if their drugs and their therapy sessions and their isolation can't save me from myself—there is always one other possibility. If George Prine hasn't demolished Morris's final cardboard maze, if it's still standing there in the basement, I could always climb in someday, and pull the flaps shut behind me. There is always that. Anything can run in families. Even disappearing.

But I'm not going to do anything with this story yet. I'm going to slide it into a manila envelope and stick it in the bottom right-hand drawer of my desk. Put it aside and try to resume my life, where I left off, just before Morris disappeared. Won't show it to anyone. Won't do anything foolish. I can go on for a while longer, pulling myself through the dark, through the tight spaces of my own memories. Who knows what may lie just around the next corner? There may be a window somewhere ahead. It may look out on a field of sunflowers.

AFTERWORD

20TH CENTURY GHOSTS: 20 YEARS ON

Am I the man who wrote these stories some
thirty years ago, or am I someone else?
—Algernon Blackwood, in his 1938 introduction
to *The Tales of Algernon Blackwood*

The oldest story in this book, "Better Than Home," was written twenty-eight years ago. I'm fifty-two now and will be fifty-three by the time this new edition of *20th Century Ghosts* lands in bookstores. Twenty-eight years. That's over half my life. I feel a tad bewildered staring at that number on the page. I have three adult sons, all men in their twenties, and I feel much the same way when I consider their baby photos: mystified and a little stunned. In the time since I wrote "Better Than Home," I was married, raised children, wrote books, got divorced, was lonely, wrote more books, remarried, and fathered twins—in short, life happened, and plenty of it.

There are flimflam artists who present themselves as new age mystics and will tell you all about your past lives: a hundred years ago, you rode with Billy the Kid and died of dysentery in Oklahoma; two thousand years ago, you made out with Cleopatra and committed suicide alongside her. (No one ever had a past life where they were a shepherd in Wales, who spent sixty years picking his nose and counting ewes and getting soaked in the drizzle—you were always a queen, or at least laid one.) I'm not much inclined to believe in reincarnation. But it certainly seems to me that I wrote these stories not half a lifetime ago, but in a different life altogether.

I've blabbed elsewhere about how I wound up a novelist (see the introduction to *Full Throttle*, my second collection of short stories, if you're curious) but will only note here that it came very close to not happening at all. I wrote several novels across my teenage years, and several more in my twenties, and I couldn't sell any of them. By the early '00s, I had more or less concluded I didn't have a novel in me. But I had one consolation: I had at least puzzled out how to write a good short story. Or, more precisely, I puzzled out how to write one good short story and then I puzzled out how to write another. I began to solve one short story after another. That's what it felt like when they were done: as if I had worked out a sticky but ultimately satisfying crossword puzzle or a clever equation. "Better Than Home" was the first and the one I lived with the longest. It wanted to be a novel, but I wouldn't let it. In first draft it was a hundred and twenty pages. In second, it was ninety. Every time I circled back to it, I lopped off another chunk. It was addition by subtraction—everything I took out made it better. The story hung around for eight or nine drafts before I submitted it to a contest for long short stories (it was still very long) and won. After I got the letter saying "Better Than Home" had been awarded the A. E. Coppard Award, I sat on the stone step of a post office in Brookline, Massachusetts, on a blowy spring day, and watched the Green Line train rattle past, trolley bell ding-dinging. I felt like I was going somewhere, too, following the rails to whatever might wait at the next stop.

What waited there was another story, "Pop Art," and another, "20th Century Ghost." It was two years between writing the former and writing the latter. But the days between good stories grew shorter with each new work. I wrote "The Widow's Breakfast" and "Dead-Wood" each in an afternoon, a month apart. Not long after I was in Florida, reading Kafka for the first time. In a careless moment, I put my bare foot down on a hill of red biting ants. In *The Metamorphosis*, Gregor Samsa turns into a cockroach and soon withers of despair and neglect, but I had a dozen inflamed bites to remind me that most insects have a lot more fight in them. I started "You Will Hear the Locust Sing" while my foot was still sore and leaking pus, and the whole thing came together in brisk fashion. It sold in brisk fashion as well to Andy Cox, the editor of a British fantasy magazine. Andy Cox bought my next one, "In the Rundown," too. You know what they say about confidence—it breeds more of itself. I had a happy afternoon reading a compilation of Gahan Wilson cartoons and then found myself wondering if I could pen a Gahan Wilson or Charles Addams gag in prose form. Turned out I could! "Last Breath" was another I wrote in just a few sittings.

By early 2004, I had maybe twelve stories that all seemed to go together, windows looking into the same dark, lonesome house . . . a house where bad things had happened. I thought, okay, maybe I don't have a novel in me, but it would still be a kind of triumph to sell a collection. *20th Century Ghosts* was turned down by all the publishers in New York and London, for perfectly sensible reasons. First collections by unknown writers rarely fly off the shelves (*Emperor of the Air* by Ethan Canin and *Interpreter of Maladies* by Jhumpa Lahiri are notable exceptions). So, I turned to the small presses, where many of these stories had first been printed, and the manuscript found its way to a boyish and big-hearted Yorkshireman named Peter Crowther, who ran a humble outfit called PS Publishing.

While Pete has many qualities, I'm not sure anyone would leap to describe him as "perfectly sensible." A horror and fantasy guy to the bone, he instantly connected with the first three tales in this book, "Best New Horror," "20th Century Ghost," and especially "Pop Art." I wrote one new story for *20th Century Ghosts*, "The Cape," in early 2005—that one is a mere twenty years old, not old enough to buy beer, but close. The collection was published that October, just in time for spooky season. Then these stories went off to live their lives and I went off to live mine.

Some of these tales have had some unexpected adventures out in the world. "Pop Art" was turned into a lovely short film directed by Amanda Boyle and starring a sad-eyed and inflatable Arthur Roth. The film made a nice ripple at film fests and caught a few award nominations after its theatrical premiere at the Jim Henson film festival.

"The Cape" was adapted for comic books by writer Jason Ciaramella and artist Zach Howard. It was something of a sensation: only one issue long, it was nominated for an Eisner Award, the comic book industry's Oscar. Jason and Zach soon expanded on the story of their soaring sociopath, and before you could say, "What the actual fuck," bears were falling out of the skies onto hapless police officers.

My family of not-so-fearless vampire killers, Van Helsing and sons, made it onto the silver screen . . . not once, but twice. A director named Dorothy Street shot a lush student film based on "Abraham's Boys" in 2009. She was assisted by two brothers, Matt and Ross Duffer. Later, the Duffer brothers—burning with love for Steven Spielberg movies and Stephen King novels—would dream *Stranger Things* into existence. At the time of this writing, Natasha Kermani, a young horror wunderkind, has finished filming a feature length version of *Abraham's Boys*, starring Titus Welliver as the Dutch Doc, and a kid named Brady Hepner as his big, conflicted, and inarticulate oldest son. The result is a work of chilling, claustrophobic suspense in the mold of classic Hitchcock (think *Psycho* or *Vertigo*).

I had trouble, going all the way back to "Better Than Home," keeping these pieces clamped down to short-story length. A bunch of them kept trying to tear free and turn into novels. The one that came closest to breaking loose was "The Black Phone." I wrote pages and pages that never made it into the final story. In first draft it was 16,000 words. The published version? Just half that. And there was even more stuff I *didn't* write, scenes I imagined but set aside. I had an idea for one sequence in which Finney escapes his basement prison, briefly, and hides under a shed behind the Grabber's house . . . only to discover himself lying among the bodies of earlier victims, their corpses chopped into pieces and rotting in Glad bags. But I didn't allow the story to slip its leash, in part because I doubted I could sell a novel, in part because I worried it might go places I didn't want to follow.

In the end, though, we got to have the fullest possible version of "The Black Phone" when Scott Derrickson made a movie out of it . . . a blisteringly scary picture with a tender heart at its core. The whole short story is there on the screen—every scene and every line of dialogue—but that's only one-third of the thing. Another third is powerfully autobiographical, offering Scott a chance to reflect on his childhood in the scuzzy seventies as they played out in North Denver. Think of it as *The 400 Blows* reimagined as grindhouse horror. Screenwriter C. Robert Cargill crafted the all-important final third, the escape-room mechanism that drives the plot. The three of us hit on a single major creative change together, transforming the Grabber from a killer klown into a murderous magician. *It: Chapter One* and *Terrifier* had already locked up the evil clown space in the popular imagination and a bad magician offered a jolting inversion on Scott's previous film, *Doctor Strange*.

The movie packed 'em in. Success may have a hundred fathers, but it also has a few children: in this case, Mason Thames, who was quietly compelling as Finney, and Madeleine McGraw, who blew the doors off as his mouthy, mildly psychic sister. Without their remarkable performances—and the work of the film's youthful ghosts, an ensemble that included future Max Van Helsing, Brady Hepner—*The Black Phone* would have sunk without a trace.

The Black Phone brought a whole new wave of readers to this book and is now probably the story for which I'm best known. Scott and Cargill cared for the source material enough to make a great film out of it, and so it isn't an exaggeration to say their enthusiasm changed the course of my life, at least a little. They were awfully good to me and this collection. So were Zach, and Jason, and Natasha, and Amanda, and all the editors and publishing folk and booksellers who championed and looked after this little book of terror tales. I was fortunate enough to be represented by the late Mickey Choate, who worked as my agent with good will, forbearance, and tireless energy for a decade without making a dime off me. He believed in these stories more than anyone, including myself.

In particular, I owe more than I can say to Peter Crowther, who decided to bring this book into the world and put it in the hands of readers, without a thought to whether he would ever see a profit. Whenever I talk to him, I'm struck by the idea that Peter's imagination is like that warehouse at the end of *Raiders of the Lost Ark*: a place so vast, one can't see to the end of it, and stacked from end to end with his knowledge of ghastly horror comics, forgotten weird television, and paperback shockers.

I have a funny story about Pete. It'll probably sound like bullshit, but it's the truth. About a year before I submitted *20th Century Ghosts* to PS Publishing, I was in a Barnes & Noble, and I came across a collection of Pete's own weird horror fiction. The stories looked great—just my kind of thing—but I thought, *Ah, I buy too many books, if I pick this up, I'll probably never get around to reading it.* So I put it down and walked away.

Then I walked back and snapped it off the shelf and took it to the register. I was thinking, *Shit, if I'm not willing to take a chance on a collection of stories by a writer I don't know, why would anyone ever take a chance on* my *collection?* At the time, I was only just beginning to submit *20th Century Ghosts* to the bigger publishers. I had no idea Pete had a press of his own or that someday I'd be sending him my stories. I read that book, *The Longest Single Note*, a few months later and it was *grand*. It was, by turns, as wistful as Bradbury, as shocking as Bloch, and as unrepentantly gruesome as Barker. It shone with all the humor, mischief, intelligence, and warmth of Pete himself. How lucky I am that my work should have fallen into his hands. How lucky that I should've enjoyed the last twenty years of his friendship.

Twenty years, man, that's a long time in a life. Long enough for a child to grow up and learn to speak for himself. These stories speak well enough for themselves, and they've had some time to live in the world and make a few friends of their own—yourself among them, I hope.

I'm grateful for them and I'm grateful for you, too.

I'm going to keep writing 'em if you'll keep reading 'em. Deal?

Joe Hill
Exeter, NH
August 2024

ACKNOWLEDGMENTS

This book was originally released by PS Publishing in England, two years ago. Thanks are owed to those who gave so much of themselves to make that first edition happen: Christopher Golden, Vincent Chong, and Nicholas Gevers. Most of all, though, I want to express my gratitude and love to publisher Peter Crowther, who took a chance on *20th Century Ghosts* without knowing anything about me except that he liked my stories.

I'm grateful to all the editors who have supported my work over the years, including but not limited to Richard Chizmar, Bill Schafer, Andy Cox, Stephen Jones, Dan Jaffe, Jeanne Cavelos, Tim Schell, Mark Apelman, Robert O. Greer Jr., Adrienne Brodeur, Wayne Edwards, Frank Smith, and Teresa Focarile. Apologies to those I might have left out. And here's a special holler of thanks to Jennifer Brehl and Jo Fletcher, my editors at William Morrow and Gollancz, respectively; two better editors a guy could not wish for.

Thanks also to my Webmaster, Shane Leonard. I appreciate, too, all the work my agent, Mickey Choate, has performed on my behalf. My thanks to my parents, my brother and sister, and of course my tribe, whom I love dearly: Leanora and the boys.

And how about a little thanks for you, the reader, for picking up this book and giving me the chance to whisper in your ear for a few hours?

Gene Wolfe and Neil Gaiman have both hidden stories in introductions, but I don't think anyone has ever buried one in their acknowledgments page. I could be the first. The only way I can think to repay you for your interest is with the offer of one more story:

SCHEHERAZADE'S TYPEWRITER

Elena's father had gone into the basement every night, after work, for as far back as she could remember, and did not come up until he had written three pages on the humming IBM electric typewriter he had bought in college, when he still believed he would someday be a famous novelist. He had been dead for three days before his daughter heard the typewriter in the basement, at the usual time: a burst of rapid bang-bang-banging, followed by a waiting silence, filled out only by the idiot hum of the machine.

Elena descended the steps, into darkness, her legs weak. The drone of his IBM filled the musty-smelling dark, so the gloom itself seemed to vibrate with electrical current, as before a thunderstorm. She reached the lamp beside her father's typewriter, and flipped it on just as the Selectric burst into another bang-bang flurry of noise. She screamed, and then screamed again when she saw the keys moving on their own, the chrome typeball lunging against the bare black platen.

That first time Elena saw the typewriter working on its own, she thought she might faint from the shock of it. Her mother almost did faint when Elena showed her, the very next night. When the typewriter jumped to life and began to write, Elena's mother threw her hands up and shrieked and her legs wobbled under her, and Elena had to grab her by the arm to keep her from going down.

But in a few days they got used to it, and then it was exciting. Her mother had the idea to roll a sheet of paper in, just before the typewriter switched itself on at 8 P.M. Elena's mother wanted to see what it was writing, if it was a message for them from beyond. *My grave is cold. I love you and I miss you.*

But it was only another of his short stories. It didn't even start at the beginning. The page began midway, right in the middle of a sentence.

It was Elena's mother who thought to call the local news.

A producer from channel five came to see the typewriter. The producer stayed until the machine turned itself on and wrote a few sentences, then she got up and briskly climbed the stairs. Elena's mother hurried after her, full of anxious questions.

"Remote control," the producer said, her tone curt. She looked back over her shoulder with an expression of distate. "When did you bury your husband, ma'am? A week ago? What's wrong with you?"

None of the other television stations were interested. The man at the newspaper said it didn't sound like their kind of thing. Even some of their relatives suspected it was a prank in bad taste. Elena's mother went to bed and stayed there for several weeks, flattened by a terrific migraine, despondent and confused. And in the basement, every night, the typewriter worked on, flinging words onto paper in noisy chattering bursts.

The dead man's daughter attended to the Selectric. She learned just when to roll a fresh sheet of paper in, so that each night the machine produced three new pages of story, just as it had when her father was alive. In fact, the machine seemed to wait for her, humming in a jovial sort of way, until it had a fresh sheet to stain with ink.

Long after no one else wanted to think about the typewriter anymore, Elena continued to go into the basement at night, to listen to the radio, and fold laundry, and roll a new sheet of paper into the IBM when it was necessary. It was a simple enough way to pass the time, mindless and sweet, rather like visiting her father's grave each day to leave fresh flowers.

Also, she had come to like reading the stories when they were finished. Stories about masks and baseball and fathers and their children . . . and ghosts. Some of them were ghost stories. She liked those the best. Wasn't that the first thing you learned in every fiction course everywhere? Write what you know? The ghost in the machine wrote about the dead with great authority.

After a while, the ribbons for the typewriter were only available by special order. Then even IBM stopped making them. The typeball wore down. She replaced it, but then the carriage started sticking. One night, it locked up, wouldn't move forward, and oily smoke began to trickle from under the iron hood of the machine. The typewriter hammered letter after letter, one right on top of the other, with a kind of mad fury, until Elena managed to scramble over and shut it off.

She brought it to a man who repaired old typewriters and other appilances. He returned it in perfect operating condition, but it never wrote on its own again. In the three weeks it was at the shop, it lost the habit.

As a little girl, Elena had asked her father why he went into the basement each night to make things up, and he had said it was because he couldn't sleep until he had written. Writing things warmed his imagination up for the work of creating an evening full of sweet dreams. Now she was unsettled by the idea that his death might be a restless, sleepless thing. But there was no help for it.

She was by then in her twenties and when her mother died—an unhappy old woman, estranged not just from her family but the entire world—she decided to move out, which meant selling the house and all that was in it. She had hardly started to sort the clutter in the basement, when she found herself sitting on the steps, rereading the stories her father had written after he died. In his life, he had given up the practice of submitting his work to publishers, had wearied of rejection. But his postmortem work seemed to the girl to be much—livelier—than his earlier work, and his stories of hauntings and the unnatural seemed especially arresting. Over the next few weeks, she collected his best into a single book, and began to send it to publishers. Most said there was no market in collections by writers of no reputation, but in time she heard from an editor at a small press who said he liked it, that her father had a fine feel for the supernatural.

"Didn't he?" she said.

Now this is the story as I first heard it myself from a friend in the publishing business. He was maddeningly ignorant of the all-important details, so I can't tell you where the book was finally published or when or, really, anything more regarding this curious collection. I wish I knew more. As a man who is fascinated with the occult, I would like to obtain a copy.

Unfortunately, the title and author of the unlikely book are not common knowledge.